THE FALL OF SUMMER

A NOVEL

TED M. ALEXANDER

GREYFIELD·MEDIA

THE FALL OF SUMMER

GREYFIELD·MEDIA

Printed in the United States of America

Published by Greyfield Media, LLC
Asheville, North Carolina
Books may be purchased in quantity and/or
special sales by contacting the publisher
GreyfieldMedia.com

Library of Congress Cataloging-in-Publication Data

Alexander, Ted M.
The Fall of Summer

1. Coming of Age—Fiction. 2. Human Interest—Fiction. I. Title
Library of Congress Control Number 2014935131

ISBN 978-0-9914237-4-3
eBook ISBN 978-0-9914237-5-0

Designed by Kim Pitman, FireflyInx.com

First Edition

10 9 8 7 6 5 4 3 2 1

Contact Author: TedMAlexander.com

For Portia

THE FALL OF SUMMER

. . . She will not care. She'll smile to see me come,
So that I think all Heaven in flower to fold me.
She'll give me all I ask, kiss me and hold me,
And open wide upon that holy air
The gates of peace, and take my tiredness home,
Kinder than God. But, heart, she will not care.

–Rupert Brooke
"Unfortunate"

JULY 1965

CHAPTER 1

Even if DJ had wanted to attend the morning funeral, he wouldn't have been able to gain admission. The homicide had been so heavily publicized that besides family, selected well-wishers and throngs of reporters, the Lieutenant Governor of New York and his entourage also appeared to pay respects, jamming the Methodist church.

Instead, he watched from across the street, hoping to locate her in the groups of mourners entering the church's vestibule.

The outer doors closed and he remained ten more minutes, then another five, until he was certain she wouldn't appear.

At home, as the afternoon funeral neared, DJ grew increasingly agitated—uncertain how he would react or maintain control. He had tried to erase the finality of the death ritual from his mind, and had toyed with the idea of not attending—instead listening to country-western tunesmith

Marty Robbins and drinking a beer or two.

But he really had no choice.

∞

Later in the day, the graveside service still fresh in his mind, DJ walked aimlessly through the overcast, vaguely heading for town.

Leslie appeared next to him. "Going any place special?" she asked. Her yellow slicker suggested innocence.

"Not really," he replied.

"Mind if I come along with you?" She was already in step.

"I guess not."

The two walked silently for a block.

Leslie glanced at DJ. "I didn't see you at the funeral this afternoon."

"I was there with Patty." Through the mist, a hint of Leslie's perfume.

She placed her hand in the crook of his arm as the two crossed the street. "Did you go this morning?"

"No," DJ said. "The church was too crowded."

"I didn't even make the attempt." Her fingers tightened around his arm. "I wouldn't even be out walking today if you weren't with me. I always thought Long Island was safe, but now I'm not going anywhere alone until they catch the killer."

"Did the police talk to you?"

"Yes, a fat detective who smoked little cigars." Leslie brushed a strand of hair from her forehead.

"Did he ask you what you were doing on the night of the murder?"

She nodded. "I told him I stayed home and watched a movie with my father. I was so upset with Bobby that I didn't go out."

DJ shrugged. "What was the name of the movie?"

"I think it was *The Best Years of Our Lives*. It was stupid even though my father liked it."

"I know," DJ said. "I saw it too."

The two continued for several blocks into the richer section of homes.

"Would you like to come over and watch TV sometime? Nobody would bother us again."

"I don't think so, Leslie."

"I've changed a lot, you know," she continued. "I'm not the same girl who went to the dances and Van Velsor's with you. I'm not as wild as I used to be."

"That's good, Les," DJ answered, meaning it. "I'm glad." He stopped to examine a cluster of pale blue hydrangea blossoms glistening in the mist, extending over the sidewalk.

"They're beautiful," Leslie said, standing behind him.

"And incomplete," DJ replied, pointing to the fragile bits of confetti locked together in bloom. "They can't attract pollen, and have no seed."

"Is that true?" Leslie asked. The mist was changing to quiet drizzle turning her yellow slicker shiny. "How do you know that?"

"Monty told me once. He learned it from my mother a long time ago."

The two stood for several more moments, then walked back toward town.

"Do you think you'll miss me?" she asked, as they approached her house.

"Sure I will, Les," DJ answered.

"We had some good times. They weren't all bad." She pulled the hood of the slicker up over her head as the rain grew heavier.

"I know."

Leslie looked up at him, uncertain. "Well, if you ever want to come by, call me."

"I will. I definitely will."

"Okay." She leaned forward and kissed him on the cheek, then looked briefly into his eyes. "It all went by so fast, didn't it?"

DJ nodded. "I think so." He watched her turn, walk up the steps and enter the house without looking back. "I think so," he repeated to the deserted street.

He stared at the closed door, then turned and retraced his steps to the house with the blue hydrangeas on the edge of the lawn.

As he stood beneath tree branches, sheltering himself from the shower, DJ watched the blue blossoms blur, then slowly draw farther away, until along with the rain they melted into the grass; fragments of a timeless cycle.

Leslie was right, he thought to himself. The time had all gone by so quickly.

He closed his eyes.

It might have been yesterday when the boys were swimming the window.

NINE MONTHS EARLIER
OCTOBER 1964

CHAPTER 2

A yellow bus eased up to the front of the high school. The driver honked, then waved for the group of boys to cross the street and join the students already boarding.

DJ lagged behind with Ike. The two were the last to make their way up the steps.

"How you doing, Ike?" the driver asked, waiting until they were settled in a nearby seat.

"Good for a guy with half a heart," Ike answered.

"Well, it's better than no heart at all."

As the bus pulled away from the high school, DJ stared out at Captain Leo's Seafood Restaurant where the boys had been acting like they were fish, pretending to swim across the outside of the long aquamarine window simply to aggravate the patrons inside—just as they had been doing since grade school.

Minutes later, entering Hardscrabble's residential area, his focus changed to the cookie-cutter Cape houses, each with a square plot of lawn and single maple tree.

Looking more closely, this time studying his own reflection in the glass, DJ noticed dark half-circles under his eyes and was immediately convinced he was dying. He gave it a few moments of deep thought, then reconsidered. No, couldn't be, he hadn't had sex yet. There was no way he would be allowed to die before that happened, especially because he was making a concerted effort for the bona fide thing and the God he'd been dealing with would certainly understand and appreciate that effort. He always bargained in good faith.

DJ shut his eyes and envisioned Leslie's basement with its water-stained maple paneling, its scratched green plastic bowl full of hundred-year-old, damp pretzels—the ones where the salt would peel off into one soggy ball—and the ancient DuMont TV resting on a table in front of the burnt-orange corduroy couch where they always sat.

She would interlace her fingers with his, or rest her head on his shoulder, and her scent of gardenias and Ivory soap aroused him to his toes. When he kissed her, DJ would move his face in front of hers, watch her close her eyes, then feel her softness and the power of her perfume.

After the first few months of being together, each time they were alone he would try to increase his familiarity with her, always to no avail despite his growing intensity. Then without any advance notice, to his amazement, Leslie let him touch her breasts. Near the end of *Queen For A Day*, while he kissed her during the commercial, almost as an afterthought, he had attempted to slip the straps of the St. Mary's green plaid uniform jumper from her shoulders. When she unexpectedly didn't resist, DJ became disoriented, but due to months of daydream rehearsal, managed to slowly begin unbuttoning her blouse with his free hand. He had reached the third button from the top, when to his astonishment, Leslie undid the remaining two, then reached behind her back and unhooked her bra.

For the first time, he had been able to feel the smoothness of her body. As his hands moved inside her blouse, touching her bare breasts, he could feel her tremble as she pressed against him.

Leslie had managed to resist his physical advances for months, either by keeping her arms pressed against her sides, turning away, or simply giving him a nasty look. For her to suddenly offer no resistance, and instead, her plaid skirt crumpled at mid-thigh, begin to kiss him more intensely than he could ever remember, unearthed an intensity in DJ he'd never felt before.

Then as surprisingly as she had begun, she stopped. Before emcee Jack Bailey could have the audience decide which pitiful creature would win all the prizes by being named Queen for that particular day, Leslie's eyes snapped open. "Get away from me, DJ." She reached behind her back, re-hooked her bra and buttoned her blouse, then stood. As she ran both hands to the back of her head to fashion a ponytail, she glared at him, then turned away. "I think it's time for you to leave. I have homework to do."

As he rose to his feet, DJ said nothing. He was embarrassed with his tumescence and used his hands as a fig leaf while he waited for an explanation. When she offered none, he knew enough not to ask.

Leslie always had reasons for what she did though it was rare that she would ever disclose what they were. And when he was unable to understand her thinking, which was most of the time, and would risk a question, she would roll her eyes, shake her head, and then change the subject, almost as if it was beneath her to dignify such a request by responding to it.

She was unsettling that way, and she was also very smart and very clean. Her green-and-white saddle shoes were always immaculate, the socks she wore over her nylons never sagged at the ankles, and even after all that kissing, he knew her breath would still be like peppermint.

As he stared down at his own hands, then glanced at Leslie's turned back, DJ used one fingernail to scoop a tiny sliver of dirt from another.

And then he was sad. It was not just being sexually

unfulfilled that bothered him, it was also the sudden sense of feeling incomplete. When Leslie had let him touch her, and his hands had moved across her body for the first time, the barrier between them had suddenly crumbled. And he realized that all their prior moments of soda fountains, hand-holding and Saturday afternoon football games had suddenly been rendered meaningless—superficial artifacts stolen from some two-bit *Archie* comic book.

He had never known Leslie suffered from red marks on her shoulders because of straps that clenched too tightly, or about a two-inch scar near the corner of her back, and that her skin was smoother just below the neckline. It was an uncharted world he had stumbled into, one that he didn't want to depart from now that he had arrived. But as the studio audience howled its approval to Jack Bailey while he crowned the chipped-front-tooth widow from Akron, and with Leslie now turned and facing him, arms crossed, cheeks flushed, DJ was suddenly uncertain anything had changed at all.

He picked up his two notebooks, said goodbye to no response and climbed the wooden stairs to the living room. As he crossed to the front door, the audience cheers below suddenly subsided, probably, he guessed, because Jack Bailey had been turned off too. He was—

The bus suddenly slammed into a pothole and DJ opened his eyes. He stared across the aisle at Lisa Havens, the high school goddess sitting next to Bobby Litchfield, the team quarterback. Bobby was whispering in Lisa's ear, his arm wrapped around her neck.

"Tonight's going to be another big night," Don Maynard said, sticking his head over the back of the seat between Ike and DJ.

Everyone knew DJ's friend, Don Maynard was having sex with his girlfriend, Frannie.

"Shut up, Maynard," an envious Rocco said from his seat behind the driver.

"Yes ma'am," Maynard responded, saluting.

"And don't salute," Rocco said, glaring at Maynard. As the town's premier greaser and last year's local Golden Gloves quarter-finalist, he was used to his directives being obeyed.

Maynard saluted.

Rocco pounced from his seat with such force his Brylcreemed hair whipped into a furry eye mask, changing him into a werewolf-like Lone Ranger. Before he could take a step, the bus driver removed one hand from the steering wheel and grabbed Rocco's arm. "Sit down, son," he said, his eyes never leaving the road.

"C'mon, that moron is giving me a lot of mouth."

"Last warning, son, sit," the driver said, "or you get off right here." He waited a moment, then released Rocco's arm.

Rocco sat, but continued to glare at Maynard.

After braking the bus at the corner of Jackson and Melville, the driver opened the door and discharged Lisa, Bobby, Maynard and a glowering Rocco. Bobby lived on the other side of town, but on Friday afternoons he had no football practice and usually went home with Lisa.

As the driver approached DJ's house, he braked again. "Last stop." He opened the door.

"Come on, Ike, let's get out of here," DJ said, lifting his books from his knees and rising.

Taking tiny breaths, his lips pursed, Ike gathered momentum, stood, then edged toward the door in small half-steps—all he could manage.

The two descended to the pavement and began to walk.

"Do you think Maynard will have sex with Frannie again tonight?" Ike asked immediately.

As he slowed to match his best friend's pace, DJ wondered if Ike would ever even get the chance for sex. And with a congenital heart defect, what would happen if he did? He suspected Ike shared similar apprehensions, and though neither would speak of the concern, DJ could feel Ike's perpetual blue undertow begin to surround and pull at him. "Probably," he answered, stopping at the sloping cement steps that crossed the patch of lawn in front of his house. "What about you?"

Ike edged the toe of his shoe against a crack in the sidewalk. "I don't know. Maybe." He thought another moment. "Do you think Maynard would tell us the truth anyway?"

"Hard to say," DJ answered. "But you know what? Maynard may lie, or he may not, but either way, who cares. Sometime down the road, we're both going to get it, and it's going to be good when we do—a lot better than having sex with Frannie in the graveyard." DJ leaned his shoulder against the lone maple that separated the sidewalk from the street and looked confidently at Ike. "And I mean it."

"Yeah, I guess you're right," Ike said, staring back, a tentative smile on his face. He looked at his watch. "Got to go. Doctor today." He started toward his house.

DJ watched Ike shuffle past the three-foot, off-white Madonna inside the turquoise clamshell that rested on his lawn, then up the steps to his front door.

"Hey, Ike," he called, "maybe I'll see you later."

Ike turned, then nodded. "Maybe."

DJ stared upward into the overhead tree branches.

If I carve my initials in the tree today, up near the top, the part that's hidden from the street, will the letters still be there in twenty years? In forty years? If I came back and looked for them, would I ever remember being seventeen? Or if I died in a car accident, or in a remote corner of the world during some bloody war, would the initials ever be seen again by anyone?

He walked up to his house, then stepped along the line of onside bricks outlining the abandoned garden. When he reached the end of the brick border, he pivoted on his heel and stared at the ground, at the blades of grass and the tiny pebbles, then with partially closed eyes, transformed himself into a circus tightrope walker.

For the next five minutes, DJ angled up and down the brick tightrope until he finally lost balance, and as the audience, cotton candy vendors, and clowns all gasped, he somersaulted into the safety net, dragging the spotlight behind him.

CHAPTER 3

Saturday afternoon, DJ was outside his house when Ike approached.

"What's going on?" Ike asked.

"Nothing much. What did the doctor say?"

"Same," Ike said, glancing away.

"I'm heading down to Van Velsor's to see Patty. Feel like going?" He already knew the answer. Ike was never doing anything.

"Yeah, all right, I'm not doing anything." Ike began walking next to DJ. "Hear anything from Maynard?"

"Nah, not a word."

As the two walked past Leslie's house, DJ thought he detected a downstairs curtain move slightly. He looked more closely at the window, but saw nothing and chalked it up to imagination. He hadn't seen her since the beginning of the week and figured she still didn't want to talk to him.

"DJ, wait." Leslie moved out the door and down the front steps. "Hi, Ike," she said, then intertwining her fingers with DJ's, she kissed him on the lips. "Where have you been hiding, stranger?"

DJ stared at her as the scent of gardenias danced around him.

"Are you mad at me?" Leslie asked, a tiny smile on her face as she looked directly into his eyes.

"Mad? No, I'm not mad," DJ said. He had never been mad, just confused.

"You want me to meet you at Van Velsor's?" Ike asked DJ while he cleaned a lens of his sunglasses with his shirttail.

"Go ahead with Ike," Leslie said. "Are we still going out tonight?"

"Sure, I guess. What time?" DJ asked. He couldn't recall making plans.

"Seven-thirty, but I can only stay out till eleven-thirty. That'll give us time." Leslie kissed him again. "Bye, Ike. See you later, DJ." She moved up the steps and disappeared into her house.

"What's that all about?" Ike asked, replacing his glasses.

"It's weird," DJ said, resuming the walk to town. "It's just weird, that's all."

∞

By the time they arrived at Van Velsor's coffee shop, lunch hour was over. DJ's sister, Patty, was wiping the counter near the grill and loading a few leftover plates into the circular dishwasher while owner Herman stacked columns of quarters by the register.

"DJ, Ike, how about a quick game of checkers?" Herman's sister Greta called. She was sitting in the first booth, a cup of coffee next to her checkerboard, a cigarette in an ivory holder held between her forefinger and thumb. In the old days, she was known for occasionally exhaling smoke and a birdcall simultaneously though DJ had never heard her in action. He had been told she specialized in the crow, the sparrow and the prairie warbler, but since Herman had spoken to her, it rarely happened anymore.

"I'll play a game," Ike said as he crossed to the booth.

DJ sat on a stool at the counter facing Patty. He studied his sister for a moment—something he rarely did—and was again surprised at how pretty she was, in an understated way. And despite people sometimes thinking she was cold, he knew she was just shy. Pretty and shy.

How about a Coke?" DJ asked.

Patty lowered her voice. "Sure, but I can't give you a freebie. Not enough people at the counter to camouflage it." She loaded another plate into the dishwasher, placed the hood down, then pressed the Start button. Wiping her hands on a damp towel, she added, "Bobby Litchfield was in here without Lisa today." Her eyes brightened when she mentioned his name.

Patty's interest was upsetting. DJ knew Bobby Litchfield would have no desire to be with his sister and he felt protective. It was his job to shield her from everyday hurt. "Yeah, well Bobby's not so hot."

Herman coughed, letting Patty know he was getting nervous that she had been standing still for ten seconds. He could be edgy at times. Herman believed his workers should do two things: breathe and wait on customers. If there were no customers, still two things: breathe and clean. And if you could only do one thing, stop breathing and continue to clean. Someone once told DJ that Herman had been baptized with a bucket of vinegar and water.

"I guess I'll take a rain check on the Coke."

"Okay, I'll talk to you later," Patty said, moving to the other end of the counter.

"So, DJ, early tomorrow morning it is?" Herman called as he thumbed through stacks of dollar bills. "Come before six o'clock. The papers might be early and we can get a jump on them. The earlier the better."

"Okay, Herman, no problem." DJ could sleepwalk through the Sunday newspaper routine. He'd bring the *New York Times, Herald Tribune, Daily News,* and *Journal American* bundles inside, insert sections, then pile them neatly on the stand. After the mounds of the newspapers were transformed to precisely stacked soldiers in front of the cash register, he was allowed to retreat behind the counter for a glass of water or a small Coke.

"See you later, Patty," DJ said, standing.

"Wait up," Ike called, leaving Greta's booth and moving toward DJ. "See you, Greta."

"Goodbye, boys," Greta called. "We'll play checkers next time too."

"I hope you'll be here first thing, DJ," Herman restated. Then as an afterthought, "Why don't you come very early so we can get an even better head start."

$$\infty$$

Ten minutes later, DJ walked into the kitchen where his father was sitting at the table, an empty bottle of Piels, a half-full glass of beer, and a chunk of cheddar resting in front of him.

"Where've you been, son?" Dale asked. He lifted the glass to his lips and swallowed the remainder of the beer, then stood and moved to the refrigerator for a refill.

"Van Velsor's," DJ said as he walked to the wastebasket and peered in, counting a total of three discarded bottles. He had learned years ago that he could gauge his father's temperament by the number of empties in the garbage.

Dale dropped his empty bottle into the wastebasket and returned to his chair. He uncapped the beer and sliced a piece of cheese from the block. "Your sister there too?" Not waiting for an answer, he continued, "What time is she coming home?"

"Same time as usual, Dad," DJ said. "She's—"

"You following this Staubach? Heisman Trophy last year, only a junior at Annapolis too. Going to be a star. Got a cannon for an arm. Doesn't have a big mouth either. I like that." He placed a forefinger between his lip and gum and loosened a piece of cheese. "I would've liked you to play football, but physically you favored your mother's side." He swallowed. "That's not your fault though."

Staring out the front window, Dale wiped the foam from his upper lip with the back of his hand. "Tough few days in court. Cliff Collins got drunk the other night and ran into the fence at the City of Glass, you know, the nursery out by the Ag School. Smashed himself up pretty good. With that kind of behavior going on, I'm glad he's still the store manager over at Mertz Brothers."

DJ nodded, not understanding the point.

"Sit," Dale said suddenly, motioning to a chair at the end of the table.

DJ was surprised and immediately apprehensive as he settled into the chair.

"Your college applications are in, right?" His father stared at him.

"Sure. Remember you had to write the checks?" DJ shifted.

"I remember." Dale said. "When do you hear?"

"March, I think, Dad. Isn't that what the guidance counselor said?"

"I don't give a damn what the guidance counselor said. If she knew anything, she wouldn't be a guidance counselor, she'd at least be attempting to teach something." He belched, covering his mouth with the back of his hand. "The reason I'm asking," he said, "is Patty will be in college the year after you—which means a lot of money."

DJ hadn't really thought much about it. He had just assumed his father would pay for college.

"So what I'm thinking," Dale continued, "is that you're going to have to assume more responsibility. You're going to have to take on some of the liability."

"What's liability?"

"Well, if you hold your horses a second, I'll tell you," Dale answered, suddenly irritated. "You're going to have to work more—plain and simple. You'll need spending money, clothes, those things, and it's going to have to be with money you earn. I'll have more than my hands full just paying for your tuition." He pulled on his ear. "Damned if I know what I'm going to do when it's time for Patty to go."

"But don't judges make a lot of money?" DJ asked.

"Not in the district court, they don't," his father snapped. "At this level, you don't make the kind of money the big-shot judges do." Fiddling with the beer bottle, rolling it between his palms, he cleared his throat. "So, I've arranged with Cliff Collins for you to work Saturdays at Mertz Bothers."

"Mertz Brothers? The department store?" DJ asked, immediately distressed. "But I don't know anything about working in a department store. How would I even get there, it's ten miles away!" He thought a second, then placed both elbows on the table. "Cliff must have really banged his head on the dashboard to come up with this idea."

"Don't get smart. It was my idea and Cliff owes me. He could've been in jail thirty days on a drunk-driving charge if it wasn't for me. He said he'll get personally involved and train you himself." Dale pushed his hair straight back in an unconscious maneuver to cover the bald spot on the back of his head. "You'll be what he calls a floating salesman."

"I don't want to be a floating salesman," DJ answered immediately, his anxiety rising.

"Well, my friend, first of all, you don't know what a floating salesman is, and second, you don't have a choice. Cliff needs someone who can work any department in the store in case someone's sick, or if they're just generally shorthanded. That'll be you, DJ: Jack of all trades—as the saying goes."

"Dad, come on," DJ moaned. "What if I have to sell shoes, or ladies underwear? I can't do that."

"Again, my friend, you'll do it if you want to go to college."

So there it was: *if* he wanted to go to college. His father had never been that candid with him before: *if* he wanted to go to college. He did, but probably not for the reasons he'd heard the other seniors describe—to be a doctor, or for freedom, or to drink a lot. It was much simpler than all of that—he was afraid *not* to go. The thought of being left behind terrified him. Nothing would be sadder than to spend the autumn alone working on some factory line next to a foreign woman with a moustache while everyone he knew had vanished to different towns and states, and the old high school juniors had become seniors, leaving him loitering around town like some overgrown mutation. He would end up shopping alone during the evening at the A&P, and eating lunch in the factory canteen—purchasing tuna sandwich halves stacked on top of each other and wrapped in cellophane—from rumbling, paint-nicked vending machines, all the time looking through grimy windows at a steady gray rain.

The whole concept was too depressing to even contemplate.

"Well, Dad, I can't walk to the store. And I don't have a car, so I don't see how this is even possible."

"You'll be able to use my car. I don't need it on Saturdays. If I have to go down to Town Hall I can walk, and you'll be home most evenings by six."

"When do I start?" DJ asked, brightening. The prospect of access to a car made the idea of becoming a floating salesman infinitely more palatable.

"Cliff said he'll train you next Saturday. He'll show you the ropes, as he calls them, then the week after, you can start officially."

Dale picked up his beer and walked to the living room. "Old Cliff should know better about his drinking and driving though. He's my friend, and I'm the judge, but I can only help him so much."

Switching on the TV, Dale slumped into his BarcaLounger and said, "Lucky he wasn't picked up by the county police—those big-shot judges aren't as willing to excuse a simple mistake as I am." Reaching for the *TV Guide* lying on the floor next to his chair, he muttered, "I sure hope this thing in Vietnam doesn't heat up. It would be a crime to lose a quarterback like Staubach."

CHAPTER 4

By the time DJ left his room and clomped down the stairs that evening, his father was snoring in his chair, reading glasses resting on his chest. Crossing the living room, DJ turned off the TV, then left the house.

Leslie was already outside when he arrived. She was perfect in navy blue sweater, white blouse, tweed skirt, and spotless loafers.

"Why don't we go to a movie," she suggested.

DJ didn't care. He was just happy to be with her again.

Walking into town, they waited at the railroad crossing while the train heading for the city chugged past them. As it slowly rolled by, Leslie suddenly threw her arms around DJ's neck, paying no attention to anyone who might be watching, and kissed him, first gently, then urgently. "That's for all the time we missed," she said.

∞

The movie, *Hootenanny Blast*, looked weak, but it was the

only option.

Moviegoers had to be at least eighteen years old to sit in the balcony, not normally a problem, but Fat Barry, the manager, who was also selling tickets that night, was friends with DJ's father and knew he was only seventeen.

Sorry, DJ," he said, rubbing the wart on his cheek, "but I got to be fair to everybody. If I let you into the balcony, I got to let all the seventeen-year-olds up there. You wouldn't want me to be unfair to everybody else would you?"

The garlic fumes wafting through the metal grill that separated their faces made DJ the prisoner. And the truth was he would not have cared one bit if Fat Barry had been unfair to other teenagers. It wasn't like he hadn't been in the balcony a million times before. Mrs. Hicks, who usually sold tickets, was always more interested in her current romance novel than anyone's age. She would have let a class of first-graders go upstairs if they had the money just so she could get back to her reading.

DJ liked the balcony too, even if it cost more. It was quiet and comfortable with just a few couples scattered around and no one paying attention to anyone else. He could rest the popcorn box on an empty seat instead of his lap and whisper in Leslie's ear without someone behind them listening. But instead, because Emperor Fat Barry had decided to be ticket seller that night, they were stuck downstairs where the floor was tacky from spilled soda and nearly every seat was packed with itchy families.

As he walked down the aisle with Leslie, DJ didn't even bother with the last row. He knew Leslie would never sit there because she didn't want people to think she was a tramp. DJ took her hand and moved to the far end of an empty row down front. Moments later, just before the lights dimmed, a mother and four kids took the remaining seats next to them. The youngest child, a five-year-old boy with a grape moustache, wouldn't take his coat off, then intermittently ate Turkish Taffy, sat on his knees, watched the screen, and stared at DJ.

Realizing that they were wedged in, with people surrounding them, DJ knew there was not much of a chance for even a kiss and had to settle for the pathetic arm around the shoulder. Resigned, and huddled in for what turned out to be a painful ninety minutes of full-screen folk music laced with lame-brained comedy, he nearly dozed off until the boy beside him, equally bored, pulled a cap pistol from his coat pocket and triggered off four rounds at the screen before his mother could grab the gun away.

∞

Later, after stopping at Van Velsor's, walking up Jackson Road with his arm draped over Leslie's shoulder, DJ gradually began to feel more relaxed. It was comfortable to be with her again.

The two stopped at the maple tree by the sidewalk in front of her house. Leslie leaned against the trunk and put her hands behind DJ's neck, pulling him toward her. She kissed him, then placed her hands on both sides of his face, gently pushing him two or three inches away, just far enough so she could focus.

"I'm sorry about what happened the other day in my basement," she said. "You know I am, don't you?"

"Sure, I know you are." He didn't, but having been able to sneak a peek at his luminous watch dial, and realizing that only twenty minutes remained until Leslie was due inside, he didn't want to begin a discussion. Resting the insides of his forearms on the tree trunk over her head, he kissed her gently, then more intensely.

"Oh, DJ," she whispered.

He ran his hands over Leslie's shoulders, then down her sides. He could feel the electricity again.

"Come on, let's go to the side of the house where no one can see us," she said, quickly taking his hand.

They moved across her lawn to the dark side of the garage. Leslie stopped and rested her back against the wall, then pulled DJ to her. "I love you, DJ." She pressed herself against him. "I love you so much."

Reaching beneath her sweater, DJ placed his hand against her blouse—touching her breast and feeling the same softness, the same excitement, the same desire. Unbuttoning the middle buttons, he moved his hand inside her blouse.

"No, DJ, no. Don't. We can't," she whispered in his ear, then kissed him fiercely.

The gardenias roared around him.

"No, DJ, please don't." Her voice was hoarse. "I can't, don't. Please don't."

"Just for a little while, Les, just for a lit—"

"We can't. No, stop."

"Come on, Les, just for a sec—"

DJ was so entangled that he never sensed it coming. When she suddenly stepped to the side and hit him, the tip of her house key protruding from her clenched fist, it was as if he had been shattered by a hidden sniper, or electrocuted, never knowing a lightning storm was on the horizon. As his eyes involuntarily welled-up, temporarily blinding him, she reared back and hit him again with the same hand, this time with such force it took his breath away. Wobbly, he sank to one knee.

"When I say no, DJ, I mean no." Leslie seethed, pacing a quick circle in front of him.

One hand over his eye, the other across his nose, DJ sank to both knees facing the wall as blood pooled across his upper lip, then dripped onto his chin.

"No, is no, is no, DJ," Leslie said, as she adjusted her blouse and sweater. "No, is no, is no. My father taught me a long time ago how to deal with boys like you," she added, pointing to the key extending through her fingers. "Just don't forget it, DJ. Just don't forget it." Leslie turned away, then strode to the front of the house and through the door. He heard the chain lock slide into place and saw the dark become deeper as she clicked off the outside light.

DJ sat against the garage wall, the sleeve of his sweater pressed against his nose. The vision in his right eye was cloudy, but when he squinted at the street light, it grew clearer.

As he struggled to his feet, his sleeve still pressed against his nose, DJ teetered down the cement driveway to the sidewalk, then turned and headed back toward town. He didn't feel like explaining how he looked to Patty or his father, and in another hour they'd both be in bed.

Maybe I deserved that, he thought. Maybe I did push her too far and shouldn't have.

But Maynard said Frannie always said no—he expected her to say no. If she didn't say no, something was wrong. That's the way it worked Maynard said: yes is yes, no is yes, or maybe yes, or maybe later, or give me a call tomorrow, but no is never no.

As he traipsed in the direction of town, DJ attempted to recall every conversation about girls he'd had with Maynard, but he couldn't remember his friend ever mentioning being smashed across the face as an integral part of foreplay.

CHAPTER 5

DJ stopped in front of the Jailhouse Rock on North Main Street, then crossed through the cars in the parking lot. As he entered the side door of the bar, he saw Monty and Wendell, his father's brothers, playing bass guitar and drums on the stage—two-thirds of the trio, The Primates. Whenever he saw them performing, he was momentarily taken aback because his father was the respected town judge and his uncles were ordinary bar musicians.

Quickly ducking into the men's room, DJ splashed water across his cheeks and eyes, then discovered the paper towel dispenser was empty. He moved blindly to the doorless stall and unrolled a handful of toilet paper. After mopping his face, he wadded the paper into a ball and tossed it into a corner garbage can that was overflowing with beer cans, whiskey bottles, and women's nylons.

DJ could hear the last chords of "Guitar Boogie Shuffle," The Primates' break song, through the wall.

Turning to the cracked mirror over the sink, he evaluated the left side of his face. It was worse than he thought. The top of his lip was puffy, giving him a snarling appearance, the corner of one eye was bright red, and dried traces of blood caked the insides of his nostrils.

As he was cleaning his nose using the tip of his little finger, the door suddenly slammed open and his uncle Monty walked in. "Hey, DJ, what are you doing here, cowboy?" He slapped him on the back and proceeded across to the urinal. "Small crowd tonight. Guess with this cool weather folks want to stay at home and watch TV."

The door kicked open again and his other uncle, Wendell, entered, a glass in his hand. "Hey, DJ, when did you get here? Hurry up, Monty, I been drinking too much of Thor's rotgut thunder." He glanced at DJ again, then came closer. "Good lord, what happened to you, son?"

Monty looked back over his shoulder.

DJ was embarrassed by his condition, but more concerned that Wendell might suspect he had been tearful. "Nothing."

"Yeah, sure thing," Wendell said, bending over and looking closely at DJ's face. "Monty, come here and take a look at this."

"For crying out loud, will you let me finish here first, Wendell," Monty answered.

"I sure hope the other guy looks worse than you do, fella," Wendell said.

Monty crossed back to DJ, zipping the fly to his black jeans as he moved. "Let me take a look here." He studied DJ's eye.

"Don't you think you should wash your hands first?" Wendell inquired, looking over Monty's shoulder and down at DJ.

Ignoring Wendell, Monty asked, "Can you see all right?"

"Yeah, I can see pretty good," DJ responded.

"Pretty good, or real good?"

"Real good."

"Does it hurt?"

"Not too much; a little when I blink."

"Don't you think you should wash your hands, Monty?" Wendell repeated. "Hell, if your fingers get too close you might give the boy a urinary infection."

"Quiet, Wendell. How about that lip? Hurt?" Monty looked closely.

"Yeah, but not too bad." DJ answered. He was beginning to feel safe.

Monty stepped back. "Well, I hate to tell you this, DJ, but when I was in the Marines, I used to look a heckuva lot worse after I'd been wrestling a bottle of Jack Daniels all night." He moved to the sink and began to wash his hands. "Who was the unlucky guy you had to whup tonight?"

"I tell you what, I'll bet it was Maynard," Wendell interrupted, his voice shrill and rising. "He's always getting into trouble. And if it was him, I'm going to kick his old man's butt just for fathering him. I'll tell you that much right now!"

"Nah, it was nobody," DJ said. "Some show-off from Amity. He just had a big mouth in front of Leslie."

"Well, you did what you had to do, " Monty said. He put his arm around DJ's shoulder. "Want to stick around a while? Come on in. Lila always likes it when you drop by and sit with her."

As the three moved through the back room of the bar, Monty steered DJ toward a corner table next to four wooden loading pallets that had been horizontally bolted together and elevated by concrete blocks to serve as a stage. Gray paper covered the outer edges, offering the people on the dance floor the impression that The Primates were playing from the top of a rock.

"Lila," Monty said, approaching her, "would you be kind enough to get some ice for Rocky Marciano's lip. Seems he's had a bout of bad luck this evening, though I figure he looks better than the unfortunate lad who ran into him."

"Are you all right, sweetie?" Lila asked, tucking a bar check into the pocket of her black-and-white striped waitress uniform before touching his lip.

"And get him a cold beer," Wendell said. "He's almost eighteen and Thor don't care."

"Isn't that against the law?" DJ asked. He'd only had Coke

at the bar before.

"Thor *is* the law," Wendell said, reminding him that the club owner and bartender was also the Hardscrabble police chief. "He don't mind long as it's family to Monty and me. And if you don't mind, Lila, I could go for another tumbler of that rotgut whiskey he's been forcing me to pour down all evening."

"All right, then," Lila said, heading toward the bar.

DJ sat at the table and rested his elbows on the red-checkered oilcloth. He looked around and noticed Jellybowl, the house bookie who lived upstairs over the bar, decked out in his usual checked coat and cheap gold. The big man was sitting on his corner stool by the pay phone, a betting slip in one hand, a drink in the other. On the other side of the dance floor, two women sat at a table, ringside. The one sitting closest to DJ was blonde and a knockout. Her girlfriend was a chunky motor mouth with frizzy brown hair.

Lila returned with a bottle of beer for DJ and a glass of thunder for Wendell. "Thor says he doesn't mind you having a beer, just don't broadcast it," she said to DJ. "Here's some ice too." She handed him a glass of cubes. "Put it on that lip every once in a while." She looked at DJ's mouth. "Whoever that guy was, he caught you good, sweetie."

Monty was already on stage, his head turned to the amplifier tuning his Fender bass as Wendell climbed up and sat behind the drums. Gordon, The Primates guitar player, adjusted the strap on his Rickenbacker six-string, then tested the audio with a clicking sound into the microphone.

As The Primates began to play, DJ sat and sipped his beer, occasionally absentmindedly placing a piece of ice against his lip. As he drank, the music became sweeter and kinder, the lyrics gained depth, and he felt older and more confident, though it hurt him to smile. He watched two stallions from the bar ask the beautiful blonde at the front table to dance, but she said no to each. The stubby brunette had smiled when each man approached the table and forced the smile to continue when each turned on his heel and left without acknowledging her. Seeing the pattern made DJ sad for a second, but Lila brought him over a fresh bottle, patted the back of his head the way he imagined his mother once did, then stood for a moment with her hand resting on his shoulder.

Slowly, as the minutes passed, he became warm and untroubled in front of his own red-checkered fireplace.

After a half hour had passed, hard as he tried, he realized he couldn't keep his eyes from the blonde woman at the front table. She watched the band, but occasionally looked restlessly around the club. DJ tried to time a smile to coincide with one of her sweeps of the room and was startled when her eyes locked briefly on his before continuing the circuit. She didn't look back again, and DJ had little doubt it was because he was seventeen—she might be as old as twenty-five—and his face was a mess.

"DJ-J-J-J." Maynard sat in a chair next to him. "What happened to you, Leslie hit you with a brick?" He laughed and smacked him on the arm.

"What're you doing here? I don't think you're allowed in here," DJ said.

"Don't worry, my old man knows Thor. Anyway, I thought you'd like to know something." He paused, smiling. "I just had a very sincere sexual relationship again. Yes, very sincere."

"Yeah, sincere all right," DJ countered.

"I just wanted to share the usual good news," Maynard said, at the same time standing and adjusting the crotch of his pants.

"Donald Maynard, you have to be eighteen to be in here," Lila said, approaching the table.

"Ah, come on, Lila, no one really cares."

"I'm sorry, Thor's rules. Enough said." Lila turned and headed for a customer who had signaled her from a rear table.

Maynard relaxed again. "Sex—really weird, really weird," he said, "but something I highly recommend if you can handle all the talking they want to do afterwards. What the hell is that all about?" He stretched his arms, then clasped his fingers behind his neck as he rocked on the hind legs of the chair and studied DJ. "So what happened, did you fall down a flight of stairs?" he asked.

"No, not really. It's a long story."

The Primates stopped playing and DJ watched the blonde stand, then place her coat over her shoulders.

"With that fat lip, you're not going to look so hot playing in the donkey basketball game next week. Major rivalry—always a big crowd. You got to look good."

DJ had forgotten about the annual juniors versus seniors basketball game played on rubber-soled donkeys in the high school gym. It was a tradition, and Maynard was right, the whole student population, along with most of the faculty, always turned out to watch.

"Well, I'd love to stay, but I really have to be running along," Maynard said, suddenly rising as Monty approached. "I don't need Thor on my butt, or Monty for that matter." He started away. "Just wanted to let you know the good news," he called over his shoulder, then hurried along the wall and banged out the side door.

Monty sauntered to the table and sat down, then straightened his legs in front of him, resting the toe of one boot into the back of the heel of the other, creating a tower. "Don Maynard's going to get himself killed one of these days," he said, then grinned. "Don't know what it is about you young fellas. You believe you're bulletproof." He thought for a minute, his forefingers arched in prayer under his nose, as he watched Lila return to the table. "Course I was never wild, was I, honey?" He raised his arm and slid it around her waist.

"Of course not." She smiled.

DJ suddenly felt uneasy and stood up. "I should go."

"You sure?" Monty asked.

DJ nodded.

"Take care of that lip, honey," Lila said.

"I will. Night." He turned and walked out the door.

Still not wanting to return home, DJ headed down North Main Street into Hardscrabble, past the darkened storefronts and drifting cardboard boxes awaiting Monday's pickup. The odd angle of a street light revealed *Carlyn Reynolds is a whore,* written in cracked, faded letters on the brick siding of the Laundromat. In the center of town, the stoplight rocked back and forth in the wind sending colored reflections rippling up the pavement.

DJ stood and watched for a full minute, then turned left and walked a block to the only light still remaining. Standing next to the Contemporary Bar and Grill's door, he peeked past the "Come On In, It's Kool Inside" penguin decal on the window and watched the bartender, a pencil-chested old-timer in a white apron, nod, then lean against the liquor shelves behind him, his arms crossed against his chest, his basset-hound eyes drooping. Further back, under the fluorescent lights, two skinny, slicked-back, watery-eyed shit-kickers in plaid shirts jabbered to each other in front of the pool table before one laughed loudly and slapped his knee, causing his cue to slip and clank on the floor.

DJ rested his forehead against the door. The wind had quit and the night was now so still he could hear the stoplight click as it changed colors. The neon sign inside the window next to him hummed, and the maple shelf below it was dotted with dried flies—raisins thrown across a baking board.

Bobby Litchfield, alone in his father's Impala convertible and wearing sunglasses, stopped at the intersection, then waited for the light to change. With the green he was gone, and as his taillights disappeared, the neon sign was switched off.

DJ turned around and hurried past Van Velsor's knowing he would have to return in less than four hours to take care of the Sunday newspapers. He crossed the railroad tracks and followed a trail of skeletal hydrangeas—moonlit guideposts leading him home.

CHAPTER 6

The Monday morning following the weekend donkey basketball game was uglier than even DJ could have imagined. In the waning moments of Saturday night's game, with the score tied, he had fallen off his donkey, become confused, jumped back on, then fired the ball into the wrong basket, scoring the winning points for the opposing team!

He knew he would never hear the end of it. The school newspaper staff had worked overtime to make certain an "extra" edition of the *Hardscrabble Skyline* would be available for the students upon arrival.

DJ could see the headline "The Shot Heard Round The World" glaring at him from a stack of papers as he entered the school building. Below the incriminating words was a picture of himself on the back of the donkey, snapped just as the basketball was leaving his fingertips. His eyes were half-closed in concentration, and for some unknown reason, the donkey had opted to turn his head and bray at the cameraman just as the photograph was taken, adding a comic touch to the humiliating disaster.

DJ grabbed a copy of the newspaper, headed for homeroom,

and slunk to his seat in the back. He attempted to appear nonchalant while he sped through the front page copy, but he could feel his heart racing and his face growing darker. The words were not kind, especially when they pointed out that due to his error, the seniors had lost the game for the first time ever. The unidentified staff writer, obviously a senior, was especially distressed at having to leave the sacred halls of Hardscrabble High School as a Donkeyball loser. He even suggested that the juniors were not worthy of such a victory and had won only because of senior negligence.

DJ folded the paper and tucked it in a book.

"Which one's the ass?" Rocco hooted as he entered the half-full homeroom holding the front page over his head. Then pointing to DJ at the back of the class, he announced, "I'll bet you can figure it out, Elders!"

∞

After school, on the bus ride home, DJ sat with his hands resting on his books, staring at his reflection in the glass. The past Saturday had been a disaster. First, Cliff Collins had trained him at Mertz Brothers and he didn't feel he had learned anything except how to unlock the cash register, then that night he had made a fool out of himself in front of the whole school at the donkey basketball game.

"What are you doing over Thanksgiving?" Ike asked, interrupting DJ's thoughts.

"Don't know exactly. Monty mentioned something about going up to his cabin in Vermont. Maybe Wendell will go too."

"But it's Thanksgiving. It's a holiday. Aren't you supposed to be home?" Ike asked.

DJ shrugged. He looked out the window. "My old man doesn't care."

Ike thought out loud. "Maybe I could go too."

DJ continued to stare out the window. He could see the

dark half-circles under his eyes in the reflection. "Okay," he said. "That would be good."

∞

In the evening, DJ walked into town alone, had a Coke, then headed home. As he passed Leslie's house, he thought about stopping and ringing the doorbell, but knew better. He had visited her moldy basement a couple of times since she had decked him and it had been the same old game: tease and stop. And when he was beginning to make progress, her father always called from the top of the stairs telling him it was time to leave. It never failed.

DJ was sure she had a silent police alarm stashed in her underwear.

It had taken a while, but he finally had Leslie figured out. She once mentioned that what she liked about the Good Humor man was not the man himself, or the ice cream, or even the truck, but instead, the chrome-plated coin changer attached to his belt. No surprises when he clicked a lever. Press the dime lever, a dime popped out; the nickel lever, a nickel. The ice cream man always knew the result in advance.

And Leslie believed DJ was her personal coin changer. Press a specific button, get a predictable response.

She was toying with him; a cat playing with a captured mouse. And when he was with her, along with the attempts to decipher her verbal gymnastics, now he always had to keep a sharp eye out for a right cross or uppercut.

DJ pulled up his jacket collar so that it covered his neck. The enclosing autumn was manipulating him too. The early darkness, the chill seeping into his sleeves, the dried leaves skating across the sidewalk in front of him—all reminders that he would have to wade through another winter before spring returned—reminders that shortened afternoons would become shorter still as cars clicked on their headlights before five o'clock, illuminating dreary figures scurrying from their offices to the protection of their houses.

And even when he was home behind locked doors, huddled beneath the blankets with the wind rattling the windows and the moon lounging on the roof, its pale, glowing tentacles stretching, probing through each room, he never felt quite safe.

It had been autumn when his mother died, and if it had not been for the lone silver-framed picture in the living room, he never would have known what she looked like.

CHAPTER 7

On Saturday morning, DJ studied himself in the mirror. He was wearing his blue suit with a white oxford cloth button-down shirt and a blue striped tie—one of two he owned. The other was pink, wide, and had a Hawaiian dancer in a grass skirt with a ketchup stain on her knee. Maynard had found it under the bed in the Holiday Inn in DeMonde, Florida, where he had been staying for his grandfather's funeral. He'd given it to DJ on his last birthday wrapped around a condom, with the note, "It'll be a piece of cake to score when you wear this baby," attached with a piece of tape.

DJ walked downstairs and picked up the car keys from the kitchen table. Patty was already at Van Velsor's, and he could hear his father snoring from the bedroom. He tiptoed out the door, opened the garage, then quickly started the Falcon and backed out into the street.

∞

Once at Mertz Brothers Department Store, DJ walked

through the security area of the employees' entrance, past a man in a blue uniform reading a Nazi novel, then directly to the store manager's office where Cliff Collins sat behind his desk talking on the phone. He motioned for DJ to sit opposite him.

"Yeah, okay, honey," Cliff spoke into the telephone as he studied some papers in his hand. He placed them on the desk in front of him and gently tugged at the strands of hair sprouting from his ears. "Feel better. Uh huh, I know." He looked over at DJ and rolled his eyes. "Well, don't you worry about that. No, you let me worry about that; nothing you can do if you're sick. Take care now, and let me know how you feel on Monday." He hung up and tapped his fingers on the desk, then frowned while he examined the papers again. "Good thing you're here, son, we got a lot of people calling in today. Some sick, some just saying they're sick. Any way you look at it, we're spread mighty thin." Cliff looked up. "Yep, it's a good thing we got you trained last week."

DJ was about to mention that he didn't think that he was trained at all, when Cliff interrupted as though he had read his mind. "Don't worry, son, as long as you have the basics, knowing how to operate the cash register, that type of thing, you'll be fine. If you have a question, just be polite and fake it until you can speak with the other salesperson working with you. As a floating salesman covering different departments, you won't be alone for at least the first month."

"At least the first month" lasted until nine-fifteen when DJ was assigned to Basement Shoes by himself.

"Mr. Collins, I don't know anything about shoes," DJ protested, genuinely alarmed.

"Learn on the job, my friend," Cliff said. "You've bought shoes. You know how to measure feet. We're short-handed today. Don't worry, I'll be checking departments—you can call me up here, and Mrs. Canova, the assistant store manager, is back from vacation and will be in later. She'll be covering all the floors to make certain everything is running smoothly.

We'll have someone down to join you shortly." Cliff gestured to the down escalator. "Go get 'em, Mr. Floating Salesman. And don't forget, we're all counting on you. Don't let us down."

DJ returned to the Security Department to pick up his cash pouch and register key, signed for both, then glided down the escalator to the ground level. After finding the Basement Shoes department in the corner, he counted the fifty dollars cash from the pouch, deposited it in the register, then took the register key and dropped it in his jacket pocket.

DJ glanced at his watch and saw he had ten minutes until the store opened at nine-thirty. He walked around the brown-carpeted area, kicked out rug wrinkles at each corner of the rectangle, then practiced zooming onto the shoe salesman's stool a couple of times, attempting to appear practiced and comfortably at ease.

He walked behind the cash register and through a curtained doorway into a storeroom containing aisles of shelves laden with hundreds of colored boxes of shoes. I'm in trouble, he thought, looking around, I'm in deep, deep trouble.

DJ checked his watch again and walked out from the storeroom in time to see the first trickle of customers on the descending escalator. As he stood behind the register, his hands resting on both sides of the counter, he forced a confident smile.

An anxious-looking mother holding her son's hand stepped onto the floor, then stopped, appearing momentarily lost. She turned and spotted Basement Shoes and began walking in DJ's direction.

While she had searched for his department, DJ used the opportunity to dive below the cash register counter to hide. He was positive she hadn't seen him.

Seconds later, a woman's voice above him on the other side of the counter called, "Hello, hellooo-o-o-o. Anybody here?" She banged the counter bell.

DJ instantly jack-in-the-boxed straight up so that his face was directly opposite the woman's, causing her to jump back a step. "Good morning," he said. "Just adjusting some of the charge slips below the counter."

"Good morning." The woman looked at him. "Are you the salesman?"

"At your service," DJ smiled.

"My, either I'm much older than I thought, or salespeople are getting much younger." She studied the Mertz Brothers employee's identification badge on his breast pocket.

DJ nodded and forced another smile.

"Well, Dale," she continued, squinting at his name, "I'm here to get shoes for my son, Philip."

The five-year-old held his mother's hand and stared at DJ. He was wearing a jumbo New York Yankees cap that had been taken in two inches, creating a navy blue wool bubble in the back of his head.

"Excellent." DJ moved around the counter so that he was standing next to the woman. "What kind of shoes?"

"Sneakers, I guess."

"Good idea," DJ said. "And fit is the most important thing," he added, parroting words he had heard every shoe salesman ever say. "Have a seat, Philip, let's measure your foot." DJ knelt, unlaced and removed both of the boys shoes, picked up the Branick device and zoomed onto the stool in front of him. He placed Philip's heel against the edge of the measuring device. "Looks to me you're about a five."

"I think that's right," his mother said. She thought a second. "We've just moved into the area. What are all the kids wearing?"

"Well, why don't I go take a look and see what we have available?" DJ hopped off the stool and disappeared behind the curtain entranceway to the storeroom.

Now what, now what, now what, he thought, as he walked quickly up and down aisles randomly opening boxes to see if he could get close to the sneaker category—sandals, loafers, moccasins, gumshoes, work boots, thermal socks. "Socks?" he questioned aloud as he rushed up another aisle opening box tops as he ran. In the last aisle he discovered adult sneakers, but nothing for kids. DJ glanced at his watch.

"Hello-o-o-o. How are you doing back there?" the woman called from in front of the curtain.

"Almost there, almost there," DJ called back. "Just a minute."

He ran down the last aisle and noticed a yellowing cardboard display showing a boy in shorts holding school books under his arm. On the cardboard boy's feet were real sneakers. DJ snatched the pair from the display, blew dust off the tops, wiped them on the back of his pants, then yelled, "Here I come."

He burst through the curtain, then slowed and walked toward the boy's mother. "I think I found just the ticket," he said, plunking the sneakers down on the floor in front of the two of them.

"Really," Philip's mother said, "Is navy the new popular color?"

"Popular as popular can be," DJ nodded. "What do you think, fella?" He lifted the sneakers and showed them to the boy, who stared at them, then at DJ.

"Are they new? They look a little tired." Philip's mother picked one up.

"Just off display. Can't get newer than that. What you say we try them on?" DJ took one of the sneakers and slid the boy's foot into it, then laced it up, quickly doing the same for the other foot. "Okay, now stand up."

When he pressed his finger on the front of each sneaker, DJ could feel at least an inch of space between the boy's toe and the end. "Seems just about right," he said. "Take a walk."

Philip clomped two steps forward, then turned around and paraded two steps back. "Feel like flippers," he said.

"They do look large," his mother observed.

"Yes, they are," DJ countered, "but let's not forget he's a growing boy."

"I don't know. Do you have anything else?"

"If money is a consideration, this is your best bet," DJ

offered. "They're on sale this week, and frankly, we have very little else in stock that would be in his size."

Philip's mother frowned. "How much are they?"

DJ didn't have a clue. "A dollar twenty-nine, plus tax," he said.

"That *is* very reasonable." She considered a second, then said, "All right, I guess we'll try them. At that price we almost have to."

"Would he like to wear them home?"

"Yes, I guess so," the woman responded.

DJ picked up Philip's shoes and returned to the cash register. He placed them in a bag retrieved from below the counter.

After he rang up the sale, DJ handed the boy's mother the change and the shoes. "Thank you for shopping at Mertz Brothers," he said.

"Thank you, Dale." She turned and walked away holding her son's hand.

DJ was relieved and started toward the storeroom when he felt a tug on the back of his jacket. He looked down and saw Philip staring up at him. "You're a real baster," he said, looking DJ straight in the eye. "You're a real mean, dirty baster," he repeated.

"Thank you, sonny," DJ replied.

Philip walked back to his mother, who was waiting beyond the rug perimeter. She smiled and waved. "He wanted to say goodbye. I think he really liked you."

DJ nodded, turned and spoke with a few browsers, praying they wouldn't want to purchase anything, then with the department empty, he crossed back into the storeroom and navigated each aisle in an attempt to familiarize himself with the inventory. After one complete circuit, he turned around and walked back through the curtain.

Standing in front of him was the stunning blonde who had sat at the front table of the Jailhouse Rock. She was more breathtaking than he recalled, and was wearing real jewelry and eye shadow. She moved her hand from behind her back and held up Philip's two navy sneakers. "Recognize these?" She wasn't smiling.

DJ stared at the sneakers, then slowly at the blonde woman. "Yes, I think I might," he mumbled.

"Didn't you just sell these to a boy and his mother?"

"Ah, if those are the ones, then they probably are and I probably did," DJ stuttered.

"I'm Carlyn Canova, the assistant store manager," she said. "Where did you locate these? And how did you manage a price?"

DJ's heart torpedoed through the flats of his feet into the Mertz Brothers' septic tank. "I got them from the storeroom," he said pointing back over his shoulder.

"And the price?"

DJ could feel his face becoming flushed. "Guessed," he disclosed softly. He knew he was going to be fired, and looked away, waited a few seconds, then after hearing nothing, slowly looked back again.

She was staring at him. "The woman who bought these sneakers had second thoughts, especially because she considered you to be so young. She stopped by my office and I issued the refund there. Show me where you got them. I haven't seen sneakers like these in years."

DJ led her to the display in the back of the storeroom and pointed to the empty cardboard feet. "There."

"You took the sneakers off that display?"

"I couldn't find any kids' sneakers. I tried." DJ glanced at her, then looked away again. "To tell you the truth, Mrs. Canova, I don't know anything about shoes or how to sell them. I didn't know what I was doing."

"I know that." She looked closely at his employee identification badge. "Is it Dale?"

"Dale or DJ," he responded.

"Well, Dale or DJ, I'm aware you were not adequately prepared, and it's our error for putting you in this type of awkward situation. I don't want to second-guess the boss, but I'm not exactly pleased that this happened." She took the sneakers and placed them back on the cardboard display. "It's not good for you, and certainly doesn't help our sales, or reputation. And reputation is everything."

DJ glanced again at Mrs. Canova. She was more beautiful than anyone he had ever seen, including all the movies and all the magazines.

"I'm going to work with you until we can get someone else down here, DJ. I checked and that should be in about an hour. Come on, let's go up front."

DJ followed Mrs. Canova back into the sales area where two or three new people were moving around. He watched how she greeted the customers, listened to their questions, then disappeared into the storeroom, returning moments later carrying two or three shoe boxes. She sat sidesaddle on the stool and chatted with people as she helped them with their shoes. The department became busier and DJ started to wait on customers again. He would ask Mrs. Canova the location of what he was looking for, and she could direct him to the correct section of each aisle.

"Mrs. Canova?" asked a bald man with lengthy strands of hair originating above one ear and stretching across his scalp. "Mr. Collins sent me down to work in this department." The man was diamond shaped, with a rep necktie hanging halfway down the fly of his pants. DJ recognized him as one of the Hardscrabble High School science teachers, though he had never been one of his students.

"Ah, yes, welcome Mr. Slavik." She nodded in DJ's direction. "This is DJ Elders. He's new and will be working with you. Please answer any of his questions, and feel free to call Mr. Collins or myself if you have any problems."

"Certainly, Mrs. Canova." He walked across to the display area to greet a woman browsing with her husband."

Mrs. Canova turned her eyes back to DJ. "You're catching on. You'll do fine. And I must say you look considerably better today than you did a couple of weeks ago at that bar." She brushed her hands together. "I hope whoever you were fighting over that night was worth it, Dale or DJ Elders."

DJ didn't know how to respond, so he said nothing. Mrs. Canova smiled and disappeared into the crowd.

CHAPTER 8

Ike's house was hot, crowded and always reeked of damp diapers laced with Cherry Blend tobacco, a sweet-and-sour concoction fermenting in humid heat.

Mr. O'Reilly rested on a lopsided sofa in the darkened living room, an unlit pipe in his mouth. His flannel shirt was buttoned to the neck and except for a fringe that grew an inch above his ears in a horseshoe, he was bald. Next to him, staring straight ahead, Mrs. O'Reilly, gray with fatigue, was holding two sleeping babies. When either partner in the suburban *American Gothic* shifted, the linoleum living room floor creaked beneath them.

"Afternoon, boys," Mr. O'Reilly said absently as he studied his pipe.

"Afternoon," DJ replied as he slowly followed Ike up the stairs to his room.

Mr. O'Reilly never smiled, and not only was DJ used to it, he knew why. One night, he had watched TV in the living room with Ike and his father. When Ike went to the bathroom, Mr. O'Reilly had forgotten he was not alone and laughed out loud. At that moment, DJ caught a glimpse of dark stretches of missing teeth. If his pipe had been a carrot, Ike's father would have been a dead ringer for Bugs Bunny.

The upstairs of the O'Reilly house was broken into tiny, unfinished Sheetrock rooms for Ike's brothers and sisters, with the twins still sleeping downstairs in the parents' bedroom. As the two walked down the narrow hallway to the cubicle at the end, Ike said, "I don't know what my parents are going to do for space when my sisters get too old to sleep with them."

Inside Ike's room was a single bed, a gray metal double door closet, and a table and chair that rested next to the only window. Scattered over the table's surface was a series of small metal springs, screws, wheels, and chains, components of a home-study watch repair course—Ike's plan for the future.

DJ knew his best friend was constantly re-examined by some up-to-the-minute doctor for his heart condition, and once in a while, if comfortable enough, Ike would share tidbits of information from the various appointments. As the years passed, DJ had been able to piece together what he figured was a fairly complete and bleak medical composite.

Ike had traveled fourteen times to New York City, twice to Philadelphia, and once to Columbus, Ohio, all for medical evaluation. The Columbus trip, when he was six, had been the worst. Ike didn't recollect much, only that his father had placed a plastic crib mattress over the back seat and he could eat animal crackers and sleep on the way home. As he fitfully dozed, he recalled being jolted awake when his father jammed on the brakes, then unable to fall back to sleep, his face coated with a crumbly drool that stuck to the mattress cover, he lay still and watched the light shadows slide across the inside of the roof, then skid out the window and disappear. Occasionally his mother would pause in her conversation and reach over the seat to touch his back—Ike later understood, to make sure he was breathing—before she continued to whisper as she lit a new cigarette from the butt of one still burning between her fingers.

He remembered lying motionless on the sticky mattress waiting for his heart to stop, waiting to skid outside and disappear with the light shadows, and as his parents' whispering lapsed off into periods of silence, he'd concentrate on the hum of the tires against the road. After a while, his father would stretch or scratch an arm or leg, and his mother would turn on the radio, pointing out an announcer's strange accent, at the same time reaching behind the seat to touch his back again.

DJ didn't ask much. He never believed it was his place to pry, but if Ike offered information, as he had about the Ohio trip, he would nod, then ask vague questions. He wasn't comfortable knowing much anyway. He could look at Ike and be reminded of the dark half-circles under his own eyes.

"Yeah, I figure I'm almost eighteen, and it's a good thing I'm thinking about tomorrow with this watch repair course," Ike said as he sat on the edge of his bed. "And I've already got almost all of the money saved for the second half. That's where you learn all the tough stuff." He motioned DJ to the chair by his desk. "Have a seat."

DJ sat while Ike leaned forward, elbows on his knees.

"I wanted to tell you something," Ike said, "I asked Patty to go to a movie with me Saturday night."

"You did?" DJ had not anticipated the statement. He knew his sister and Ike cared for each other as friends, but he had always figured that was just next door neighbor convenience. Plus, he had never thought of Ike going out with anyone.

"Just needed to tell you."

DJ paused a second, then nodded. "Hey, it's up to Patty. I don't care."

That seemed to satisfy Ike, so the two spent the next hour talking about Maynard, Frannie, and how they'd all gotten so old. Then neither spoke as they sat absorbing the dusk, until Ike said, "Seems like it was just yesterday when we were all in third grade together, DJ. Now Maynard's having sex with

Frannie, and pretty soon everyone's going off to college." He rubbed his hand against the sleeve of his madras shirt. "Yeah, everybody's leaving town."

It was true. DJ would be off to college next year, and could learn to run a mile, or chase girls if he wanted to, but Ike, debilitated by his heart condition, would still be sitting in his cubicle, fossilized by the Cherry Blend, dirty diaper heat.

Ike and his room always managed to submerge DJ— the sadness, always the profound sadness, always the blue undertow his friend unintentionally initiated just by relating bits and pieces of his life story. And DJ always wanted to make it right for him, just as he did for Patty, but he didn't know how except to listen and nod—something he figured no one else attempted.

Later, when it was dark and Ike switched on his desk light, DJ walked down the stairs. "Goodnight, Mr. O'Reilly," he said, heading for the door.

"Goodnight, now," Ike's father replied from his seat on the sofa, his pipe tobacco glowing in the dark.

∞

When DJ walked in his front door, Patty told him Leslie had called. "Please call her back," she said from in front of the kitchen sink where she was washing dishes.

Dale sat at the table, a beer bottle clutched in his hand.

DJ had been over at Leslie's house again the night before, and it was ridiculous. All she wanted to do was hold hands. He tried for more, only to have her give him a dirty look and say she hoped there was more to their relationship than just his desire to touch her.

He didn't think so, but didn't say so.

"Did you know Ike wanted me to go to a movie with him?" Patty asked.

"Just heard about it. You going?"

Patty hesitated, then said, "I didn't think I could say no to Ike. I mean I'm not doing anything, and he is a friend. But I wouldn't want him to think it's more than that."

"Maybe he doesn't. Maybe he just wants another friend himself. He's probably tired of spending Saturday nights alone. I mean, I'm never around."

"Any TV dinners left?" Dale asked.

"Yes, Dad," Patty responded, "I picked up a whole bunch last night. Would you like me to put one in the oven for you?"

"Got chicken?" Dale asked.

"Yes, we have chicken," Patty answered.

DJ picked up the telephone to call Leslie, then hung up.

Instead, he climbed the stairs to his room and reached into a stack of record albums, lifting Marty Robbins's *Gunfighter Ballads and Trail Songs* from near the top. He slipped the record from the jacket, placed it on the turntable and lowered the needle. With his back against the wall, DJ slid downward until his knees hunched up against his chest. The opening acoustic runs led to Marty's voice which poured from between the guitars, as fresh and pure as spring water gushing over the stones in a mountain stream.

Marty Robbins—an old friend, a trail boss who allowed DJ's escape from Leslie's sexual treadmill and his father's inebriation, setting him free to meander through the terra cotta canyons that led to the wide-open plains and the distant violet mountains.

"Thanks, Marty," DJ whispered. "Thanks, pal."

CHAPTER 9

As DJ drove home from Mertz Brothers Saturday night, he caught flashes of trick-or-treaters in his headlights: orange and black groups, white ghosts and skeletons, all carrying brown paper bags, running from one house to the next.

When he walked in the door, Patty said, "Herman called and said to come a little early tomorrow morning. Then Leslie called and she wants you to call her back. She says it's important."

"It's always important with Leslie," DJ muttered. "What time are you leaving with Ike tonight?"

"I don't know. I guess about 7:30. Why, do you want to go?"

"No, no. Just wondered." He was tired, and anyway, he suspected Ike wanted to be alone with Patty. "Where's Dad?"

"Sleeping." Patty pointed to the bedroom.

"That's a surprise," DJ said as he headed up the stairs to his room.

"Don't forget to call Leslie."

"Okay," DJ said, closing the door behind him. "I won't."

He didn't forget. He decided not to.

The phone rang downstairs.

"DJ," Patty called, "it's Leslie for you."

"Tell her I'll call her back," he yelled back through his door.

"She says it's important."

"I'll call her back."

After Ike had stopped by for Patty, DJ sat in the darkness of his room, rocking on the back legs of the desk chair. An occasional group of trick-or-treaters would ring the bell and then run away seconds later when no one answered. He could hear the storm door slam shut, then muffled shouts and laughter moving away down the street.

As he listened to the house creak and the wind gust against the window panes, DJ heard the phone downstairs. He counted twenty-eight rings before his father lumbered from the bedroom into the kitchen. "God Almighty," he heard him mutter, "Jesus, God Almighty," as he picked up the telephone. "Hello. No, no, he's not here. No, Leslie, if he was here, don't you think he would have answered the phone by now?" Dale paused. "No, I don't think so. All right, I'll give him the message." He slammed the receiver into its cradle, "God Almighty." DJ heard his father walk to the back of the house and the springs groan as he climbed into bed.

A half-hour later, DJ sneaked down the stairs and out the front door. As he approached Leslie's house, he crouched below the front hedges and darted past.

Once through the side door of the Jailhouse Rock, he stopped in the men's room to check his appearance in the mirror. On his way out, he passed the wastebasket jammed with empty beer cans, liquor bottles, and women's nylons.

Thor never emptied the garbage.

He crossed directly to Lila's corner table by the stage, pulled out a chair and sat down. The place was so jammed for Halloween that Jellybowl was helping Thor behind the bar.

As DJ scanned the room hoping to see Mrs. Canova, it seemed everyone was in costume. Monty had on a football uniform, and Wendell was a duck, with only the circle of his face showing beneath an orange bill jutting from his forehead. In front of them, the dance floor was writhing with adults in embarrassing, homemade outfits.

"Hi, sweetheart," Lila said. "Monty said you might be stopping in tonight."

"No costume?" DJ asked.

"Isn't this costume Thor makes me wear every weekend bad enough?" Lila asked, pointing to the prisoner's stripes of her cocktail uniform. "Can I get you anything?"

"A Coke would be good."

Lila shoved her checks into her apron pocket. "Okay. Better for you than beer. I'll be right back. We're real busy tonight."

Out of the corner of his eye, DJ spotted Mrs. Canova as she returned to the table from the dance floor, followed by a clown with a painted face and orange wig.

Hard to believe he'd wear that circus outfit, DJ thought.

She wasn't wearing a Halloween costume either which made DJ a little more at ease. Clarabel asked her something, she shook her head, then as he departed for the bar, she turned her attention to her girlfriend sitting at the table.

"What the hell you rushing 'Guitar Boogie Shuffle' for?" Wendell barked at Gordon five minutes later after the song ended and the three climbed down from the stage. "Your damn chords was pulling the drum part faster."

Gordon ignored Wendell and moved directly to Mrs. Canova's table beating Clarabel by five seconds. The sweating clown sat down anyway and immediately knocked back a mug of beer.

"How you doing, cowboy?" Monty slapped DJ on the back,

as he walked back to the men's room. Then over his shoulder, he called, "Hey, Wendell and I are definitely heading up to the cabin over Thanksgiving. Let me know if you want to go."

Wendell arrived at the table and watched Monty walk away, then turned and stood in front of DJ in his duck suit. "Am I a jerk or what?" he asked, swiveling his neck and surveying as much of himself as he could view. His tail feathers swooped out five feet behind him. "Ever try hitting the bass pedal with webbed feet? I tell you what, if Thor wasn't the boss, I'd tell him what he could do with his duck suit."

"Wendell, who's your guitar player?" DJ asked.

"Hell, that's Gordon. I thought you knew him."

"No, not really," DJ answered.

"Yup, Gordon Erario, the fastest hands in Hardscrabble— part-time musician, full-time mechanic." He scratched his arm feathers. "I'm going over to the bar. Want anything?"

"Thanks, but I think Lila's bringing me a Coke."

"To hell with Coke, I'll sneak you back a beer." He toddled off through the tables, his tail feathers dusting the backs of people's heads as he passed.

Out of the corner of his eye, DJ watched Gordon and the clown vie for Mrs. Canova's attention while her girlfriend sitting next to her stared absently away. After a while DJ stared away too.

Halfway through the last set of the night, he was feeling wobbly. The day at Mertz Brothers had worn him out, it was one o'clock in the morning and the three beers Wendell had smuggled him turned the costumed crowd surreal.

"Would you tell Monty and Wendell I said thanks," he said to Lila, when she returned to the table to light up a Newport.

"Of course, honey." Lila inhaled, then shook the match out.

DJ rose and slipped into his jacket.

"Safe home, sweetheart," Lila said as she rested her cigarette on the ashtray's rim and headed for another table.

DJ zipped up his jacket and walked outside through the parking lot. All the trick-or-treaters were asleep and he couldn't deal with the thought of the morning and Herman waiting at the door of Van Velsor's staring at his watch. And the nylons and empty liquor bottles in the wastebasket that had been there for months, the pathetic clown, Lila's beehive hairstyle, Leslie's phone calls—they were all depressing.

DJ crossed Main Street and moved left on to Melville Road. He was about to turn right on to Jackson Road when a car came to a crawl behind him and suddenly clicked on the high beams, elongating his shadow. Turning quickly, DJ raised his arm to shield his eyes, but could only see glaring white light and the silhouette of a roof. The headlights abruptly flicked back to low and the car surged next to him.

The horn beeped, then the window closest to him rolled down. "Can I give you a lift?"

"Mrs. Canova, is that you?" DJ asked, though as soon as the question was out of his mouth, it was obvious that it was and that he was an idiot for asking.

"Yes it is. Hop in. I'll give you a ride home." She leaned across the console and opened the door."

"Is this the new Mustang?" DJ asked.

"What do you think of it?"

"It's great," DJ said. "I like the bucket seats."

Mrs. Canova smiled. "Which way?"

"Turn right here, then go to the end of the street where it forks, and you can let me out by the stop sign. Thanks a lot for the ride."

"It's too cold to have to walk anywhere tonight." When she shifted into first gear her coat fell away from her legs.

DJ glanced at her skirt inches above her knees.

"Did Basement Shoes work out all right today with Mr. Slavik?"

"Yeah, it was fine." DJ felt very nervous. "Where's your girlfriend?"

"Oh, we always take separate cars. It's just easier that way. She likes to go her way, and I go mine." She shifted into third gear. "I'm glad the job went well. All you needed was more hands-on training and some inventory knowledge." She approached the stop sign. "Which house is yours?"

"That one straight ahead." He pointed to the gray Cape.

Mrs. Canova swung the Mustang around in front of the house and pulled up next to the curb. "Here you are, DJ." She smiled. Her lips were slightly cracked from the cold and her blonde hair hung loosely around her forehead.

"Was the clown your husband, Mrs. Canova?" DJ asked.

She stared at him for a moment, then laughed out loud. "My husband is a clown all right, but not that particular one." She continued to regard DJ as she had the first time they met. "Why?"

"I don't know, I was just thinking about it." Impulsively, he added, "I bet Gordon would be interested to know though."

"Gordon, the guitar player?" She laughed again, then abruptly stopped. "Oh, I'm sure there's a lot Gordon would be interested in. He knows my first name, but he doesn't have my last name or phone number, which is what he's after." She thought a moment, her hands resting on the steering wheel. "Poor Gordon, he'll never get to first base." She depressed the clutch, then shifted into first gear. "Well, DJ, I have to be going. I guess I'll see you again next Saturday."

"Sure, I'll be there, Mrs. Canova." He fumbled for the door handle.

"Carlyn," she said. "You can call me Carlyn when we're not in the store."

When we're not in the store? "Okay, uh, Carlyn," DJ said uneasily. "Thanks again for the ride."

"You're more than welcome, Mr. Elders." She smiled. "I'll see you next week."

DJ stepped out of the Mustang and closed the door behind him. He stood on the sidewalk while Carlyn pulled away from the curb and drove back down Jackson Road.

CHAPTER 10

Herman had just finished placing the coffee filters in the urns and was still in his overcoat counting cash at the register when DJ walked in, earlier than he had ever arrived before. He saluted Herman, but said nothing as he marched past him on his way to the rear of the coffee shop. Caught by surprise, Herman saluted back, then glanced at his watch, twice.

Getting out of bed that morning had been easy. Most of the night had been spent kicking the blankets around and thinking of Mrs. Canova. It had been a relief to finally roll from between the sheets and head to work.

And surprisingly, in spite of a night filled only with catnaps and half-dreams, DJ was full of energy. As he brought the bundles of papers in on the handcart, he even began to whistle, but quickly stopped when he remembered Herman was the only one allowed to determine each day's cheerfulness level.

"It's always good to get an early start," Herman said as he glanced at his watch again. His level of joy approached pure rapture as he watched DJ quickly assemble the newspapers with military precision.

"It sure is, Herman," DJ said, completing one stack of the

New York Times and carrying the pile to the stand near the front door.

Herman watched DJ and looked at his watch for the fourth time. "This is very exciting, DJ," he said, scratching his chest through the opening between two buttons of his shirt. "We'll be able to open forty minutes before opening time."

∞

Later in the morning, Greta stopped by after church. She sat in her booth with the checkerboard and a coffee cup in front of her. After the rush of people from the last Catholic Mass had slowed, she asked, "DJ, how about a game?"

DJ nodded. He had known Greta for years—her checkers, the cigarette holder, the chocolate figures she created in Van Velsor's cellar to sell during the holidays, but he wasn't aware of much else. He thought he recalled Patty once mentioning that she lived alone in an apartment on the street behind the A&P, but he wasn't positive. And he had witnessed the cheerless image of her in a dark winter coat, shopping for greeting cards by herself in the stationery store one night. The vision had gnawed at him, producing a vague sense of sadness—for her, for himself, though he didn't know why.

"Sure, Greta, I'll play a game," he answered.

"As long as he's off the clock," Herman interrupted from behind the cash register while he added a long column of figures using his black marking pencil.

"Am I off?" DJ asked.

Herman looked at his watch. "Yes, all right."

DJ walked to the booth and sat down opposite Greta.

"So, you are well, DJ?" she asked as she moved a black checker forward.

DJ pushed a red checker opposite hers. "I'm pretty good, Greta." The two concentrated in silence, then interchanged four moves, after which Greta jumped one of DJ's checkers.

"How did you do that?" He hadn't anticipated the move and something that simple should have been obvious. It wasn't brain surgery. "I mean, how did I miss that?"

Greta smiled. "I had a thought the other day. Would you and Patty like to come to dinner at my apartment Thursday night?"

DJ was unprepared for the question. "Dinner at your apartment?"

"I've already invited Ike though, unfortunately, he's unavailable. I would invite your father too, but I suspect he might not be able to make it." She moved another checker.

DJ considered the invitation. "That would be great, Greta. Thank you. I'll ask Patty."

They continued to focus on the game, but within five minutes DJ conceded. "One day, Greta, one day," he said laughing.

"Yes, one day," she said, sipping her coffee.

DJ was ready to leave—the lack of sleep was beginning to catch up with him—when Bobby Litchfield walked in holding hands with Lisa.

After he picked up a *Daily News*, Bobby walked to the counter, then noticed DJ in the booth with Greta. "Hey Shooter, is it true that if a bird had your brain he'd fly backwards? Where did you learn to throw basketballs at the wrong basket? Even the donkeys wouldn't have been that stupid."

"Stop it, Bobby," Lisa said, a casual smile edging across her face. "It was only a game."

Bobby walked over to the booth. "Hi, Greta." He leaned over and grabbed DJ easily around the neck. "I ought to kill you, pal," he said, pretending to apply pressure before he pulled his hands away and slapped DJ on the back. "Just kidding, DJ. You should be proud. We'll be known as the only senior team in school history to lose to the juniors."

"Come on, Bobby. We're late." Lisa was standing by the counter.

"Better late than never. Isn't that right, Shooter?" Bobby

slapped DJ on the back again. "See you. Bye, Greta." He crossed to Lisa and the two headed for the door. "So long, Herman. Hope our boy gets a basketball scholarship to UCLA. I'm tired of them winning every year."

Lisa laughed and playfully tapped Bobby's arm as if she was swishing at a gnat on his sleeve. Bobby smirked and ran his hand down her side.

DJ hadn't moved, even when his neck was being wrung.

"Boys like Bobby," Greta said, "they have too much power."

CHAPTER 11

On Thursday, at two minutes before six, Patty and DJ arrived at Greta's door. The hallway was cool with a scent of mothballs and fresh paint. "Don't lean anywhere," DJ said.

"This seems like a strange thing to do even though she's nice," Patty said, "like we're orphans or something. I mean we don't really even know her."

"Yeah, it is kind of crazy." DJ pressed the buzzer, waited, then heard the weight of Greta's steps as she approached the entrance.

"Welcome," Greta said, swinging the door open. "Come in, come in. I'm so happy to see you." She wore a gray silk dress and a gold necklace.

"I hope we're on time," Patty said.

"You couldn't be more perfect," Greta responded. She closed the door and lifted the steel bar from the lock and placed it in a corner against the wall. As she turned back, Greta caught DJ and Patty watching her. "I'm sorry about this ridiculous lock, but as long as it came with the apartment, I concluded I might as well use it."

"I've never seen one before," Patty said. And the bar is a

strange color blue. Kind of blue and purple."

Greta lifted it from the corner. "Yes, it is a ridiculous color." She nodded to Patty. "See, this curved end fits in the lock on the back of the door." She slid the tip of the bar into the lock. "And the straight end fits into this metal groove in the floor behind the door. Now if Attila The Hun attempts to crash through using a battering ram during dinner, the bar is heavy enough that he won't come close to getting in." She placed it in the corner. "I suppose he'll just have to invade Europe all over again."

"Well, I feel safe," Patty said.

"Trust me, you are." Greta smiled. "Now hand me your coats and I'll hang them up."

As he watched Greta, DJ noticed she looked sunny, almost radiant. Her gray hair shimmered under the lights.

"This way," Greta said as she extended her arm.

Patty and DJ followed her into an extended living room highlighted with antique furniture, oriental rugs, and city night scenes painted in oil. In the corner, just through the entranceway, hanging over a country side table next to a hurricane lamp, was a canvas that immediately caught DJ's eye—a Fourth of July celebration filled with fireworks, rockets, and streamers cascading through a pitch-black sky.

Against the far wall, two large walnut JBL speakers sat on either side of a cabinet containing an amplifier, receiver, and turntable. Facing the speakers, against the opposite wall, were two leather recliner chairs separated by a teak cocktail table. Chamber music stirred faintly in the background.

"They're rather obtrusive, aren't they?" Greta said, indicating the speakers. "I refer to them as Greta's folly."

"This is wonderful," Patty said.

"And those are speakers?" DJ asked, immediately wondering how his records would sound. He'd never seen speakers that large, even in the high school auditorium.

"Indeed they are." Greta crossed her arms. "And believe me, DJ, it's a long story, something I'll tell at another time if you're ever interested." She extended her arms to the two leather chairs. "Please sit. Please."

"What about you?" DJ asked.

"Oh, I'll slide a chair over in a moment. Please."

"These look so comfortable, Greta," Patty said, running her hand across an arm as she sat down.

"Would you like Coke, or lemonade, and, well, I guess you wouldn't care for milk." She hovered, her hands pressed together.

"Anything is fine, Greta," Patty said.

DJ nodded.

Greta disappeared into the kitchen and moments later returned carrying a silver tray with two Coke bottles, an ice bucket, and two crystal glasses. She set it on the table between them, and using tongs, gingerly placed ice cubes in each glass. "Please pour the Coke yourself. I'm going to get a touch of sherry."

Greta departed into the kitchen once more and returned carrying a stemmed cordial glass. She slid over a chair, then raised her hand in a toast. "To Patty." She looked at her and smiled. "And to DJ," she said, her smile unbroken. "To friends."

DJ was self-conscious—he had never made a toast—but was able to follow Patty's lead and lift his glass. He gestured to Greta and nodded self-consciously.

∞

During dinner, Patty looked at Greta. "This is such a beautiful apartment. Have you lived here a long time?"

"Several years," Greta replied, "though it seems a great deal longer than it actually has been."

"And before that?" Patty asked.

"Ah, yes, before that it was New York City." She sipped from a Waterford glass. "Many years in New York City."

"And what was that like?" Patty continued. "What did you

do there?"

"Doing was never a problem. Doing is never a concern in Manhattan—just finding the hours in the day to accomplish it all is where the difficulty lies." She nodded at Patty. "I went to many plays, and I had, and still have for that matter, a favorite French restaurant called Cheval Blanc. It's all very wonderful."

"I would love to see it," Patty said.

"Then you will, my dear, then you will."

For dessert Greta brought a foot-high strawberry shortcake to the table. "It's been ages since I made one of these," she said.

"When did you find the time?" Patty asked.

"In Hardscrabble, when your brother is a business owner, and you share the disbursements of a trust fund, time takes care of itself." Greta placed a Players cigarette in an ivory holder, lit it, and sipped black coffee as she wound a lock of hair around her forefinger.

"Maybe we should break out the checkerboard," DJ suggested when the conversation lagged.

"Ah, DJ, even the checkerboard has its place. And tonight it's locked up in the coffee shop." She placed the cigarette in a Steuben ashtray. "It's odd isn't it, an old woman filling her days with coffee and checkers. You children must think I'm very odd."

"No, that's not true," Patty said.

"Well, thank you for the reassurance," Greta replied, "but at least I know I'm nutty. It helps when you're aware of these things."

Patty gradually opened up, talking about school and plans for college. She mentioned that she had seen a movie with Ike, strictly as a friend, but that she would love to spend time with Bobby Litchfield, though she knew she'd never have a chance.

DJ drew comfort from watching Patty and listening to her talk about herself. To see his sister's eyes shine, and to discover Greta's interest in her, was a relief.

Gradually, Patty ran out of words, and Greta turned to DJ. "And you, dear boy?" she asked.

"And me, nothing. I'm talked out."

Greta nodded. "You should know that I've observed you in the coffee shop and watched you here tonight. I can see how much you care for your sister. It's marvelous. Simply marvelous." She stood and cut DJ another piece of shortcake.

"No, really, I couldn't, Greta." DJ held up his hand.

"Patty?"

"No thank you, Greta, but it was delicious. And we really should go."

Minutes later as they were leaving, DJ glanced back at the oil painting of the soaring orange and gold skyrockets, spitting, flaring, and simmering against the dark night.

Once on the stairwell, he heard the bar of the lock slip into place behind them.

∞

"I'm not sure what just happened," DJ said as the two walked across the parking lot behind the A&P.

"She's very nice, isn't she?" Patty asked. "I think she's also very religious. Sometimes I see her coming to five o'clock Mass on Saturday night."

"Do you still go?"

"Actually, I'm over there at 4:30 when the church is empty. I like it better."

"And Herman doesn't mind you taking time off?" DJ asked.

"No, it's slow then, but I don't get paid."

"Surprise, surprise."

The two moved through the alley next to the A&P, then up Main Street and across the railroad tracks. "Isn't it funny that I've worked at Van Velsor's all this time, but never knew anything about Greta before tonight?" Patty asked.

"Hey, same with me," DJ replied. "But I like her."

"Me too," Patty said. "It was weird when she said she was watching you."

"Yeah, I know."

When they entered the house ten minutes later, Dale was snoring in his lounger in front of a flickering western. DJ walked over and turned off the TV.

"I think Ike's going to ask me to another movie," Patty whispered as they stared down at their father.

"Is that good?" DJ asked.

Patty glanced briefly at DJ. "I don't know what it is. I think it's sad more than anything. If I had to pick one thing, it would be sad."

"For who?"

"For me. For Ike." She paused. "Maybe even for you. I don't know, it's hard to explain." A faint smile. "Is being with Leslie sad for you?"

"No, just crazy. But I haven't seen her much lately."

"Not having a mother is sad for me," Patty said.

"We had a mother."

Patty stared back at her brother. "I don't feel like we did. I don't feel like I ever had a mother." She crossed the living room and walked to her bedroom. At the doorway, now a white and blue porcelain figure, breakable, resigned, she turned and whispered, "Goodnight," then closed the door behind her.

Moments later, DJ heard the first faint notes of Johnny Mathis sweep from under her door and float across the living room, gently burying their sleeping father alive.

CHAPTER 12

DJ arrived at Mertz Brothers on Saturday morning five minutes before the security guard unlocked the employees' entrance. He stood outside, alone, and looked through the parking lot for the Mustang, but Mrs. Canova hadn't arrived yet—only his gray Falcon, a Buick, and Cliff's junker.

"Okay, everyone in." The guard swung the steel door open with one hand. "Or at least you, buddy."

DJ moved past the guard and headed for Cliff's office.

"Sit, DJ." Cliff nodded at the chair opposite his desk. "I've got to figure out who's not showing up today before I put you anywhere." His eyes were red road maps and DJ could smell his sour breath across the room. "Want a cup of coffee?"

"No thanks, Mr. Collins," he responded.

"How did it go last week? I didn't hear of any problems." Cliff was studying his notes as he spoke.

"There were no problems, DJ did a wonderful job," Carlyn said as she entered Cliff's office. "I think he continued to learn a good deal about shoes in the process too. What do you think, DJ?"

DJ had been anticipating this moment all week—to see her

again, to say something charming, to make a Steve McQueen impression, but with the moment at hand, her presence was too overwhelming. "Yes," he murmured.

"Where are we going to use DJ this week, Cliff?" Carlyn asked. "With a couple more weeks' experience, he's going to be invaluable to us."

"Well," Cliff said, perusing the papers lying on his desk, "I could probably use him in Basement Shoes again, although I'd rather give him more experience. Don't believe he'd be comfortable in Foundations."

Carlyn looked over Cliff's shoulder. "Bob's out today. I bet DJ would be perfect for The Ivy League Shop." She glanced at DJ. "You're going to college next year, aren't you?"

DJ rediscovered part of his voice. "I hope to."

"What do you think, Cliff, The Ivy League Shop?" Carlyn asked.

"Sure, that'll work." Cliff picked up a chart and made a notation on it. "Think you can handle that, son?"

DJ nodded.

"Off you go, buddy. Main floor."

As DJ rose, Carlyn continued to look over Cliff's shoulder. "Have a good day, DJ," she said, her eyes remaining on the papers in Cliff's hand.

"Thank you. Thanks a lot," he said, then headed down to Security for his money pouch and register key.

∞

The Ivy League Shop was upscale and smelled like cedar shavings, unlike anything he was accustomed to.

Mannequins with Madison Avenue haircuts were wearing broad-striped shirts, knit neckties, corduroys, blue blazers, and winter coats with wooden barrels for buttons. Plus scarves; piles of scarves. Nobody DJ had ever known wore a scarf—they just zipped to the neck and plunged ahead.

The striped shirts were not a total shock—he'd seen them before on The Beach Boys album covers, but having them for sale right here, right next door to Hardscrabble, surprised him. He thought that was only a California look.

DJ stared down at his black shoes and rubbed the front of each on the back of his pants. He approached the necktie table, thumbed through a few, then moved to the shoe section. He discovered the department carried only a limited selection, mostly loafers, and thick-soled dragons with holes running in patterns across the leather called wing-tips—all completely different from what he'd sold in the basement.

"Mr. Elders, it looks like we're together again." Mr. Slavik approached, the flat of his hand pressed against the top of his head in a moderately successful attempt to keep the breeze from rustling the hair strands stretched across his scalp. "Mrs. Canova said we're a good team."

"Have you ever worked here before, Mr. Slavik?"

"Many times, Mr. Elders, and it's much easier than Basement Shoes. Different class of people. They don't have as much difficulty parting with the buck."

"You don't have to call me Mr. Elders, Mr. Slavik." He paused. "You're a teacher at Hardscrabble, aren't you?"

Mr. Slavik studied DJ. "I thought you looked familiar. You were never in one of my classes, were you?"

DJ shook his head.

"I didn't think so. You're a senior. Am I correct?"

DJ nodded.

"Well, when you graduate and you're no longer a student, we can share some Hardscrabble High School horror stories," Mr. Slavik said, now unconsciously patting the top of his head, keeping his hair in place. "Have you got the register in order?"

"All set, I think."

The first customers began drifting through the main floor and DJ was much more comfortable than during the previous weeks, mainly because of Mr. Slavik, but also because he liked The Ivy League Shop—its cedar smell, all the wool, the lime cologne, and Royal Copenhagen cufflinks. He wandered past the main counter and straightened a stack of crew socks as he passed.

"DJ-J-J-J!" Maynard walked over holding Frannie's hand. "DJ-J-J-J, the salesman." He was pleased he surprised DJ. "Give me two dozen neckties and a box of shirts. No, make that a box of neckties and two dozen shirts. No, make that two dozen shirts, two dozen neckties, a box of condoms, and a carton of cigarettes."

Mr. Slavik, patting his hair in place again, appeared behind DJ. "Do you need any assistance, Mr. Elders?"

"I bet you can't do that and rub your stomach at the same time," Maynard said staring at Mr. Slavik.

"Excuse me, Mr. Maynard?" Mr. Slavik said, removing his hand from his head. "I haven't had the pleasure of your company since, what has it been, the ninth grade? It's amazing how certain names remain with me."

Frannie tugged at Maynard. "I'm going over to the Women's Department. Come on, Don." She walked to the main aisle dragging him behind her.

Maynard stared back at DJ as he walked away. "See what happens? All your control goes out the window, right out the frigging window and you turn into a moron."

The customer traffic increased and DJ didn't see Mrs. Canova the entire morning. When it was almost time for his lunch hour, he casually asked Mr. Slavik where she was. "Mrs. Canova usually only shows up when there's a problem," he said. "Most of the time she's up with Mr. Collins in his office." Then he added, "She's pretty, isn't she?" and turned away.

∞

Before he left the store that evening, DJ bought a blue necktie with gold stripes he had been studying from a distance for most of the day. Around four o'clock, he had taken the tie and placed it below the counter so that no one else would purchase it.

Navy and gold, safe colors that made him feel new.

∞

By the time DJ had showered, Ike was already at the front door. He'd heard him step inside so he slid into his bathrobe and walked into the living room. "Where you headed tonight?" he asked.

"What have we got a chaperon now?" Ike laughed. The fragrance of English Leather wafted from his coat. "Boy, I mean it's cold out there." His hands were shaking.

"We're going to another movie, right, Ike?" Patty asked.

"Sure, I think that's what we'll do. Then probably stop at Van Velsor's if you want to meet us there later, DJ."

"Kind of a postman's holiday," Patty added. "I hope Herman won't want me to clean."

"I don't think he would do that," Ike answered, then thought a second. "But I'm not sure."

"Maybe I'll see you later," DJ said though he knew he wouldn't.

Patty put her hand in Ike's arm. "If Dad wakes up later, I bought a new supply of TV dinners. He probably won't like them though—no chicken."

"In his shape, he couldn't tell the difference between chicken and Spam," DJ answered. "So who cares?"

CHAPTER 13

DJ didn't want to make Ike's mistake and put on too much cologne. Some behind his neck, across his chest, and a splash across his knees, though the knees were a last-minute call.

He sat in his room for a while doing nothing, then went downstairs and turned off all the lights except for one in the living room. He didn't want to be blamed if his father stumbled and cracked his head open. Once outside, he pulled the door shut.

At the side entrance to the Jailhouse Rock, DJ realized it was too early to go inside and walked down Main Street to the high school, then slowly returned. He glanced at his watch and moved across the Rock's parking lot.

"DJ?" Carlyn was stepping out of her Mustang.

His heart jumped. He hadn't noticed her car parked in the corner.

He stopped. "Hi, Mrs. Canova."

"Carlyn, remember?" She laughed and adjusted her pocketbook strap over her shoulder. "Are you going in?" She nodded at the front entrance to the Jailhouse Rock.

"I have to use the side door. I'm not officially allowed inside because I'm not eighteen. Thor just lets me stay at the corner table with Lila because Monty and Wendell are my uncles."

"Monty and Wendell?" Carlyn asked.

"The two men in the band with Gordon."

"Ah." She thought a minute, her thumb locked beneath the pocketbook strap. "You know, DJ," she said, "I've been coming here almost every Saturday night for a couple of months, but I almost didn't make it tonight—I needed a change. Then I thought a little more about it and remembered I don't like to be alone so I came along anyway. Now I'm standing here and I still don't want to go inside." She considered another second, then said, "Do you feel like going for a ride? Maybe heading somewhere else tonight?"

"Me?" DJ was shocked. "You mean me and you? I'm not allowed out too late."

Carlyn smiled kindly. "I know. I won't keep you out till all hours. I was just thinking of going for a ride, maybe to a restaurant down on the south shore. I know one that's right on the ocean, a place that I haven't been to in years. She tugged at her coat collar. "I think it's still there. You can look out the windows and see the waves. If it's high tide, it's wonderful."

DJ had been caught off guard and immensely regretted how he had Beaver Cleavered his response by mentioning any kind of a curfew. His plan had been to sit at Lila's table in the corner, and when Carlyn wasn't looking, to shoot furtive, lust-laden glances at her during the night. With a little luck, he might be able to coordinate his departure so that she would give him another ride home. The possibility of being alone with her for any period of time had never entered his head. He rocked slowly back and forth on his heels. "Won't your husband mind?"

"No." She hesitated. "I guess it was a dumb idea. It makes more sense to go inside."

"No, no, I don't think it was a dumb idea," DJ quickly interrupted. "I'd like to go. Let's go."

"Are you sure?" Carlyn asked, cocking her head to the side.

"Yes, I'm absolutely sure," DJ responded. She was an all-American beauty, right out of a shampoo ad. "Absolutely, positively sure. I am really one-hundred-percent sure." He grinned and continued, "I really am, believe me. Let's go."

Carlyn slowly smiled back at him. "I believe you. That's nice. I like that. I knew you were a good salesman." She turned in the direction of her car. "Let's go."

DJ followed her back to the Mustang feeling like it was his first day in Basement Shoes. He had no idea what he was doing.

As the car crept out of the parking lot, Carlyn said, "Duck down, there's Gordon coming out the front door. I'm sure he's looking to see if I'm here."

DJ put his head between his knees.

"All clear," Carlyn said, as she spun out of the lot and on to Melville Road. "Let's go out to Route 110 and head south. God, I feel so free." She loosened the top of her coat. "It's wonderful. Thank you, DJ." She reached over and patted him on the back of his neck. "I hope you don't mind being with an older woman tonight." Her coat had fallen away from her leg and DJ could see the top of her thigh.

"No, I don't mind." He thought a moment. "I like it, as a matter of fact."

"You're sweet." She glanced quickly over at him.

"Won't your husband be mad that you're driving around with me? I mean we're, you know, together, and you're married."

"Are we doing something wrong? Taking a car ride?" She adjusted the rearview mirror. "I've never heard that driving together was a crime, or anything to feel guilty about."

DJ nodded, trying to ignore her foot on the accelerator and the leg stretching above it. He'd never seen such a sensual leg—a leg with a stocking that ran across her calf and ended in a place he couldn't even contemplate.

"Never pay no attention to women's legs," Wendell had once counseled him. "Them legs only distract you from the real truth. And the real truth isn't near as pretty."

Carlyn turned right on to Route 110 and headed south past the Hardscrabble Drive-In. "Kind of cold for that, don't you think?" she asked, indicating the theater.

"Yeah, I think they're about ready to close for the season."

"How about some music?" She flicked on the radio, then twisted the tuning knob. "It always relaxes me."

"Have you been a manager at Mertz Brothers long?" DJ asked.

"It's unusual to see a woman in my position, isn't it? I know. Cliff Collins knew my mother when she was alive, and I had enough education and experience for him to arrange the job after I moved back to Hardscrabble. Even so, it wasn't easy. People aren't used to a woman as a manager. I think it just makes everyone uncomfortable. For a while there, the company president was watching every step I took." She reached across to the radio and changed stations. "But it's all worked out. At least for the time being."

DJ looked out the window. As they continued south, drawing closer to the ocean, the traffic was growing increasingly sparse. In the distance on the horizon, he could sense the ocean merging into the sky. Carlyn slowed down for a four-lane bridge that extended over a marsh, then kicked the accelerator again.

"Where's the restaurant?" DJ asked.

"If I remember correctly, it's about a mile away. Off the road and up on the right."

The highway was growing darker as they approached the ocean.

"Not a lot of cars out for dinner tonight," DJ said.

"I'm sure it's here unless it closed down and I didn't know about it. We should be seeing the lights any second." Carlyn was glancing out the right of the windshield as she drove.

Straight ahead, a blinker warned that the highway turned into two single-lane roads, one bearing left, one right. "I think it's to the right," Carlyn said, slowing down and swinging the

Mustang in that direction.

"Are you sure? Maybe we're in the wrong place or something," DJ said. A vague uneasiness began to creep up the back of his spine. It was pitch black, he hadn't seen a car for miles, and he had no idea where he was. It was hard to believe any type of restaurant was near them.

A half-mile later, they approached a yellow, metallic dead-end sign nailed to the top of a weathered piece of two-by-four. Broken red reflectors ran up the front of the wood. Behind the sign, a turnaround extended off the pavement and onto the compacted beach sand.

"I think I blew it," Carlyn said. She stepped on the brake and slowed to a stop. "What do you think?" She looked across at DJ.

"It looks that way. Maybe we passed the restaurant and didn't see it." The headlights cut a narrow tunnel through the dark while the wind rocked the car. "I guess we should turn around and head back."

"Do you want to?" Carlyn's features were shadowy in the dashboard lights as she looked beyond the dead-end sign.

"What do you mean? What else would we do?"

"Oh, I don't know. As long as we're here, we might as well take a look at the ocean. It's just a little past the sign. Want to?" She looked over at DJ.

"Seriously? Just past the sign?" His anxiety grew.

"Sure. I'll bet if I open the window, I can hear the waves." She rolled the window down an inch. "Listen."

DJ held his breath, but heard nothing. "It's kind of cold to go out there," he said.

"Listen," Carlyn repeated, "the ocean's right there." She opened the door. "Come on."

DJ opened his door and moved outside. Carlyn was already past the dead-end sign and walking on the beach toward the ocean. He could barely see her though she was only several feet in front of him, her blonde hair blowing straight back in his direction. As he moved into the darkness, DJ realized that if he didn't stay close to Carlyn, she would disappear in seconds. After jogging a couple of steps, he caught up.

"See, right over there," she yelled as she pointed her finger.

The wind was ferocious. DJ could barely make out Carlyn's words. He followed her pointed finger and could see the white caps as they crashed onto the beach.

He was freezing.

He turned back to Carlyn.

She had disappeared!

DJ looked right and left and saw nothing. "Carlyn," he called. All he could hear were his own words nearly lost in the howling wind. "Carlyn," he yelled again, but this time his voice was totally drowned out as a monster wave thundered onto the beach spraying icy needles across his face. "Carlyn, where are you?" Panic was beginning to erupt. "Carlyn!"

Freezing fingers suddenly covered his eyes from behind. "Gotcha," she said, her mouth close to his ear. "Let's go, it's too scary here." Carlyn took DJ's hand and pulled him back with her to the Mustang.

Inside, she turned on the engine and cranked up the heater, then made a three-point turn and headed back north. "Now let's find that restaurant."

∞

They had made the wrong turn. The Atlantic Fish House turned out to be on the left fork of the road.

"Well, I almost got us there the first time," Carlyn said, pulling into a nearly empty parking lot.

DJ didn't reply. He had forgotten about momentarily losing her on the beach and was thinking about her lips next to his ear, and how she held his hand on the way back to the Mustang.

"Glad you folks made it," said a white-haired man in a double-breasted blazer. "Last night of the season. After tonight, you won't see us till Memorial Day." He picked up two menus. "Pick anywhere you like that's open."

"How about over there," Carlyn said, pointing to a table next to a copper porthole.

"Looks as good as any though it might be a bit drafty," the white-haired man said.

"I suspect we'll survive."

"Very good," he replied.

After they were seated, DJ looked nervously around. "I don't think I have enough money for this."

"My idea, I'll pay," Carlyn responded. She took the napkin and placed it on her lap. "I'll bet you were beginning to think there was no restaurant here at all, that I was making this whole thing up."

"No, I didn't think so," DJ lied. He looked at Carlyn across the table. Her cheeks were still pink from the cold.

"You're staring at me," she said, "and I can't believe it, but I might just blush." She looked away.

When dinner arrived, DJ studied how Carlyn used the different pieces of silverware, and while attempting to imitate her, to his total humiliation, he managed to drop his knife on the floor twice during the meal. The weather-beaten waiter, who looked as if he had spent the day catching the fish they were eating, sauntered over each time, and smirking, replaced the knife. "Looks like you're from the squat-and-gobble school of eating, huh?" he said to DJ the second time.

"Excuse me," Carlyn said, partially standing.

The waiter looked at her.

"I don't appreciate your sense of humor, if that's what you call it," she said. "Save it for someone else next time." She sat down and dismissed him by turning her back.

$$\infty$$

Following dinner, Carlyn sat and ran her finger up the

stem of the wine glass. "You know, you remind me of my first boyfriend. I guess that's why I felt like I was blushing." She rested her chin on her hand as she looked at him. "How old are you, DJ? Seventeen?" She gently shook her head. "I cannot believe it's been ten years since I was your age."

"You don't look like you're twenty-seven," DJ offered.

"And aren't you sweet for saying so." Carlyn reached across and patted his hand, then ran her fingers through her hair as she looked around the empty dining room. Outside, the wind picked up and as quickly subsided before revving up again.

"Why are you having dinner with me tonight instead of your husband?" It had taken him the entire meal to ask.

Carlyn's eyes focused on DJ. "Because my husband has gone to South Carolina and is on his way to Vietnam. He's in the army." She slid the base of the wine glass back and forth on the tablecloth. "Just like that, DJ, gone. I started going to the Jailhouse Rock the week after he left rather than go just plain crazy."

"And you don't wear a wedding ring?"

"Neither one of us ever has. That's just the way we decided to do it."

The maitre d' walked to the table. "May I bring you anything else?"

"Well, that's not too subtle a way of letting us know that you're ready to go home," Carlyn laughed, "but now that you're here, you can ask the waiter to bring our check."

She paid with an American Express card—something DJ had never seen done before—but he didn't mention it because he didn't want to appear unworldly.

∞

Driving north on Route 110, Carlyn glanced at her watch, "twelve-thirty—an early night."

"We could always stop at the Rock," DJ offered.

"Wouldn't that just look too cute, the two of us parading into the Jailhouse Rock together," Carlyn said. "I think Gordon would fall off the stage." She glanced into the rearview mirror. "If I'd had another glass of wine, I would probably do it."

"Well, if you want to stop for a while, I could go in the side door and nobody would know."

Carlyn thought a second. "I think I'm going to call it a night, DJ. But I can drop you off there if you like. Or I can drive you home."

DJ didn't want to be at the Jailhouse Rock if Carlyn wasn't there. He liked it once in a while when there was nothing else to do, but he got tired of sitting by himself in Lila's smoke, his elbows resting next to the glass-sweat puddles. "I guess you could drop me off at home if you don't mind. I've got to get up early for work tomorrow anyway."

"Work tomorrow?"

"I do the Sunday papers at Van Velsor's. It starts real early and Herman likes me to get there earlier." DJ looked out the window, attempting to see Carlyn's leg in the reflection.

"That's strange, having to get there earlier than early." She studied the street signs. "I know I'm supposed to turn somewhere around here."

"Second right up ahead. Jackson Road."

Carlyn made the turn and drove up the block, slowing as she approached DJ's house. "It was nice of you to take all this time to entertain me tonight," she said, pulling the Mustang over to the curb. "I hope it wasn't too boring for you."

DJ put his hand on the door handle. "Oh no, it wasn't boring for me at all. I liked it. A lot. And thanks for buying me dinner." The overhead light flicked on as he swung the door open.

"DJ?"

He turned toward her.

"Close the door for a second."

He pulled the door shut, extinguishing the overhead light, then looked at her.

"Come here," she said. Reaching across the space between

them, she gently placed her hand behind his head. "Come here."

"Where?"

"Here." Carlyn applied pressure to the back of DJ's neck until his face was in front of hers. She kissed him, easily, softly. As she moved her lips from his, she ran the back of a finger down the side of his face. "English Leather. It's all so familiar," she murmured. Her eyes were next to his. "I shouldn't be doing this, should I?" She slid her finger down his face again. "Am I blushing?"

"No, I don't think so." He ran his tongue across his top lip. "Are you sure your husband's in Vietnam?"

"On his way. We're safe." She kissed him again, contemplated his eyes once more, then let her hands drop. "But I should go now."

DJ didn't move. "Okay, I guess so. If you have to." He slowly reached for the door handle again, briefly hesitated, glanced at Carlyn, then pushed the door open. "Okay, I guess so," he repeated as he stepped out of the car and closed the door behind him. Carlyn sat for several seconds before she pulled the Mustang away from the curb.

∞

Patty was at the kitchen table drinking a glass of chocolate milk. "Do you want some?" she asked.

"No thanks." DJ leaned against the doorway, his hands in his pockets.

"I saw you get out of one of those new Mustangs, but I don't know anyone who owns one."

"My boss at Mertz Brothers. She was at the Jailhouse Rock tonight and offered to drop me off."

"That was nice of her." Patty sipped from the glass. "Ike got sick tonight. We were at Van Velsor's and he said his chest hurt, but he didn't want to do anything like call an ambulance.

Then in a few minutes, the pain went away. I think he was more embarrassed than anything."

"But he's okay?"

"It only lasted about a minute. He seemed fine afterwards. I thought he looked a little more pale than usual, but sometimes he is a little more pale than usual." Patty put the empty glass in the sink and filled it with water. "He asked me to another movie."

DJ didn't respond.

"I told him I'd go." She studied a fingernail. "Do you think I'm wrong?"

"I'm not sure," DJ said.

"I just don't want him to be misled," Patty said. "That's all. I don't want him to get the wrong idea."

"Then don't give him the wrong idea."

Patty stared at him. She slowly nodded. "Okay, I won't."

CHAPTER 14

It had been three weeks since the kiss. Three weeks that seemed like three years. DJ had seen Carlyn at the Jailhouse Rock a couple of times and she had smiled at him, but never offered him another ride home. He'd hung around, even walked into the parking lot when she was leaving, but the Mustang never stopped. At Mertz Brothers, she was rarely near the department he was working in, and when he did catch a glimpse of her, he thought about that night in the front seat of her car and was immediately depressed. He'd end up looking away.

As the November days grew shorter, with each new one further separating him from Carlyn, he would lie on his bed after school staring at the orange-sailed, eighteenth-century ship hanging on the wall next to the window. He would focus on the setting sun reflected in the sails and ignore the low winter skies soaking into the dark branches of the next-door maple tree.

With his hands folded behind his neck, DJ spent hours reviewing the kiss, all the while continually staring at the orange-sailed ship. He could see himself as the captain barking orders and at the same time clutching Carlyn around her tiny waist. He'd almost get there—he could see Carlyn perfectly in her tattered blouse—but when it came time to focus on his own image, he always ended up looking like Mr. Clean. The earring and muscles were perfect, but the bald head and goofy smile blew up the whole scene.

"I've been watching too much TV," DJ muttered to himself when Mr. Clean materialized for the third time in five minutes.

He strode downstairs, went to the closet and put on his coat. "Going over to Leslie's, Dad," he said. He didn't bother with the charade of taking his school books with him.

Dale sat at the kitchen table reading the *Daily News*. "Fine," he said. "You saving your money?"

"Sure am," DJ responded.

DJ hadn't seen Leslie in weeks, but when she had called in the afternoon to ask him to come over that evening, he couldn't think of any reason not to.

Her father answered the door. "Leslie's in the basement, DJ, go on down." He stretched, then picked up his gun and holster that was slung over the railing post. Climbing the stairs, he muttered under his breath, "The New York City Police Department owns me. Take all my time; risk my life. For what? Those bastards own me."

Leslie's father complained a lot. DJ was used to it.

She was leaning back on the couch watching TV. Only the end-table lamp was on, with the TV volume barely audible.

"Hi, Leslie," DJ said, taking off his jacket. "Haven't seen you in a long time." He remained standing.

"Too long, don't you think? What have you been doing?" Leslie appraised him. "Come here." She patted a place next to her on the couch.

DJ walked over to her and sat.

"I hear you're going away tomorrow."

"Yeah, that's right, with Monty, Wendell and Ike. We're going up to Monty's cabin in Vermont for the weekend. He wants to make a trip there before the place gets snowed in."

"But over Thanksgiving?"

"Thor always closes the Rock during Thanksgiving so he can visit his sister in Florida. Wendell and Monty have the weekend off." DJ cautiously leaned back against the couch, but kept his hands resting on his knees.

Leslie looked at her fingernails, rubbed them against her skirt and held them up to the light. "I don't know why we do these things to each other," she said finally. "After all the time we've spent together, we have these inane separations."

DJ wasn't positive what inane meant, but could get a decent grasp from the context. "Yeah, it's been pretty inane," he responded.

"Did you think about me during these weeks we've been apart?" Leslie subtly shifted so her hip was touching his.

"Sure, I did," DJ responded.

Leslie thought for a few seconds. "I like your shoes," she said, indicating his new loafers from The Ivy League Shop. "They're different from your other ones. These are much more classic."

Now he was in trouble, and the context wasn't helping him. He thought classic always referred to books like *Robin Hood*, or *Ivanhoe*, not shoes. "I like classics," he offered and stared at the TV.

"You really are changing, you know," Leslie said, her face suddenly close to his. "I think it's important that we both change, don't you?" She rested the side of her arm on the back of the couch, her hand on DJ's shoulder. "That's a sign of growing up. Changing. Knowing more about each other." She ran her finger against the edge of his ear. "We're not kids, are we, DJ?"

The scent of gardenias surrounded him. "No, we're not kids," he replied, still facing forward.

"Do you want to touch me?" she whispered. "Like you haven't touched me before?"

DJ slowly turned to her. She took his hand and placed it under her blouse. She had already disposed of her bra. "Come here," she said leaning backward, unbuttoning her blouse. Pulling him over her, she slid her hips further forward on the couch until he was directly on top of her. "Oh God, DJ," she murmured, taking a quick look at her watch.

He knew he wasn't supposed to, but he caught the glance. "Is this more of the same, Leslie?"

"You like it, don't you?" she answered.

"I like it until your father comes to the top of the stairs and stops us."

"Don't worry about my father," she whispered. "He won't do anything."

"But he did last time. And all the times before that."

"He won't, he won't," Leslie insisted, running her fingers through DJ's hair. "Don't worry, he won't." She let her hands glide down his neck, then ran her nails softly across his back. "You always worry too much."

"I only worry when there's a reason to worry. And there's a reason to worry."

Leslie put her hands on the sides of his face. "And what's that supposed to mean? What's your problem anyway, DJ?"

"It's inane what you do to me."

"I don't have any control over what my father does," Leslie said. "You know that."

"What time was he going to call from the top of the stairs?" DJ asked, glancing at his watch. "It's eight twenty-five. What did I have left, five minutes? A half hour?"

Leslie stared at him, a disgusted look crossing her face. "Get off me," she said, pushing him away. She quickly buttoned her blouse and tucked it into her skirt. "I'll be back in a minute." She ran up the stairs.

DJ studied the prehistoric pretzels in the green plastic bowl, picked one up and dropped it, then leaned back and gazed at the ceiling.

Leslie quickly descended the stairs. "My father's asleep. I just checked." She sat down next to DJ again. "Now where were we?" she asked.

DJ had long envisioned the opportunity before him, but now that it had arrived, he was already gone, rolling with Marty Robbins and the sagebrush into the sunset, sailing away on the orange ship. The image of Carlyn pierced every thought, and though he knew the idea of ever being with her was hopeless, pursuing Leslie's body in the dank basement just made him weary and unresponsive.

"Well?" Leslie asked, leaning back on the couch again. "No one is going to disturb us." She reached and took both of DJ's hands and placed them under her blouse. "Just the two of us alone, DJ."

DJ held his hands against Leslie's breasts, unmoving.

"Come on, DJ," she whispered, a questioning look creeping into her eyes, "what are you waiting for?"

DJ pulled his hands away. "You know what, Leslie," he said, "maybe this isn't such a good idea."

Leslie stared at him, incredulous. "You're not serious."

"Yeah, I think so," he answered, then sighed. "I'm serious. Maybe I'll just go on home." He stood up.

"What is it you don't like, DJ?" Leslie asked quickly, still on the couch. "What is it you all of a sudden don't like?"

"I'm not sure." He slid into his jacket.

"Don't you dare walk out on me!" She rose and unbuttoned her blouse, letting it fall to the floor. "How about this?" she asked, facing him.

"I've got to go, Les," DJ said, looking toward the stairs.

"No," Leslie blurted, pulling his arm until he was back on the couch. "No, you're not going anywhere."

Her strength was alarming.

"You're not leaving." Leslie stared down at him, her chest heaving, waiting for DJ to move, to try and escape. When he didn't stir, she reached up and touched her breasts. What's the matter, DJ, these aren't good enough for you now?" She laughed, never letting her eyes stray from his. "Then how about something else? I bet you'd like a little more, wouldn't you, DJ?"

DJ started to rise again.

"No," Leslie seethed, pushing him back. "I said you're not leaving. You're not going anywhere."

He remained seated, uncertain, and now, intimidated.

"You want more. That's it, isn't it, DJ? You want more." Her eyes still locked with his, Leslie reached to her side and unbuttoned her skirt, let it drop to the floor, then slipped out of her panties.

She stood in front of him fully naked.

"Leslie, your father might come downstairs," DJ whispered urgently as he looked over her shoulder at the stairwell. "Put your stuff back on. Don't do this. It's too crazy."

"Getting good, isn't it, DJ?"

"Leslie, please don't, this is craz—"

"I told you he's not coming down!" A slight smile crossed her face. "All this," she said, running her fingers down her body, "wasn't too crazy when you were trying to get at it yourself. It wasn't crazy then, was it, DJ?" Leslie moved so that she was within inches. "Touch me, DJ. Anywhere. You're allowed now." She placed her hands on his shoulders then lowered herself until she was sitting on his knee. "Touch me, come on, touch me. I want you to."

DJ stared away. "This is no good, Les."

"Yes, it is good," Leslie answered, shifting slightly and placing her hands on the sides of his face. Leaning forward, she kissed him. "You know it's good. You've been waiting for this, DJ."

"I can't," DJ said.

Leslie was back on her feet, suddenly furious. "What do you mean you can't? You've wanted to do this forever."

"I've got to go, Leslie." He stood, looking away, unwilling to catch her eye and ignite the fury that he knew could be waiting for him.

Leslie hadn't moved. "Please, DJ. Please don't go." She self-consciously crossed her legs and covered her breasts with her arms. "We don't even have to do this. I just thought you wanted to." She hesitated again. "You did, didn't you?"

It was the first time he'd seen any vulnerability from Leslie—a piece of her, like the scar on her back, that he had never known existed.

And he no longer cared.

"I wanted to do this once, Les. Tonight, I've just got to go." He took a step toward the stairway.

"No, no, you don't, you're not going." She was on him in a second, tearing at his hair and scratching with her fingernails. "No, you're not going," she cried. "You're not going. You think you can just walk away like that? I'll kill you before that happens." She stepped back and took a swing with her right hand.

He anticipated the punch and ducked away, then instinctively swung back, slapping her so hard across the face that it scared him.

Leslie instantly halted, looked up at DJ, stared briefly, then lowered her head. She stood silent, swaying, her hands at her sides, then leaned forward, allowing her forehead to briefly rest against his chest—for once, fragile. Moments later, she turned and quietly retraced her steps, gathering her clothes before dressing. Returning to the couch, she sat with her knees together, staring at her shoes.

DJ hadn't moved, and had studied the floor to avoid watching her dress. "I . . . I'm sorry, Les," he said, "I didn't mean to do that." Now that she was silent and diminished, he felt protective of her.

Leslie stood. "Just go, DJ. Just leave."

"I didn't mean to have that happen, Leslie. I don't do things like that."

"You just did, DJ. Just go."

"Okay." DJ turned and started up the stairs and crossed the living room. Back in the basement, the TV volume had been turned up slightly and canned laughter filtered through the floor.

He stopped at the front door and listened to the sudden

hilarity below.

What had just happened?

In the beginning, when they were discovering each other, he would sometimes lie awake at night wondering what she was doing at that exact second. He could recall the gardenias being subtle and pleasing, and moments when he was satisfied to hold her hand in the balcony, then kiss her at the doorstep, all the time feeling just plain lucky to be part of her life.

What had just happened?

He considered climbing the wall between them once more, and maybe walking together down to Van Velsor's for some hot chocolate. He looked at his watch. There was still time. Leslie might place her hands in his coat pocket to stay warm, then laugh just like she used to at the beginning, when it all seemed effortless.

DJ crossed the living room and opened the door to the basement. He walked down the steps.

Leslie was on the couch, her arms folded across her breast, intently watching TV. "What?" she challenged, looking up, her voice rising above *The Beverly Hillbillies*.

He stood, unmoving, now uncertain what to say.

"What?" Not waiting for an answer, she returned her eyes to the TV.

Still unsure, DJ watched her, cleared his throat, paused, then said, "Nothing, Leslie." He climbed back up the stairs, walked through the living room and out the front door.

CHAPTER 15

"Yesiree Bob, we're on our way. Thanksgiving in Vermont and a sunny day to boot," Wendell crowed from the front seat of Monty's Chevy as the car headed out of Hardscrabble. He took a church key from his jacket pocket and pried the cap loose from a beer bottle. "What do you think about that, big brother?" He punched Monty in the arm and took a gulp. "I feel like I've died and gone to heaven."

"You'll be going to heaven all right if you keep juicing that way, especially while it's still morning," Monty said.

"Late morning. Very late morning. Anyhow, a man's got to have a little fun. You should know that better than most, big brother." Wendell took another swig and turned to DJ and Ike in the backseat. "Help yourselves fellas," he added, nodding to the case of beer resting between them. "We got more than enough to go around." He chugged three-quarters of the bottle, then repeated, "Yesiree, Bob," and placed both feet on the dashboard.

"How'd you finally manage to get away from Mertz Brothers this weekend, DJ?" Monty asked over his shoulder.

"Mr. Collins and Mrs. Canova said I could take the day off. I haven't missed any time so far since I started." DJ stared at his reflection in the glass to see if he had dark half-circles under his eyes. "They told me they're going to be training another floating salesman like me. I don't know who it's going to be, but they said they like how I'm working out."

"Damn tooting, you're working out," Wendell said. "Price is right."

"I know Cliff Collins. Do I know Mrs. Canova?" Monty asked.

"I think so. She comes into the Rock a lot."

"Oh yeah?" Wendell said, suddenly interested. "What does she look like?" He handed his empty bottle over the back of the seat to Ike. "Another brew, if you don't mind, General Ike Eisenhower."

DJ hesitated. "She's blonde. Pretty good looking. You know, regular stuff." It was difficult to even think about her.

"She comes in a lot?" Wendell asked. "Only blonde I know that's there all the time is the one Gordon has the hots for. That's not her, right?"

DJ hesitated again. "Yeah, that's her."

"That's her! You serious?" Wendell paused, holding the fresh bottle of beer in mid-air. "You kidding me?" He studied DJ. "All this time you been working for that gorgeous blonde and you been keeping us in the dark? What the hell is that supposed to mean?" A frown broke out on his forehead as he lowered the bottle. "That is no way right, DJ. We brought you up better than to keep secrets from family. We're all for one, and one for all." He looked at Ike. "Ain't that right, General Ike?"

Ike nodded. "I guess so."

"I don't think she likes Gordon," DJ said.

"Then why in the heck does she sit front and center every weekend eyeing the band like she's some kind of man-eater?" Wendell asked. "And if she's a Mrs., what the hell is she doing there by herself in the first place?"

"Her husband's in Vietnam," DJ said. "She likes the music."

Monty scratched the back of his head. "Is her first name Carlyn?"

DJ was surprised. "How did you know?"

Monty thought a moment. "I guess her face has been bothering me for a long time. She's not the Carlyn Reynolds that used to live near town when Rosie and you first moved to your house, is she, Wendell?"

Carlyn Reynolds is a whore. The faded white paint on the brick wall flashed through DJ's mind. He had forgotten about it.

Wendell considered Monty's question as he opened the beer bottle. "That Carlyn was only a teenager, and she wasn't a blonde." He took a lazy gulp from the long-neck. "Course that don't matter, no reason collars and cuffs got to match. I'll tell you right now though, if it's the same Carlyn, she grew up in a crazy house. Father dead. Mother had a ton of boyfriends before she passed on. Always a racket over there."

"The reason I ask," Monty said, "is because when I think about it, and get past the hair color, they do kind of look the same. And how many Carlyns can there be in Hardscrabble?"

"Well, I tell you what, if it's the same Carlyn that lived on my block, she must be married to her second husband. First one disappeared, best as I can recall," Wendell said, balancing the bottle on his knee. "Isn't that right, Monty?"

"Believe so. Seems to me he just vanished into thin air. Didn't show up for work one day and was never seen again. Thor told me he'd heard the guy had mental problems and took to drifting. Of course, you never know what to believe. Someone else said he'd just had enough of married life and headed south. All I really know is that he disappeared." Monty reached over and turned on the radio. "Then after a while, I heard she left town too." He shook his head and stretched. "Are they the same person? I don't know. It was a long time ago."

∞

Later in the day, across the Vermont state line, Wendell was asleep, his head resting against the side window, while Ike listened to his transistor radio, the earplug in place.

"We're getting there now," Monty said over his shoulder.

The two-lane roads, the bare trees, and the stone fences preoccupied DJ. Occasionally, he would see a ramshackle house, sometimes with cardboard in the windows and rusted farm machinery in the backyard, and once he noticed a tiny, solitary turquoise trailer in a meadow, smoke rising from a stovepipe chimney.

"Can't get much reception," Ike said, turning off the radio. "I wonder how Patty's doing?"

"Fine, I'm sure," Monty answered.

Ike stared out the window. "It's cold up here."

"Yeah, it's always cold. We're about as far north as we're going though. A couple more miles."

Five minutes later as they drove past the "Entering Braxton" sign, Monty elbowed Wendell.

"Don't do that," Wendell complained irritably as he opened his eyes. "I tell you what, for a second there, I thought I was in the service, or back with Rosie. And I don't appreciate either of them thoughts." He stretched. "I need a pit stop."

"Here's the plan," Monty said as they passed the outskirts of town. "We'll stop at the IGA and pick up some groceries, then head out to the cabin. It's pretty well stocked, but this way we can get milk, eggs, that kind of stuff." He looked back at the boys. "Anything special you fellows want? We're going to be up here for a couple of days."

"Nothing I can think of," DJ said. He reached into his pocket. "My father gave me five dollars for food."

"Don't worry about it," Monty said. "By the looks of you two, I doubt either one is going to eat enough to break the bank."

Slamming through a couple of potholes, the Chevy plowed into the grocery parking lot, then halted against one of the tarred telephone poles lying in the gravel in front of the store entrance.

∞

Dusk was gathering, bleeding in from the woods, when they pulled up in front of the cabin. Monty jumped out. "First thing," he said, "is we have to get a fire going. Feels like snow."

DJ could hear the wind whipping through the pines and pulled his collar up as he climbed out of the Chevy. Wendell and he unloaded the car while Monty and Ike went inside.

By the time the trunk was empty and Wendell had lugged in the case of beer, Monty had the kindling in flames. "Give us a couple of minutes and we'll be warm," he said, squatting as he fed pieces of bark to the fire.

While Ike stood frozen next to the fireplace, hands in his coat pockets, DJ walked around inside. It was the first time he had been to the cabin though Monty had been describing it for years, usually mentioning how it had been the first thing he ever bought after his stint in the Marines. "Two hundred down," he had said to DJ, "and the smartest move I ever made in my life."

The space was little more than one large room containing a kitchen corner, fireplace and stairs leading to a loft. DJ went to the window on the back wall, looked out, then turned and climbed the stairs to the loft where a double bed rested next to four single cots.

"DJ," Monty called, "while you're up there, do me a favor and throw a sleeping bag on each bed. Pile of them in the corner."

DJ unrolled four sleeping bags, then headed down the steps, jumping the last three. He could feel the heat begin to permeate the cabin.

Wendell lit three candles and placed them around the downstairs, then took a fourth and planted it on the table in front of the stove.

"That's it," Monty said as he knelt in front of the fireplace and pushed another log over the flames. "All perishables go in this ice chest. I'll keep it outside. The stove works on propane, and the best news is we still have running water. When we leave, I'll drain the pipes and shut it down." He turned to Ike and DJ. "You boys must be starving. Wendell, go get a couple of flashlights out of that cardboard box in the corner."

"You got it, boss," Wendell answered, then uncapped a beer.

∞

After dinner, DJ washed the dishes in the sink. He was beginning to feel at ease and more accustomed to the shadows flickering in the far reaches of the downstairs, more comfortable with the blasts of wind outdoors. Behind him, Wendell dried the last plate using a hand and a half, the leftover fingers clasping a beer bottle.

"Believe it or not fellas, I have a working toilet too," Monty said, pointing to the far corner of the cabin. "Open that door and it'll smack you in the face."

"And I'm just the guy who can use it," Wendell said, throwing down the dish towel and heading across the floor. "Better than the damn tree by the front porch where I'd be peeing ice cubes."

A minute later, returning from the bathroom, Wendell seated himself on the couch. "Heck of a nice fire you made, big brother. Real pleasant," he said. Smiling at Monty, the bottom of the beer bottle resting on his stomach, feet extended in front of him, he slowly yawned. "Yep, I'm like a cow in high clover, just tickled to be here."

CHAPTER 16

Later that evening, Wendell and Ike headed up to the loft.

"I'm tired," Ike said shuffling across the room.

"I'm drunk," Wendell murmured, walking after him.

Silence slipped into the cabin. Monty blew out all the candles except for the one on the table in front of the stove. He held a cup of coffee in his hand as he sat in a chair. "Come on over closer to the fire," he said to DJ, indicating the couch.

DJ moved and sat facing the fireplace.

Monty sipped from his coffee cup as he stared into the flames. "Wendell concerns me. He drinks too much. Runs in the family, I'm afraid."

DJ considered Monty's words. "My father drinks a lot too. At least it seems like he's drinking most of the time."

"Most of the time means all of the time he isn't working or sleeping," Monty said. "Like I said, runs in the family. Been there, I should know."

"Was my mother that way too?"

The question caught Monty by surprise. He glanced over at DJ, then back at the fire. After a few seconds, slowly, carefully, he said, "You know, DJ, there's something agreeable about staring at the fire— the warmth, the smell of the wood. You get to speak without seeing anyone. It's comfortable, almost natural. Easy, I guess is the word." He sipped from his coffee cup again. "But in answer to your question, no, your mom was not the same way. I rarely ever saw her even take a drink. Champagne once on New Year's Eve, maybe. That was about it. Some folks just don't care for it."

A log crackled, fired off sparks and flared against the back wall of the fireplace.

DJ hesitated. "I don't remember her that well, and my father never says much."

"That doesn't surprise me. Patty and you were tiny when she left us." Monty shook his head. "A terrible loss. Hard to even describe." He turned slightly in his chair so he partially faced DJ, but was still able to watch the fire. "Your mother was a wonderful person. And I know her biggest regret, the one that tore at her more than the cancer, was leaving the two of you behind. I know how she loved you both."

"How do you know she did?" DJ was staring deep into the flames, past the orange, past the blue, past the rising smoke.

Monty perched the toe of one boot into the heel of the other. "Because she was my best friend and she told me so. You kids were everything to her."

"But did she ever say so?"

Monty looked at DJ. "That she loved you? Of course she did. Many times. But even if she hadn't, it wouldn't have mattered because I knew she did." He continued to stare at DJ. "You know that, don't you? Because if you don't, you should. Your sister and you were the world to her. There was nothing else that fulfilled her life more than the two of you."

DJ unexpectedly felt his eyes begin to sting. He coughed, then stared to his left, away from Monty, away from the flames, to the shelter of the darkness.

"I want you to understand," Monty continued, his voice hushed, "she didn't leave you because she wanted to." He hesitated, selecting his words. "She left you because she had no choice." His voice grew softer still as he stared into the fire. "She left all of us because it was out of her hands, out of our hands." He paused again, then slowly continued. "And all the praying and bargaining and doctoring couldn't stop her from drifting away. Much as we all tried to keep her, and hard as she tried to stay, one morning we woke up in our beds, turned off our alarm clocks like always, only to discover she'd been taken from us during the night."

"Was I with her when she died?" DJ asked.

"No, I don't believe you were," Monty answered. "Dale once told me that the last few days when she was in the hospital, you two little guys would crawl into the sack with him at night. He'd tuck you in your own beds, but you both would stay awake and come to his bedroom when he turned out the lights. I suspect some part of you knew that being next to him was as close as you could get to her.

"Everyone suffered the loss. You, me, even Dale." Monty unconsciously rubbed the top of his knee. "Forgive me, of course, Dale." He shook his head slowly side to side. "But I think it affected Patty the most. She was always an outgoing child—you were the shy one—and she seemed to withdraw after your mother's death. Hard to read little kids, but I sensed it right away. Broke my heart watching her, almost as if she had moved into a cave with just those bright eyes peering out at me, giving me no idea what she was thinking." He shook his head again. "But I guarantee the need you both had for your mother was mild compared to her yearning for the two of you. Nothing sadder in this whole world than a mom unable to take care of her babies."

"I don't remember much," DJ said, visualizing the lonely, silver-framed picture of her in the living room.

"I would guess not," Monty said. "But I was there as a grown-up, or at least in the body of one, and I have a bank full of recollections, memory insurance I gathered day to day, almost as if I knew sometime I might need it." He licked his finger and rubbed at a smudge on the toe of his boot. "I don't want to preach, but I'll tell you how it was in those days, if you want." He glanced over at his nephew.

DJ nodded.

"All right," Monty said. "Before your father was a judge, he was involved in local politics most of the time. Kept him real busy; meetings at night too. And he never hung around with Wendell and me much. He's always been a loner. I wasn't married, didn't have a girl, so I'd come over and visit. Always enjoyed Patty and you, plus your mom was kind. We'd spend some evenings talking at the kitchen table. She'd drink tea, I'd drink coffee or bring over some beer, depending on how much money I had. Dale never cared, after all I was his brother, and in a funny kind of way, it took some pressure off of him. Freed him up to be more involved with all the comings and goings at Town Hall, I suppose."

Monty nodded slightly as he thought back. "As I see it now, I cared a great deal for your mother, though we were always just close friends. And you need to know, DJ, that's all we ever were—just real good buddies. Nothing beyond that. Ever." He thought a long moment. "It's just that I never had a better one." Monty reached into his pocket, pulled out a handkerchief, and blew his nose. "No, I sure never did."

He tucked the handkerchief back into his jeans and leaned back. "I recall a Saturday afternoon during the fall when we were sitting on one of those carved-up benches in the Hardscrabble town green watching you two knuckleheads play in the sand. It was one of those bright afternoons, clear, you know, like crystal, with the maples gold and orange. Patty and you had those healthy apple cheeks and were toddling around at ninety miles an hour, and your mother was smiling, pretty as could be in a blue dress. I'd watch the three of you and was just pleased to be alive." He hesitated. "That's when she told me she was going to die."

Monty paused again and shifted in the chair. "Course I couldn't believe it. Would never have allowed myself to think it possible. I wasn't capable of those kinds of feelings back then." He shifted again. "Your mother sensed that, seemed to know instinctively that I was not prepared to respond, or be helpful, or comforting, and she let the subject be. After that one moment, we never talked about it again. Never once. And later on, as she grew weaker, most of her time was spent trying to comfort me." He shook his head. "And isn't that just one of the most pathetic things you've ever heard? A full-grown woman, sick beyond words, trying to reassure some dud like me."

DJ stood and walked past the kitchen table, and for no reason, ran the water from the sink faucet over his hands before returning to the couch.

"I remember," Monty continued, "walking home with her from the village green that afternoon because the two of you had to be put down for a nap. Your mother smiled at me at the front door and said, 'Thank you for sharing the day,' then went inside. Yeah, quiet as could be, she went inside and closed the door, just like any other hour of any other day."

"I went back to the bench. Stopped at the liquor store on the way, naturally. Then I drank from a whiskey bottle the rest of the afternoon. People passed by—folks I even knew—but they didn't say anything. A couple of kids stared a little, but no one called Thor. And I wouldn't have cared if they had. All I wanted to do was fade away, to become part of the bench, or be absorbed by the trees, or the church across the green. I needed to be shotgunned, filtered, then scattered among the leaves, so not to ever feel the pain I knew was brewing deep in me. And as I sat there drinking, watching those loud, orange leaves on the trees turn into a bonfire, the more I could focus on the past and become that piece of dust in the beam of sunlight in front of me—and that dust became your mother, and Dale, and me, laughing and dancing at the church Christmas party—until that finally floated away too, and I forgot my name, or what I was even thinking. Then I sat in my car and watched the clouds bringing in the rain, and I thought I'd left the window open, but it was my nose bleeding, across my lips, down onto my shirt, down onto my belt buckle."

Monty looked over at DJ and stared away for a moment before continuing, his voice now strained, "And I'm still here, and she's still gone. And all the booze I drank that day, and all the pain growing inside me weren't going to change that. Much as I'd like to say it isn't so, it is." He turned away.

DJ was silent. After a few minutes had passed, he asked, "What about Lila?"

Monty picked up his coffee cup. "Ah, good, old Lila. She came along years later. She's my pal, but it's not the same." He stood, picked up the poker and rustled the wood in the fireplace. "Lila's a good gal. She's got a good heart, and I love her to death, but it'll never be the same."

"I wish she was here," DJ said.

"Lila? She comes up sometimes."

"No, my mother. I wish she was here." Then unexpectedly, embarrassingly, DJ felt his eyes begin to well up. As he leaned forward and gently rocked on his knees, a few tears, ones he was unable to deter, washed down his cheeks and fell to the plank floor.

Monty stood and took his coffee cup over to the sink. He rinsed it out, turned and sat at the kitchen table, facing the wall until DJ had calmed. "I suspect it's time to go to bed now," he said, rising to his feet, "what do you say, son?"

"Okay," DJ answered. "I guess I feel better."

"Well, that's fine. Nothing wrong with cleaning out some of those old closets every once in a while."

Later, with the three asleep on their cots around him, DJ slipped out of bed and picked up Ike's transistor radio from the floor. He placed the plug in his ear, adjusted the thumbwheel, then twisted the dial till he faintly heard one station just as it was ending its nightly broadcast. The crackling reminded him of the final scene of the short story "The Birds," after the birds had taken control, and the wireless played "God Save The Queen" before it went off the air for the final time, or staying up late with Patty and watching the TV station end its nightly programming with "The Star Spangled Banner." As the chorale sang the sweet, final notes, the American flag that had been rippling across the screen faded, and four jets in formation rocketed into view, then quickly disappeared trailing gray clouds of smoke that gradually turned to snow as the station transmitters shut down for the night.

All at once, DJ was floating. The sensation was familiar, and though he couldn't recall the first time it had occurred, if he had to guess, it was shortly after his mother died. Rising, then floating, he was able to detach from any emotional discomfort, and from a remote, overhead vantage point, gradually grow tranquil and at ease. As far back as he could remember, distance had been his refuge.

With his back to the moon, DJ lingered over the cabin, floated above the trees.

This night he could sense his mother as he hung suspended, could feel her breath and the tingling of her fingertips as she touched him, held him. For seconds, he was part of her, safer in her embrace, content to view the world through her eyes.

Until Monty's words echoed through the hushed night and he realized he was drifting downward.

Yes, it was true, he was still here. And yes it was true, she was still gone. And all the pain he felt would change nothing.

DJ stood and watched from the window as snowflakes began to fall in front of the dark trees: first a black-and-white screen, then a wedding veil, and finally . . . a white wall.

DECEMBER 1964

CHAPTER 17

Everyone in the high school knew that Lisa dumped Bobby Litchfield. On Thanksgiving Day, a lantern-jawed Harvard sophomore whom Lisa had secretly been writing to for a year, stopped by and offered her what he considered the opportunity of a lifetime—himself. Lisa gave the proposition two minutes of modest soul-searching, in tandem with a hurried income-projection analysis, and Bobby was instant history.

While the breakup of the king and queen of both the Junior Prom and the Inaugural Ball was a shocker to most, Maynard, the All-Knowing, claimed he had predicted the dissolution months before. "She just got bored going out with some big jock," he whispered in study hall. "The guy offered her nothing up here," he added, pointing to his forehead.

"And I'm sure you could offer her a lot more," DJ answered.

"I think that's fairly obvious," Maynard replied, cleaning his ear with his pencil eraser.

What the All-Knowing had failed to mention, simply because he was clueless, was that following his dismissal by Lisa, Bobby Litchfield immediately unearthed a new girlfriend: Leslie.

When DJ heard the news during gym class, he was so deep in thought that he ran an extra lap without being forced to, something no one had ever seen happen before in the history of Hardscrabble High School. It doesn't make sense, he thought to himself as he labored around the gymnasium, the rubber of his sneakers slapping against the polished floor. Less than a week ago, Leslie had been standing stark naked in front of him in her basement, and now she already had a new boyfriend.

Yet only part of him was surprised, and most of him wasn't unhappy.

"Don't know why you would ever be crazy enough to walk away from her," Bobby said to DJ as they stood next to each other, their feet up on a locker room bench, untying their Keds. "She told me the two of you were through." He looked over at DJ. "So I guess Leslie being with me isn't a problem, right?"

"I guess not," DJ mumbled. Actually, he thought it was the elimination of one. Now Bobby would be in the cellar with the Jurassic pretzels, the fuzzy DuMont TV, and Leslie's Rocky Marciano alter ego .

After dressing quickly, DJ left the locker room. At the end of the corridor he spied Rocco parading hand-in-hand with his new girlfriend, Ann Tompkins. "That happened over Thanksgiving too?" he asked Ike, who had just stepped alongside him.

Rocco had never even been out on a date before and Ann Tompkins, who worked weekends in her father's auto body shop, had always intimidated any potential boyfriend. "Is he that desperate?" DJ reconsidered his question. "Is *she* that desperate?"

"They both are. Desperation runs wild in this school, in case you hadn't noticed." Ike stopped, then leaned over and pulled up a sock. "If you don't think so, look at Maynard."

"All this is hard to believe," DJ repeated, thinking about Rocco and Ann, then Leslie. He turned toward Maynard, who had joined them. "You skating?"

"Sure," Maynard answered. "Frannie's staying for Home Ec club. I'll meet her after we're done."

"You coming, Ike?" DJ asked. Sometimes he watched from the bleachers.

"No, can't. I've got to take the bus. Doctor at four-thirty. Maybe I'll call you later and talk to Patty. See what's going on." He headed for the line of buses in the front of the school.

DJ and Maynard walked down the hallway toward the gymnasium.

"Rocco's brother, Artie, is going in the army," Maynard said matter-of-factly. "After Basic, he thinks he's headed right to Vietnam."

The mention of Vietnam ignited an internal flare that made DJ nervous. Suddenly, seemingly overnight, the war was creeping closer and closer. In the past, he had never given it too much thought. Sporadic, vague stories in magazines had caught his eye, and occasionally he'd hear some report from a distant source, but it had never meant much. The conflict seemed to be a far-off accident, barely visible on the horizon. Yet with Rocco's brother expecting to head to Southeast Asia, that faraway billboard was rapidly coming into focus.

"They have punji sticks on the trails over there," Maynard said. "Bamboo sticks with human shit on them. They're sharp and can go right through your boot and poison you."

"Where do you hear this stuff?" DJ asked as they approached the gymnasium door.

"Artie. He has friends over there. One guy got jabbed and his leg blew up like a blimp. They almost had to cut it off." Maynard swung open the door.

"Maybe they should look where they're walking."

"Running. Believe me, you go to war, you're running."

The two crossed the gymnasium and picked up their roller skates. The Booster Club and a few local businessmen sponsored the skating every month, claiming it to be an all-encompassing cure for juvenile delinquency, but most townsfolk knew it was bogus goodwill designed strictly to generate business.

After lacing up their skates, DJ and Maynard cast themselves gingerly out into the growing crowd circling the perimeter of the gymnasium. Skating in the pack with the rest of the amateurs, DJ was pleased he could navigate around the floor as well as anyone else. Of course, there was always some show-off who skated backward, his arms folded behind him, a smug look on his face, but DJ wasn't even jealous. The pretty girls were only interested in the football and baseball players. Roller skating, like bowling, was minor league and just a step above being a member of the pathetic audio-visual squad.

As he glided around the floor, DJ began to sense a lightness, an airiness, a newfound freedom mushrooming inside him, a feeling that he could only attribute to being liberated from Leslie's basement. She would now have someone else to focus her anger, impatience and perfection on, and he could sneak away into the night, a smiling rat backstroking away from the sinking ship.

∞

After the turkey TV dinners that evening, DJ went to the closet and reached for his coat.

"Where are you going?" Patty asked.

"Over to Greta's. Feel like coming along?"

She paused, then said, "No, not tonight. I've got too much homework and I promised Ike we could talk on the phone later."

"Okay," DJ said, walking to the door. "See you later, Dad." He waved to his father as he left the house.

Since the first night Patty and DJ had visited Greta, he had been back several times, with and without his sister. And occasionally, Patty dropped by alone. Greta never seemed to tire of their presence and welcomed them whenever they appeared. This evening DJ had self-consciously brought two Marty Robbins record albums with him.

After the second one was completed, Greta refilled her sherry glass and brought DJ a new bottle of Coke. "Are you Marty Robbins?" she asked, returning to her chair.

"How could I be Marty Robbins?"

"Identification," she said. "Sometimes I imagine myself to be Kirsten Flagstad singing Wagner in Carnegie Hall." She smiled. "The mind is magical, and we're never quite sure what exists and what doesn't."

DJ nodded. He had no idea what she was talking about.

Greta placed a new cigarette in the ivory holder and lit it. "How's Leslie?"

She hadn't heard about the breakup. DJ didn't give any details, saying they had just grown tired of being together, but added that she already had a new boyfriend, Bobby.

"She's with Bobby Litchfield?" Greta asked. "And Bobby is without Lisa?"

"That's what I hear," DJ said. "I haven't seen them together though."

"And you're happy with that?" Greta asked.

DJ shrugged. "I don't know, there was a lot of stuff going on between Leslie and me."

"Poor girl," Greta said. "A stern father she could never please and a mother who hibernates. It must take its toll on her. I should think it's a wonder she has a boyfriend at all." Greta paused. "Of course, Leslie is attractive and that always makes a difference."

"Do you know her parents?" DJ asked.

"Not personally, but you would be surprised what you overhear sitting alone in a coffee shop booth day after day."

DJ poured the remainder of his Coke into the glass. He was feeling more relaxed than he could ever remember. The exhilaration of being apart from Leslie kept bubbling up from out of nowhere, washing over him, drinking him in. "Greta, who's the man in the picture?" he asked, indicating a framed photograph on the side table resting below the fireworks oil painting.

Greta sighed, then briefly looked away. "The last time I saw him was 1939. He sent me the picture after he had gone to war." She ran her hand across the back of her neck, then gazed at the image. "And now I am old. And it could have been yesterday when I read the poetry he wrote for me:"

> *If I should die, think only this of me:*
> *there's some corner of a foreign field*
> *That is forever England . . .*

DJ watched as the words flowed from some deep reservoir, just as he now imagined Kirsten Flagstad must sing. "He wrote poetry to you?"

"Only for me—no one else." A satisfied look crossed Greta's face. "And the irony, of course, is that he died from an insect bite on a remote island without ever being published."

"Who was he?" DJ asked.

Greta looked across the room, then back at DJ, a ghost of a smile tracing her lips. "Another time, perhaps, dear boy, another time."

DJ was embarrassed by his question—afraid that he had been prying. He glanced at his watch and saw it was almost ten o'clock. "I really have to go, Greta."

"I know," she answered, rising, "and you were very kind to come by."

As he descended the stairs outside her apartment door, he heard the lock bar slip into place behind him.

CHAPTER 18

Saturday morning, DJ met the new floating salesman at Mertz Brothers. Bobby Litchfield grinned at him when he entered Cliff Collins' office. "Forgot to mention this during school," he said. "I needed the money and I'm between football and baseball seasons. My old man limited me to two sports senior year. He said it shouldn't be all fun anymore, but that goes to show you what he knows because I was trained last weekend by a drop-dead, go-to-hell knockout. You must know her, Mrs. Canova?"

"Too bad you're going with Leslie," DJ said.

"Yeah, too bad," Bobby said, watching DJ. "Too bad for you, that is."

"How did you get the job?"

"Same way as you, I bet," Bobby answered. "My old man knows Mr. Collins. I guess you've been working out well enough so they thought they could add another slave. Here I am."

"How you doing, fellas? You know each other?" Cliff asked, straining through his bloodshot eyes as he entered his office carrying his scheduling charts.

"Yeah," DJ answered. "We do."

∞

Bobby was sent to The Ivy League Shop and DJ was assigned to the Kitchen Appliances department.

During his lunch break, DJ walked out into the mall. As he strolled to the far end, he picked up his usual hot dog, then stared at a crepe-paper Santa Claus propped up in a variety store window.

He walked inside and stopped at a rack of children's Christmas books. He picked up an oversized *The Night Before Christmas* and turned to the last page where Santa stood on a snow-covered roof, a wrapped piece of bubble gum attached to his sled—a bonus to the purchaser. The book seemed carefree and comforting, reminiscent of what he had wanted his family to be, so DJ bought it. He decided he would keep it in the top drawer of his bedroom dresser and open it every once in a while to pretend he was a kid.

∞

"Mrs. Canova was looking for you," Mr. Slavik said, when he returned to Kitchen Appliances. "She wants you to stop by her office and bring your time sheets."

DJ was nervous, then concerned. "Why would I have to do that?"

"Don't know, it's never happened to me." He shrugged. "Maybe there's an error somewhere."

"How could there be an error?" DJ asked. "You work, you fill in your time sheets. How could there be a mistake?"

Mr. Slavik straightened a row of product brochures on a rack by the cash register. "I don't know. I'm just passing along the message."

DJ rode the escalator to Mrs. Canova's office. After tightening his tie, he knocked on the closed door.

"Come in." She was sitting behind her desk, a fountain pen in her hand. "Oh yes, DJ, come in. Please close the door."

DJ turned and gently shut the door behind him, then stood in front of it.

"Did you bring the time sheets?" she asked.

"Yes, they're right here, Mrs. Canova," he answered, holding up the papers in his hand.

"Slide a seat over please."

DJ pushed an aluminum-framed chair to the front of her desk.

"No, bring it around to my side so we can check the numbers together." She signaled with her forefinger. "Come on, I won't bite."

DJ moved his chair and placed the sheets in front of her.

Mrs. Canova glanced at the papers DJ had placed on her desk. "How is the floating salesman doing?" Not waiting for a reply, she asked, "Are you happy with the job?"

"It's fine," DJ answered tentatively. He remembered touching her and the back of her finger running down the side of his face, her eyes reaching for his.

"The reports I have indicate you're doing very well." She looked over at him. "The reason I called you is that Mertz Brothers is prepared to increase your salary twenty-five cents an hour. Is that something you would find agreeable?"

The way she had placed her hand behind his head, pulling him closer, the darkness outside, the softness of her lips. He couldn't turn to her. He was too near. Instead he looked away. Nodding to the wall, he said, "That would be good. Thank you."

Silence pervaded the office. Outside, far in the distance, a fire truck's siren moved even farther away.

"But you can't look at me?" she asked gently.

DJ hesitated, then shifted toward her. "Yes, I can," he said. "I can look at you." She was close again, as she was at the beach, as she had been in the car.

"It's very difficult for me, DJ," she said softly. "I've missed you."

His voice was raspy. "Me? Why would you miss me?"

Carlyn bit her bottom lip. "I don't know why. But I have. More than I care to admit to myself." She touched his shoulder with the tips of her fingers, then reached behind his head and brought her lips to his, kissing him. Running her finger across his face, just as she had in the Mustang, she brushed her lips against his again, then asked, "Do you feel this way?"

"Yes," DJ mumbled, his face flushed, his eyes cast downward.

"But this shouldn't be happening," Carlyn said slowly. "I should know better than to be doing something this foolish."

DJ didn't answer, then raised his eyes until they were in contact with Carlyn's. Leaving the palms of his hands placed on the top of the desk, trembling, he leaned forward and kissed her.

"We can't do this," Carlyn said, a moment later, her voice uncertain as she looked at him. "It makes no sense. And certainly not here." She lingered on DJ. "Would you meet me tonight? Is that even possible?"

DJ hesitated, then said, "I could do that," fumbling with the words, "but what about your husband?"

"He's in Vietnam. He's been there a week." She hesitated and looked briefly away, then returned her gaze to DJ. "But I suppose we should talk about that too." She glanced at her watch. "Do you want to meet me in the parking lot of the Jailhouse Rock?"

DJ nodded.

"Is nine o'clock all right for you?"

DJ nodded again. "Yes." He was unable to look at her.

"Okay. Until nine o'clock then."

DJ stood and replaced the chair by the door. Looking over his shoulder, he gave a tentative wave to Carlyn, then walked out and returned to Kitchen Appliances.

"What did Mrs. Canova want?" Mr. Slavik asked as he rang

up a blender.

"She just had a question about the number of hours I had worked. I think the bookkeeping department made a mistake."

"Well that's easy enough," Mr. Slavik replied, handing change and a receipt to a bearded man in a buffalo plaid shirt. "I don't know about you, but I have a hard time concentrating when she's around. Her husband, he's some lucky guy."

"Yeah," DJ said, "I guess he is."

CHAPTER 19

Carlyn was waiting in the corner of the parking lot. DJ had half expected the space to be empty. He walked over to the Mustang, opened the door and stepped inside.

"You made it," Carlyn said, a smile on her face. She waited until he was settled in his seat. "Where to?"

"I don't know. Anywhere is fine."

Carlyn started the car. "Okay."

As they drove out of the Jailhouse Rock parking lot, DJ could hear the thumping of Wendell's bass drum as The Primates began their first song of the night.

"I could show you my house," Carlyn volunteered. "I'll bet you don't even know where I live."

"Is it near here?"

Carlyn glanced over at him, a quick smile crossing her face. "Sure it is. I don't make it public information, that's all. Just a few miles." She headed south on Main Street, out of Hardscrabble and down toward Amity. After ten minutes, Carlyn turned left and drove several blocks. She pulled into the driveway of a neighborhood home. "This is it." She opened the car door. "My little oasis, small, but it works. Come on inside."

DJ wasn't sure he should be at the house. It was hard to believe what was happening, but he followed Carlyn across the slate walkway, then waited while she opened the storm door and inserted the key in the front lock. Twisting the door knob, she pushed forward. He followed her and closed the inside door behind him. As it clicked shut, at the moment he turned to face her, Carlyn put her arms around his neck, kissing him. "I can't wait any longer, DJ. I want you right now," she whispered in his ear. "Now. Not later." She dropped her coat to the floor. "I know you want me too." She quickly lifted her sweater over her head, reached behind her back and unhooked her bra, then released his belt buckle and unzipped his corduroys. As his pants slid from his hips to the floor, she unbottoned the side of her skirt and let it slither down her legs, then drew DJ to the rug next to the door. She slid off her underwear, then his, and pulled him on top of her. Carlyn ran her tongue across his lips and at the same time reached downward bringing them together. "We've got to be careful, we don't want this over too quickly," she whispered, her eyes half-closed. She slowly moved her hips beneath him. "This is what we should really be teaching at Mertz Brothers."

The remark so surprised DJ, he began to lose focus.

"I was just joking. Really," Carlyn said, her voice increasingly distant. "Relax, it's okay. It's okay." Quietly struggling, she gasped, and ran her fingers across his back.

"I can't believe this," she whispered again and again as she slowly arched her back, moving her head to one side. "I can't believe it, I can't believe it," she repeated to no one, her voice rising. Her fingers ran wildly through DJ's hair, over and over, then suddenly she was frozen, locked against him for several fluttery seconds until she slowly, inch by inch, pooled down onto the rug, her arms thrown to her sides. As her breathing gradually evened, she scratched her ankle with the toe of her opposite foot. "Are you good?" she asked.

DJ nodded, fairly certain he knew what she meant. Armed

with a hair trigger, he'd been "good" very quickly, maybe too quickly for Carlyn. And he was still wearing his shirt and jacket. He moved so he lay next to her on the hallway throw rug, his head resting against one of her shoes.

Carlyn jumped up and gathered her clothes. "So much for foreplay," she said, then added, "I wish I wasn't like that sometimes. How about a beer?" She flicked on a light and disappeared across the living room.

Uncomfortable with his own nudity as well as Carlyn's, DJ hurriedly dressed and followed after her.

By the time he walked into the kitchen, she was standing at the open refrigerator wearing a robe. "Beer out of a bottle or glass?"

"Bottle's good," DJ answered.

"Bet you wonder what happened back there," Carlyn said as she uncapped the beer and handed it to him. She switched on the radio perched on the shelf over the sink, twisted the dial until she tuned in a local station, then moved to DJ and wrapped an arm around his neck. She kissed him as she rumpled his hair. "Me too. I wonder what happened too. But I liked it."

DJ sat on a stool at the end of a counter as Carlyn returned to the refrigerator and took out a bottle of wine. After filling half a glass, she walked over and stood next to him, her arm leaning against the counter. "This is much more civilized than beer," she said. "Beer is only for animals like you."

"I hope your husband really went to Vietnam."

"Believe me, he's in Vietnam. I had a letter this morning." She sipped from her glass. "But we shouldn't concern ourselves about him. Out of sight, out of mind."

"Do you do this a lot?" DJ asked, then stopped abruptly. "I mean do you—"

Carlyn laughed. "You really are a funny boy," she said, then with her eyes wide, her mouth open in mock chagrin, added, "I mean, you're not a boy, I know that, but still, you can be funny." She ran her fingers through DJ's hair. "No, I do not do this a lot. I do this never as a matter of fact. That's why I'm more surprised with myself than you are. I couldn't believe what happened at Mertz Brothers this morning. I'm a professional woman kissing a high school boy in my office behind closed doors." She shook her head. "I mean, really." Her face grew darker, the color seeping down her neck with the thought. "Then this, tonight." She sipped the wine. "And yes, I know it might be hard for you to believe, but I do love my husband. Of course, after this, it might make sense to ask myself how much."

Carlyn placed the glass of wine on the counter and rested her hand next to it. "It's strange how things can change so quickly." She reached over and unbuttoned the top two buttons of DJ's shirt and shoved her hand inside. As her fingers ran across his chest, she brushed her lips across his mouth. "I've got a bed much more comfortable than the floor."

∞

Later, as Carlyn lay in the crook of his arm, and the street light needled its way through the partially closed Venetian blinds, they listened to the Beatles on the faraway kitchen radio. After a while, just as he was getting drowsy, she said, "Thank you."

Like most of the important times in his life that he could remember, DJ didn't know how to respond. As he covered himself with an edge of the sheet, he kissed her on the cheek. "That's okay," he said. "That's okay."

CHAPTER 20

Dale was happy. It occurred annually, every second or third week in December, though Nostradamus would have been hard pressed to pinpoint the exact date the joy train would pull into the Elders' station.

Dale claimed his turnabout each year was a result of the rediscovery of the Christmas spirit.

As children, Patty and DJ quickly realized their father was a changed man once that spirit was in his possession, so each year they toddled around the house in early December in search of that wily ghost, aware that if they found the spirit, then presented it to him, he would become a new man—kind, easy, and most important, interested. The problem was that neither Patty nor DJ knew what the Christmas spirit looked like so they searched everywhere—in the attic, under the beds, behind the toilet paper roll, even in the crack between the bottom of the oil burner and the cement floor in the cellar. Any unusual-looking object they couldn't identify, a stick, a dead insect, a fuse, they'd take to their father and say, "Here's the Christmas spirit for you," then wait for his pronouncement while their grubby fingers twisted behind their backs. Most of the time he would ignore them, or tell them to go play, but once Patty had found a five-dollar bill under the cushion in his recliner and Dale had been so pleased with her discovery that Christmas joy immediately descended upon him, turning the three into a family of friends.

Yet as easily as they adapted to their newfound father at Christmastime, as they grew older, his accompanying British accent took some getting used to. Along with his newly-discovered benevolence to his fellow man, Dale also began to speak in precise, clipped tones, referring to himself as a barrister instead of the town judge, and would proceed to drink Scotch whiskey, neat, ignoring the cases of beer in the cellar. One year, he even attempted to grow a Bengal Lancer moustache, though he quickly shaved it off when his less-than-charitable court officer told him he looked like a walrus.

"I tell you what, your father wanted to study law in Cambridge, or somewhere in England. He needed that snob appeal," Wendell said when DJ had inquired about the accent a couple of years earlier. "Dale was always smart, he just wasn't smart enough for that highfalutin' stuff. City college was about all he could handle, though he'll never in a million years admit it. He ought to own up to it instead of sitting on his butt in Hardscrabble settling parking ticket squabbles, all the time thinking he belonged on the Su-preme Court." He hesitated. "And I'll tell you what else. Dale doesn't spend practically any time with Monty and me. What kind of a brother is that?"

Wendell was probably right on all counts, DJ thought, but he currently wasn't complaining because the Christmas spirit had at last arrived, the giveaway being his father traveling to a specialty shop in the mall and returning with a genuine English plum pudding in a tin. "Paid a bloody fortune for it," he said, depositing the package next to the quart of Johnny Walker on the kitchen table. "But what the hell, it's Christmas."

But what the hell, it's Christmas. There was a certain irrational logic in the statement that DJ understood. Even the teachers were easing off, a couple of them discovering the Christmas spirit themselves. And he heard the annual Living Nativity planned for Christmas Eve under spotlights outside St. Mary's—a ritual he loved—was proceeding without a hitch.

DJ had a sense it was going to be a memorable holiday. Since the first night together with Carlyn, they had been meeting secretly, most of the time returning to her house, though once they went to an old harbor motel and spent three hours in a tiny box room containing a flimsy mattress that rolled them together in the middle, tiny soaps next to the sink, and according to Carlyn, a freezing toilet seat.

They'd pretend to be strictly business associates at Mertz Brothers, rarely even acknowledging each other's presence, and then for no reason that he could imagine, Carlyn would do something he considered to be very risky right in the store. One afternoon in Basement Shoes, she walked into the back of the storeroom where he was searching for a size fourteen extra wide outdoor boot and began to undress him in the middle of the aisle. DJ had kissed her a little, but was so concerned that they might be caught, he pulled away. Carlyn had pouted for a split second, told him he was no fun, then adjusted her makeup, pinched him on the rear and walked out through the curtains to the front, saying, "Check on that size for next week, DJ," over her shoulder, just as Mr. Slavik was returning from lunch.

"How come Mrs. Canova only comes to visit when I'm not around?" Mr. Slavik asked DJ, mildly annoyed.

"Bad luck, I guess," DJ responded.

∞

Being alone during the upcoming weekend was a new experience. Carlyn told him she was going to visit her sister's family in Albany before the holiday, and though she knew Cliff was furious with her for taking a day of vacation on the weekend before Christmas, it was an obligation she wanted to complete so that she might be with DJ during the holidays.

Her concern about being with him was satisfying, and her absence created a love-lost, pining feeling that was not totally unpleasant. Also, he was feeling a little worn down from all their bedroom activity and thought he could probably use an industrial Geritol power boost.

After working at Mertz Brothers on Saturday, DJ showered, then decided to stop at the Jailhouse Rock. Patty wanted him to join Ike and her at a movie, but he wasn't in the mood. Also he could see that Ike was getting more and more possessive about being alone with his sister. Instead, he felt like relaxing and letting the day splash over him, then getting enough sleep so Herman would cease to be an irritant in the morning.

DJ slipped in the side entrance to the Rock and sat at Lila's table. "Hi, sweetheart," she said, inhaling a Newport. "Wendell's at the bar and Monty's getting something out of his car." She rested the cigarette on the lip of the ashtray, then moved off to take a drink order. Moments later, Gordon walked out of the restroom and over to DJ, his Rickenbacker guitar strapped across his chest. Gordon took the guitar with him everywhere—he was paranoid someone was going to steal it. He lifted his drink off the corner of the stage. "DJ, you know that great-looking blonde, Carlyn, was her name, the one that used to come in here? I don't see her around anymore. I wonder what happened."

DJ shrugged. "Gee, how would I know?"

"I was driving through Amity the other night and I thought I saw her sitting at a stoplight in a Mustang, and I was sure it was you riding next to her."

DJ looked at Gordon. "Me? You're kidding. Why would I be in her car?" He paused and then grinned. "It's not a bad idea though. Could you make it happen?"

"Yeah, I wish," Gordon said, climbing the steps up to the stage, "I wish I could get it done for myself." He plugged his guitar into the amplifier and began to tune.

Monty walked up to the table. "And what do we owe this special occasion to?" he asked, clapping DJ on the shoulder.

"Good to see you, son."

"I tell you what, ole Dale's gotten around to this year's Christmas spirit," Wendell said, appearing behind Monty. He sat next to DJ. "I guess you're more than a little pleased about that."

DJ nodded.

"Yeah, I tell you what, DJ," Wendell continued, "ole Dale called me up to see how I was doing which was the first inkling that the Christmas spirit had landed—then he called me a bloke. He said, 'Talk to you later, old bloke.'" Slowly, a contented look crossed Wendell's face and he sighed. "Yeah, I tell you what, it's Christmas all right."

The Primates played and sang wearing Santa Claus caps, without Wendell complaining once. "Don't care as long as it's not a duck suit," he said, when he sat at the table during the next break. "But I ain't playing that British crap that's coming into the U-nited States. I'll tell you that right now. Beatles, Dave Clark, screw 'em, they're a bunch of weirdos. You check out their hair? I don't care what Thor says." He turned to Lila who was standing next to the table adding up a check. "Lila, honey, would you bring me another drink, and see if you can find a beer for DJ."

Lila nodded and headed to the bar.

Ten minutes later, DJ watched his uncles return to the stage and begin to play.

He thought about Carlyn for the hundredth time that night. He didn't ask about her husband anymore—not even his first name—mostly because he hated him. DJ knew the guy would be muscular, tan, wearing combat fatigues, and dog tags that clanked on a hairy chest; a monster gladiator who owned Carlyn, or at least had first claim to her, which was more than he could bear. The thought of someone else touching her was impossible to fathom. He loved her too much himself.

DJ constantly struggled to put the problem out of his mind, recognizing his competition was in Vietnam, feeling certain that any married woman who was in love with her husband wouldn't do what Carlyn was doing. But once past that hurdle, he had to deal with another nagging cloud of anxiety—a fear of what the man would do if he ever returned and caught them together.

His empty beer bottle in hand, DJ walked to the front of the Rock. With most everyone on the dance floor, Thor was resting behind the bar talking with Jellybowl, who was peeling an apple using a jackknife blade. "Merry Christmas, son," Thor said, as DJ approached. "But, hey, don't let anyone see you with that beer. One of my own deputies might arrest me."

"Okay, I won't," DJ answered.

"Hey, Thor, how about some service," two locals called from down at the end of the bar.

"On my way," Thor answered as he wiped his hands on a rag and moved toward them. "I thought you guys were coming back late this afternoon. You can only hunt for so long."

"We were supposed to be back earlier. Roadblock on the Thruway in Albany. Cop killed. They're tearing the place apart looking for the murderer. Slowed us down a ton. Normally takes us four hours to get home—took us six today."

"No kidding? That's bad." Thor shook his head. "Well, don't worry, they'll catch the guy. Cop killers never escape. You kill a policeman, it's like writing your own death sentence."

Overhearing the conversation, DJ instantly thought about Carlyn being in Albany and began to worry, but then quickly dismissed his concern. After all, Albany was the capitol of New York, with millions of people living in the area. She'd be safe. Odds of her being hurt were zero to none.

He was sure.

CHAPTER 21

As he left the Rock, DJ considered the following week. He knew he wasn't going to have much spare time because Carlyn wanted him to work at Mertz Brothers whenever he wasn't in school, right through December 23rd. She said if the store didn't make money now, it never would, and that she needed him. Actually, he liked the idea of being that busy, with her filling in the remainder of his time. Most of his life had been a series of empty spaces, missing boards in a picket fence—but with Carlyn everything was complete and stable.

As he walked through the silence of his street, past the colored lights outlining the perimeters of the houses—a blue-collar Broadway—Ike's home stood out under the street light. Every year, Mrs. O'Reilly used nearly identical decorations—a wreath on the door and all the windows littered with taped, construction paper Santas standing next to white angels with glitter halos hovering over their heads,

At home, DJ closed the front door quietly behind him. Patty was sitting at the kitchen table. "I've been waiting for you," she said.

"How was the movie?" DJ asked, hanging up his coat.

"Okay. Herman called. He said to come in a little early tomorrow."

"Great," DJ said as he joined Patty at the table.

"Look at this," Patty said snapping open a small box.

"What is it?" He reached across the table and lifted a simple gold band with pearl from the black velvet.

"Ike gave it to me tonight," Patty said, her face expressionless. "He said he couldn't wait until Christmas."

"Ike gave you this?" DJ asked, studying the ring. "He doesn't have any money." DJ looked again. "Is it real gold?"

"I guess so. He said it was. I told him right away that I couldn't take it, but he said I had to."

DJ thought a second. "You aren't getting married, are you?"

"No, nothing like that." Patty took the ring back and put it on her finger. "It does look nice though, don't you think?"

"Patty, you can't keep that. Ike doesn't have any money."

She removed the ring and placed it back in the box. "I know, but it was nice of him to think of me." She glanced at DJ. "I know, I know, I can't keep it." She snapped the lid closed. "I just didn't know how to tell him I couldn't." She thought for a moment. "I still don't."

"Why do you think Ike did that?"

"He's thinking about the two of us—me and him—all the time. That's what's going on." Patty pushed the box across the Formica table with the tip of her finger. "And I didn't do anything to encourage him. I went to the movies, but not on a boy-girl real thing, you know? It's just about being with a friend, like going out with you and Maynard." She paused for a second. "But Ike has it all turned around, DJ. He thinks we're more than that." She sighed, then picked up the box again. "Look at this," she said, snapping the lid open, "I bet Dad never gave anything like this to Mom. I'll bet he never gave her anything close to it." She pointed at their snoring father in the other room. "Look at him, the sleeping Winston Churchill. What a joke."

"Yeah, I know." DJ said. "Wendell was talking about him

and his English accent at the Rock tonight."

"Wendell's no better. I don't know why he should be passing judgment about anyone else." She yawned, then abruptly laughed. "And look at me. Here I am a junior in high school and the only guy I've ever been out with is Ike." Her laughter slowly froze, then collapsed mid-air. "It really is pitiful. And you know what, DJ," she added, her voice suddenly soft, "I'm ashamed to admit it, but I don't even like to be with Ike. I know he's your friend, but I can't help it. Everybody stares at us. They know something's wrong with him because he's pale, but then they think something's wrong with me because I'm the one with him." She looked over at DJ, then stared away. "Am I terrible?"

"Patty, Ike can't control how he looks."

"I know that," she said, her voice rising, "I didn't say he could help it, but it's not my fault either." She snapped the box lid closed again. "I'm sorry. I don't mean to be this way. Sometimes I just wish I had a normal boyfriend and lived in a normal house." Patty thought for a moment and studied DJ. "Do you have a new girlfriend?"

The question caught him off guard. "New girlfriend? Why?"

"I just wondered. This is the first Saturday night you've been home early in a while and I know you're not with Leslie."

DJ didn't answer.

"And I've seen the Mustang with the blonde girl drop you off a couple of times—the one you said was your boss at Mertz Brothers. Actually she looks older than a girl." Patty stared at him. "You don't have to tell me if you don't want to."

DJ thought. "Well, I sort of have a new girlfriend," he said, then proceeded to give Patty an abridged version of his relationship with Carlyn.

"Sounds okay to me," Patty said, after he was finished. "Is Carlyn a lot older?"

DJ nervously laughed out loud. "Not really." He rose and crossed to the refrigerator, "a little older, that's all."

∞

Later, in the dark, after they had retired to their bedrooms, Patty put the Johnny Mathis *Merry Christmas* album on her record player, turning the volume up so the music would wind around the corner and up the stairs to DJ's room.

He knew it was her way of sharing herself with him, her way of saying she loved him without having to wade through the awkwardness of mentioning it face to face.

Despite Patty's outer sweetness, DJ had never been sure about her emotional equilibrium. In the past, he had wondered if the shy, but outwardly friendly demeanor she offered to all passersby was merely camouflage erected as a shield to protect her.

And sometimes he thought Patty was afraid to react because of the unpredictability of their father's drunkenness, but now, more than that, he was beginning to wonder if she was able to feel anything at all.

With their mother dead, leaving the two of them behind to struggle on, he had long ago discovered how to float above the emotional terrain. Maybe Patty was so numbed from the loss of their mother and the mercurial relationship with their father, that despite her frequent smiles, internally, she was forever staring down the barrel of another rainy day.

She often spoke in emotional codes, and DJ always felt relieved and less responsible for her well being after a personal message had been deciphered. Sharing Johnny Mathis signaled that at least for the foreseeable future she was going to be all right, that a beam of light could still be injected and fanned out through her depths.

Following the refrain of "Blue Christmas," his ankles, his knees, then his chest began to loosen, and gradually he floated away from Patty's gravity.

CHAPTER 22

After school Monday, DJ stopped at Town Hall and picked up the Falcon to drive to Mertz Brothers. Dale's court officer had agreed to take him home for the next two evenings while DJ was working at the store.

When DJ walked into Cliff Collins' office, the first person he saw was Bobby Litchfield with an inch-long bruise under his eye.

"Bobby, I want you in Kitchen Appliances," Cliff said. "You'll be with two other fellas who've been here for a while. Listen and learn." He looked closer at him. "What happened to your eye?"

"Banged it on the car door." Bobby laughed. "I've got to watch where I'm going."

"Looks like the car got the better half of it," Cliff said, absentmindedly flicking his left earlobe. "Well, don't tell anyone it happened here."

Bobby walked out the door. "How you doing?" he said to DJ as he passed.

"DJ, I'm putting you back in The Ivy League Shop with Ben Slavik again. If it gets too busy, which it might, call, and I'll send someone else over."

"Okay," DJ said. He was pleased. Keeping his voice neutral, he asked, "Where's Mrs. Canova? I haven't seen her around for awhile."

Cliff spoke over his charts. "Mrs. Canova was just here. She was away over the weekend."

It was approaching dinner hour, but the store was crawling with people. Once in The Ivy League Shop, DJ immediately took position behind the cash register and was busy, nonstop, until seven-thirty.

Carlyn suddenly appeared. "Mr. Slavik," she asked, "would you please take these receipts up to Mr. Collins."

"Sure," he said and departed.

The Ivy League Shop was quiet except for a couple of browsers.

"I'm sorry, I didn't get home until late last night," Carlyn said. My sister wanted me to stay for an early dinner before she put the kids to bed."

"Did you get caught in the roadblock?" DJ asked.

Carlyn appeared startled. "Roadblock? What roadblock?"

"I heard there was one up around Albany. It took some hunters a long time to get back to Hardscrabble. State police were looking for a cop killer."

Carlyn slid her tongue across her lips. "No, I didn't run into anything like that." She smiled and stepped closer, then behind the register, where no one would be able to see, ran her hand along the back of his thigh. "Don't worry about roadblocks, big shot, what's more important, do you have a few minutes after work tonight?"

DJ felt the excitement charge through him, but then remembered that Greta had invited Patty and him to trim her Christmas tree. "I can't," he mumbled. "I'm going over to Greta's with my sister."

"You have another girlfriend? I'm away for one weekend and you're already with someone else?" Carlyn's eyes sparkled.

"No," DJ said, "Greta's just a friend."

"I'm teasing you, DJ," Carlyn said. "I know who Greta is. She's an institution in Hardscrabble."

"Maybe we could meet tomorrow night?" DJ suggested.

Carlyn smiled and rubbed the back of his thigh again, then ran her fingers across the zipper of his pants. "Maybe we can," she said, "but the question is, if we do, are you man enough to handle a woman who hasn't been with you in more than a week?"

"I could try," he said sheepishly as Mr. Slavik approached.

"Ah, a true swordsman," Carlyn said, then turning, "Yes, Mr. Slavik, any problems?"

"None," he said, "but Mr. Collins would like you in the office when you get a second."

"Thank you, I'm headed there now," Carlyn said. "And DJ, see if we have any more of those neckties, would you please?" She turned and walked in the direction of Mr. Collins's office.

Mr. Slavik walked to the register and opened it with his key. "What kind of necktie is she looking for?"

DJ was momentarily stumped, then said, "Blue striped."

Mr. Slavik pointed to the tie table. "We've only got about twenty dozen left," he said, then closed the register. "How many husbands has she got?"

CHAPTER 23

Greta opened the door and placed the lock bar against the wall. "Christmas is such a wonderful time," she said. "I heard tonight we may get snow before the twenty-fifth. Wouldn't that be marvelous?"

She took Patty and DJ's coats and returned to the living room. "Your Cokes are right there," she said, indicating the cocktail table. "Now I have a dilemma that I hope you both can help me with. But first, we must have some Christmas music, then I'll share my predicament." She crossed to the stereo and placed a record album on the turntable. After adjusting the volume, she listened intently, then readjusted the tone before returning to DJ and Patty. "Yes, and now, the predicament. Please, if you would, look at the tree."

Patty and DJ stared across the room at the naked evergreen standing in front of the two stereo speakers.

"What do you see?" she asked.

"It needs ornaments," DJ said, referring to the three cardboard boxes sitting next to it.

"What else?" Greta asked.

"It's crooked," Patty said.

"Precisely. Thank you, Patty. Herman helped me bring the tree home and put it in the stand, then he left. After he was gone, I went into the kitchen to get water for it, then walked back into the room and there it was, infuriatingly tilted."

"That should be easy enough to fix," DJ said. "I'll crawl underneath, loosen the screws. Patty, you can adjust the tree, and I'll re-tighten everything. Easy."

Greta was clearly relieved. "Do you mind this kind of inconvenience, dear boy? I certainly didn't invite you here to work."

"It's not work," DJ said. "Do you have any pliers?"

"Yes, I think I do. In the kitchen drawer." She returned in seconds and handed them to DJ. He crawled under the tree and loosened the screws around the base of the trunk.

"Patty, you steady the tree and let me stand back and look." Greta moved to the far end of the room. "A little to the left." She moved to the other side. "More, more. Yes, right there. Perfect. Okay, DJ."

DJ tightened the screws around the base. "Good?" he called. "I can come up?"

"I believe so," Greta said as DJ clambered to his feet. "No, no, no, it shifted again. It's not straight again!"

"Then we should get it right," DJ answered, crawling back under the branches. He loosened the screws again and Patty held the tree until Greta was satisfied.

"Yes?" he called.

"Finally," Greta said.

DJ tightened the screws and slid from beneath the tree.

"I'm so sorry to put you both through this," Greta said.

"Anyway, it's done," Patty replied.

"And now the ornaments," Greta said as she turned over the record album. "I have some that are quite old and are very beautiful. I don't think many of them are even manufactured anymore."

The three spent the next forty-five minutes decorating the tree. Once the cardboard storage boxes were empty, Greta handed DJ and Patty strands of silvery, lead foil icicles to drape over the branches.

As she admired the handiwork, her sherry glass in hand, Greta said, "It looks like rain from the angels. Come let's move further back for perspective."

As he stood next to Greta, DJ watched reflections from the fireworks oil painting flickering in the glass ornaments—liquid flames dancing across the tree.

"No, it's not right," Greta announced, her voice forced. "It's tilted again. It's not right."

DJ couldn't tell. "Are you sure, Greta?" he asked.

"I am quite sure," she answered, her voice tense. "Don't you see?"

"Well, then I'll go back underneath—"

"You will do no such thing," Greta said. She walked to the closet and picked up a broom. "I think we just need a small push on the bottom of the trunk to get the correct balance. It should be quite simple, actually. It wouldn't make sense for you to attempt to straighten it again with those inferior screws."

Greta took the end of the broom handle and poked it through the branches until it rested against the trunk. She gave a slight push. "Tell me when it's straight."

"I can't tell. What do you think, Patty?"

Patty appeared equally baffled. "I think that it's okay now, Greta. Come look."

Greta stepped away from the tree and returned to the back of the room. Moving her head from one side to the other to gain perspective, she said, "Yes, I think—"

This time DJ saw the tree slightly shift.

"No, no, no," Greta said, her anger now resonating through the room. She crossed to the tree and jammed the broom end through the branches until it rested against the trunk. Pushing again, the tree visibly moved.

"Now?" she asked, her back to DJ and Patty. "Now is it right?"

"Yes," DJ and Patty answered in unison.

"Good," Greta said, straightening up and returning to the back of the room, the broom in hand.

The tree shifted.

Greta lunged forward swinging the broom handle as if it were a baseball bat, smashing the side of the tree with such force that it toppled over and crashed to the floor, scattering broken glass and tinsel across the rug and into the hardwood corners.

DJ quickly pulled Patty out of striking range and then stood still, his heart pounding while Patty leaned against him.

Standing with her back to the two, the handle still held in the follow-through position of a home-run swing, Greta surveyed the demolition before slowly, deliberately, lowering the broom. Shaking her head, she turned to DJ and Patty. "I'm such an old fool. No patience, no grace, and an ill temper to boot."

Then slowly, she began to chuckle. "You must think I've lost my mind. You do, don't you?" Greta chuckled louder. "I have hated those ornaments as long as I have owned them, but one might have thought I would've simply thrown them away." She began to laugh. "Oh, what an old fool I am." Sitting on the edge of one of the leather chairs, the broom handle resting against the fold of her dress, she laughed harder and shook her head.

DJ remained frozen next to Patty.

Greta gradually regained her composure and stood. "Forgive me, children. I apologize for frightening you with my behavior."

"Are you all right?" Patty asked.

"Yes, of course, dear," Greta responded. "Now if you and your brother can stand to remain in this chamber of horrors for a few more minutes, I truly do have a wonderful chocolate-raspberry torte for us to hopefully, enjoy, if you're not already too traumatized."

"Let me sweep up," DJ said reaching for the broom.

Greta looked at him. "You're very kind as always, DJ, but no, I'll clean up the mess I've created. And I assure you, it won't be the first time." She laughed again, then sighed. "My, my, my, what have I done, what have I done?"

CHAPTER 24

Tuesday, December 22nd—the last school day before the Christmas vacation—was chaos. DJ drove to the mall following his last class and parked the car behind Mertz Brothers. He had rushed, supposedly because Cliff Collins needed him right away, but his hurrying had little to do with the store's needs and everything to do with Carlyn.

Because everyone he knew in Hardscrabble was scarfless and shivered through the winter, he had decided to give scarves for Christmas. Smooth, wool scarves; rich, warm, wool scarves from Scotland and England. For Monty, navy blue, for Wendell, black-and-white checked, and for Patty, soft red wool mixed with cashmere. He had figured green for Greta because he knew it was her favorite color, gray for his father, for no reason, and blue-green checked for Ike. He had chosen each individually before the holiday rush, and using his store discount had accumulated a stack of scarves he'd hidden in his closet at home.

He even bought one with navy and black checks for himself. Standing in the storeroom of The Ivy League Shop, he draped it around his neck and stared into the mirror. It looks good, he thought. Carlyn's going to like it a lot.

And she did. Once inside her house, she slipped it from his neck and ran her fingers across his cheek as she had the first night in the Mustang. Her lips were so close to his that he could feel her breathe.

She walked into the bedroom and leaving the bureau lamp lit, slowly undressed in front of him, then sat on the edge of the bed. DJ slid out of his clothes and moved next to her. He touched her cheek with the backs of his fingers, just as she had touched his, and moved with her under the quilt where the two huddled until she was warm.

Later, as they lay together, Carlyn's head resting against his shoulder, DJ slid from beneath the quilt and walked to his shirt. He took a small, rectangular box from the pocket and moved back under the quilt next to her. "I love you," he said, handing her the gift. He'd been considering the moment for a month, but even so, had to look away when he made the simple declaration.

Carlyn said nothing, then lifted both arms outside the comforter, untied the ribbon and snapped open the lid. The gold ankle bracelet had two attached hearts inscribed with the initials CC and DE, and had cost DJ eighteen dollars plus an extra two dollars for the engraving.

"And I love you too, DJ," Carlyn whispered as she ran the tip of her finger across the two entwined hearts, "but I don't know what to do about it."

CHAPTER 25

December 23rd was continued chaos at Mertz Brothers, with no one sure whether the pandemonium was increasing or declining.

DJ had driven the Falcon home from Carlyn's the night before and crept into the darkened house, but then had lain awake until two o'clock. Over and over, he watched her place the bracelet around her ankle. Then she had kissed him, rested her perfumed hair on his chest, and to his surprise, fallen asleep.

He'd hoped to speak with her at the store in the morning, but she was so overwhelmed with the crowds he caught her eye only once.

Throngs of anxious buyers swarmed through the different departments—locusts demanding his attention—ravaging him, threatening to overrun him, until he was set free at four o'clock. As he walked through the parking lot, lines of brake lights blinked on and off as drivers played chicken for vacant parking spaces.

∞

DJ was barely in the door when Ike called and wanted to walk into town. "Tradition," he said. "Have to keep the annual tradition going. What else have we got? Be over in a few minutes."

Dale was sitting at the kitchen table sipping Johnny Walker, wearing a tartan vest. "Lovely feeling this Christmastime, isn't it just?" he asked, glancing at DJ. "Might consider installing a fireplace so the family could enjoy a Yule log." He added a splash of the scotch to his glass, then spun the top back on the bottle with a flick of his wrist.

"Good idea, Dad," DJ said, pulling his coat off a hanger.

"Where's your sister? I haven't seen her."

"Working. Busy time at Van Velsor's with all the shoppers in town."

"Ah, yes, the Christmas season," Dale intoned. "Well then, perhaps I should jaunt down and have a peek. It's always great fun to watch the locals make fools out of themselves at this time of year. Perhaps I might even find some reason to place a wager with Jellybowl should I stop at the Jailhouse Rock."

"What would you bet on?" DJ inquired.

"There's always something. Quite." Dale answered, turning his attention back to the bottle.

The doorbell rang and DJ let Ike inside.

"Is that you, Master Dwight O'Reilly?" Dale called from the kitchen.

"Yes, it is, Judge Elders. Merry Christmas."

"And to you, lad. Have a good night out. Cheers!"

∞

"Let's go down to Van Velsor's," DJ said as he closed the front door and descended the steps.

"I'll bet you're glad the Christmas spirit is here."

"Oh, yeah," DJ answered. "Get it while you can."

"Boy, it's cold," Ike said minutes later.

"Sure wish I had a scarf," DJ replied as they crossed the railroad tracks.

"Only old ladies wear scarves," Ike answered while they traipsed down Main Street. In the distance "Jingle Bell Rock" was being piped over speakers hanging outside Monty's TV Repair Shop.

"Let's take a look at the Living Nativity layout before we hit Van Velsor's," DJ said.

The boys crossed the street to the brick church and stood where workmen were erecting spotlights around the crèche.

"It should be real nice tomorrow night," DJ said. "Seems like we've been doing this for a long time."

"We have," Ike responded. They stood and watched the workmen until Ike began to shiver. "What do you say we head over to see Patty?"

"Right," DJ answered, staring at Ike's neck. "You could use a scarf. Keep you from being so cold."

"Never wear it," Ike answered.

Not good, DJ thought.

All the booths were filled when they entered Van Velsor's, so Ike sat at the counter and drank hot chocolate while DJ joined Greta in her booth for a game of checkers. To his surprise, he eventually managed a king. Greta slowly raised her eyes and smiled, "That's my gift to atone for my atrocious behavior the other night."

∞

Twenty minutes later when DJ returned to the counter, Ike wanted to wait until Patty was done for the night.

Overhearing the conversation, Patty shook her head. "You would be here for hours. Too much cleaning up to do."

∞

"How come Greta doesn't work when they're that busy?" Ike asked, as they trudged back across the railroad tracks.

"Don't know. She does sometimes. I guess she just waits on tables when she wants to. Look who the owner is." DJ pulled his collar up tighter around his neck.

"Did you see the ring I gave Patty for Christmas?" Ike asked.

"Yeah, she showed me."

"What did she think?"

"It was nice. A real nice present." DJ paused. "Looked expensive though."

Ike shrugged, then mumbled, "Well, Patty's worth it."

"I mean, I just wonder where, not just you, but, you know, where anyone would get that kind of money."

"Easy," Ike answered, "I used the money I saved for the second half of the watch repair course."

"You used *that* money." DJ stopped. "You mean the money you've been saving?" He kicked at the snow. "You can't do that, Ike, you need that money. You've got to learn all that stuff for next year!"

"I wanted to buy it," Ike said, still shuffling along, "I wanted to and I'm glad I did."

DJ caught up. "Patty can't take that ring, you know."

Ike continued to move forward. "But she did, DJ. She took it."

The two walked another three blocks.

Ike stared straight ahead as he approached his house, then slowly climbed the front steps, opened the door and stepped inside, never once looking back.

CHAPTER 26

Early next morning, Patty and DJ decorated the tree Dale's court officer had dropped off the night before. And despite Ike's negative comments about scarves, DJ was committed and descended into the cellar to wrap them. He'd bought the paper and ribbon at Mertz Brothers, but even with his employee discount, it was more expensive than Woolworth's. By the time he was finished, Patty had already placed her presents under the tree, and even with her gifts combined with his own, DJ thought the pile looked skimpy, especially compared to all those Kodak "Open Me First" families on TV.

On Christmas Eve, a frigid weather front was gripping the Northeast, accompanied by light snow and icy wind. For the Living Nativity, it was a trade-off: arrive early, have a good standing position for the pageant, and freeze—or arrive late, not be able to see what was going on, and still freeze, only for a shorter duration.

DJ, Ike and Patty decided to compromise, arriving twenty minutes before the spectacle, and though they managed front-row standing room, it was right of the crèche, close to the street-side of the church. "This won't be so bad," DJ said, hoping to inspire Patty and Ike, "we'll still be able to see everything."

The choir sang "Oh, Little Town of Bethlehem," and DJ thought the lyrics were more moving than he could ever remember. As the second verse began, a churchwoman walked forward and placed her newborn child in the manger for authenticity. The baby, wrapped in a snowsuit and covered with a blanket, briefly opened his eyes, recognized nothing, then so bundled he was unable to move, fell back to sleep.

While Father Hill, wearing black earmuffs similar to mouse ears, began the Christmas story, little puffs of white smoke emerged from his lips with every syllable he spoke, and as he continued, the mood turned magical, tranquil and holy.

Minutes later, as the choir was singing "Joy To The World," DJ studied the surrounding crowd of people, all standing in the freezing cold, celebrating together, leaning against one another. Back to the left, Rocco, no longer wearing his black leather jacket, but instead a navy wool coat, stood with his arm draped over Ann's shoulders while they sang together. He had never seen Rocco sing before, not even in kindergarten when they all learned their first song, "The More We Get Together." Behind them, Monty and Lila were radiant, smiles on their faces. Lila had covered her hair with a red scarf and her arm entwined with Monty's. Next to Monty stood Wendell, a toothpick between his teeth, a somber look across his face. Dale, wearing a gray Sherlock Holmes hat purchased mail order from a Bond Street haberdasher years before, rested his hand on Wendell's shoulder. Back by the trees, Leslie and Bobby stared straight ahead, hands shoved in their pockets, and next to them, Maynard kissed Frannie on the cheek, then ran his hand along her back while she pretended not to notice.

All at once DJ couldn't stop examining the crowd. He

needed to memorize the scene at that exact moment because somehow he knew his life was about to change forever. He realized he was viewing a snapshot that would never be his again, a moment that could someday, perhaps be repeated, but never, ever duplicated. Monty had always told him that nothing changes, but now he wasn't sure.

DJ could feel the panic rising as he understood that even the initials he had carved at the top of the old maple tree in front of his house would someday gnarl together and be unrecognizable, and that the tree would eventually be destroyed. The joy-to-the-world moment that he was grasping at, the one that he was intent on capturing and keeping forever, would finally begin to fade too, eventually slipping through the bars of the cage that held it, and then one day, the cage itself, rusted, forgotten, would shift slightly and blow away, spinning, unraveling, disintegrating in flight.

And even his babies' babies would die.

Then she was behind him. Her hand touched his briefly, leaving a note. And she was gone.

> *Could we be together tomorrow evening? Parking lot,*
> *Jailhouse Rock, 5:00?*
> *Merry Christmas. I love you.*
> *C.*

And when he lay with Carlyn the following night, her naked skin resting against his, and with the sleet ticking against the window pane, she told him she would be his forever.

CHAPTER 27

"You must wonder about me, dear boy," Greta said, her sherry glass poised in front of her lips.

Greta and DJ sat in the leather armchairs listening to Kirsten Flagstad's "An die Hoffnung."

"September 8, 1954," Greta sighed, turning her eyes to the speakers. "Just a marvelous performance, and such passion."

DJ nodded as if he understood. He had only begun to comprehend the breadth of opera, and although Greta perceived his musical shortcomings and graciously answered any questions, he still was not able to absorb the intricate beauty that she described. As easily as he understood the clarity and emotion of his music, the magic of Wagner circled around him, tantalizingly out of reach.

"Are you enjoying the sherry?" Greta asked. "I really shouldn't allow it, you know, but it is a lovely experience."

"I am." DJ answered as he ran his finger along the edges of the stem. He wasn't wild about the taste, but he loved the idea of it. And more than that, he liked being with Greta, cocooned in a retrospective comfort zone of music and gentility.

"You know," Greta said as she stared down at her shoes,

"there is really more of me than meets the eye."

DJ looked across at her. "I don't understand."

She nodded at the framed photograph on the side table. "Have you read the inscription?"

"No."

"Please." She nodded toward the table.

DJ stood and walked over and lifted the picture. In the corner, written in script so faded as to be barely legible, were the words:

For Greta.
My love, Rupert

DJ stared at the photograph of a handsome, sandy-haired young man in a tweed jacket. His tie was loosened from his neck and the studio lighting shadowed parts of his face making it difficult to tell his age. The image could have been a teacher in high school, or someone born a hundred years before.

"Who is he?" DJ asked, examining the photograph more closely.

Greta looked across the room at him while she reached for her box of Players. Placing a cigarette in the holder, she lit the end, then shook the match, extinguishing it.

DJ placed the picture back on the table and sat down.

"He was everything to me, you know."

"Who was he?" DJ asked.

"I don't mean to flatter myself that you might ever wonder about me, dear boy, but you do know so little. A woman of my age sitting in her brother's restaurant all day, working intermittently and at her pleasure, living alone at night— wouldn't you think pieces of the puzzle might be missing?"

DJ wasn't sure how to respond.

"There was more, you know," Greta continued, as she sipped her sherry. "Not a great deal, but there was more."

"More of what, Greta?" DJ asked.

"More of me, dear boy." She stared at DJ. "Though I must confess it's difficult to recall being near your age. But seeing you here in all your magnificent youth, I realize I was only several years older when my life was complete." Her mouth sagged slightly as she studied the photograph from a distance. "That's Rupert at the time when I was truly alive. And of course, now that moment is long gone." She touched a corner of her eye. "I blinked once and it was gone." As Greta sat and studied the photograph on the side table, the lamplight melted her features, rendering her unrecognizable. "I'm so sorry to bore you," she said suddenly.

"You're not boring me. Please tell me."

Greta looked at DJ, sighed, and reached into her memory. She spoke from a faraway place. "I heard the screen door slam on that summer morning, then listened to his footsteps moving down to the street as he left for the train station. It was so early I could hear the echo of his heels as he walked away. I couldn't move, nor could I even change from my bedclothes. Then I slept until I could sleep no longer. I awoke, and through the panes of glass, I saw the shadows of the day crossing the clusters of autumn hydrangeas, and from the fields behind the building, I heard children laughing. And I still had not left our bed. I think now that it must have been the children's voices that finally forced me to move because very slowly I managed to concentrate on pushing first one foot, then the next, to the floor. And I moved ever so slowly to the lavatory where I stared into the mirror, then looked away before staring again."

Greta placed the two fingers holding the cigarette holder to the side of her face and twisted a lock of hair with her forefinger. As she spoke, smoke curled in a funnel to the ceiling. "I found a shirt he had left behind and for the first time tears came to my eyes." She paused in midstream to think, to reflect. "Then I cradled the shirt as if it were a baby, our baby, and moved back to the bed he had shared just hours before."

Her fingers remained on her cheek; the cigarette ash

grew longer. "So I curled up under the sheets, cradling our child, and with his scent surrounding me, I forced myself to sleep. And as my eyes closed, I gradually sank into that great gray field below the surface—that void that waits for us all—until slowly the pressure surrounded me, compressed me, destroyed me, and I was lost, dear boy." Greta turned to DJ. "I was lost."

DJ stared back at her. He was lost too. At last, he simply nodded.

Greta crushed out the cigarette, then delicately picked the stub from the holder. "He had gone to war. It was 1939, and, as simple as that, he was gone. And eventually what I feared the very most came to pass. I would never have believed that when he left me that morning, it was the last goodbye, the last moment I would ever touch him again, or hear his voice. Had I known that to be true, I would never have been able to leave my bed at all." She touched the match's flame to the tip of a new cigarette. "But, indeed, it was true, and thankfully, God was merciful, shielding me in ignorance, allowing me to carry on for months until I was notified of Rupert's death. Before then, I had naively dared to hope."

Greta's words were massaging the current year away, transporting DJ through decades in an intoxicating time capsule she had created. He could hear the screen door swing shut and Rupert's footsteps disappearing into the distance. He could see the dying hydrangea globes resting against lime leaves, and could feel the brisk fall morning as the early sun poured into the uncovered spaces.

He remained silent.

"Rupert was not even buried at home as he should have been," Greta continued. "Instead, the government made a singular decision to lay him to rest on Skyros. His grave was very beautiful—many pale blue anemones, orchids and rock hyacinths."

"Skyros?"

"A distant island, dear boy. An island so remote that I have never traveled to it. She hesitated, then pointed. "The Fourth of July fireworks canvas hanging over the side table, the one that you have admired in the past, is a product of Monsieur Ozenfont. I bought that in Rupert's memory many years ago, a tribute to how we lived and how he died. That for me is far better than any picture of a sterile cross weathering in an olive grove." Greta considered her statement. "Or perhaps I bought it because we should all die on the Fourth of July. Perhaps that's it after all. I don't know. But I look at the painting and wonder why I was not taken too, why Rupert departed as a near-child, and I, an old lady, sit here remembering and wandering through the past." She slowly shook her head. "And then after years of listening to the clock on the mantle tick, waiting only for the afternoon paper, or the evening news, I ask which of the two of us is the lucky one."

Greta rested her head back against the chair and closed her eyes for a brief moment before leaning forward again. In a hoarse whisper, she said, "I'm sorry for having imposed upon you this evening, DJ. It was all long ago and has no relevance to your life."

"I didn't know."

"Only Herman and Patty know," Greta replied. She crushed out her cigarette.

"Patty knows about Rupert?"

"Patty and I have grown very close."

DJ knew that to be true, but was surprised his sister had never mentioned anything to him.

Greta slowly straightened in the chair and glanced over at DJ. Softly, after some deliberation, she said, "I have watched you, and of course, you must realize you are not responsible for Patty." She paused. "Or Ike."

DJ was taken aback by her statement. He had been thinking about Rupert, and had to refocus. "What do you mean? Patty and Ike have no one to look out for them."

"And who looks out for DJ?"

Caught off guard again, DJ stared down at his hands, then

thought of his mother, the essence of whom he couldn't quite grasp, which created an emptiness he couldn't quite shovel fast enough to fill. And his father—his father sitting at the kitchen table staring blankly out the window. "Some people do," he finally said.

"Patty and Ike must learn to—"

"They can't, they can't, Greta," DJ interrupted. "Look at them. My sister has no mother and Ike can hardly walk, and nobody listens to him anyway."

"Did you make that happen?" she asked.

"No. You know that."

"Then why are you responsible for them?" She stared at him, a challenge issued.

"Because if I'm not, nobody will be. Just look at them. Look at my father. Look at Ike's father. Patty and Ike need me to watch out for them. And I'm strong. I can."

"Did either of them ask for you to assume the responsibility?"

"They didn't have to ask. I know."

"Your compassion is inspiring, dear boy, but caretaking can be an overwhelming responsibility and is not always appreciated."

"It's appreciated."

"And when all is fully realized," Greta continued, "everyone involved is usually done a disservice. Being so accommodating is stressful, and one way or another, the helping hand always manages to cast a shadow, blocking out the light, stunting growth if it's not withdrawn."

Greta reached across and patted DJ's arm. "I've seen your need to protect Ike and Patty, even at the coffee shop. I've heard your words. I've watched your behavior." She hesitated. "But don't you think your personal world resting on your shoulders is quite enough for any one person?"

A part of DJ wanted to believe her, but didn't know how. In his mind, Patty and Ike had been his responsibility forever. They depended on him. They needed him. It had always been that way. He couldn't change it. He could never change it.

∞

Later, when he walked home from Greta's, the sky was clear, and the stars were spiky and burned near, as if hanging on threads held from the fingertips of Van Gogh.

CHAPTER 28

DJ spent his Christmas vacation days at Mertz Brothers and his evenings with Carlyn. They visited little-known restaurants she had discovered or just wandered around in the Mustang, traveling through winterized seaside hamlets and unmapped back roads. She knew of a house twenty miles away that was decorated with ten thousand Christmas lights, so they drove to view it. Carlyn parked across the street and they listened to the blaring Christmas carols funneled through all-weather speakers planted in the front lawn.

New Year's Eve day, they were both free, Carlyn because she had worked five straight iron days, and DJ because the store didn't need him. The two were meandering around in the Mustang during the afternoon when it occurred to DJ that no one was at his house. Patty was working until five o'clock and his father was glad-handing at the Town Board's annual holiday party in the Municipal Building, which lasted until seven or eight o'clock, or until Dale was ready to pass out.

"We could go over to my house. I could show it to you," DJ suggested while they were stopped at a red light.

Carlyn looked over at him, amused. "For some odd reason,

I don't think that's such a good idea."

"Nobody's home this afternoon." He looked at his watch. "It's only two o'clock. The house will be empty at least until five o'clock."

"And what would we do in your house?" Carlyn asked, a smile tracing the corners of her lips.

Captain Steve McQueen, not Captain Mr. Clean, would rule the orange-sailed ship, that's what they would do. A naked, muscular Steve McQueen in command of his twin bed, would lie next to a naked, adoring damsel, creating a sexual encounter that traveled far beyond most of the erotic fantasies he'd ever conceived of—not counting last year's Miss April. "Nothing much," DJ answered as he looked out the window.

"It would be okay with me," Carlyn said, "but where can I hide the car?"

"In the garage," DJ responded too quickly. "My father's not home. I'll get out and open the door, then you just drive in."

∞

By the time Carlyn was out of the Mustang and leaving the garage, DJ had the doors closed and the house key in his hand.

Once inside, he took a deep breath to calm his nerves.

"Smells like a brewery in here," Carlyn said, taking off her coat.

DJ noticed three empty beer bottles on the kitchen table in place of the Scotch bottle—the end of his father's Christmas spirit. "Yeah, surprise." He reached for her coat and hung it in the closet. "Do you want to look around?"

"No, I've got the idea," she said. "Just show me where you live."

DJ was still nervous. "Up the stair—"

The telephone abruptly rang, jarring the silence, causing them both to jump.

"It's hard to believe I'm acting like a scared teenager," Carlyn said, giggling like one.

"I know," DJ said, trembling as he picked up the receiver. "Hello." He paused. "Hello." Shrugging his shoulders, he hung up the receiver.

"Who was it?" Carlyn asked, leaning against the stairwell wall, arms crossed.

DJ shook his head. "Nobody." He shrugged. "Nobody was on the line."

"That's odd," Carlyn said.

The phone rang again. DJ grabbed the receiver off the hook. "Hello." He hesitated. "No, that's the wrong number. No, sorry, you have the wrong number." Hanging up the phone, he smiled at Carlyn. "You heard it, wrong number."

"Man or woman's voice?" she asked.

"Man's. Didn't recognize it."

Carlyn nodded.

"Just a wrong number—nothing to worry about," DJ said, as he led her up the stairs.

Once in his bedroom, she seemed more excited than he was. Tugging at their clothes until they were both naked under the covers of his twin bed, Carlyn rolled on top. "This is like being a teenager all over again," she whispered as her knee rubbed the inside of his thigh. "All over again."

DJ let Carlyn dictate the tempo, and afterward, as she shared his pillow, her shoulder resting against him, she reached across to the bedside table and picked up his high school senior picture proofs, flicking through them one at a time, studying each. "Have you decided yet?" she asked after examining all of them.

"Not really, I don't like them," he said. "I look bad. I've got dark half-circles under my eyes."

"Not in these pictures." Carlyn turned her head so she could look at him. "Not in real life either."

"Well, sort of, I do," DJ said, secretly pleased she didn't think so.

"How about this one?" she asked, picking out a different pose than DJ would have selected.

"For the yearbook?"

"No, I could care less about the yearbook. For me."

"I think we have to hand them all in when we choose the one we want." DJ said.

"And with mountains of photographs they get back, they're going to miss one little picture of DJ Elders?" She reached over and squeezed his cheek. "I don't think so, sweetie. I'm in retail, and I just don't think so."

DJ nodded though he wasn't sure she was right.

"Forget the proof, just get me a great big eight-by-ten of your smiling face so I can put it on my bureau. How about that?"

DJ nodded again. He was happy she had asked. "I could do that," he said.

Later, Carlyn suggested they take a shower together which immediately rocketed his erotic fantasy level into a new orbit, leaving even Miss April pale and earthbound.

∞

She smoothed the soap across his chest, then slid it around his stomach and down along his legs. He watched the water drip across her flattened hair, roll off the end of her nose and across her lips, then spin from her chin and disappear between her breasts. Carlyn's skin was white and translucent, the edges of her cheeks barely pink, and DJ thought she had never been more beautiful.

She moved one hand gently upward from DJ's thigh and halted. "Just wanted to see if you were ready." She smiled, while she leaned backward against the tile wall and watched his eyes. "You are ready, aren't you DJ Elders, my little lover boy. You are ready, aren't you?" She laughed softly and pulled him inward. As the shower's spray crashed on his back, DJ could feel the roller coaster climbing the track faster than he could ever recall, faster than he could comprehend, and just as he reached the top and stared out from the dizzying heights, ready to plunge down the first hill, Carlyn pulled away from him. "Not yet, not yet," she giggled. Then suddenly, "Now, DJ, now!"

Several seconds passed before he realized that the water splashing across his back was lukewarm and Carlyn was still tugging at his hair. "Whoa," she whispered, her eyes slowly focusing. "I wonder if that's what Olympic swimmers do in their spare time."

"I better adjust this water," DJ answered, slowly reaching back to the faucet.

"Whoa," Carlyn repeated, as she gradually disentangled herself from him. "Where did you learn how to do that, sailor?"

He hadn't thought he'd done anything. As a matter of fact, it felt like she'd done it all. And though sailor wasn't as good as captain, DJ was pleased with her assessment. "Natural, I guess."

"I guess." She let out a long, slow breath, leaned back against the wall and looked around, "Whoa," she repeated for the third time before sliding down the tile so that the edge of her back was resting on the lip of the tub.

Carlyn looked around and said, "Well, you know, as long as I'm starting to recover, and as long as I'm here, maybe I should get clean, if that's even possible."

DJ handed her the bar of Ivory. "It's possible." He stepped from the shower and picked up a towel.

Moments later, Carlyn rinsed the soap from her body, turned off the water, stepped out and crossed to the mirror over the sink. Using her forefinger to write in the steam on the glass, she printed "Carlyn loves DJ," accenting the inscription with an exclamation mark. Turning to him, she smiled. "What do you think?"

Her name printed on the mirror triggered his memory again: *Carlyn Reynolds is a whore.* And Monty's assertion on their trip to Vermont that Carlyn Canova might be Carlyn Reynolds from years ago—the person whose husband had disappeared—flashed through his mind. "Are you Carlyn Reynolds?" DJ blurted out.

"Was," she answered casually. "Why?"

As he rested his elbow against the wall, DJ was immediately uncomfortable. "Uh . . . no real reason. Monty thought he recognized you from West Hardscrabble a long time ago. That's all."

"Well, if it was West Hardscrabble, it must've been me. I lived there with my mother before she died. I don't know of any other Carlyn Reynolds that was around then."

DJ hesitated. He knew it wasn't smart to ask, that based on previous attempts, the subject was already strained, but he forged ahead anyway. "How's your husband doing?"

Carlyn turned away from him. "Kind of an odd time to ask about my husband, don't you think? I can barely walk, and you ask about my husband."

"It's always an odd time to ask about him. You never want to talk about him."

"Let me tell you something, DJ," Carlyn said, turning in front of him, running a finger across his chest. "I don't love my husband. I thought I did, but I was wrong. I love you, and you really shouldn't forget that. I don't like it when you forget." She quickly kissed him. "And now if you'll excuse me, I'm getting cold standing here." She wrapped a towel around her shoulders, turned, and wiped the message from the mirror using the palm of her hand.

Nothing with Carlyn ever seemed to quite fit. Yet on the surface, everything he observed appeared complete and in place. "Is your husband in Vietnam your first or second husband?"

Carlyn whirled around. "DJ, stop. There is no reason to carry on this kind of ridiculous conversation."

"I'm just curious."

"Well, there's nothing to be curious about. Enough is

enough." She dropped the towel, then stretched her arms out. "What you see is what you get." She lowered her eyes. "Take it or leave it."

In spite of himself, DJ had to smile. No matter what she said, he realized he never wanted to be without her. He knew it. He sensed she knew it. "I love you," he suddenly whispered.

"Well, you read the writing on the mirror," Carlyn answered.

That evening in New York City, while Guy Lombardo and his Royal Canadians rang in 1965, the two sat on the couch in her house watching TV and holding hands. After midnight, Carlyn opened a bottle of champagne, then dragged out some old record albums. While Sonny Til and The Orioles warbled in the background, they danced slowly in the kitchen, each with a half-empty champagne glass resting against the other's back, early morning silhouettes welcoming the New Year.

MAY, 1965

CHAPTER 29

DJ couldn't believe it! Frannie being pregnant was bad news, actually terrifying news. The whole concept of being tied down with a wife and a child seemed much worse than his own recurring nightmare of graduating from high school and working on a factory assembly line.

At least Carlyn had taken care of birth control. It had been one of their earliest conversations.

But how stupid could Maynard get?

And now that his friend's path was so clearly defined, DJ began to wonder what his future with Carlyn would be. Their relationship seemed to be changing and he didn't know why. They had been inseparable since before Christmas, yet over the past month she had not been quite as accessible—a Saturday night they missed, a weekend when she had to visit her sister again, a couple of times he thought she should be home when he called, but there was no answer. Not enough to add up to anything, but enough to cause concern. And any change of pattern in his life made him nervous, but when it involved Carlyn, the anxiety intensified. She was in his blood, pumping through his heart, minute by minute, hour by hour—with his desire for her relentless. Once, early in the relationship, he thought he was strong enough to consider breaking up and starting with someone from his class—after all, he was seventeen and Carlyn was almost thirty—but he quickly realized that the idea of being without her was unthinkable. And with that recognition his obsession escalated. The need for her seethed through his veins, with relief arriving only after they had gyrated on her bed and he was convinced she still loved him.

In the meantime, Carlyn appeared to recognize his compulsion for her and wore it like a badge of honor while she laughed away any concern about her husband returning, or her feelings changing.

Except once. Driving along the south shore on a Sunday afternoon, DJ was feeling particularly unsure of himself and brought up the subject of her husband in Vietnam again, and how, according to Monty and Wendell, there was another husband years before. His unexpected statement surprised her and she didn't respond. Then later, breaking the silence between the two of them, she said, "DJ, don't be weak. Don't whimper around me."

"I'm not whimpering," he replied quietly. "I just asked a question."

In the past, Carlyn would have pulled him against her breast to reassure him. Instead she turned on the radio and stared ahead, refusing to discuss her husband in Southeast Asia and never denying the existence of a first husband, a man Monty claimed had mysteriously disappeared, never to be seen or heard from again.

CHAPTER 30

The Mustang crunched into the parking lot and moved slowly across the gravel. "Hi, baby," Carlyn said to DJ through the open window. "Let's go, we've only got half the night to get to and from the city."

"Seriously? New York City? On a Sunday night?" That made him nervous. Manhattan seemed almost as distant as Vietnam.

Carlyn looked over, a quick smile crossing her face. "Hop in. Don't worry. I'll get you home in time to be all rested up for those nasty teachers tomorrow. You're a big boy now. You're playing in the big leagues."

"Okay," he said and stepped inside the Mustang. Big leagues or not, DJ stayed nervous because Carlyn drove the entire distance to the city using the left-hand lane of the expressway as her personal roadway. At eighty-five miles per hour, she tailgated any vehicle in front of her, usually causing it to pull over to the center lane, allowing her to pass.

When they entered the tunnel under the East River, she reached across and rested her hand on DJ's thigh. "Scared?"

DJ placed his hand on top of hers. "No, are you kidding?" he answered. "Where are we going?"

"Nowhere really," Carlyn replied, "I just felt like getting away from the sticks and spending some time in the city." Once through the tunnel, she turned left on 45th Street and headed across town. At Seventh Avenue she drove the car into a small parking lot. "Come on," she said, handing the keys to the attendant, "I could use a drink."

Following her across Seventh Avenue, DJ hurried as streams of taxis bore down on them. "Don't worry," Carlyn said, "they always slow down to take a look."

DJ followed her into a corner Irish tavern that was noisy, crowded, and had a thick coating of sawdust on the floor. Carlyn pushed her way between two men leaning on the bar.

"Excuse me, Miss," a bar-tanned tree trunk in a denim jacket said, "How about a seat?" He stood and slid the stool to Carlyn, then took his drink and moved to the right, allowing enough space for DJ to stand next to her.

"This place is really packed," DJ said, looking around. "Do people always do this on a Sunday night?"

"Every place isn't like Hardscrabble," Carlyn answered.

A surly-looking bartender wearing a floor-length apron and a black bow tie over a frayed white collar stood in front of them. "What'll it be?"

"Scotch and water for me, and what about you, DJ?"

"A beer."

"You got proof?" Surly asked.

"He's going to start basic training for Vietnam in three days, I hardly think he needs proof. You ought to be able to sell a beer to a soldier putting his life on the line for his country."

Carlyn's sudden intensity startled the bartender.

"That right?" he asked DJ.

DJ nodded. "That's about it."

"What branch?" Surly asked.

"Now what do we have, a military interrogation?" Carlyn asked, her fingers drumming against the bar.

"Just curious, lady, calm down. A lot of the fellas who are regulars in here been in the service, that's all."

"Marines," DJ said. "The best." He'd heard Monty call the Marines the best all his life.

Surly studied DJ a moment, taking a bullshit pulse, then said, "Bless you, son, I'm an old leatherneck myself." He reached out to shake DJ's hand. "You going to make me proud over there, you can have all the beer you want tonight." He scratched the back of his head. "I was about your age when I joined up myself. Best experience of my life. And you're right, son, they only take the best." He pointed down the bar. "Couple of the boys down there are ex-Marines themselves. They'll be mighty happy we got a new recruit that's got his priorities in life straight. And with a beautiful lady to boot." Surly smiled for a brief second. "Finest days of my life. That much I do know."

DJ placed a ten-dollar bill on the bar. "I wonder if we can drink this up tonight," he said.

"Could be tough if I'm buying for the Marine Corps," Surly answered.

After his second beer, DJ was more relaxed. Surly had told the two ex-Marines about the new recruit and they had looked his way, nodded and raised their glasses in a toast.

Maybe I should join the Marines instead of going to college. I never had this much attention anywhere, DJ thought. He took off his coat and hung it over the back of the stool Carlyn was resting on. He took a deep swallow of his next beer, rolled up his sleeves and when Carlyn wasn't looking, quickly flexed his biceps. He was beginning to feel more like a Marine every minute. Maybe he'd get an eagle tattoo on his arm. Or a snake wrapped around a bleeding heart with Carlyn inscribed in the center. When he flexed again, he saw Carlyn watching him in the mirror hanging behind the bar. Instantly embarrassed, he pretended the flex was just the beginning of a motion to scratch his face. He let his hand continue to his jaw, where he scratched, then for emphasis scratched some more.

"Itchy in here tonight, isn't it?" she said, continuing to watch him in the mirror. After a minute, she leaned toward

DJ, put her arm around his neck and kissed him. "It's nice to be able to do this in public, where nobody cares, where nobody's going to talk."

Normally DJ would have been uncomfortable with such a blatant demonstration of affection, but surprisingly, he discovered he was aroused. The overt sexuality of Carlyn's skirt at mid-thigh, the public place, the fact that all the other men found her to be desirable, combined with the beer, hacked away at his inhibitions. Ordering another round from Surly, he rested his hand on Carlyn's thigh. She held it there, against her bare skin, her hand on top of his, then moved it slowly up and down.

An hour later, as they slipped into their coats, then walked across the sawdust to the door, Surly called, "Hey!"

DJ stopped and looked back as the bartender pulled himself to attention, his belly hanging over his white apron. Gravely, ceremoniously, he offered a solemn salute.

Bringing himself to attention, DJ returned the salute as best he knew how. It was good enough because it brought a smile to Surly's face. "Attaboy!" he called.

The two darted across Seventh Avenue and got into the Mustang. With her foot heavy on the accelerator, Carlyn powered through the maze. "Let's go home a different way," she said, making a screeching right-hand turn.

"Fine," DJ said. He was busy figuring out whether he was going to be sick from the two shots of whiskey Surly had bought him.

Within minutes, after passing through a tunnel, they were on a parkway running next to the water.

"Where are we?" DJ asked.

"Belt Parkway," Carlyn said. "Aren't the lights on the water beautiful?"

"Where's the Belt Parkway?"

"Brooklyn, good old Brooklyn," she said.

"Are we on the way back to Hardscrabble?" DJ asked as he stared blankly out the window.

"With a little detour," Carlyn said, slowing down and swinging the Mustang into a rest area by the water. She turned off the lights and killed the motor, leaving them in dark silence except for the hum of the cars passing behind them on the parkway. The water in front of the car was black, but sprinkled with the reflections of parkway lights. To their left and right, only empty space.

"Why are we stopping?" DJ asked.

Carlyn looked over at him. "Because I want to. Because it's time."

"Time for what?"

"What do you think, baby?"

"I don't know."

"Yes, you do. You know what time it is." She reached across and ran her hand across his thigh.

"You don't mean here?" DJ stared at her. "We can't do anything here, Carlyn, that would be crazy, plus it's cold."

"The crazier it is, the more I like it." She crawled over the console.

DJ could feel her breath, sweet with liquor, against his neck as she unzipped his jeans, lifted her skirt and slowly moved on top of him. The windows were already fogged.

"Oh, God, I love this," Carlyn breathed in his ear.

DJ paused. He thought he heard a tapping on the car. "What was that?" he asked. "What the heck was that?"

"What was what?" Carlyn asked, paying no attention. "Don't worry, baby. Just relax."

"I heard something."

The tapping occurred again, louder, and this time Carlyn caught it. "What is that?" She was losing her concentration. "Who's out there?" she called, her body suddenly frozen on top of DJ.

This time the rapping was against the windshield. Louder still.

"Who's out there?" she called again.

"Open the door," a harsh male voice called.

"Quick, lock the doors," Carlyn whispered while she reached across to the driver's side and pressed down the button. At the same time DJ managed to twist around and lock the passenger's door.

Carlyn pushed herself away from DJ.

"Who's in there?" the voice repeated. "Open up."

"Who are you?" DJ asked, buying time, fumbling with his pants.

"I'm the damned police, and if you don't identify yourself, I'll call for backup."

Carlyn pushed into the driver's seat, her bare feet scraping the radio knobs, then reached the window and rolled it down. "What can I do for you, officer?"

The flashlight's beam focused first on Carlyn, then on DJ. "You kids screwing, or killing each other in there?" the voice asked. His flashlight raked across them both again. "By the looks of things it was more screwing then killing."

"Are we breaking the law, officer?" Carlyn asked, her voice pure silk. DJ had heard the tone before. It was one of the voices she used whenever he asked about her husband.

"If you're screwing in a public place, you're breaking the law, surer than shit." he answered. "Let's have a look at your license and registration."

Carlyn reached across and opened the glove compartment, took out an envelope with the registration, then removed her license from her wallet and handed both to the policeman.

Reading the registration and the license, he wrote some information on a notepad, then handed them back to Carlyn. "I'm going to have to write you up for illegal parking anyway," he said. "No one allowed here after nine o'clock at night." He paused, and in a quieter tone said, "Course, if one day I was able to be as lucky as that youngster next to you was tonight, there would be no reason for any kind of summons."

Carlyn eyed the policeman. "And what is that supposed to mean?"

It suddenly occurred to DJ that he was about to be sick.

"Well, it's not too hard to figure out now, is it?" the officer asked, bending down and leaning in the window, a lazy smile on his face. His nose was dead-on WC Fields. He sniffed. "You know, you might even have more of a problem than I guessed earlier. Smells like a gin mill in here." He took his summons pad from his back pocket. "Let's see, illegal parking, indecent exposure, drunk driving. You've got enough points here, little lady, to keep you off the road for a while."

"I'm not driving," Carlyn said, "so you can forget about writing me up for that."

DJ lurched from the car and vomited, but still heard most of the conversation behind him.

"Looks like whatever got to him was more than he could handle. Probably wasn't man enough to take care of things in the right way, so everyone is satisfied."

"What are you suggesting?"

"Just so you know, getting back to the drunk driving, as long as the keys are in the ignition, it means the same thing whether the motor's on or not. It's the law. Read it. You might learn something. Give you something to do instead of taking advantage of young boys." He paused. "You could have a bunch of tickets, not be able to drive for six months, or a year, or we could get together one of these nights and work something out. We can just start out with your phone number if you like. You decide."

Carlyn stared at the officer and smiled slowly. "Why not, you've already written down my address."

∞

As DJ stepped back into the car, he saw the cop give Carlyn a tepid salute, then walk back to his cruiser. He switched on his headlights, pulled out of the rest area and back on to the Belt Parkway, quickly merging into the traffic flow. DJ rested his head against the window.

"You all right, baby?" Carlyn asked.

He wasn't. Every time he closed his eyes, he was spinning out of control. "Yeah, I'm okay," he answered.

"Time to get us home," Carlyn said, starting the Mustang and accelerating out of the rest area.

"How many tickets did he give you?" DJ asked.

"None," Carlyn said. "He let me off with a warning."

DJ clutched the tops of his knees, attempting to control the dizziness. "I only heard part of what he said, but it sounded like he wanted to be with you."

"Those types are all alike," Carlyn answered. "They think they know it all, that they have enough power to make you do what's good for them." She laughed softly. "I wish I could frame the look on their faces when they discover at the last minute they're wrong." She chuckled again. "They just never figure it out until it's too late."

CHAPTER 31

It took DJ nearly a week to recover from his Sunday night in New York City. As he approached the Mertz Brothers' cafeteria during his lunch hour, the thought of all that alcohol still made his stomach lurch.

The employees' cafeteria wasn't much more than jumbled tables, cardboard sandwiches, and a bulletin board, but at least there were no vending machines. DJ picked up a tuna fish on white bread, a bag of potato chips and a Coke, then paid Josie, the cashier in the turquoise uniform, hairnet, and stockings rolled down below her knees—an unpleasant sight on the best of days. He walked over and sat at a corner table by himself. He hadn't seen Carlyn all morning and was back in Basement Shoes—both scenarios irritating.

Five minutes later, Bobby Litchfield appeared. "Mind if I join you?" he asked, placing the tray on the table opposite DJ.

"Suit yourself." Bobby hadn't said more than five sentences to him since they had been working together at Mertz Brothers.

"Food stinks here," he said, sitting down. "Hey, but what do you expect in a place like this?"

"I guess," DJ said. "I thought you weren't going to be here in the spring. Aren't you on the baseball team?"

"Was," Bobby said. "No more. The old man said making money is more important now. I need it for college. What a pain." He lifted his sandwich off the tray. "At least he didn't make me quit football last fall. That's where all the glory is anyway."

"That was a break," DJ said sarcastically.

"Yeah, it was." Bobby missed DJ's tone. "Hear you're going to community college next year." He took a bite out of his sandwich.

"Yep, I figured I wanted to stick around the area." DJ opened the bag of potato chips and poured them onto the paper plate. "Where you going to school?" He knew. Everyone in the high school knew, but he didn't want to give Bobby the satisfaction of thinking he was impressed.

"I thought I was going to get into Princeton, but I'm not. Shocked me. I thought my old man was going to croak. You know he's an alum."

"So where are you going?"

"Yale," Bobby said. "First Yalie from Hardscrabble High School."

"You couldn't get into Princeton, but you got into Yale?"

"Weird, huh?" Bobby said. "But I'm not asking questions. Figure I'll go to law school, make decent money within five years, then get out of this half-assed town."

"Well, good luck," DJ said. He crumpled his napkin into the potato chip bag.

"Let me ask you something," Bobby said, lowering his voice. "You got a minute?"

DJ glanced at his watch. "I guess so. Why?"

Bobby looked around, over his shoulder, then said, "Ah, I don't mean to pry or anything, but when you were going with Leslie, ah, did you find anything a little strange about her?"

DJ had a good inclination where Bobby might be heading, but he didn't let on. "What do you mean?"

Bobby looked at DJ and hesitated a second. "I mean, did you have any problems with Leslie?"

"What kind of problems?"

"Problems. You know, like when she gets, ah, you know, physical." Bobby looked around the room again.

"Physical?" DJ took an ice cube and chewed it. "What do you mean?"

"I mean did she ever like try and take a swing at you?"

"A swing? Why would she do that?"

"That's exactly what I can't figure out. I don't know why, but most of the time when we get you know, romantic, she ends up hitting me, or clawing me, or kicking me—whatever is easiest."

"Did you hit her first?" DJ asked.

"Oh, come on," Bobby answered. "I'm just doing normal things, what any guy would do, and boom, out of left field, she pulls some stunt. Look." He slid his collar down his neck, displaying scratch marks. "That's from last night." As he brushed crumbs off his hands, he looked directly at DJ. "I don't get it."

"Why don't you break up with—"

"You know what she said?" Bobby interrupted, a note of caution appearing in his voice. "She said if I ever broke up with her, I'd regret it." He laughed a little too loudly. "Can you believe that? If I broke up with her she was implying she would do something to me." He shook his head. "Crazy, no?"

"Leslie told me that too, only she was a little more specific. She said she was going to kill me," DJ said.

"That's right, me too!" Bobby blurted out. "You do know what I'm talking about."

DJ nodded. "And look, here I am."

"Yeah, look, we're both here. That's a relief." He leaned back in his chair, a smile on his face. "A big relief. She did all that stuff to you?"

DJ nodded. "It sounds the same. I got to the point where I couldn't stand it anymore and broke up with her."

"And she said she was going to kill you?"

"More than once," DJ confided. "I was happy the two of you became a couple. Took her mind off of me."

Bobby laughed, this time more openly. "I'll bet you were happy." He leaned in, his face closer to DJ's. "But you know, I'm going to hang in there a little longer. She has such a great body, and what's really crazy is that sometimes she doesn't mind what I try and do. Even encourages it. Then other times, she goes nuts. And I never know which way she's going to be in advance."

"My Uncle Wendell told me it's worse when you're married."

Bobby leaned back, his hands clasped behind his head. "Trust me, I have no interest in getting married. And you know, so what if I don't get anywhere? I'll be off to New Haven in the fall and I won't have to deal with her again." He slapped DJ on the shoulder and stood. "Well, got to head back to The Ivy League Shop. What say we keep our little discussion to ourselves?"

"Okay," DJ said, still sitting.

"See you. Thanks for the conversation. Wish me luck." He started across the cafeteria to deposit his tray.

∞

Sunday afternoon was humid and lifeless, and though he had been with Carlyn until midnight, and had worked for Herman with only a few hours sleep, DJ was restless.

Like a majority of the seniors, he'd stopped studying—most of the teachers were letting them breeze through class—except for reviewing old Regents examinations in preparation for the upcoming tests. As DJ rocked back in his desk chair, his feet on the side of his bed, he listened to the new Marty Robbins album Greta had given him. After side two, he went downstairs and collected Patty, then picked up

Ike. The trio slowly walked the half mile to the Hardscrabble Rural Cemetery. As they sat on the wood fence surrounding the graveyard, Ike turned his face upward. "It feels like spring is really here after all."

"I guess so," DJ said, his hand resting on a fence post. Then he added, "I can't believe Maynard is really getting married next week."

Ike shook his head. "But knowing Maynard, somehow it's not a surprise."

"I know," DJ answered. "It fits."

Patty studied the two briefly. "It's May. And next year I'll be a senior. I can't believe that."

"Believe it. It happens," DJ answered over his shoulder as he walked into the graveyard leaving the two behind. He could feel the fatigue from the night's lack of sleep creeping into his peripheral vision: black dots dancing off to the side when he glanced a certain way, swirling atoms locked in orbit, always there when he was fighting fatigue.

DJ took small steps. He could smell the winter's thaw and saw tiny buds peeking out from the ground. Near the back gate, two Monarch butterflies skittered back and forth across the marble wings of an angel gazing toward heaven, but tethered to the ground. Real early for butterflies. Must be some weird breed, DJ thought.

As he walked around the inside perimeter of the fence, DJ kicked three or four blue 4X condom capsules into a shrub so that Patty wouldn't come across them. He knew Maynard and some of the Ag School students used the graveyard as a late-night bedroom. Maynard claimed that after dark it was the safest place in town. He mentioned once having sex with Frannie on the ground in front of the McClellan's family monument when she suddenly became panicky, asking if he had felt something beneath him move. "One thing I know for sure," Maynard retorted, "it wasn't you."

DJ glanced back over his shoulder and saw Ike kissing Patty. She was sitting on the top rail of the fence, her hands resting on the wooden bar, leaning toward Ike, whose face was turned upward. DJ quickly looked away, startled.

Moments later, the two joined him, and the three walked single-file through the tombstones. As they passed a grave, each took a turn reading the inscribed name, then tried to guess the appearance of the long since departed. They had played the game together for years, and since the cemetery was small, with no new bodies buried in decades, each name was immediately recognizable.

After walking past a dozen graves, Ike said, "This is depressing, let's forget about it."

In his room that night, it was not the image of the ancient gravestones, or even the surprising picture of Ike kissing Patty that kept DJ awake. Instead, over and over again, he watched the two Monarch butterflies, their liquid gold splashing against the blue sky as they danced as one, darted apart, then resumed their courtship just beyond the reach of the holy angel with the chiseled marble eyes.

CHAPTER 32

As DJ stood next to the Falcon in the nearly-deserted Jailhouse Rock parking lot Wednesday evening, he could still feel a chill in the air though the days were growing longer. He stepped behind the fire escape, a place where he could watch Main Street, but still be hidden.

A twilight return for no reason except that it was the spot where he had first begun with Carlyn—the starting point of their first drive into the night. In the distance, he heard a car downshift as it powered its way out Melville Road toward the Ag School. Then silence—a rare instance of absolute quiet, with no cars, no birds, no noise at all. He could hear his fingers run across the back of his neck, and as he shuffled his feet, the echo reverberated through him, as if he was underwater.

Hardscrabble looked hollow and one-dimensional in the closing dark. Outsiders made fun of the Revolutionary heritage of the town's name, but DJ didn't care. He just didn't want to leave for anywhere else, and he sure wasn't ready to head to Vietnam and step on a punji stick, then have his leg chopped off, a result of some raging infection.

He was going to college, but what if he failed in those

classes, or his father lost his job and couldn't pay for him? He'd be headed to Vietnam on a boat with everyone sleeping in hammocks next to each other. He'd seen that picture in *Life* magazine—and knew it was true. Or, worse yet, what if he ran into Carlyn's husband in Vietnam and he knew what DJ had been doing with his wife. DJ could visualize himself stabbed in both eyes with a steel bayonet, then stomped into the rice patties and left for the water buffalo to feed on.

Just as he had felt Christmas Eve, the night of the Living Nativity, he couldn't bear the thought of change, of not seeing Ike, or Patty. He didn't want to grow older. Instead, he needed to be with Leslie, holding hands in the balcony—that stretch of time when her anger was manageable. He wanted high school to remain a vast ocean waiting to be crossed, just as it had appeared when he was a freshman. And he needed Maynard to keep his pants on forever so he wouldn't have to worry about him too.

Dusk: a surreal line between light and dark, awake and asleep; illusory, and not to be trusted.

Carlyn.

He was grasping the side of a hot-air balloon's basket, a balloon that had already risen too quickly for him to jump to safety. And though feeling he was losing his grip, slipping, slowly slipping, he didn't have the strength to pull himself inside or the courage to let go.

Dusk and Carlyn.

∞

While there was still a glint of light left in the air, DJ stepped back into the Falcon to pick up Ike, then drove by for Maynard. As they had done many nights before, the three cruised around Main Street, mostly in second gear with the windows wide open and the sweet night air rushing in on them. In the background, Cousin Brucie's voice boomed through the dashboard radio as he played the Top 40.

From the corner of his eye, DJ watched Maynard sitting next to him, checking for any girls walking down the street. His glasses slid down the oily bridge of his nose and his hair sported the classic Dennis the Menace cowlick. Way too young for his upcoming wedding, DJ thought. Way too young.

In the rearview mirror, DJ could see Ike as he looked tentatively around—a fawn at a creek bed—before he coughed softly, his hand covering his mouth.

The three circled the downtown blocks several times, then drove north on Main Street and out of town. After prowling through the quiet neighborhood streets, DJ headed to Route 110, past the Jesus Saves church.

For as long as he could remember, every Halloween a couple of the high school boys hung an S&H Green Stamps banner below the Jesus Saves sign. The parishioners were kind and good-natured, as they believed their Savior to have been, and the following day, a church member always took the banner down, but left it in the grass next to the sign so the boys could pick it up to use the following year.

As DJ circled back into town, he stopped at a red light.

Maynard suddenly called, "Swim the window! Hey, we've got to swim the window."

"I don't think that's such a good idea," DJ said, "Captain Leo is losing his sense of humor."

"He's been losing it for years," Maynard answered.

"Swim the window," Ike said. "Swim the window."

"Come on, DJ, for old times sake, let's swim the window," Maynard said.

DJ slowly nodded, then drove the Falcon down Main Street and parked opposite Captain Leo's Seafood Restaurant in front of the high school. The three crossed the street. Lined up on one side of the restaurant's twenty-foot window, the boys, pretending to be fish, half-walked, half-swam past the front of the transparent aquamarine glass, immediately attracting the attention of the patrons dining inside. Maynard was a frenzied, four-eyed shark with pointed hands as the fin, DJ a barracuda with a thousand teeth, and Ike, as always, because of his heart condition, brought up the rear as King Neptune, walking slowly, an imaginary spear in his hand.

Maynard abruptly fired across again as a blowfish, his cheeks expanding and contracting as he stared at the unsettled diners watching him through the window.

Captain Leo walked out the front door wearing a blue blazer and his captain's hat. "Very, very funny, boys," he said, "but not funny enough to continue. You and your classmates have been doing this for too many years. Hit the road, or I'll have to call the police."

"Thor is the chief of police and he's tending bar at the Rock," Maynard said, "I don't think the chances are very good he'll close up and come down here."

"Ah, but there are always deputies on duty." Captain Leo smiled.

"Come on," Ike said, turning, "we've had our fun. Let's go." He started moving across the street.

"How did you get out here so fast?" Maynard asked Captain Leo.

"Timing is everything," Captain Leo answered. "You of all people should have learned that by now, Mr. Maynard, Mr. Shark Man Maynard." He winked. "It's a small town and everybody knows everyone else's business."

Maynard turned and walked away with DJ.

Once inside the Falcon, Ike said, "Don't worry about it, we did all right. We got a lap or two across the window. When we were kids doing that, Captain Leo was usually outside before we could get started. He's slowing down."

"He's still fast for an old man," Maynard said. "And, by the way, he's still a moron."

As DJ pulled away from the curb, he thought to himself, true, they had done all right, and yes, Captain Leo, along with everyone else was aging. But he also recognized the echo from deep recesses warning him that the moments they had just spent swimming the window, like the night of the Living Nativity, were gone, never to be seen again. The boys were shadows of themselves, play-acting and attempting to recreate a sense of where they had once traveled: a time when the hydrangea bushes were only knee high, the Dodgers were in Brooklyn, and their fathers still lusted after their mothers.

CHAPTER 33

Sunday morning, DJ placed the *Daily News* on the kitchen table. The newspaper headline announced that a New York City policeman had been killed. Below that, in smaller, less alarming print, a prediction that bus and subway fares would be raised within thirty days, and at the bottom of the page, an agonizing forecast that the New York Mets would continue to go down swinging.

DJ opened the newspaper and stared at the face of the murdered police officer, the *same* face that had peered through the window of the Mustang when Carlyn and he had been parking in the rest area off the Belt Parkway! DJ felt his stomach tighten as he stared at the photograph. It *was* him: the dark hair, the W.C. Fields nose—both were exactly as he remembered. He could hear the brassy voice demanding to know what they were doing in the Mustang. DJ quickly turned to the copy below the picture.

The body of patrolman Edmund Dixon was discovered late Friday night near the Exit 3 service area of the Belt Parkway when a pedestrian walking a dog noticed an arm protruding from beneath weeds and underbrush. Patrolman Dixon's uniform was reportedly in a state of disarray, but both his service revolver and nightstick remained in his possession. Cause of death remains undetermined, with further information to be made available from the New York City Deputy Commissioner's Office following autopsy results.

The rest of the story mentioned that Patrolman Dixon had left a wife and three children, and that twelve detectives were assigned to the case.

DJ studied the photograph. He was sure it was the same policeman

Dusk and Carlyn.

He continued to stare at the picture until the grainy newsprint began to jiggle in front of him and he was no longer certain it was the same individual after all. He took a Coke from the refrigerator, then returned to the paper and scrutinized the photograph again. He was absolutely positive it was the same cop.

His father was asleep, and though it was risky, DJ took the car keys off the kitchen table and with the *Daily News* tucked under his arm, left the house.

∞

As he pulled up to the curb in front of Carlyn's, he was relieved to see the Mustang was in the driveway.

He rang the doorbell and waited. After a few seconds had passed with no answer, he rang the bell again. Still no response. He walked down the steps and around the side of the garage to the back of the house. After letting himself in through a chain-link fence gate, he spotted Carlyn lying on a chaise, sunning herself in a two-piece bathing suit. Dark glasses covered her eyes and he couldn't tell whether they were open or not.

He stopped. "Carlyn."

She remained motionless on the recliner.

DJ took a step closer. "Carlyn."

"What are you doing here, baby?" she asked, moving her head so she was facing his direction. "I didn't know you were coming over."

"I've got to show you something," DJ said, walking over to her.

"Sit, baby," she said, sliding her leg to make space on the chaise. "But give me a kiss first."

DJ looked at the two houses bordering her backyard. "What about the neighbors?"

"Screw the neighbors. I haven't seen you since Thursday. That's too long." Carlyn pushed up on an elbow until her face was close to his. She lifted her glasses so they rested in her hair, leaned forward and touched her lips to his. "There," she said, lying down again, placing her sunglasses back over her eyes. "Now I feel better." She looked at him, the corners of her mouth lifting slightly. "Couldn't wait for tonight, huh?"

When she kissed him, he had smelled the cocoa butter from the suntan oil. He ran his tongue across his top lip, tasting the hint of her perspiration. "Actually—"

"Actually, nothing." Her smile was larger. "I'm game. I'm tired of the sun anyway."

"No, Carlyn, really," DJ stammered. "Here, look." He opened the copy of the newspaper to the third page and held it up so she could see it.

"What?" she asked. "The picture? I saw it this morning. It's a tragedy." She raised herself on her elbow again. "You don't mean to tell me you came over here to show me a photograph of a cop." Her smile broadened. "Pretty lame, Elders. You must think I'm senile if I'm falling for that sorry excuse for dropping by. I may be too old for you, but I'm not that far gone."

"Doesn't he look familiar?" DJ insisted, still holding the picture in her face.

Carlyn paused. "What do you mean, familiar?"

"Look, he's the policeman who stopped us a couple of weeks ago when we were parking in that rest area off the Belt Parkway." He held the picture closer. "See, it's the same guy."

Carlyn lifted her sunglasses and stared at the photograph for a moment, then covered her eyes again. "You aren't serious, are you?"

"Of course I'm serious. That's the guy." He pointed to the picture again. "It's the same guy."

"DJ, trust me, it's not. Now that you mention it, there's a slight resemblance, especially the nose, but for the most part, it's not even close."

DJ put the newspaper on his lap and stared at the photograph again. He squinted. "Are you sure?"

"Let's not forget your condition that night, baby, which I still have some guilt about causing. Come here." She put her hand behind his head and pulled him closer, kissing him again. "You worry too much, and that worries me."

She lay back and droplets of sweat turned into tiny streams running down her sides.

"I still think it's him," DJ said. "It has to be him."

Carlyn didn't respond and turned her face toward the sun.

"Do you remember the policeman's name who stopped us that night?" he asked.

"No, but I wish I did, then we could put an end to this game you're playing."

DJ sat motionless, then reached over and ran his finger across Carlyn's stomach. Before he could reconsider the question, he blurted out, "What happened to your first husband?"

Though he couldn't be sure because of the sunglasses, Carlyn appeared to be staring at him. Unexpectedly she laughed. "You don't give up, do you? That's why I'm crazy about you, Mr. Elders, you're going to ferret something out of me if it takes a lifetime." She shook her head. "Well, since it's the hundred and tenth time you've asked me, and because you've even got the bright interrogation light glaring in my face now," she said pointing to the sun, "I've decided to tell you although it's not considered good form to discuss former relationships with existing ones." She lifted her sunglasses again and looked at him. "First of all, yes, there was a husband before my present one." She smiled. "And what happened to him?" She stared directly into DJ's eyes. "Nothing is your answer. Absolutely nothing happened to him, or to me. We split up, that's all." She placed the glasses back on the bridge of her nose. "Satisfied?"

"Well, I mean, how did you break up? Where did he go?"

"You're beginning to sweat like a dog who's doing too much digging." She reached across and unbuttoned his shirt. "You can take it off if you like."

DJ left the shirt in place. He dropped the newspaper on the ground next to his feet. "Seriously, Carlyn, I'm just interested. Was he younger than you, like me?"

Carlyn turned her head away again. "No, he wasn't. We were the same age. Familiar story, we got married too young, and before we were even old enough to vote, we'd lost interest in each other. He went his way, I went mine."

"Where is he now?"

Carlyn turned back in his direction. "Why do you want to know?"

"Just curious. I think someone said he just stopped going to work one day. They never saw him again." DJ wiped his forehead on his sleeve.

"Someone just said that? And who is someone?"

"I think it was Monty. He said he seemed to remember hearing that your husband just left, you know, disappeared."

"Well, I suppose there is a grain of truth to that. He did just leave, and I didn't hear from him for six months." She thought a moment, then ran her fingers through her hair. "I was very concerned. I didn't love him, but I did care about him, if that makes any sense—at least as much as I cared about anyone. We'd gone together a long time before we got married." She absentmindedly moved her hands from her hair then ran them across her cheeks. "But he was okay."

DJ stared. "Where did he go?"

"Away. Just away. I don't think it's healthy to dwell in the past. Why don't we just leave it at that. He went away."

"What was his name?"

Carlyn abruptly sat up, tucking her feet under her knees. "What's going on, DJ?"

"Nothing's going on. I'm just curious that's all. If I had been married once, wouldn't you want to know about my wife?"

Carlyn took her sunglasses off and tossed them to the grass. "No."

"And I don't even know about your new husband. I mean the one who's in Vietnam." DJ could feel his voice starting to squeak. "I mean, I don't know anything about him. Nothing. He might come home any minute and shoot my butt off. Or maybe yours too. I don't think it's stupid for me to wonder about that stuff. Do you think it's stupid?" He paused. "Why is it stupid?"

"Come here, baby," she said, pulling him toward her.

DJ resisted for a moment, then allowed himself to be pulled to her breast. The nylon was hot against his cheek. "And I don't see why you would want to be with a seventeen-year-old," he struggled to find the right word to use, not boy, not man, "ah, person, when you could get anybody you wanted."

Carlyn kissed the top of his head, then put her hand up under his shirt and ran her fingers down his spine. "Everyone is so concerned about age and other people's business. Why do I have to apologize for caring about someone?"

DJ noticed immediately that Carlyn used *caring* in place of the word *loving*. It should have been the word *loving*! His mind was racing. "I'm not, you know, crazy, but I need to know some things, that's all."

Carlyn continued to stroke his back. "Wel-l-l-l-l, if it's really that important to you, how about my ex-husband's phone number? You can call him and talk as long as you want. His name's Ed. Just plain Ed." She lightly bit into his shoulder. "Will that get you started in the right direction?"

DJ was relieved, almost elated. And safer, much safer. "You wouldn't mind if I talked to him?"

"Look, DJ, like I said, I don't believe in reliving the past, but if it means that much to you, I wouldn't care if you talked to God."

Carlyn stood, and with DJ following, walked to the back door and entered the kitchen. She crossed to a cabinet drawer and pulled out a green leather book. After flipping through several pages, she took a pad and a pen, then scribbled some numbers. She ripped off the piece of paper and handed it to DJ. "Here he is in all his glory, Edward Lynch, the Third. I have no idea what you would ever want to talk about, but that's how you can get a hold of him." She replaced the book in the drawer. "Feel better now?"

He did. It was remarkable how much better he felt. "Yeah, I guess so."

"Good," Carlyn said, approaching him, "as long as you feel better." She reached down and touched his thigh. "But let's talk about what you really stopped by for."

DJ's arousal was instantaneous. He had been excited from the first moment he had seen her in the two-piece bathing suit. "I have the car and my father doesn't know it. I should get back—"

"Or else the law will get you?" Carlyn interrupted. She reached behind and unfastened the top to her swimsuit, letting it fall to the floor. Her breasts were pale against her dark skin, and she gently pushed herself against his bare chest. "The law's loss is my gain," she said, reaching over and sliding out of the bottom of the swimsuit. "Don't worry about the law. I don't."

∞

Later, in Carlyn's bed, his head propped-up on the pillow, DJ studied the framed eight-by-ten photograph of himself on her bureau. More than anything, he was pleased it was there. And she was right, there were no dark half-circles under his eyes.

∞

When he arrived home that evening, his father had already retired to his bedroom and hadn't missed the car. Patty had left a note saying she was visiting Greta. DJ took a shower, then went to the telephone and dialed just plain Edward Lynch, the Third. Nervous, uncertain what to say, he listened as the phone rang and rang. After two minutes, he quietly hung up and climbed the stairs to his room. He tucked the slip of paper with the phone number into his top desk drawer.

The thought of the spontaneous day with Carlyn ran through him. He could still taste the cocoa butter and feel the softness of her beneath him. Her first husband had a phone number, so he had to be alive, her second husband wasn't due back from Vietnam any time soon, and now he was confident he had made a mistake about the murdered New York City policeman.

It was all good.

CHAPTER 34

Maynard and Frannie's Saturday afternoon wedding ceremony included two families, two bridesmaids and two best men—Ike, and DJ, who had the day off from Mertz Brothers.

Watching the ceremony with Dale from a back pew, Wendell later related that Maynard looked like he had just been electrocuted. "Yep, it was a pitiful sight," he told friends. "Just like leading a damn lamb to slaughter. Same as I felt when I married Rosie."

Following the brief ceremony, the wedding party and Father Hill adjourned to the Knights of Columbus hall for tea sandwiches and punch prepared by two ladies from the Women's Guild. During the self-conscious celebration, the good Father put on a *Sing Along With Mitch* album, and the strolling photographer, who could cover the entire affair in a twenty-second walk around, took several candid shots, then posed the entire group together in front of a mammoth scroll of the Ten Commandments.

"Kiss the bride," the photographer urged. Maynard did as instructed, then as Mitch and the Gang sang "I Found A

Million Dollar Baby (In A Five and Ten Cent Store)," he excused himself and left the party for the men's room.

Never to return.

∞

"Wonder where he went," Ike thought out loud an hour later as DJ and he exited the Knights of Columbus hall leaving behind a strained gathering.

DJ scratched his head. "What I wonder is if he'll ever come back."

As they passed Van Velsor's, Herman was placing a *Congratulations Hardscrabble High School Class of 1965* sign in the window. He stepped down off his ladder and stuck his head out the front door. "Come early tomorrow morning, DJ," he called, "we might need extra time with the newspapers."

"You know me, Herman," DJ answered, "I'm always early."

"I know," Herman acknowledged. "Early is good. Very early is better."

"Patty and I are going to the movies tonight," Ike said, when they reached their houses. "What are you doing?"

DJ looked around at the bushes, half expecting to see Maynard's face peek out and signal for him to come hide too. "Nothing," he answered. He couldn't see Carlyn until tomorrow. She said she had too much paperwork to catch up on at home. "Maybe go down to the Rock for a while. Heck, I'm almost legal."

"See you," Ike said, shuffling away.

∞

Later in the evening, DJ walked down to the Jailhouse Rock and slipped in through the side door, taking a seat at Lila's table while The Primates were on stage.

"Hi, sweetheart," Lila said, touching his shoulder. "Haven't seen you around in a while. You been all right?"

"Yeah, I'm fine," he said, wondering how much paperwork Carlyn had that couldn't wait until Monday.

"Can I get you something?" She placed her Newport on the lip of the ashtray.

"Would it be all right to have a beer?"

"That'll be fine if you really want one." She rolled up the sleeve of her uniform.

"I do. I'll pay."

"That's all right, sweetie, Thor's not about to take your money. I'll be right back." She headed off to the bar and was back in five minutes.

DJ felt much better and less alone by the time The Primates finished their first set of the evening.

"DJ, where you been, son?" Monty asked, approaching the table. "Everything all right?" He stared into DJ's eyes.

"Fine, just fine."

"Glad to hear it," Monty replied, patting him on the shoulder before crossing to the bar.

"I tell you what, I'm tired of playing the drums." Wendell stood by the table, fired back the rest of the whiskey he had been nursing, then slammed the glass on the table before sauntering over to the bar behind Monty.

Moments later, Wendell returned and placed a beer in front of DJ. "Here's a backup for you, partner. Each one makes the world a little softer."

After the band began again, DJ walked up to the bar. He caught Thor's eye. "Mind if I stay here?" he asked.

Thor nodded, then added, "Only a little while," and pointed to an empty stool in the far corner against the wall underneath the Schaeffer beer clock.

DJ sat and looked around. After a few minutes had passed, Thor took his empty and placed a beer in front of him before moving away.

Rocco's older brother, Artie, slid onto the stool next to DJ.

His arms and palms were bandaged. He sat still, his fingers intertwined on the bar in front of him.

Thor walked over and stretched out his hand. "How you feeling, Artie?" he asked.

Artie reached out to Thor. "Glad to be home, Chief."

"Glad to have you home. Thank you for going over to that hell hole for us." Thor brought him a beer, then moved to the other end of the bar to fill Lila's drink orders.

DJ hesitated, then turned on the stool. "Home from Nam for good?" He hoped using the term Nam instead of Vietnam would add to his own credibility.

"Who wants to know?" Artie lit a Lucky Strike.

"DJ Elders. I'm a friend of Rocco's."

Artie stared at DJ, sipped his beer and looked away. "I'm out all right." He placed the Lucky in the corner of his mouth and raised his two arms over his head as he turned back to DJ. "See these bandages? They go down my arms, down my chest, down my stomach, across my balls, down the insides of my legs, and across my ankles. I'm all torn up." He continued to hold his hands over his head, then gradually brought them to his waist, resting them back on the bar. "It hurts too. Every day it still hurts. There was blood everywhere. My mind hurts too." A dribble of beer slipped from the side of his mouth.

"Did you get shot?" DJ asked.

Artie sat a full minute, not speaking, then took the cigarette from his mouth and drank the rest of his beer in one gulp. "Got to go," he said before inching out his wallet and leaving a dollar on the bar. "Stay away from Nam, DJ, stay away." He left his cigarette burning in the ashtray, stood and carefully oriented himself before cautiously moving toward the front door.

DJ watched him, then quickly stood and followed. "Hey, Artie." He caught up with him. "When you were over in Nam, did you ever meet a guy named Canova? A guy from Hardscrabble?"

Artie leaned against the door and considered the question.

"No, I never did," he said after a long moment. He lit a cigarette. "And I knew all of the guys from here. Army?"

"I think so," DJ responded.

Artie touched a bandage on his neck. "Nope, never heard of him. And it's just as well, especially if he's dead."

"Are you sure?"

Artie nodded. "Positive." He walked through the front door. "Positive," he repeated before disappearing into the night.

DJ moved through the thinning crowd back to Lila's table. She was sitting, her feet out, resting.

"I'm leaving," DJ said.

"I know, sweetheart," Lila said. "Take good care." She reached up and squeezed his hand.

DJ couldn't get Artie from his mind as he walked home. Why didn't he know Carlyn's husband?

And Maynard. Where was Maynard and what was he doing? He might just be foolish enough to visit a recruiter and head to Vietnam.

Bobby Litchfield's Impala was parked in front of Leslie's house, and from a distance, from the reflections of a street lamp, he could see their shadows huddled close together in the front seat.

He crossed and walked on the other side of the street.

"That you, Elders?" Bobby called, as DJ went past.

"How you doing, Bobby?" He kept walking.

"Couldn't be better, my friend," Bobby called. "Couldn't be better. See you at the Mertz boys."

"Sounds good," DJ called back. He could hear Leslie giggling.

Bobby and DJ were both working more hours at Mertz Brothers. Cliff Collins was pleased with his student-floating-salesman program and according to Carlyn, wanted to use them both full time after they graduated from high school.

DJ crossed the street in front of his house and saw Ike and Patty sitting on the front steps, holding hands, quietly talking. In the background, Ike's transistor radio was softly spinning music through the layers of darkness, creating a private, intimate room for the two. When Patty saw DJ, she quickly pulled her hand from Ike's.

"Any word from Maynard?" DJ asked, sitting down next to Patty.

"Nothing," she said.

"I heard that if he doesn't turn up tomorrow, Frannie's going to file a Missing Person's Report. Everyone's getting real concerned," Ike said.

DJ looked at the bushes near the steps, still expecting Maynard to appear. "You don't think he would do anything stupid like join the army, do you?"

Neither Patty or Ike responded.

"Hope he shows up," DJ said, then stood. "Hope he doesn't go to Nam. I ran into Rocco's brother, Artie, and he said it's terrible there."

"I saw him yesterday in town," Patty said. "He doesn't look so good. Herman said that he's taking medicine that calms him down."

"He doesn't sound so good either," DJ said as he climbed the steps and walked inside the house. He looked at his watch, saw that it was one in the morning, then walked to the phone. He dialed Carlyn's number and listened as it rang, twice, three times. After six rings, he hung up.

CHAPTER 35

Sunday morning, the front page of the *Daily News* screamed: *Police Killer Suspect Nabbed*, with the lead story describing how the New York City cop killer had been caught. DJ couldn't stop to read the article until his break, so he stared at the murderer over and over again as he inserted the different sections into the middle of each newspaper. The suspect had dark, curly hair, a shirt open to the waist, and entrapped in a phalanx of detectives, was being dragged to the police station.

DJ now felt foolish about rushing over to Carlyn's with the newspaper and harboring suspicions about her—that she might have somehow been involved. What was he thinking?

Sipping a Coke during his ten-minute break, he read the full story about the capture and arrest. Vincent L. Biondi, who had been police commissioner only since the beginning of the month, tried to tone down the significance of the arrest, but was clearly pleased with the department's detective work. "Just old-fashioned police tenacity," he was quoted as saying, a smile on his face in spite of himself.

According to police statements, the suspect, Albert

DeVries, held a grudge for years because of the way Police Officer Dixon had once confronted him in the presence of his girlfriend. According to official reports and assorted testimonials, DeVries had vowed to "get" Officer Dixon when he "least expected it." Old records and interviews with neighbors had led to the suspect. The police were jubilant and the press both satisfied and impressed with the swiftness of the collar.

And DJ was more relaxed than he had been in weeks. Relief flowed over him. He was meeting Carlyn later that evening, and was grateful he hadn't done something really stupid the night before, like knocking on her window, awakening her, simply because she hadn't answered the telephone. It would have ruined everything.

∞

Later, when the Mustang pulled into the Jailhouse Rock parking lot, Carlyn appeared more beautiful and radiant than ever. They traveled directly to her bedroom where she poured herself over him and apologized for her neglect, for not seeing him as frequently as she had in the past.

"Just think, DJ, we have the whole summer," Carlyn said later as she lay on her side staring at him. "And I love you so." She reached over and ran her fingertips down the side of his face. "You'll be at Mertz Brothers, and I can adjust our schedules so they're compatible. Cliff won't figure it out. No one will know but you and me."

∞

The following day, home from the department store, DJ glanced through the mail on the corner of the kitchen table.

"What're you looking for?" Dale asked.

"Nothing, just looking," DJ answered.

He opened a form letter from the school district, addressed to his parents, congratulating them for their son's/daughter's imminent graduation from Hardscrabble High School, and stating that because the size of the class was so large, the graduation would be held in the parking lot behind the school. Graduation rehearsal was in the auditorium on Thursday, June 24th, at ten o'clock in the morning, with no one excused. Caps and gowns would be issued to seniors in the high school gymnasium following rehearsal, and all flowers on graduation day should be sent to the cafeteria.

DJ leaned against the wall in the kitchen while he stared at the letter. There it was: short, concise, in black and white. It was almost over. The announcement had arrived. One more official handshake and it *was* over. After all the years, growing up with the same people, becoming comfortable with familiar surroundings, the last day was finally near.

He stood still, thinking, until Dale turned toward him.

"What's the matter with you? Do I have to check you into the state mental hospital, DJ? You're standing there like you're a zombie."

DJ forced a laugh. "Sometimes I wonder, Dad," he said. "Has anyone heard about Don Maynard?"

"Nope," Dale said. "His wife, what's her name, Francine? filed a Missing Persons Report, and his family is out looking for him, but if you ask me, he just got cold feet. He'll turn up. It takes forever to get used to being a married man."

∞

The following morning before the store opened, Cliff sent DJ downstairs to Basement Shoes, and in what seemed an increasing pattern, assigned Bobby to The Ivy League Shop.

As he was organizing the shoe boxes on the shelves in the storeroom, Carlyn walked in and without saying a word, started to unbuckle his belt.

"Carlyn, cut it out," DJ said, quickly looking over his shoulder.

"Oh, come on, baby, take a chance once in a while," she said, kissing him. "How about a little fun before your customers get here." She placed her hand on the front of his pants. "I'm your customer, and the customer's always right," she whispered.

"No, no, we can't," DJ said, attempting to move away. As she pushed herself against him, two or three shoe boxes suddenly slid backwards and crashed to the cement floor.

Her breath surged into his ear as she rubbed against him and fumbled with his belt.

"Stop it, Carlyn," DJ whispered, "we can't do this."

"Anybody here?" Mr. Slavik called from the register out front.

Carlyn quickly bit DJ's ear, then darted backward. "So I would appreciate it if you would continue with the straightening back here until Mr. Slavik becomes too busy and—"

Mr. Slavik stepped in through the curtain. "Good morning."

"Ah, good morning, Mr. Slavik," Carlyn said. "DJ is going to continue to organize the stock while you work out front. If you need help, DJ, just call." She nodded at him, then at Mr. Slavik. "Have a good day, gentlemen." She walked through the curtain and out into the sales area.

Mr. Slavik stared at DJ, who was crouched in front of one of the shelves, picking up the boxes that had fallen. "Lipstick coming into fashion for men?" he asked.

DJ quickly looked up from where he was kneeling. "What?"

"I was just wondering about lipstick. Wondered if it was a new fad I didn't know about."

DJ stood. "I don't understand what you mean, Mr. Slavik."

"You've got lipstick all over your face, son. That's all." He smiled, and added, "You're either a very strange or a very lucky boy." He started toward the exit of the backroom. As he was about to walk through the curtain, he turned. "Don't worry, I won't say anything, I need the job." He shrugged. "Anyway, at my age it's vicarious gratification."

DJ took a Kleenex from his jacket pocket and hurriedly wiped at his face, then before any customers arrived, he rushed to the men's room to finish mopping up any remaining lipstick.

∞

At lunchtime, DJ wandered out into the mall and strolled down one side, passing several stores. He stopped for a hot dog before sitting on one of the shopper's benches. As he scanned the stores opposite him, he noticed a book shop with a few people, all of them wearing glasses, perusing the aisles while a single employee sat reading behind the cash register. DJ scanned the bookstore window, the bakery next door, and was continuing on to the children's store, Harvey's House of Toys, when he suddenly stopped. Sweeping quickly back to the bookstore window, past the piles of bestsellers on prominent display, to the window's far corner, he saw an enlarged black-and-white photograph and immediately recognized a familiar face. DJ rose from the bench and moved across the mall to the window. Three photographs were featured, but he recognized only one. On a banner above them were the words:

Come And Join Us As We Celebrate The World War I Poets.

Each photograph had a name below it: Alan Seeger 1888-1916, John McCrae 1872-1918, Rupert Brooke 1887-1915. Below Alan Seeger's photograph was a handwritten message, *June 22, Happy Birthday, Alan Seeger*, but it was the face of Rupert Brooke that DJ stared at. *Rupert*, the identical photograph that was sitting in a bronze frame on the table in Greta's apartment—the same half-shadowed features, loosened tie, and sandy hair. DJ looked closely for the inscription to Greta, but the bottom of the portrait was bare. He studied the picture, then considered the years, 1887 to 1915, and realized the dates made no sense. According to Greta, Rupert had soldiered in the Second World War, then died on some remote island. And she said his poetry was written for her alone.

He walked into the bookstore and approached the young woman reading behind the cash register.

"Excuse me."

She looked up. "Yes, may I help you?"

"I have a question about Rupert Brooke."

She marked her place in her book and slid it under the counter. "I'll see if I know the answer. Are you a devotee?"

"I'm not sure." DJ hesitated. Actually, he wasn't sure what a devotee was. "I thought Rupert Brooke fought in the Second World War."

"Well, that answers my question, now with regard to yours, I don't know who your sources were, but Rupert Brooke fought and died in the First World War. It was a terrible tragedy."

"You're positive?" DJ asked.

"Follow me, please." Now with a superior intellectual attitude accompanying her, the woman led DJ down an aisle to the poetry section. "Brooke, Brooke, Brooke," she repeated as she ran her fingers across the spines of the books. "Ah, yes, see for yourself." She pulled a hard-covered edition from the shelf and handed DJ a copy of *The Collected Poems of Rupert Brooke*. "This will give you a brief biography and should answer any questions you might have."

"Thank you," DJ responded as he leafed through the pages while the clerk returned to her perch. Rupert Brooke *had* fought in the First World War which DJ figured was almost before Greta had even been born. As he thumbed through the pages, he recognized "The Soldier" as the poem she had recited. According to the inside notes, it was one of his most famous.

DJ walked to the counter and purchased the book, then after thanking the woman again, returned to his bench in the mall. Nothing made sense. Maybe he had misunderstood Greta's story, but when he carefully retraced their conversations, he was certain he hadn't.

Before he headed back to Basement Shoes, he stopped at the men's room.

"Elders" Bobby Litchfield said, looking back over his shoulder as he stood in front of the urinal. "What's going on?"

"Not much. Heading back to Basement Shoes."

"You hear I broke up with Leslie? She's too crazy for me."

DJ hadn't heard. "When did that happen?"

"Last night. God Almighty, I'm probably scarred for life from going with her all this time. Usually I could block the punches if I saw them coming, but last night she actually bit me. I never anticipated that at all." Bobby turned away from the urinal, zipping his fly as he walked to the sink. "Did she ever do that to you?"

"Punches and scratches mostly. After a while I got around to figuring out it wasn't worth it."

"I can understand that."

"What did she say when you broke up with her?"

"She didn't say anything, just went nuts instead. You've been there, right? Charged me, swinging both arms. Like a windmill or one of those boxing kangaroos."

"Did she say she was going to kill you again?" DJ asked.

"Yeah, she said it, then she killed me." Bobby grinned. "You're talking to a ghost." He shook his head. "She's just a mental case." Glancing at his watch, he asked, "What time you got to head back?"

DJ turned toward the sink, zipping his trousers before washing his hands. "Right about now. How's The Ivy League Shop working out?"

"Great," Bobby said. "I think they like me there because I look good in the clothes. Probably adds to the sales. Everybody thinks they'll look that way."

"Yeah, that's probably it," DJ answered. As much as he hated to admit it, Bobby's assessment was probably the truth.

The two headed out of the men's room.

"See you at graduation, Elders. We're almost free!"

∞

That evening, when Dale was snoring in his lounger, DJ and Patty slipped outside and walked to Greta's. DJ considered telling Patty about the Rupert Brooke fraud he had discovered at the mall, but then decided not to ruin her evening. Another time.

Later, after listening to Kirsten Flagstad while Greta sipped sherry, DJ slowly began to lose sight of the disparity between Rupert Brooke and the two World Wars. The fact that the poet was born in England, not the United States, and that his verse had been written, published, and targeted for an international audience, not solely for a single woman currently residing in Hardscrabble, gradually began to trickle away.

DJ rested his head against the back of the chair and watched Greta knead her fingers together as she explained Flagstad's interpretation of Grieg.

Why bring up inconsistencies? He felt perfect and whole, and recognized that discrepancies were merely misunderstandings to be dealt with further down the road, if at all.

CHAPTER 36

Saturday night, DJ sat with Ike and Patty on the front steps listening to Ike's radio. Carlyn wasn't free again, but she said she'd try to make his graduation the next day.

"The king returns," Maynard said, stepping out of the darkness and plunking down next to DJ.

"Maynard!" DJ said, slapping him on the back, overjoyed. "Where you been?"

"I have to tell you," Maynard responded as he lit a cigarette, "it's been interesting."

"Do they know you're back?" DJ stammered. "I mean, do Frannie and your family know you're home?"

"Yeah, they know I'm back," Maynard responded, a sly smile on his face.

"After you took off like that, I'm surprised you're allowed out tonight," Ike observed.

Maynard stared over at Ike. "I'm married, a father-to-be, and they're going to put me on some kind of curfew?"

"Well," DJ said, "where did—"

"Where did I go?" Maynard finished the question. He laughed quietly to himself, his elbows resting on his knees, then looked over at the group. "You really want to know?"

They nodded.

"Let's see, I hated the thought of being married, so I started out going to the bathroom at the Knights of Columbus, then headed to New York City where I tried to enlist, but couldn't because of my age. So I just stayed there until my money ran out." He flicked the half-smoked cigarette butt into the street. The sparks showered the gravel before flickering out. "That's it."

"That's it?" DJ asked.

"That's it," Maynard answered.

"Was Frannie happy to see you?" Patty asked.

Maynard hesitated, lighting another cigarette. "Couldn't tell. For a change, she's not speaking to me. I'm back in my old cellar bedroom at my house."

"That's not so good," Ike said as he leaned back and adjusted the radio.

"Wrong again," Maynard said. "That's the biggest break I've had all year."

The four sat in silence as Maynard chain-smoked, then cracked his knuckles, each one independently, right down the line.

"Are you going to graduation?" DJ finally asked.

"Wouldn't miss it for the world," Maynard answered. "My old man already picked up my cap and gown." He paused. "Hey, what is it with the robe? It's in a fold-up pack. It's like a tarp. Did I get leftovers? Or maybe I'm supposed to go into the house painting business after graduation."

"Disposable robe," Ike said. "Rayon. I read the label. Green for guys, white for girls."

"What the heck is rayon? Ah, who cares," Maynard interrupted. "If it's hot enough, maybe we'll all melt. One big oozing puddle in the school parking lot." He stood and headed up the street. "See you tomorrow."

∞

Maynard wasn't wrong about the puddle in the school parking lot. The late afternoon sun bore down on the seated graduates, with the temperature hovering at ninety-eight degrees. DJ stared around and couldn't see an inch of shade anywhere except under the speaker's platform that had been constructed for the ceremony. Even the grass on the football field behind the parking lot had bleached to hay.

The two girls he was alphabetically assigned to sit between stared straight ahead, only occasionally glancing at their white hands folded on their white rayon laps. First Communion, graduation, wedding day; DJ figured it was all the same for them. They looked fresh—he could smell the hairspray—and only the half-circle mirrors of perspiration under both pairs of eyes betrayed their reaction to the weather. As Father Hill gave the invocation, at the same time mopping his florid face with a sodden, white handkerchief, the two prayed. While DJ sagged, the sweat running from under his arms and down his sides, cleanly, crisply, coolly, the girls sitting on either side of him promised their best intentions to the good Father.

As he looked back over his shoulder, DJ saw Patty, Monty, Lila, Wendell and Dale through the waves of green and white. Patty blew him a kiss, which caused his eyes to fill though he didn't know why, and he quickly turned to face the dais.

DJ became convinced the graduation ceremony was designed to run through the end of time. Everyone who spoke announced that they would make it short because of the sweltering heat, but each ended up wanting his day in the sun.

"What are you doing after graduation?" DJ whispered to the girl to his right.

She glanced over at him, obviously concerned that she would be speaking when she should be paying attention. "I'm going home. My parents are having a party for me."

"No, I mean after graduation. Not tonight. After graduation." DJ slid the fronts of his hands across his forehead then wiped them on the robe, creating puddle-streaks that ran perpendicular to the fold lines.

"I'm getting married," she said.

"Really?" DJ answered. "To who?"

She stared ahead and didn't respond.

Bobby Litchfield's valedictory speech was quasi-intellectual, patriotic, fittingly homespun, and aside from his all-American looks, he was even more impressive to the audience because they knew he was going to Yale. When he finished, the students gave him a standing ovation.

DJ received mild applause as he walked across the platform to receive his diploma. He'd hoped for more, but then figured most people, including a lot of students, didn't know who he was. As he walked down the steps, grateful that he hadn't tripped on the way to his diploma, he thought he caught a glimpse of Carlyn standing far in the back, behind the last row of parents—just a flash of her blonde hair. He couldn't stare, he had to keep walking, but he was excited that she planned to surprise him.

Bobby Litchfield got a large round of applause as he received his diploma, but by far the biggest ovation went to Ike as he shuffled across the stage before shaking the superintendent's hand. Grinning and with a surprised look on his face at the public reaction, he descended the stairs, letting the railing slide through his fingers.

And then it was over: the moment, the afternoon, the four years, the life.

$$\infty$$

"I'll see you at home later," Dale said. "Do you need anything?"

"No, nothing, thanks, Dad," DJ replied, as he ripped off the robe. They were jammed into the riotous cafeteria crammed with students, parents and families.

"Here, have some fun tonight," Dale said, handing him a ten-dollar bill.

DJ stared up at his father, surprised. "Thanks, Dad," he said.

"I'll see you later," Dale said. "You need the car, come on back and get it. Patty's across the way with the O'Reillys." He turned and eased his way through the throngs of people.

"Congratulations," Wendell said, crowding into the space Dale had vacated.

"You're a man now," Monty said, shaking DJ's hand.

"We're heading out of here. Feel like coming along with us?" Wendell asked.

DJ's eyes were darting around the cafeteria searching for Carlyn. He wasn't sure she planned to come to the graduation, but if it was her, he was excited with the prospect. "Ah, no, thanks, Wendell. But I appreciate the offer."

"Well, if you want to drop by the house later, please come ahead," Monty said.

"I will," DJ promised.

As soon as Wendell and Monty left, he meandered through the crowd in the cafeteria looking for Carlyn, but was unable to locate her. After a few minutes of searching, he spotted the O'Reillys standing near one of the windows, chatting with Ike and Patty. DJ gave a final glance around, then walked over to join them. Mr. O'Reilly was holding his elbow, his free hand clutching his unlit pipe as he nervously clenched and unclenched his fingers around the bowl. Mrs. O'Reilly, whom DJ had seen just weeks ago, appeared as if she had gained ten pounds across her hips and waist. Her dress was tight and the fabric stretched across her broad behind while her tiny breasts barely nudged the material across her chest.

"Well, DJ," Mr. O'Reilly said, struggling to make conversation, "it looks like the two of you made it."

"Barely," DJ answered.

"Barely is right," Ike said, then looked at Patty and smiled.

Patty laughed. "I don't know how they did it myself."

Mrs. O'Reilly looked anxiously at her husband's watch. "We really should be getting home for the babysitter." She looked at the three. "How about a ride?"

DJ wasn't sure what he was doing yet because there were a lot of graduation parties going on across town, but he knew for sure he wasn't going to sit in the cookie-crusted, urine-laced, station wagon spittoon belonging to the O'Reillys.

"I think we're just going to hang around here for a while, Mom," Ike said. "Parties are going to be starting everywhere pretty soon."

"Let the kids have some fun," Mr. O'Reilly said, steering his wife away. "It's their night to howl." He put the stem of his pipe in the side of his mouth. "You kids go ahead and tear up the town now. We'll see you later." He turned to his wife who had not moved. "Come on now, honey, let's us head home."

The two crossed the cafeteria toward the parking lot.

With his parents gone, Ike asked, "Now what?"

"Now me," Maynard answered, appearing over Ike's shoulder.

"You just keep turning up," Patty said, a smile crossing her face.

"At your service," Maynard bowed. "And I have the chariot outside with no Frannie."

"Where is she?" Ike asked.

"She has her diploma, but didn't want to graduate with the class. 'Too hot, she said.'"

"Don't you want to go home and be with her?" Patty asked.

"Sure I do. I also want to hammer tacks into my forehead," Maynard answered, pushing his glasses back on the bridge of his nose. "What I want to do is go to every party in town. I've asked around and I know where they are."

"Good," DJ said, still glimpsing around the cafeteria for Carlyn.

"Then we're out of here," Maynard said. "I'm in the side parking lot."

∞

Most of the celebrations were strictly backyard affairs with citronella candles covered with decorative fish netting, packs of kids chasing each other, and groups of family members eating sausages and potato chips. The older men, in white, short-sleeved shirts, rested against cyclone fences, drinking beer they had hand-pumped from aluminum kegs sitting in tubs of ice.

"Should have primed the pump better," DJ heard one of them say. "Too much damn foam."

At one of the stops, DJ recognized the girl who had been sitting next to him during graduation. Parked on a redwood picnic table bench, she was holding hands with a greasy character sporting rolled up short-sleeves, tattoos and a world-class pompadour.

Once back in the car, Ike said, "We're going to all these parties and I don't know anybody. I feel like we're, you know, intruding."

"We are," Maynard said, lighting a cigarette and flicking the match out the window. "But who cares. Free beer, and nobody knows we don't belong." He floored the accelerator, fishtailing around the corner.

∞

In the car after their fifth stop, Patty said, "Starting to get late, maybe we should head home."

"What time is it?" Maynard asked, turning on the radio.

"Eleven o'clock," Ike answered, staring at the dial of his watch.

"Can you find some music?" Patty asked.

"In five minutes," Maynard answered. "Nothing but news right now."

"And locally," the radio announcer said, "Albert DeVries, the suspect in the murder of Patrolman Edmund Dixon, has been released due to lack of evidence. According to New York City Police Commissioner, Vincent Biondi, DeVries has proven to be elsewhere at the time of the homicide—an airtight alibi. The commissioner has stated that currently there are no other suspects... In other news, according to the US Weather Bureau, the heat wave will continue. Look for temperatures in the high 90s..."

"What did he say?" DJ asked. He had only been half-listening.

"Hot, hot, hot," Maynard answered, squinting into the rearview mirror.

"No, about the police killer."

"Whoever done the deed is still out there," Maynard said.

"That's weird, I thought they had him," DJ answered. "That's what they said last week. They said they had him."

"Well, *they*, whoever *they* are, were wrong," Maynard said. "Who cares anyway. It's all in the city and doesn't have anything to do with us out here."

The Fall of Summer

CHAPTER 37

Later in the week, DJ mentioned to Greta that he had discovered some students had already left for college or started their full-time jobs. He was upset all over again—the splintering of friends, each going their separate ways, developing new worlds. He'd known it had to happen, but he still wasn't ready.

"Ah, dear boy," Greta said, peeling a leaf from an artichoke, "as we strip away the layers and erode our protection, we confront our fears." She pointed at the artichoke in the porcelain dish in front of DJ. "But once we do, we are, surprisingly, quite able to carry on. We gain strength as a result." She studied DJ. "And you, dear boy, are in the springtime of your life, with worlds to conquer—and conquer you must. I, on the other hand, am in the fall of summer." Her eyes met his, "Yes, dear boy, the fall of summer, and if I'm candid, far beyond, which despite public relations efforts to the contrary, is not a pleasant place to be." She nodded at the table. "But enough of that, you must try your artichoke now. Chilled, it's very good, you know."

DJ watched her dip the edge of the leaf into a mixture of

vinegar and oil, then slip the end between her teeth. "Delicate and unique," she added, placing the leaf in a discreet Tiffany's silver bowl. "Go on, now you must try."

"Where did you learn about artichokes?" DJ asked, following her example, sliding a corner of a leaf into his mouth.

"From Rupert, of course. Artichokes were always one of his favorites."

"Of course," DJ answered. The World War I picture of Rupert he had seen at the mall crossed his mind. "I should have guessed that."

"Yes, you should have," Greta said, smiling approvingly.

∞

An hour later, DJ walked with Greta to the station. After she boarded, he stood and watched as the train eased away from the platform, headed for New York City.

If she had offered to let him stay in her apartment, listening to Haydn as he sipped sherry by himself, he would have accepted. The interior was comfortable with an old-fashioned decor containing the oversized contemporary speakers, thick walls retaining the cool temperature from the previous night, and a settling calm that seemed to satisfy his chronic emptiness. He wasn't certain if the feeling would be the same without Greta actually there, but he realized that over the months of his senior year, her home had become a sanctuary, a haven where everything flawless, beautiful and holy was heeded, and that which was not, ignored.

CHAPTER 38

With the beginning of the long Fourth of July weekend underway, DJ was beginning to feel less tense and more accepting. The thought of the police killer still being on the loose was disturbing, but that whole incident now seemed far away, unrelated to Carlyn and no longer personal.

The night before he had stayed with her until six in the morning, even sleeping some of the time, then had slipped the Falcon back into the garage. He was happy and she appeared to be content and more at ease as well.

DJ was beginning to admit that his high school years were behind him, and for the first time conceded that might not be so bad after all. And though he never mentioned it, in a corner of his abstract vision of lifelong plans, he imagined a future with Carlyn, no matter how unorthodox the rest of the world might perceive the match to be.

"Hi, baby," Carlyn whispered under her breath, as she passed him in Men's Furnishings on route to another department. "See you tonight."

∞

After a slow morning, during his lunch break, DJ walked out into the mall.

Approaching from behind, Bobby Litchfield clapped him on the shoulder. "Hey, Elders, how are things in cuff links?"

"Somebody's got to sell them," DJ answered, glancing back at Bobby.

"Fair enough." Bobby was wearing a blue, gray and gold madras sports jacket, charcoal gray slacks, and Weejuns. The sun from his days off at the beach had made his hair even blonder. "Where we eating today?"

"I don't know." DJ shrugged. "I was just kind of walking around."

"Hot dog good? I'm buying. I got a story you're not going to believe."

"It must be some story if you're buying."

The two approached the hot dog vendor.

"Two," Bobby said, then handed over a dollar, "with mustard." He handed one of the hot dogs to DJ.

The two leaned against the wall and watched the shoppers drift by. After a minute had passed, DJ said, "Okay, so what's the big news?"

"Before I forget, I wanted to check with you on something," Bobby said. "I was thinking of asking your sister out. You wouldn't mind would you?"

DJ was surprised. "Patty? Why would you want to do that?"

Bobby thought a minute as he chewed the hot dog. "I don't know. She's a good kid. Kind of quiet, but real quality, you know what I mean. I'm sick of these psychos I always end up with. Lisa wasn't as bad as Leslie, but even she wasn't so great." He licked mustard from the side of his hand. "I guess I'd just like to be with someone normal for a change. Somebody nice, if you know what I mean."

"I don't kn—"

"She's not going with anyone, is she?" Bobby asked.

"No, not exactly."

"Good. I didn't think you'd mind, but I wanted to check."

DJ hesitated, then was silent.

"Did you go to any graduation parties last week?" Bobby asked.

"Yeah, a few. Mostly boring." He paused, trying to figure out what Bobby was up to. "You?"

"I went to one helluva graduation party all right. A one-on-one party if you know what I mean." Bobby had a smug smile on his face. "You get where I'm going with this, right?" Having a second thought, he added, "Oh yeah, and don't think I would ever try anything like that with your sister. That's different."

DJ eyed Bobby. He didn't really feel like listening to his conquests, especially after he had just mentioned he wanted to spend time with Patty. "As long as it's different with Patty, and yeah, I know what a one-on-one party is," DJ said. He focused on the shoppers moving past. "I thought you and Leslie had broken up."

"It wasn't Leslie," Bobby said.

"Really? Who then?" DJ glanced briefly at Bobby, mildly interested, then turned back to the crowds.

"Canova," Bobby said, his eyes wide.

"Canova?" DJ turned his head. "What do you mean Canova?" He felt a sense of foreboding rumble through his stomach.

"How many Canovas do you know? Mrs. Canova. Mertz Brothers' Mrs. Canova. Her first name is Carlyn. I'll bet you didn't even know that."

DJ turned and faced Bobby. He could feel the blood rushing to his face. "What are you talking about? What about her?"

"Let me tell you something," Bobby answered, "you probably think she's a corporate manager, straight-laced—all that stuff. We all did." He leaned over and rubbed a spot off the top of his loafer. "Let me tell you what she really is, my man. She's an animal—a sex machine."

"Ah, don't give me that," DJ whispered. He was an exposed animal frozen in white spotlights.

"I'm not giving you anything but the truth," Bobby said. "And I don't want you to say anything, nothing at all, understand? And I mean to anybody—I'm sworn to secrecy. Fact is, she's been kind of coming on to me in the store the past couple of weeks—you know in the back room, rubbing up against me, giving directions real close, that kind of thing. I thought I was crazy at first, but after a while I began to believe it. Then she said she wanted to have a drink after graduation, to celebrate, so I went through the nonsense with my parents, you know twenty minutes in the cafeteria, that garbage, then I went outside and she was waiting around the corner for me in her Mustang." He paused. "Have you seen that car? It's amazing."

DJ could feel his ears ringing, his fingers trembling. "This is all bullshit."

"You think so, huh? She lives down in Amity. She drove directly to her house and once we got inside, I could barely get the door closed before she attacked me. She was all over me, ripping my clothes off, ripping her own off, right there on the floor by the door." Bobby hesitated and shook his head. "I screwed her right in the hallway. Right in the damn hallway— she couldn't even wait to get to the bedroom."

DJ put his hands in the side pockets of his suit jacket, closing and unclosing his fingers.

"Then she went into the kitchen to have something to drink, and even though I hardly had my clothes back on, she started up again. Practically dragged me into her bedroom. Wouldn't leave me alone for the next two hours." He chuckled. "Afterwards, I could hear the radio from the kitchen playing all this soft, background music and I almost fell asleep which would have been a disaster. My old man would have killed me if I hadn't come home that night." Bobby reached down and pulled up a sock. "I have to tell you, Elders, I was beat the whole next day." He smiled. "But that kind of beat is worth it.

And, the good news, is that she wants to get together again Sunday night."

DJ pulled his hands from his pockets. He stopped listening.

"What a piece of ass though. I can get her, I can get anybody." Bobby paused. "She even said we should do it in some exotic place like the woods or the bathtub next time. You believe that? Does this all of a sudden happen once you graduate?"

DJ walked into the crowds, disappearing into the waves of window shoppers.

"Hey, Elders, where are you going?" Bobby called. "Don't worry, I wouldn't try anything with your sister. Don't get nervous on me about that now."

Once in the sun-baked employees' parking lot, DJ unlocked the Falcon. Inside, with the windows rolled up, the heat body-slammed him, encapsulated him, making it difficult to breathe. Pressing the tip of his finger on the dashboard, he felt the metal sear his skin.

And still he couldn't neutralize the agony.

He forced his finger to remain against the dashboard, allowing the pain to rush through his arm as he stared at his own eyes in the rearview mirror.

The reflected savage was unrecognizable.

Abruptly pulling his finger from the dashboard, he cranked down both windows, started the engine, and headed out of the parking lot.

CHAPTER 39

An hour passed, then two, before DJ pulled into the shady corner of the empty Jailhouse Rock parking lot and turned off the engine.

Twenty minutes later, Jellybowl approached the Falcon. "Whatcha doing, sonny boy?" he asked, jingling the change in the front pockets of his pants. "I seen you sitting out here."

DJ looked out at Jellybowl, then stepped from the car. "Where are you going?"

"Where am I going?" Jellybowl was bewildered. "Why I'm going back to the side porch of the Rock where I was sitting before. I just came over to see whatcha doing. I heard the car come in a while ago and came out to look when I didn't hear no door slam." He looked at DJ. "Whatcha doing?"

"I'll come with you," DJ said.

Jellybowl hesitated. "With me to the porch?" He thought a second as he rubbed his chin with two fingers. "Well, okay, that'll be fine," he responded and started across the parking lot.

DJ followed him around to the far side of the building, then sat down in a mint-green, iron rocking chair.

Jellybowl sat still for several minutes, then without speaking took out a pocket knife and began to peel an apple. As he worked, with his tongue lodged in the corner of his mouth, one long peel uncoiled from the apple to the tops of his white shoes. "Learned to do that from my mama," he said after a while. "Want a piece?"

DJ nodded.

"Well, here then." Jellybowl cut the apple in two and handed over half.

DJ held the soft cool apple against his burnt fingertip. His finger was blazing, the flames raging all the way up the back of his wrist.

"My mama showed me how to make a Christmas tree from rolled-up newspapers too," Jellybowl added, "but I forgot how to do that." He took a bite then looked up from his apple. "Guess that's because I eat apples all the time and Christmas only comes once a year."

DJ stared across at Jellybowl, then down at his own shoes.

"Yankees ain't doing much," Jellybowl continued. "And forget about those Mets. Bunch of losers." He picked an apple seed from his mouth. "Action on the trotters and flats too slow. Makes it hard to make a living these days." Jellybowl took another bite from his half of the apple, then used his thumb and forefinger to clean the corners of his mouth. "This is pretty good though. Sitting here, you know, this ain't bad living."

DJ looked over at the big man, then stared at the apple. He nodded.

Jellybowl ate the remainder of his half in silence, excused himself and walked inside the Jailhouse Rock to the pay telephone. After dialing and talking, he returned to the porch. "Thought you'd be working today," he said, as he sat down again.

"I know," DJ answered.

"Go ahead and eat that apple now," Jellybowl said, staring at the half in DJ's hand. "Makes no sense to let it go to waste."

DJ looked at the apple. "I'm not hungry. You can have it back."

Jellybowl shrugged. "If you don't want it, I might as well."

DJ handed the piece of apple back.

The two sat in silence, Jellybowl chewing, DJ unmoving in the rocking chair.

After Jellybowl finished eating and folded up his pocketknife, he cleared his throat. "See them puffy, white flowers," he said, pointing to the hydrangeas next to the porch. "Reason they're drooping is because they're hot and thirsty. And they're lonely too. They might even be crying."

DJ stared at the flowers and didn't respond.

Several minutes later, Monty walked up on to the porch. "How you doing, cowboy?" he asked. "See you still got your suit on."

DJ looked up at Monty, then away. "Yeah, I do," he said. His voice felt hoarse and his entire arm throbbed. Staring down, he saw the tip of the finger had turned to a white blister.

"Well, least you can do is take your jacket off in this heat," Monty said, scraping a rocking chair across the porch to DJ.

DJ removed his suit jacket and laid it on the floor in front of him.

"They let you go early today?" Monty asked. He laced his fingers behind his neck and stretched his legs in front of him. "Nice to get a holiday once in a while."

"I got to go," DJ said, standing. "Better get the car home."

Monty looked at his watch. "Heck, Dale isn't due home himself for another hour or two. What's your rush? Too hot to be scampering around."

DJ hesitated, sat down, then stood again. "No, I have to go," he said, standing and reaching down to retrieve his jacket.

Monty followed him to the parking lot. "Why don't you stop by the Rock tonight? Lila hasn't seen you since graduation, and she's always talking about how grown up you've gotten. She keeps telling me what a fine man you're turning out to be."

DJ opened the Falcon door and stepped inside. "Bye." He started the engine, shifted the car into first gear and drove away leaving Monty standing with his hands stuck in his back pockets.

CHAPTER 40

That evening, DJ waited in the parking lot of the Jailhouse Rock for Carlyn to come by.

"DJ, where were you?" she asked through the open window. "Ben Slavik said you never came back from lunch." She reached across and opened the door of the Mustang.

"Got sick," DJ said, sliding in beside her.

"You all right, baby?" Carlyn placed her hand on his forehead. "You've got to let me know though. You just can't get up and leave. People get fired that way."

DJ looked across at her. "You wouldn't fire me, would you, Carlyn?"

"Of course not, baby, but I have to know what's happening so that I can protect both of us." She turned on the radio.

"Okay," DJ answered.

"Well, it's Friday night," she said, changing the subject as she drove out of the parking lot. "A nice long weekend. We can head down to my house, then maybe go for a ride. We haven't done that in a while." She tuned in the radio. "I've always loved the Fourth of July. Are you all ready for the Fireama Sunday?" Carlyn hitched her skirt so it was above her knee and didn't wait for an answer. "By the way, I have bad news. I won't be able to go with you Sunday. My sister called from Albany and I have to go up there again. She's having problems with her husband and, as usual, is looking for some moral support." She looked over and ran her hand across DJ's knee. "I knew you would understand."

She was too beautiful. Even her profile spilling over with lies was beautiful.

"I had lunch with Bobby today."

"Great. How is the boy wonder?"

"He's happy."

Carlyn glanced in the rearview mirror, then out the side window. "He should be. Valedictorian, going to Yale. Attractive, smart. He should be very happy."

"He said graduation was great. Best time he's ever had." DJ's finger throbbed. He pressed his thumb against it.

"I guess it's nice to be in the spotlight," Carlyn said. "I wouldn't know, it's never happened to me."

"He said the best part of the whole day was after graduation. After the ceremony, after he left the school."

Carlyn hesitated for the briefest of seconds. "I'm glad. He's a bright boy and a good worker." She glanced over at DJ. "But not as good as you." She slid her hand along his thigh again. "No one's as good as you." Carlyn turned the knob of the radio, changing the station. "After our, ah, rest stop at my house, where do you feel like going?"

DJ looked out the window, then back across at Carlyn.

"What's the matter, DJ?" She glanced across at him.

"Bobby said you picked him up after graduation. Outside the school."

Carlyn glanced again. "You're kidding. Why would I ever pick up Bobby Litchfield?" She shook her head and changed the radio station again.

"I don't know, why would you?"

Carlyn's voice rose. Subtly. Faintly. "I wouldn't, I didn't. I don't know what he's talking about. It sounds like he has a lot of fantasies." She became matter of fact. "I guess sometimes when people are born with too much, they think they're entitled to everything. Maybe that's what's going on in his mind."

DJ took a deep breath to steady his voice, to quiet his anguish. "Bobby said he went with you down to your house."

Carlyn placed both hands on the steering wheel. "And what is that supposed to mean?"

"I don't know why you did it, Carlyn," DJ said, his voice shaky in spite of his effort to keep it even and under control.

"Did what? What are you talking about?"

"Why you did everything with Bobby that you did with me." He halted, clutching his burned fingertip with his free hand, then repeated, "I don't understand why."

"You're ridiculous, DJ. And I can't believe Bobby Litchfield is making up these insane stories." She stepped on the accelerator. "Now what's his plan, to tell everyone he's screwing me? Is that supposed to make him larger than life?"

"Everything you did with him was the same as you did with me." DJ rested his head against the side window. "In the hallway, in the bedroom. Exactly the same way. And next time outdoors or in the bathtub. That's what he told me you said, next time in the bathtub."

Carlyn abruptly pulled the Mustang to the side of the road, bringing it to a skidding halt. She turned down the radio as she faced DJ. "Is that what he told you? Is that what he said?"

"Yes. That, and not to tell anybody."

"Do you believe him?" Her expression briefly softened. "Do you?"

DJ hesitated. "I don't want to. But it's all the same. You even had a glass of wine in the kitchen between, you know, times." He stared over at Carlyn. "Bobby couldn't make that up." His voice faltered. "And the radio was on in the kitchen when you were in the bedroom. Just like it always is with us." He looked away, then slowly turned back. "And I don't know why you did it."

Carlyn stared over DJ's shoulder, her fingers tapping on the steering wheel. After a moment passed, she sighed, and instead of the consoling denial DJ expected, she said, "It infuriates me that he opened his mouth. I don't believe how some people never learn." She shook her head, then studied her nails. "I just wish I could frame the look on their faces when they discover at the last minute they're wrong. They just never figure it out until it's too late."

Carlyn's sudden admission that his accusations were accurate left him instantly naked and against all of his wishes, on display, as if some tuxedoed TV magician had suddenly yanked the cloth from a table, leaving the settings in place, but the wood exposed.

Barely able to hear himself, DJ whispered, "You said you loved me." He could no longer look at her. The tip of his finger was white-gray and ached to his toes.

Carlyn was silent for several seconds, then stepped on the accelerator and pulled the Mustang back onto the road, leaving a smoke screen behind them. "I do love you, DJ. But that's not the beginning and end of everything else."

"It is for me."

"Oh, don't be pathetic. It doesn't become you." She turned up the radio. "Look, this doesn't have to be a big deal. We can still go on. Life goes on; just relax. I'm sorry Bobby mentioned what happened. He should have known better."

"If you're married, why would you do this at all?"

Carlyn flashed. "Oh, I see, now because you don't have exclusive rights, it's become a morality play. That's perfect."

"I just wondered about your husband, that's all."

"Well, as long as we're being candid, my husband doesn't care about you, or Bobby, or anybody for that matter."

"I don't underst—"

"And the reason he doesn't care," Carlyn continued, her voice beginning to rise again, "is because he doesn't exist."

DJ hesitated, then leaned forward. "What do you mean he doesn't exist? He's in Vietnam."

Carlyn slid her hand behind DJ's neck, her tone softening. "Dale Elders, you poor, lovable thing." She glanced at him, the fire still smoldering in her eyes. "Despite how this may all appear, I do have a special place in my heart for you. You really are a sweet boy. And such innocence." She smiled, briefly, almost sadly. "If anything could reach me, that would probably be it."

"I don't understand what you're talking about, Carlyn."

"Oh, come on, DJ, listen to what I just said," she snapped, her smile disappearing as she retracted her hand. "There is no husband in Vietnam. That's really easy enough to grasp, isn't it? The husband is nothing but crap I made up to keep the men I don't want to associate with at arm's length. I especially hate the sloppy, sniveling types. And as it turns out, the ones that I do choose don't care whether I'm married or not, they just don't want to get caught themselves." She brushed her fingers through her hair. "That describes you pretty well too, doesn't it, DJ? You couldn't say no, but even though you're not married like most of them are, you didn't want anyone else to know what you were up to because of your age." Carlyn paused for a moment. "This may sound cruel, but one way or another, it's the way you all are."

"All are?"

"Yes, all. I could write a book. The patterns are the same, except most everyone has the sense to keep their mouths shut. For my own good, and theirs." She stared ahead. "Bobby should have known better. I don't need a reputation around this town." She flicked on the car headlights. "And I don't like it. Not a bit."

The softness DJ thought he remembered was no longer evident. Or more likely, as he was beginning to realize, never existed. He concentrated on the pain in his finger—focused on the burning. "I don't understand you," he said tentatively.

"Oh, DJ, relax," Carlyn shot back at him. "I like doing what I do. That's all. I like it. You liked it too, otherwise you wouldn't have kept coming around. Birds do it, bees do it. They do it in the trees in Australia. Does that mean everyone's in love? I don't think so. That's all human-initiated garbage."

"Then why did you pretend?" he asked slowly. "I didn't pretend."

Carlyn sighed wearily. "As I said, DJ, I do have a special place for you. And I don't think it's my intention to hurt you, or anybody else. It just seems to work out that way." She tilted her head slightly. "People have the need to hear certain words. They expect me to say certain things, so I go through the motions and say those words, mostly because it makes everyone more comfortable." She looked across at him and said, "You're sweet, DJ, and one of my favorites." Turning back to watch the road, she added, "But you're no exception."

After a while, DJ murmured, "Oh." He stared out the window and attempted to revisit all the powerful, forceful anchors in his life to cling to: the Cub Scout follows Akela, an image of the Duke of Flatbush patrolling center field, defying anyone to infiltrate his territory, Monty speaking the truth. But despite his efforts and his resolve to endure, he felt himself collapsing from a slow, indefatigable leak of sadness.

They drove for several more miles until he realized he was only vaguely familiar with the area. "Where are we going?"

"To the beach. Now that you've been mortally wounded, I suspect you wouldn't have wanted to stop by my house."

"Why the beach? It's dark out."

"Why not?" Carlyn smiled. "It's different."

DJ thought again of the faint lettering, *Carlyn Reynolds is a whore*, printed on the brick wall in town. "How come you changed your name to Canova?"

"My mother always liked Judy Canova, the comedienne." She glanced over at DJ. "You've got to have a sense of humor."

As the Mustang pulled up and stopped at the final red light before the causeway leading to the ocean, DJ opened his door and stepped outside. Closing it behind him, he began walking back in the direction they had traveled.

When the light changed, Carlyn drove away.

CHAPTER 41

DJ walked for twenty minutes, one foot on the pavement, one on the weeds, broken glass and cigarette butts bordering the road. A pickup passed, then screeched to a halt and backed up.

"What the heck are you doing down here on the south shore walking along this road anyway?" Wendell asked. "Shit, son, it's dark and dangerous."

"Don't know," DJ said as he settled into the cab next to his uncle. He thought of the Mustang traveling across the causeway, its taillights disappearing into the darkness.

"What do you mean you don't know, huh? What does that mean, 'don't know?'"

DJ stared out the window, watching the highway lights stream by, then closed his eyes.

"You're lucky I was out late fishing," Wendell said, tugging at his chin. "I tell you what though, DJ, walking when it's dark like this just ain't safe." He glanced at his nephew and seeing no response changed the subject. "Them flukes and blue-bellies biting like crazy today. Got a cooler full in the trunk if you want to take a couple home to Dale."

"Thanks, Wendell," DJ said.

Wendell studied DJ another moment, then focused back on the road. "Well, then, okay. You don't have to answer me about what you were doing down here. When I was your age I didn't talk much either. Just don't get yourself in trouble, that's all." Wendell cracked the window. "Sorry I smell like low tide. Happens when you're around the water all day." He rolled the window down further, then reached over and lowered DJ's window an inch.

Wendell drove a few miles before breaking the silence. "I tell you what, I sure wish your father could be more like family once in a while, like look at me, bringing him some fish. I tell you what, he never was though, even when we were little brothers. His idea of fun was to catch a live frog, stuff a firecracker down its throat, light it, then watch it hop away and explode. I never much cared for that type of stuff. Wasn't enjoyable for me, or Monty for that matter." Wendell touched the brim of his ball cap. "Funny I should remember that about Dale."

DJ listened to his uncle ramble on until the two arrived in front of his house. Wendell jumped out, opened the cooler in the rear of the truck and wrapped two blue-bellies in newspaper. "These are prime," he said, handing the wrapped fish to DJ.

"Right," DJ murmured, "thanks for the lift."

"You okay, son?"

"Good," DJ answered, "I'm good."

"Okay, you know better than I do." Wendell climbed into the driver's seat, started the truck, and headed back toward town.

As the pickup disappeared, DJ took the fish and slid them through the sewer grate, then walked to the front of the house where Patty sat alone on the steps, her transistor radio sitting next to her.

"I've been waiting for you," she said, her hands clasped around one knee.

"Yeah, huh?" DJ looked vacantly around. "Where's Ike?"

"He went home."

"Oh. Well, I think I'll go in," DJ said. Pressing ice against his finger was the only way he could think of stopping the pain.

"Before you do," Patty said, her eyes gleaming, "I want to tell you something."

DJ waited.

"Bobby Litchfield asked me out for tomorrow night." She stared up at DJ, an expectant look on her face. When he didn't respond, she said, "Did you hear me?"

DJ leaned against the railing. He was bone tired. "Yeah, well, what about Ike?"

"What about Ike?"

"I thought you two were together." DJ needed to sit for a moment, but didn't want to stay. "Why are you going to be with Bobby if Ike and you are together?"

"We're not together," Patty protested. "What gave you that idea?"

"The way you acted," DJ said. "I just thought you were together by the way you both behaved."

"Well, we're not. We were never 'together,' as you call it." Patty turned off the transistor radio. "I thought you'd be happy for me."

"What about the ring he gave you?"

"That was just a friendship ring. You know that. Anyway, I gave it back to him tonight." She stood and walked into the house, then proceeded to her bedroom.

DJ followed her inside and crossed to the bathroom. He closed the door behind him, switched on the light and stared at himself in the mirror. Duke Snider—the Duke of Flatbush. Always in control in the field and at the plate. No one dared fool around with the Duke.

"Someone knocked at the front door. Will you get it?" Patty called from her room.

His heart soared. Carlyn was back, and somehow he knew he would discover a way to forgive her. He needed to discover a way. In fifteen minutes, they would be in her bedroom and she would tell him why it had all been a lie. He could feel tears of relief welling up in his eyes.

Wendell stood inside the house. "DJ, I brought you some more fish for Dale. I can hear his snoring so I don't want to wake him." He hiked his pants. "See what happened, I got to thinking that I had a ton and I only left him two. I am his brother, you know, and he doesn't deserve just two or three. I got to set the family example. Know what I mean?" He lifted the newspaper-wrapped bundle out from under his arm and handed it to DJ. "Now you got a whole boatload."

Wendell turned and left the house. "See you at the Fireama," he called over his shoulder.

DJ walked into the kichen and stuffed the fish into the refrigerator. Moments later Patty joined him.

He leaned against the wall and held out his finger. "What do I put on a burn?"

"Lord, DJ, that looks awful. What happened?" She took his hand.

DJ stood motionless, helpless. "It's a long story. I'll explain it sometime."

"Come here, I'll show you what to do." Patty led him to the bathroom and held his finger under cold water, then applied some first-aid cream. "That ought to take care of it, at least for the time being." She looked up at DJ, reading his eyes, monitoring his mood. "Are you excited for me?"

"I guess, yeah, I am." He stared at his finger. "I'm just real tired and worried about Ike."

"Oh, you don't have to worry, he understands." She thought a second. "Now I've got to figure out what to wear, and how to get off early tomorrow night so I can have enough time to get ready."

"Right," DJ answered, "that's right." He headed upstairs to his room, then sat on the edge of his bed. His suit reeked of flukes and blue-bellies, and whatever else had been crawling over Wendell all day. DJ threw his jacket on the floor before slowly lying back. After a while, he pulled the sheets across himself, and as he stared at the ceiling, he gradually felt his ache for Carlyn degenerate into hatred for Bobby.

CHAPTER 42

"Do you know why I got all that applause at graduation?" Ike asked on Saturday afternoon. "I can tell you right now it had nothing to do with everyone liking me so much." He stared at DJ, a belligerent look in his eyes. "You know why I got all that applause? Because I made it to graduation—I lived long enough to graduate, and nobody thought I would." Ike assumed a 1920s fighter's pose, then shadow-boxed a step. "That's what all that phony clapping was about."

Abruptly halting the exercise, his lips white from the tiny expenditure of energy, he asked, "Did Patty tell you she gave me the ring back last night?" He began the shadow-boxing again. "She's with Bobby Litchfield and all of a sudden I'm out of the picture." He dropped his hands once more and turned away. "Just means I was never in the picture in the first place." As his chest heaved up and down, Ike leaned against the railed fence that surrounded the Hardscrabble Rural Cemetery. "I knew that." He looked away. "I knew that all along." Moments later, he asked, "Why do you think Bobby called Patty anyway? He could have anyone."

"Don't know, Ike," DJ responded. All he'd heard was

Bobby's explanation and it had sounded lame.

"Your sister has a real good figure, you know," Ike said. "But he wouldn't be stupid enough to try anything." He rested his arms along the fence rails—a wisp of Cassius Clay laying his arms along the ropes.

"No, I don't think so," DJ answered. "I don't think he would be that stupid."

"Because if he ever tried something, weak guys like me can suddenly get strong. I read about someone my size who lifted a car off a guy after the jack had collapsed. They said it was adrenalin, and I got as much of that as the next guy."

"You're probably right," DJ answered.

"Damn straight I'm right."

"I know you are."

Ike hesitated. "How come you're not working?"

"My suit smelled like fish."

"Oh." Ike suddenly squatted. "Man, I feel awful."

"Do you want me to call somebody?" DJ searched for a passing car.

"Not my heart, my mind. Just doesn't feel too good." He slid further down so he sat with his back against a fence post, his knees touching his chin. "You know, I'm crazy to think I can make a living repairing watches."

"No, you're not—that'll work. You're almost there."

Ike smiled. "Yeah, that's right. I'm almost there. It'll work all right. Maybe get a little office upstairs with my brothers and sisters running everywhere. Lot of people will want to drop off their watches. Maybe my father's nightclub personality can entertain them while they're waiting." He shook his head. "Yeah, I'm almost there."

DJ climbed to the top railing of the fence and sat. "Maybe you could share a bench with one of the jewelers in town. Monty knows the guy next to his repair shop. I think his name is Sid."

"So where do you think Bobby's going to take her?" Ike asked.

"Don't know," DJ answered.

"What time's he picking her up?"

"I think eight o'clock. I think. I'm not sure."

"In the convertible, I bet."

"Yeah, probably."

Ike picked a blade of grass and stuck the end into his mouth. "Well, I won't be outside my house when he comes by. That would be the best thing."

DJ hesitated, then said, "I guess."

Ike struggled to his feet and the two walked slowly from the cemetery which suited DJ fine. Like Ike, he was vacant—just stumbling along—with only a burned finger and a fish suit in the cleaners setting them apart.

The night before, he'd awakened in the darkness—numb from Carlyn—and felt his way down to the refrigerator. He'd taken a bottle of beer, opened it, and crept back to his room. Still wearing his shirt, suit pants and shoes, he had crawled back into bed. After drinking half the beer, just as he was at last beginning to relax, a hidden trapdoor in his subconscious sprang open, catapulting the entirety of his pain into view, arcing his misery with a precision and clarity that brought tears to his eyes.

He lay stone still, unable to move.

He never knew such depths existed.

Later that night, still unable to sleep, he had attempted to view the orange ship on the wall—the orange ship he had once McQueened—but all he could manage was a fraction of the moonlight reflected in a corner of the frame. He waited motionless until the sun crept around the corner, until he could see the ship, faint and faraway, then he was immediately aboard, sleeping until noon without a single call from anyone at Mertz Brothers inquiring as to his whereabouts.

CHAPTER 43

Saturday night, at eight thirty, Ike knocked on the front door. "Are they gone?"

"Yeah, they left about an hour ago."

"Was she happy? You know, laughing, or talking a lot?"

"I don't know, Ike, I was upstairs. I didn't listen. I didn't watch."

"You know it's very possible she might not have a good time," Ike added hurriedly. "Litchfield can be a real jerk." He shadow-boxed for a brief second. "You know that, right?"

DJ was still holding the front door open. "Yeah, I know that. Want to go somewhere?"

"How about Van Velsor's?" Ike answered. "Who knows, they might even come in there." He looked up at DJ, his lips dry and faint blue. "What do you think?"

"Yeah, okay, we could do that." DJ stepped outside and closed the door behind him.

The two walked into town and ran into Leslie leaving the drugstore. "Hi, DJ, Ike. Where're you headed?"

"Van Velsor's," Ike answered. "Feel like coming along?"

Leslie looked at DJ. "Van Velsor's? I don't know." She

glanced at her watch. "I'm not doing anything, I guess. Do you mind me tagging along, DJ?"

He was surprised at Ike's invitation, but felt detached from her. It didn't matter. "Okay," he said, "why not."

Leslie nodded. "If you really don't mind."

When the three walked into Van Velsor's, most of the booths were taken. The weekend of the Fourth of July was always busy.

DJ knew that Herman had been furious at Patty's request to leave early, but after some prodding from Greta, he relented.

Greta was so involved with checkers solitaire—playing both red and black by rotating the board after each move—she didn't notice DJ as he walked in. He stopped next to her. "Who's going to win this one?"

Greta glanced up and smiled. "Oh, dear boy, each team has the intelligence of a duck. They'll probably both lose."

Ike, Leslie, and DJ sat in the last empty booth near the rear of the coffee shop, Ike next to DJ, facing the door.

DJ stood and walked over to the jukebox and selected several tunes, then back in the booth, he yawned and stretched. After listening to Leslie ramble on for awhile, and with his Coke finished, he announced, "Seems like it's getting to be that time to head—"

Ike tapped his shoulder. "They're here."

"Who's here?" Leslie asked.

DJ glanced at the front door in time to see Patty and Bobby walk in. Both appeared despondent. Patty's arms crossed her chest as she stared at the floor and slid into a front booth that had just been vacated. Bobby sat opposite her facing the street.

"Don't tell me Bobby's going out with your sister," Leslie said, following Ike's gaze. Her face flushed. "I can't believe he would embarrass me that way."

"They're not talking," Ike noticed immediately. "They're not happy. Look at that, Patty's had a bad time." He looked triumphantly at Leslie, then at DJ. "I told you it wouldn't work."

DJ glanced at the two. Ike was right, they weren't talking. Patty was looking downward at the table. The cotton cardigan she had bought for the evening hung limply off her shoulders.

"I think something's wrong," Ike said.

Using the back of her left forefinger, Patty brushed under her eye.

"Ah, I don't think there's anything wrong," DJ replied as the jukebox clunked to silence. He could see Bobby's shoulders adjusting, his head tilting to the right. The menus were still on the side of the table.

With the jukebox quiet, only the buzz of conversation filled the coffee shop.

"So that's what I'm talking about! Get it?"

DJ heard Bobby's voice.

"Did you hear Bobby say something?" Ike asked.

"I'll tell you where you get off. And don't tell me what to do." Bobby's voice was louder, more belligerent. He seemed unaware the music had stopped.

"Sounds like he's losing his temper again," Leslie seethed. "We just barely broke up and he dares to show up with someone else. What a bastard."

Patty continued to stare at the table, and again lifted her forefinger to brush under her eye.

"Don't act like you're something special." Bobby picked up the menus, then slammed them down on the table. "Give me a break, huh."

Patty didn't move. DJ was frozen.

As more people became aware of the commotion up front, the conversation in the coffee shop grew quiet.

Bobby reached across the table and grabbed Patty's cardigan, ripping it from her shoulders, throwing it on the seat next to her. "I asked you once, 'Who do you think you are?' I can get Canova, and you give me a hard time. Grow up." He reached over and grabbed the cardigan again, this time throwing it on the floor.

Ike was on his feet, slowly shuffling to their booth. Reaching

Bobby's back, he tapped him on the shoulder. Without turning to see who was behind him, Bobby savagely shoved Ike away, sending him sprawling backward on to the seat of his pants, then his back. Ike tried to rise, then lay still, his head on the black and white linoleum floor, his mouth open.

"You shouldn't have done that," Patty screamed as she rushed toward Ike.

DJ jumped up and charged past his sister, then with a strength he didn't know he possessed, slammed Bobby into a full nelson and wrestled him toward the front of the store.

"Let me go," Bobby bellowed, struggling violently against the control hold DJ had him locked in.

"What's that, Litchfield? I can't hear you?" DJ shouted, as he forced Bobby toward the front door. "What's that, what're you saying, I can't hear you? I can't hear you, Litchfield." Tightening his grasp, he smashed Bobby's face into the plate glass front door using the golden boy's nose as the battering ram.

Once outside, DJ released Bobby with a violent shove, sending him tumbling into the street.

"You're a dead man, Elders," Bobby cried, jumping to his feet, blood streaming from his nose. Wildly swinging his fists, he charged DJ, but was intercepted by Herman who had been in the backroom until he heard the commotion.

Clamping Bobby's arms to his sides, Herman said, "Go home, Bobby. Have your father call me. I don't want you around here until I've spoken with him. And maybe not even then."

Wild with rage, Bobby ripped his arms free and made another lunge at DJ. Herman grabbed him again.

"I told you to go home, Bobby," Herman said, his voice tense. "Next step is Thor."

As he pushed Herman away, Bobby glared at DJ, then abruptly turned and jumped into the Impala, slamming the door. "You're all a bunch of hick town, lowlife fucking losers," he yelled, "a bunch of fucking losers." He started the engine, screeched out of the parking space and sped away down Main Street.

Herman and DJ stood and waited until the car was out of sight before going inside.

Patty and Greta were kneeling next to Ike, who was conscious.

"I've called an ambulance," Greta said to Herman. As she spoke, a siren echoed in the distance.

DJ picked up Patty's sweater as Herman moved to kneel next to Ike.

Leslie walked out the door, her eyes cast downward.

Minutes later, after the emergency medical crew had arrived and carted Ike away, Greta stood with her arm around Patty's shoulders. "Let's talk tomorrow."

Patty nodded.

Both were trembling.

"It's been a difficult night for everyone," Herman said. "DJ, you only have to come in fifteen minutes early tomorrow. Sleep in. Enjoy."

DJ looked blankly at Herman. "Okay."

"But, if you feel like it, and you're already up, earlier than that wouldn't hurt." He slapped him on the back.

"Would you like to stay here a while longer?" Greta asked Patty.

"Thank you, no," DJ answered for both of them as the two headed for the door. "Patty and I should go. Bye, Greta. Bye, Herman."

CHAPTER 44

"I don't think I'm ready to head home," Patty said.

The two walked to the town green and sat on a bench in the dark.

"Bobby wanted me to do things that I didn't want to do..." Her voice trailed off.

"Here, Patty, put your sweater on," DJ said, handing her the cardigan. When she made no attempt to take it, he placed it over her shoulders.

Two or three cars drove by, bumper to bumper, as if connected, before the street was silent again.

"I told him I wouldn't, and he kept pushing me, leaning on me, saying I had to. He was drinking too. He was very rough with me, DJ. He was stronger than I was."

DJ could feel his anger rising. He felt inadequate and responsible for Patty, responsible for Ike, and increasingly furious with himself for his own failure to intercept Bobby's actions.

"He tried to unbutton my blouse, then he pushed me down in the front se-"

"I know, Patty, I know," DJ interrupted. "I know." He couldn't bear the details.

"I didn't know what to do and I finally got away. He chased me in the car, and then," Patty shook her head, "we ended up in Van Velsor's." She looked at DJ, "I don't understand why he would do that, go to Van Velsor's, I mean, after what happened."

DJ slowly shook his head. "I don't know, Patty."

"Did I make him behave the way he did? I thought we were going to drive to Jones Beach." She slowly slid her arms into the cardigan and wept silently, gently, the fingers of one hand covering both eyes.

DJ reached across and put his arm around her shoulders.

He began to float. From overhead, hovering in the warm summer breeze, he could see the two of them sitting on the bench in the dark, and if he had not known they were brother and sister, he would have thought they were lovers attempting to resolve a mutual difference that was destroying them.

The scene slowly changed to the same park bench, only years before when the brother and sister were children in shorts playing in the sand. Monty sat and talked with their mother, who was young and vibrant in her blue dress.

How he wished she was alive for the nearly-grown siblings sitting in the dark, not just for the children in the sand. How he wished she would enclose Patty in her arms, taking responsibility for her, comforting her, guiding her.

How he wished she would set him free.

"DJ, DJ."

He was staring at the boulder with the copper plaque honoring the World War II and Korean War veterans. The angle of the streetlight turned the letters into dark and forbidding crevasses.

"We should go," Patty said, as she blotted beneath her eyes with a tissue. "It's getting late. I know Herman said you only have to be a little early, but tomorrow's the Fourth and he'll want you there earlier than that."

"Are you all right?" DJ's arm still rested on her shoulder.

"Am I all right?" Patty glanced away, back toward Main Street. "No," she answered. "No, I don't think I'm all right." She looked directly at her brother, resigned. "And I don't think Ike is either."

"Ike will forgive you," DJ said.

"I did everything very badly with him, didn't I?"

DJ slowly nodded. "I think so."

"I'm never sure what to do."

DJ nodded again. "I know."

Patty buttoned the front of her sweater, then sat for a moment before rising. "We ought to go," she said. "I need to call the hospital and see how Ike is."

CHAPTER 45

As they approached the front of their house, Patty noticed the kitchen light was on. "He usually turns that off before he lands in the recliner."

"He's getting worse," DJ responded. "He probably forgot. I don't think he remembers anything anymore."

When DJ and Patty entered the house, Dale was sitting at the kitchen table. He rose, beer glass in hand, entered the hallway and sat on the steps leading up to DJ's room. "I had a call from Rob Litchfield, Bobby's father. What happened, Patty?" he asked.

Patty unbuttoned her cardigan and folded it tentatively over her arm. "What did he say?"

"Don't worry about what he said, I want to hear what you have to say."

"Dad," DJ interrupted, "this is really embarrassing for Pat—"

"Let me decide that," Dale countered. He sipped from his beer glass. "I just want to know what happened."

Patty stared at the floor. DJ could see her begin to tremble again. "It's very uncomfortable," she said. "Could we just not

262 | Ted M. Alexander

talk about it? At least tonight?" She slowly lifted her eyes to meet Dale's. "Would that be okay?"

"I don't think so, Patty," Dale answered. "That's not the way things are done. In a court of law we don't say something is uncomfortable and postpone it until the next day. That's what cowards do, cowards and those who are guilty."

"Dad, for God's sake, Patty's neither one. It's just been a bad night an—"

"Shut up, DJ." He turned so that he was staring away from Patty—impartially away—as he spoke. "Now tell me. I want to hear what happened."

Patty moved her fingers, rubbing the nail of one with the nail of another as she stood in front of him. "Okay," she said slowly, and then, in a quiet voice, told her father of the incidents of the entire evening—Bobby's aggressiveness, her sense of being nearly raped, her running from him in desperation to get away—many details she had omitted from DJ, ugly aspects of a violent encounter that began with surprise and ended with terror. When she was finished, tears were streaming down her cheeks again. Cautiously, Patty sat down next to her father on the stairs.

Dale stared away into the distance.

"I didn't know what to do, and then he caught up with me and said he would leave me alone, that we could go to Van Velsor's as if nothing had happened, as long as I didn't tell. He promised. I didn't know where we were—some place in the woods—and I didn't dare not get in the car. It was dark, and I was scared, so I did what he said. And he left me alone, and we did go to Van Velsor's like he promised."

"That's where the fight broke out?" Dale asked.

"Yeah, that's exactly where it happened," DJ said. "And he's lucky somebody didn't kill him."

Patty rested the side of her face on her father's knee. "I didn't know what to do. All I could think of was to run." Her tears left dark spots on the leg of his olive green trousers.

Dale drained the rest of the beer in his glass. "Well, that's not the story that was told to me."

DJ watched his father's face.

"What do you mean?"Patty asked, raising her cheek from his knee. "That's what happened."

"The way Bobby told it to his father was that you came on to him pretty strong. The two of you were supposed to drive to Jones Beach, but you wanted to do something else. He said that it was your idea to, how do you say it, 'go parking.' You thought that way you could keep him as a boyfriend."

"Oh, please," DJ said, his voice rising in disgust.

Patty studied her father. "You don't believe that, do you?"

"Quite honestly, I don't know what to believe, Patty. Rob's an outstanding attorney in this town, with an excellent reputation and known for his integrity. Bobby was class president and valedictorian. Never has had a problem before and now suddenly, out of the blue, this? Doesn't add up."

"What doesn't add up?" DJ said, his voice rising. "She told you what happened. What's the matter with you? What she says happened is what happened. Why don't you act like her father for a change?"

"I wouldn't travel in that direction if I were you," Dale said, staring at his son.

"But what I told you is the truth," Patty said. "I couldn't make it up if I wanted to."

"Look, Patty," Dale said, his voice taking a conciliatory tone, "the truth can be stretched and interpreted in any number of ways. Maybe you didn't know what you were doing. Maybe you were sending signals, unconscious signals to Bobby."

"But, I wasn't," Patty said, "I thought we were going to the beach. All I did was get in the car."

"I'm sure that's what you thought, but you probably got close to him, or—"

"What the hell is this, the third degree?" DJ took a step forward. "Look, she told you what happened. Whose side are you on?"

Dale visibly restrained himself before responding. "It's

not a question of sides, it's a question of the truth."

"Well, you got the truth! Right before your very eyes, you got the truth. Now leave her alone." The rage was bubbling, churning so close to the surface DJ could taste the bile rising in the back of his throat. "That's the whole truth, the whole damned truth! You got it? You finally got it? Huh?"

After gently placing his glass on the stair, Dale slowly got to his feet and walked toward DJ. Without breaking stride, in a sweeping motion, he grabbed his son's throat and one leg, then jerking him off the ground, heaved him ten feet through the air. DJ's lower back smashed against the arm of the recliner, reverse jackknifing him before he crashed to the floor. Sitting, dazed, one leg twisted under the other, he stared up at his father.

Patty lurched toward DJ and knelt, tears streaming down her cheeks,

Dale walked into the kitchen and took a bottle of beer from the refrigerator.

"I'm okay," DJ said to Patty. "Just let me sit here for a couple of minutes." He moved both of his legs, pulling one from beneath the other. "Honest, I'm okay."

Returning to the hallway, Dale peered intently at DJ. "Next time it'll be worse." He ran his hand across the top of his head. "But maybe we'll all get lucky, you'll get smart, and there won't have to be a next time."

Pressing a hand against DJ's knee to right herself, Patty slowly rose and approached her father. "You do believe me, don't you?" she whispered. Reaching out and placing her arms around Dale's neck, resting her head against his chest, she said, "Tell me you believe me. Please." Her voice had been reduced to the singsong of a child's. "Please."

Dale's arms hung awkwardly at his sides, one hand holding a beer bottle. "Instead of worrying about what I think, why don't—"

"Please . . ."

". . . you do something to better yourself, something to

make me proud, something that will make you appealing, or smart enough to attract someone like Bobby instead—"

"Please . . ." Patty's hands began to loosen from Dale's neck as her face turned toward the floor.

". . .instead of having to show off your physical assets to get attention and . . ."

As Dale continued, Patty slid from his chest, down across his side, until her arms were wrapped around his knee. DJ watched, his back against the recliner, until his father shook his leg loose and walked back into the kitchen, screeching the legs of the chair against the floor as he seated himself at the table. After a minute had passed, he called, "You two have never understood that I can't be both a father and mother to you. It's damn difficult enough just being a father." The legs of the chair scraped along the floor again. "It wasn't my fault she died, and it's about time both of you grew up and faced the facts of life. They may not be pretty, but they're real."

DJ rose slowly from the floor, his lower back sore and tingling. He leaned over and helped Patty to her feet. As she stood next to him, her eyes swollen, he placed his arms around her. She rested her head against his shoulder. "It'll be fine," he whispered, after a moment had passed. "And the Christmas spirit isn't that far away."

"I know," Patty murmured, patting his arm with two fingers. "I know."

CHAPTER 46

During his break at Van Velsor's Sunday morning, DJ leaned on the counter and read an article from the *New York Times* about the escalating war in Vietnam. Defense Secretary McNamara had announced eight battalions were being added to the 173rd Airborne Brigade and the Third Marine Division, bringing the total US forces to eighty thousand, with a construction and supply program underway to eventually accommodate as many as a quarter of a million men.

DJ looked over at Herman who was behind the counter pouring a cup of coffee. "What's going on in Vietnam?" he called.

Herman looked up briefly. "We're going to war. Unofficially." He shook his head. "I've seen it all before, DJ, and we should be very cautious."

Vietnam was closer then ever to Hardscrabble. Artie, the emotionally battered eyewitness to the misery, now at home and on exhibition, was a living testament that the battles were genuine.

DJ rose from the counter and crossed to the bathroom at the back of the coffee shop. His back ached from landing against the Barcalounger the night before, but aside from a bruise on his knee, it was the only physical damage.

Returning to the front of the coffee shop, he stood at the window and watched as a town employee walked behind a flatbed stacked with rolled-up, six-foot American flags. As the truck crept down Main Street, the worker reached into the back, then planted flags in the metal holders attached to the parking meters and telephone poles. When the truck reached the end of the street and creaked out of sight around the corner, the sun tumbled down on an empty town ablaze with rippling red, white and blue.

Herman stood behind DJ. "Don't worry about Vietnam. When you go to college or are married, you don't have to go to war."

"Are you sure?" DJ asked, looking up at Herman.

Herman shrugged. "Unless everything gets bigger than it's supposed to."

∞

After leaving Van Velsor's, DJ walked up the street toward home. From a distance, Ike was a speck sitting next to his house. As he drew closer, DJ could see he was resting in a rusted, green-and-yellow plastic woven lawn chair, an army blanket tucked over his lap.

"When did you get home?" DJ asked as he reached Ike's side.

"They let me out this morning."

"Are you all right? When Patty called last night they said you were okay, but right now you don't look so hot." DJ sat down on the grass next to the chair.

"I'm the same." Ike shifted slightly.

DJ nodded.

"How's Patty doing?"

DJ spread his fingers through the grass. "I haven't seen her today. Last night she was pretty upset. I guess she'll be okay."

Ike sat quietly for a few moments, his hands folded on his lap. "That's good," he finally said. "I'm glad she'll be okay."

Down the block, Leslie's father emerged from his front door, coffee cup in hand, and placed the American flag in its holder next to the mailbox. He sipped from the cup, stretched and returned to the house.

"You going to the Fireama?" DJ asked.

"What time?"

DJ looked at his watch. "About an hour. I'll stop by when I'm ready if you want."

"I tell you, DJ," Ike said, "maybe I'll meet you down there later. I'm not sure my mother would let me go anyway after last night."

"Really?" DJ asked.

"I think so. I'm going to rest here a little bit first. I'm still kind of shook up."

DJ stared briefly at Ike. "Okay. I'll be there. You'll be able to find me—either near Van Velsor's or across from the Rock. Figure I'll stay through the fireworks anyway." He pushed himself to his feet.

"Right," Ike said.

"You sure you don't want me to stop by before I head into town?"

Ike nodded. "I'm sure." He tucked his hands under the blanket.

"Okay. I'll see you later." DJ crossed to the sidewalk and headed toward his house.

"You know what I wish?" Ike suddenly called.

DJ turned. "No, what's that?"

"I wish," Ike answered, "that just once, when we swam the window, I didn't have to be King Neptune."

DJ stood and tugged at his shirt collar, then nodded. "I know that," he said to himself before taking another step. "I've known that forever."

CHAPTER 47

Hardscrabble's July 4th Fireama was considered the spectacle of the year. By the time DJ returned to town, Main Street had been closed off to all traffic except for the parade. Merchants were in the midst of gala sidewalk sales and fly-by-night vendors in tricornered caps rolled carts loaded with souvenirs and cotton candy up and down the street. The firehouse had already turned into a wild keg party for the volunteer firemen, and crowds swarmed the downtown blocks as two bands played continually at each end of Main Street.

Settling on the curb in front of Van Velsor's, DJ remembered lying with Leslie on the football field last year. As he held her hand they stared up at the whistling skyrockets that flared into sunflowers before evaporating into sonic booms that rocked the pit of his stomach.

During the winter, he had believed that Carlyn and he would be doing the same thing—lying in the dark, shoulder to shoulder, whispering back and forth. After her bedroom, the motels, and the department store's back rooms, he'd never thought that it would be different.

270 Ted M. Alexander

From his seat on the curb, he scanned the crowd to see if she might be there, maybe looking for him. But no, mostly just families, high school kids running together, and men in military uniforms looking for their assigned meeting points.

When the parade began, as town judge and self-appointed marshal, Dale led the procession. Attired in blue suit accented by a red, white and blue necktie, he walked directly behind the color guard, waving and smiling at the crowds that lined both sides of Main Street. From the look of pleasure on his face, DJ might have thought the Christmas spirit had arrived in July, but he knew his father was being especially personable because it was an election year.

Behind Dale, local dignitaries waved from the back seats of convertibles and World War II vets marched by, their medals reflecting the sun's rays, while the Hardscrabble High School band played, "On, Brave Old Army Team."

DJ stood and walked north on Main Street, then watched the rest of the parade from a vantage point opposite the Jailhouse Rock. When the fire trucks bringing up the rear headed out of town and the crowds moved back toward the heart of the business district, DJ remained behind, leaning against a parking meter.

"DJ-J-J-J," Maynard said as he tapped him on the shoulder. "Bet you thought I was missing in action." He was holding hands with Frannie.

"Hey," DJ said, his spirits rising.

"Where is everybody?" Maynard looked around, then without waiting for an answer, said, "We're going to get something to eat. Come on."

DJ followed Maynard and Frannie through the crowds of people back into the center of town. They stopped opposite the high school where a vendor was cooking sausages on a colossal, futuristic chrome grill.

"I'm buying," Maynard said, turning and pushing his way through the swarms of people. He returned ten minutes later with three greasy packages.

After they finished eating, Frannie excused herself, looking for a restroom.

Once she was gone, DJ said, "I didn't know Frannie and you were back together. I thought you were still living with your parents."

Maynard wiped his mouth with the greasy wax paper the sausage had been wrapped in. "When you're married, you're always kind of together."

"Oh." DJ thought that through. "When did 'kind of together' happen?"

Maynard crumpled up the wax paper and pushed it into his pocket. "Ah, I don't know, we got together in the past couple of days, I guess. I just got to feeling sorry for her. You know, she didn't do this thing all by herself. I figured I had better assume some responsibility too." He pushed his glasses back up to the bridge of his nose and smiled sheepishly. "Know what I mean?"

DJ had never known Maynard to assume responsibility for one iota of anything in the history of civilization. "Not exactly," he replied.

Maynard hesitated and tapped his foot in the sand by the curb. "Did you see Artie, now that he's home from Vietnam? That's what I mean."

"I don't get it."

"I saw him yesterday walking down the street talking to himself. He's cracked! Totally gone. And that's my alternative. Get a divorce, go to Vietnam and become an Artie—if I'm lucky that is—or stay at home, have sex maybe once a month, and work at D'Aloisio Mills across town." Maynard ran his hand across his forehead, pushing his hair to the side. "I mean, what would you do? I already tried running away and that doesn't work. I never was a genius, but you don't have to be one to figure out the way to go."

"I don't know what you're talking about. We're going to college together. That keeps us out of Vietnam."

Maynard shrugged. "Yeah, well, I've been meaning to

tell you—I thought I was going to college." He looked down, then shook his head. "I can't, DJ. No money, got a kid on the way. Parents aren't going to pay for everything. I don't have a choice."

"Can't you get a loan or something?"

"Nah, and to tell you the truth, I never did want to go very much in the first place. Just kind of thought I had to." He licked his lips. "What I want is to have some real money."

DJ looked away.

Maynard grabbed him by his shoulders. "Hey, buddy, it's not so bad. We can still have some fun. Just because I'm married doesn't mean I can't fool around. Know what I mean? That goes without saying, huh?"

"Look who I found," Frannie said, arriving with Greta and Patty. "We met on the line to the ladies room."

"Ah, yes, the Two Musketeers," Greta said. "Mr. Maynard, of course, lest I ever forget, and how are you, dear boy?" She squinted at DJ.

"Good, Greta," DJ answered. "How about you, Patty? I didn't see you this morning. Are you okay?"

"I'm better, DJ," she said. "Greta always figures out a way to cheer me up. And Herman let me take tonight off."

DJ studied her and wasn't convinced. She couldn't make eye contact.

In the background, from up the block, a roaring interpretation of "Danny Boy" was in the process of being rendered en masse by the Fire Department. As the firemen approached the finale, lowering their volume two decibels and sliding into the sentimental "Oh, Danny boy, oh, Danny boy, I love you so," DJ could feel goose bumps spring up along his shoulders. The sweet final note was immediately followed by prehistoric bellows and the crashing together of beer mugs.

"We're going over to the football field to get a spot for the fireworks," Patty said. "Want to come along?"

The five crossed the street, then walked behind the high school and sat on the grass of the nearly empty football field.

Gradually, they were joined by hundreds of others. As the sky slowly grew darker and the crowd denser, voices grew muted as all eyes focused overhead.

When the first skyrockets flared, DJ unsuccessfully tried to stare beyond them into the blackness. For ten minutes on his back he watched as the kaleidoscope tugged at him, then growing dizzy and fearful of his unsteadiness, he slowly let himself rise, float, and become part of the power. In the dark sky, as the glittering gold rockets crashed around him, over him, beyond him, he recognized Carlyn's Shalimar perfume, and when he whirled with the iridescent streamers, he rested his lips on the nape of her neck, tasting the salt of her skin, then ran his hand along her thigh, pulling her closer to him. Twisted and flushed between her sheets, his fingers ran across her breasts while his eyes memorized her face.

And Carlyn was there, below. With each flash of color she was illuminated, her arms around Bobby's neck, her body against his. Then she was walking from the school to the lake behind the football field, her arm around his waist, her hand tucked in his rear pocket. And she kissed him, her back against a fence, her hands slipping through his blonde hair, the heel of her foot wrapped around his calf, drawing him inward.

DJ closed his eyes, and when he reopened them, he was staring upward again, watching the kaleidoscope flare and shatter, then unravel. Rising unsteadily to his feet, DJ said, "I'll see you later," and walked through the crowds out past the goalposts. As he approached the lake, he looked closely, but couldn't see Carlyn or Bobby, then moving back past the football field and the side of the school building, he headed up Main Street.

Ten minutes later, as he approached the steps to his house, he saw the empty lawn chair sitting next to Ike's front porch. He walked over and folded it, then placed it against the front steps before returning and entering his own home. The kitchen light was out and he was certain his father was already sleeping so he closed the door quietly.

"How did I look in the parade today?" Dale asked from the kitchen.

"Sorry, I didn't know you were up. Light's off." DJ reached inside the doorway and turned on the wall switch.

"I tried to look damn good. Word has it the Liberty Party is eying me for a state judgeship. All I need is their support and I'm elected. Not bad, huh?"

"That would be good, Dad," DJ said.

"Have a beer," Dale said. "Why aren't you watching the fireworks?"

"Didn't feel like it." He grimaced as he took a sudden step and felt a jolt of pain in his lower back.

Dale frowned. "What's happened to you? Did you hurt yourself?"

DJ stared at his father. "Yeah, you know that."

"I do? What happened?" Dale turned to look at the bottle of beer as he emptied it into his glass.

DJ continued to stare. "Last night, Dad, you know what happened."

"I was here all night, son, I wasn't with you. I have no idea."

"You don't?"

"Of course I don't. This is a ridiculous conversation. What's important is your physical condition."

"I'm all right." DJ ran his finger across the molding on the doorway. "Dad, could I borrow the car for a little while?"

His father glanced at his watch, then scrutinized DJ. "I guess so. You haven't been drinking, have you? I won't allow drinking and driving."

"No," DJ answered, "not at all."

Dale slid the keys across the table. "Go on, have some fun." He ran his hand along the back of his head. "How about me being a state judge, huh?" He stood, walked to the refrigerator, opened the door and took out a beer bottle. "Wouldn't that just be about the greatest thing you ever heard of?" He reached into the cupboard over the sink and took down a bottle of scotch. "Hell, I feel like celebrating. Can't blame me now, can you?"

"Nope, I can't," DJ answered, taking the keys as he left the house. Under his breath, he added, "And I'd never vote for you, that's for sure."

CHAPTER 48

DJ avoided town on his way to Amity, then approaching Carlyn's street, apprehensive that he would see Bobby's Impala, he slowed to a crawl before making the turn. As he passed her house, he saw no cars at all—even her Mustang was missing from the driveway. After circling the block, he drove slowly past again, but still saw nothing, only the glare of the kitchen night light reflecting into the front room.

For the next hour, DJ drove aimlessly around Hardscrabble and by the time he returned home, his father was asleep in the bedroom.

DJ took a beer from the refrigerator and returned to the living room. He checked the *TV Guide* and saw that because it was the Fourth of July, Million Dollar Movie was showing *The Best Years of Our Lives.* After he clicked on the television, he settled back in the BarcaLounger, the footrest lifting his feet into the air. About the time Myrna Loy began escorting an increasingly intoxicated Fredric March around town, DJ was fully relaxed. When an Anacin commercial interrupted the movie, he walked to the kitchen for another beer, burying the empty bottle in the wastebasket so his father couldn't keep count.

He was settling in again when Patty arrived home. She closed the door behind her and walked into the living room. "It looks like you're becoming him," she said, staring at DJ and his bottle of beer.

"I'm not becoming him." He stared at his sister. "Are you okay?"

"I guess," Patty said looking away. "Greta and I went back to her apartment for a while after the fireworks. Then I just got tired and came home. Why did you leave early?"

"I don't know. Wasn't in the mood." DJ sipped from the beer bottle. "Feel like watching?" He nodded to the screen. "It's not bad for an old movie."

"I don't think so, DJ," Patty answered. "I'm just going to take a shower and go to bed. Try to sleep." She crossed to her bedroom and closed the door.

After the shower ended, DJ heard Patty walk into her bedroom and close the door quietly behind her. With the blue-white light from the TV encircling him, the house became silent except for the distant snoring of his father, the audio from the TV, and a couple of moths batting at the window screens.

When the movie ended as he always imagined his movie with Carlyn would end, arms wrapped around each other, DJ stood up and turned off the TV. After burying the empty beer bottle in the kitchen wastebasket, he walked to the bathroom, brushed his teeth and headed upstairs. Removing all his clothes to sleep naked, something he had never done before, even with Carlyn, he turned out the light and crawled under the sheet.

∞

At first, he thought he was on his front steps, listening to an approaching ice cream truck: a bell; no, a series of bells ringing, stopping and ringing again. Then as DJ opened his eyes and saw the morning light slipping into his room, he realized it was the phone he was hearing. The ringing persisted and DJ was about to go downstairs when he heard his father crashing through the living room on his way to the kitchen to pick up the receiver. "Who is it?" Dale asked, his voice dry and irritated. "What?" A long silence. "Are you sure?" The annoyance had disappeared and he was momentarily quiet. "Holy Mother of Christ," he said slowly. "Holy sweet Mother of Christ." Dale listened again for several seconds. "I'll be down. Give me ten minutes." He slammed the phone down.

DJ jumped from his bed. "Dad," he called from the top of the stairs, "who was that?"

"Thor," his father replied tersely as he continued through the living room. "The Litchfield boy's been murdered. They found him next to the lake behind the high school."

CHAPTER 49

DJ didn't attempt to go back to sleep and when Dale hadn't returned by seven o'clock, he took a shower, then knocked on Patty's door.

"DJ?" she called.

"Can I come in?"

"Sure." Patty was under the covers when he entered the room. Pushing her hair from her eyes, she sat up and rested the back of her head against the wall. She studied her brother. "What's up?"

"Dad got a call this morning." DJ hesitated. He wasn't sure how to proceed. "He said," DJ paused again, his voice wavering, "he said Bobby Litchfield was murdered last night. They found him next to the lake behind the high school."

Patty's eyes widened. "Are you serious?" She surveyed him, unsure. "You're not serious, are you?" She slowly covered her mouth with her hand. "My God, DJ, I can't believe it."

"Thor called Dad this morning. He's been gone since six o'clock."

Patty continued to study DJ, her face ashen. "You're not kidding. It's true?" Slowly shaking her head, she slid from beneath the covers. "Bobby's a liar and a creep, but that's insane—that couldn't happen." She rose to her feet. "Let me get dressed, then we should go into town. It must be true to get Dad out of bed at six o'clock in the morning."

DJ went outside and stood under the maple tree in front of the house.

Carlyn.

Returning to the front steps, he sat down and waited.

The Brooklyn cop. Now Bobby.

Carlyn.

He was afraid to think what he was thinking.

Carlyn.

"That's ridiculous," he said out loud, "totally ridic—"

"Let's go," Patty said, closing the front door behind her.

∞

It was seven-fifteen when Patty and DJ crossed the tracks on Main Street. Hardscrabble was in an uproar. Local and Nassau County police cars lined both sides of the street while pockets of men in suits or uniforms stood next to storefronts, writing on notepads, or talking into hand-held, two-way radios.

Patty and DJ walked down to Van Velsor's and saw Herman standing outside the shop talking with some locals. He saw them approach and excused himself from the men. "You two are all right?" he said, putting an arm around each of their shoulders. "You have to be very careful now with this incident. We don't know what's happening."

"Herman," Patty said, "what did happen?"

"I know very little," he replied, "except that Bobby Litchfield's body was found very early this morning next to the lake behind the high school. The police won't discuss any more details."

"Do they know who did it?" DJ asked. "They must have

clues."

"As I said, I know very little. Greta has just walked down to Town Hall to see if she can uncover any more information."

"I can't believe it," Patty said, her eyes wide. "How could something like this happen in Hardscrabble?"

"I want you both to be very careful," Herman repeated. "We'll have to be vigilant until we have more news."

"S'cuse me, Herman," an elderly man interrupted, sticking his head outside the door of the coffee shop. "Could I trouble you for a cup of tea."

"Of course," Herman answered. "Patty, you're working this afternoon?"

Patty nodded.

"I'll see you then." He turned and entered the coffee shop.

"Let's head down to the school and see what we can find out," DJ said.

They walked toward the end of Main Street, but couldn't get within a block of the high school before one of the local police stopped them. "Sorry, kids," he said, "restricted area. No one allowed except the detectives."

"Does anyone know what happened?" Patty asked.

"Local boy dead. Appears as if it's a homicide," the officer replied. "Crying shame too. I didn't know him, but people claimed he was an All-Star." He shrugged. "Haven't heard much else."

DJ and Patty turned and walked back to the village green, then sat on a bench facing the street. A TV station van arrived and three men climbed out, opened the rear doors, then started removing equipment.

The two watched the film crew place a long line of cameras, cords, and steel boxes on the sidewalk.

"Come on," DJ said, rising. "Let's go."

As they walked up Main Street, DJ looked back and saw his father working the policeman, slapping one on the back while he shook hands with others.

∞

At home, changing for work at Mertz Brothers, DJ pulled his pressed suit off the hanger. No dead-fish, low-tide smell. He descended the stairs tugging his tie around his neck. "I'll see you later, Patty. You working until closing tonight?"

"Yes," Patty responded from her bedroom. "Be careful."

"You too, I'm locking the door behind me. And make sure Herman drives you home."

∞

When DJ pulled into the employee parking lot, he caught a momentary glimpse of Carlyn walking into the store through the security entrance.

Cliff Collins was alone when DJ entered his office. He looked up from his desk, expressionless. "I'm going to use you in The Ivy League Shop today. Pick up your cash and register key."

"You've heard?" DJ asked.

Cliff placed the papers on his desk. "Yeah, I have. And I'm as stunned as the next guy. Just makes no sense. A great kid like that." He shook his head. "Makes no sense."

As the morning dragged on, when DJ spoke with a friendly customer, he asked if they had heard anything new about the murder over in Hardscrabble. He got no information and a couple of strange looks.

Around noon, with The Ivy League Shop empty, DJ stood at the cash register organizing the charge slips.

"DJ?"

He looked up, then placed the slips on the top of the register drawer. "Hi, Carlyn."

"I want you to know that I'm sorry about the other night.

You know, what happened in the car. Maybe we should talk some more."

"What would we talk about that you haven't already said?" He was surprised at the boldness of his words.

Carlyn stepped closer and ran the tip of her finger across the back of one of his hands. "I think there's a lot we haven't said. Maybe some things I should have been more honest about at the beginning. We should be together. We owe that to each other."

"And what about Bobby, Carlyn?"

She moved her hand across her breast so that it rested on her opposite shoulder. "I don't know what to say. I don't know how to respond, DJ. I have no idea what happened to Bobby, or how anyone could have done such a horrible thing." She stared at him. "I truly don't."

DJ wanted to place his arm around her waist, to bring her closer so that her body rested against his. Instead he stared back.

"Could we meet tonight?" A smile barely touched the corners of her mouth, and she dropped her eyes. "Maybe, begin again."

DJ tapped the charge slips on the counter and looked away. "I don't know, Carlyn."

"We have to, DJ. We really have to be together." She inched closer. "This whole thing with Bobby is so upsetting to me and I need to be with you."

"It just doesn't seem right."

"We have to." She placed her hand over his. "DJ, we have to be together."

It had been weeks since DJ had noticed dark half-circles under his own eyes, but they were clearly present under Carlyn's; shadows through skin as translucent as Ike's.

But it wasn't the half-circles or her overall appearance being just a degree off that disturbed DJ the most. Instead, it was Carlyn's subtle change of demeanor, her sudden urgency to be with him that triggered a remote alarm. She had always been a tease, and the aggressor, but nothing they had ever done together had been out of necessity or a result of a demand.

It wasn't any part of the Carlyn he knew.

Or trusted.

Moving his hand from Carlyn's, then tucking the charge receipts back into the register drawer, he said, "I don't think so, Carlyn."

"You don't think so?" Her tongue ran quickly across her lips. "Why don't you think so?"

DJ placed his fingers on the cool steel of the cash register. "It's not good right now. I don't know, it's just not good." He closed the register drawer, then looked back at her. "I don't know why."

Carlyn adjusted her blouse, straightening the sleeves, then abruptly turned and walked to the edge of The Ivy League Shop's carpeting before pivoting by the tennis sweaters and facing him. "You'll think it's a good idea again," she said. "One way or the other, it'll be a good idea again. It was before and it will be again."

DJ stood, unmoving, listening to the sound of Carlyn's high heels clicking away through the main corridor of the store.

CHAPTER 50

After six o'clock, DJ closed out his register and left Mertz Brothers. He climbed into the Falcon, started the engine and switched on the radio, then headed home. The news offered nothing new concerning the homicide in Hardscrabble except that Nassau County had assigned five detectives to the case full-time.

Twenty minutes later, as he drove up Jackson Road toward his house, DJ noticed small pockets of neighbors standing on the sidewalks. Two or three here, four there, a couple more standing in front of the O'Reilly house. After easing the car into the garage, he closed the door and walked down to the sidewalk. "What's going on?" he asked Leslie's father, who was standing near the driveway.

"The ambulance just took Ike," he said as he slid his hand across the smudged anchor tattoo on his forearm. "About fifteen minutes ago. Maybe twenty."

DJ shook his head. "Not again. Ike never gets a break. He just got back from the hospital yesterday. "What did they say?"

Leslie's father lit a Camel and exhaled through his nose and mouth, then hung a thumb through the strap of his undershirt.

"What they said, DJ, was that he's gone."

"I know, but did they say how long they would keep him this time?"

Leslie's father ran a sun-scraped hand across his brow. "I wasn't clear, I guess. He's gone for good, son. He's dead. They took him away fifteen or twenty minutes ago." He flicked an ash onto the sidewalk. "I know he was a friend of yours so I'm sorry it turns out I have to be the one to tell you."

DJ dropped his head and stared down at an anthill by the root of the maple tree. The ants went in and out, scurrying from one place to another. Up the hill carrying crumbs, down the hill empty-handed. Never stopping. Never looking forward. Never looking back. DJ raised his head and faced Leslie's father. As he stared, he could feel his face contorting, his eyes blinking wildly, as if he too was emerging from the black ant tunnel into the daylight. "Is that the truth that he's dead?"

"I saw the body slumped over," Leslie's father said, pointing to the lawn chair next to the O'Reilly house. The army blanket was next to it on the grass. "The technicians put Ike on a stretcher, covered him with a sheet, and took him away in the ambulance." He exhaled through his nose and mouth again. "And from what other people have been saying, it was close to a miracle that he survived this long."

DJ took off his suit jacket and hung it over his shoulder. "Maybe so," he said finally before walking halfway up his front steps and sitting down, stretching his jacket across his knees.

He watched as the clumps of neighbors gradually drifted apart and returned to their pastel Cape Cods, murmuring, touching, glancing back over their shoulders.

Leslie's father waved as he walked back down to his house. "Sorry, son," he called.

Across the street, from an open kitchen window, DJ could hear pots being rattled in the sink as cars drove up and down the block, braking at the stop sign—strangers, alive and unaware that his best friend, Ike O'Reilly was dead.

∞

Later, in the dusk, DJ rose from the steps and walked over to the O'Reilly patch of front lawn. He folded the aluminum chair, leaned it against the house, then returned to the same spot and picked up the blanket, folding that too. Beneath the blanket on the ground, nearly invisible in the enveloping dark, was a Bible. DJ reached for it, and was about to walk over and place it next to the chair when he decided to see if any pages had been dog-eared, to try and discover where Ike's mind had been in his last few minutes on earth. He opened the book, but instead of seeing the biblical text, in a hollowed-out space in the New Testament, he discovered a paperback copy of *Lady Chatterley's Lover.*

As he flipped through the pages of the book, he made no further attempt to retrace Ike's thought waves. Instead, in what he thought would be an act of kindness for his departed friend, he ripped all the pages from the Bible and stuffed them, along with the paperback, into the front of his shirt. He left the Bible's front and back covers on the grass, then walked to his front steps, assured that the final memory of Ike in Hardscrabble would remain sanctified and undiminished.

His own house was empty. He was certain his father was still in town, working the crowds, redefining himself as the critical local leader, tireless and decisive in the midst of an unprecedented crisis.

DJ placed a Marty Robbins album on the turntable in his room. He returned to the kitchen and listened as the faraway singer became an echo from a cave's darkness; a moan spiraling across the desert; a coyote's howl under pinpoint stars.

DJ took Lady Chatterley and the remaining Bible pages and buried them under the empties in the wastebasket, then sat at the kitchen table in the dark. With Ike. Left, right, up, down, it was all about Ike. Little, pale Ike, who could barely walk and scarcely breathe, had formulated a minimalist life plan to repair watches. He would spend his hours and days sitting quietly using tiny tools and magnifying lenses, chatting with customers, listening to the radio.

And somewhere along the way his plan included Patty by his side.

DJ had harbored similar dreams with Carlyn—the only difference was that he was slumped down in a darkened kitchen next to a refrigerator, alive, and Ike, Ike, the watch repairman with the defective heart, was on his back in a refrigerator, paler than pale and newly dead.

The cars outside passed the house, their headlight beams flashing across the kitchen window, the occupants oblivious, the ants continuing. None of them knew what had happened to Ike O'Reilly. And when most people would finally hear, they'd mumble a silent prayer for his salvation, then a heartfelt thanks they were still alive.

DJ placed his cheek on the side of the Formica table and felt the coolness seep into his skin. As he stared sideways at the wall, tears slid to the table creating shallow puddles.

Another car's headlights flashed through the kitchen exposing cracks in the plaster.

Maybe he had just grown too accustomed to Ike living, and unwisely assumed it would remain that way. Every day, since the first grade, he had awakened in the morning and traveled to school with him.

Perhaps he should have listened more closely to the doctor stories or believed his father years ago when he told him that Ike would never survive to twelve, much less eighteen.

DJ turned his face on the table and stared at the opposite wall.

The truth was that it wouldn't have mattered what anyone said. DJ had never accepted the fact that Ike was hopeless, that his early finish had been preordained.

And he had never been prepared for an ordinary day

in July when his own heart would be as broken as his best friend's.

CHAPTER 51

An hour later, leaving the house, a bottle of beer in his hand, DJ locked the front door behind him. A steady stream of ants carrying crumbs was moving in and out of the O'Reilly house and though DJ knew he should be one of them, he figured he could wait until tomorrow. By then he would be more composed, more restrained, more in control. And when Patty returned from work at Van Velsor's, he knew she would drop by for both of them.

As he descended the front steps, DJ realized he was heading to Greta's sanctuary of calm and beauty—a place where he could feel safe and cared for. A murderer on the loose concerned him, but he decided to go anyway. Moving slowly in the direction of her apartment, he looked carefully into shadows for any stranger lurking, waiting to attack. As he approached Greta's street, a squad car pulled up behind him, its bright lights suddenly illuminating the surrounding area.

"You all right, son?" a voice called.

DJ turned around, shielding his eyes with his hand. "I'm fine."

"That you, DJ?" the voice called. He was one of the local police, one of Thor's men.

"Yeah, that's right," DJ answered. "I'm headed over to Greta's."

The policeman lowered his high beams. "Well, you look out now. None of us knows what's going on around this town. Aren't even sure what we're looking for, but nobody can be too careful. Know what I mean?"

"I do," DJ answered.

"And don't be walking around the streets with an open beer bottle in your hand, otherwise I'll have to be telling Dale. Anyhow, it's against the law."

"Okay," DJ said, looking for a place to ditch the bottle.

"You started it, so you can finish it," the policeman continued, "but don't be doing it anymore." He began to raise the window and added, "Like I say, you be careful now." He sped away.

After dropping the empty beer bottle in an outside garbage can, DJ walked into the foyer of Greta's building and rang her doorbell.

Greta nodded quietly as she opened the door. "You must come in." The two walked to her living room. "Perhaps some sherry tonight?"

DJ nodded.

She hurried away to the kitchen, returning with two crystal cordial glasses. "Here," she said, extending her hand. "Now, you must sit."

"Thank you," DJ said, taking the glass before moving to one of the leather chairs.

"Some music, perhaps?" Greta asked.

"I guess so."

Greta sat, placed her glass on the table between them, and studied DJ. "Sometimes the silence is preferable," she responded. "Occasionally it makes things clearer, and perhaps that's what we need tonight. Clarity. I think we could all use that considering this terrible tragedy with Bobby."

"You heard about Ike?" DJ asked suddenly. He stared at the floor.

"No, dear boy, I've been in the apartment all afternoon. What about Ike?"

DJ sipped the sherry, but could barely taste it, barely swallow. "He died today." His voice cracked. "He's gone too."

Greta looked at him, unblinking. "That can't be true."

Guarding his loss, locking in his despair, DJ studied the rainbow colors reflected through the Waterford glass. "It is though. Leslie's father told me." DJ half-coughed, half-choked. "He saw them take Ike away. And I saw the chair, and the blanket, and the Bible. It's true all right."

Greta sat on the edge of her chair, her back straight. "Dear, sweet, Ike. I can't believe it." She looked away toward the darkened hallway, then whispered, "He should never have been born into this vile world." Her palms pressed together in prayer, she was silent for several seconds. "And then, of course, Bobby, who had everything to live for." Her eyes shifted away again. "I don't know what is happening, or why. I simply don't understand." She hesitated. "Was there any suggestion of foul play with Ike as there was with Bobby?"

DJ thought for a moment then shook his head. "I think he just, you know . . . died."

Greta touched the crook of her forefinger to her chin. "I'm sure." She reached for her glass, sipped, then placed it back on the table. She leaned forward, focusing her attention on DJ. "And how are you, dear boy? How are you with all of this?"

"How should I be?"

"Very sad, very disturbed, I would imagine. Just as I am increasingly becoming." Greta stood and walked to the kitchen, returning with the bottle of sherry. Filling DJ's glass again, she added a drop to her own. "And when was the last time Ike and you were together, if you don't mind me asking?"

DJ immediately sipped the sherry. "Yesterday afternoon before I went to the parade. He was sitting in the lawn chair by the side of his house."

Greta nodded imperceptibly. "Did he say anything to you?" she asked gently. "Did he know what was happening to him?"

"I'm trying to remember," DJ thought aloud. He could feel his throat begin to constrict again, his grief begin to rumble from deeper reaches. "He looked little . . . that's all. Like he was small . . . and broken."

"Resigned? I wonder." Greta held the stemmed glass on her knee and stared over it. "The poor, dear boy." She briefly closed her eyes. "There is so much that makes me weary. And though we all struggle with a last goodbye, the true impact remains unrecognized until an hour, a week, or a month has passed—until there's an unexpected lull in the day, or we are about to fall asleep, and for the first time realize what it feels like to be truly alone." Greta slowly shook her head. "We never understand the power of the last goodbye until long after it's been seen or heard."

"He said he was tired of being King Neptune. Those were the last words." DJ could feel the internal ache revving. "He was worn out from being King Neptune."

"And what could that mean?" Greta asked, a puzzled expression slipping across her face.

DJ used his thumb and forefinger from one hand to dam the corners of his eyes. "He wanted to be able to swim the window like the rest of us. He wanted to be able to swim it, and not have to walk like King Neptune because of his heart."

"You mean when all you boys pretended you were fish in front of Captain Leo's window?"

DJ nodded, then leaned forward, resting his forehead in his hands. "That's what he wanted—not to be King Neptune, and to be like everyone else."

"Yes, I'm certain that's correct," Greta said.

"And he couldn't do it. He couldn't even come close." DJ's voice cracked as his grief began to upset his equilibrium. "He just wanted to fix watches and have Patty. Then she's not even nice to him, and before I can turn around and do anything about it, he goes out and dies." DJ couldn't contain the pain and covered his face with both hands. "Just like that, he goes out and dies."

"It's not your fault that happened, DJ. You must know that."

"I don't know that. I don't know what to do, where to go, who to believe—everyone lies to me. I have a girlfriend, then I don't, because she lies to me. My father lies, except at Christmastime, and what he becomes then is a lie. Maynard lies—he's not going to college with me, and Ike," he said, "lied to me for eighteen years. I thought he was always going to be my friend." He brushed his eyes with the heels of his hands and stared at the floor. "I thought that . . . " His voice trailed off.

Greta leaned forward on the edge of her chair. "I will be your friend, DJ, and I never lie to you."

DJ stared back at her, his despair, coupled with the sherry, erasing boundaries. "Why would you say that, Greta?" He was nearly hoarse. "How could you ever say that?"

Greta appeared perplexed. "I say it for only one reason, because it's true."

DJ shook his head. "No, it's not. It's not true at all. You've lied to me like everyone else."

Greta leaned back. "That's not so, DJ. I'm surprised at you for making an accusation like that."

"There's nothing to be surprised about. It's not an accusation, it's a fact." He pointed to the picture of Rupert Brooke on the side table. "Just who the heck is that? Huh, who is that?"

Greta tilted her head. "I've told you who he is. You don't have to repeat the question."

DJ's control was disintegrating, his anger and pain with losing Ike and Carlyn eroding any margin of civility. "No, let me tell *you* who that is." DJ jumped to his feet. "That is Rupert Brooke from England and World War I. That is Rupert Brooke, the internationally famous poet from World War I, not World War II. Did you hear me, Greta? From World War I—somebody who probably died before you were even born." He lunged to the table and grabbed the picture. "See this guy?" DJ stabbed his finger at the portrait. "See this guy here? He was dead before you even existed! Or close to it. He died in 1915. It's 1965. When were you born? 1900? 1910? So what's all this lover bullshit you've been talking about? You were a kid while this guy was living in another part of the world writing poetry for England. He didn't even know you! What a joke!"

DJ slammed the picture back on the table, then turned away and began to pace the room, his hands in the air. "What's the matter with everybody? What's the matter with you, Greta? I don't understand why people keep making up stuff as they go along. What they want to be, that's what they tell everyone they are." DJ snapped his fingers. "Like my father wants to be a high-class English lawyer, so he dresses up like Sherlock Holmes, looking like the village idiot in the process, and develops an English accent to boot. But even though he drinks British booze, he still gets drunk every night and forgets everything except that he's a *barrister*! A *barrister*! You believe that?

"Ike wants to stay alive, so he pretends that's what he's going to do, then he dies reading dirty books disguised as the Bible. Maynard can't keep his pants on so I'm going to college by myself. You want to be in love with a poet, and you want him to be in love with you, so you find a picture, *write an inscription to yourself,* then tell everyone it's true. And everyone, including me," he said hammering his chest with his thumb, "is so dumb we believe it. What kind of craziness is all this? Tell me, what? What?" He turned to Greta. "For God's sake, tell me what's going on!"

Greta was silent, unmoving, her hands resting across her knees. After several moments, she said, "I think of him, and he is beautiful, so he is mine. I would not expect you to understand."

DJ froze, his anger slowly abating, then turned and picked up the picture of Rupert Brooke, placing it in a standing position again. Facing Greta again, he continued, "And you would be right to expect me not to understand. And I don't. And you know why, Greta? Because it's crazy, that's why. You're in some kind of dream world." DJ halted and stared at her. "I believed you as much as I do Monty. And you're just like everyone else. You wouldn't know the truth if it slapped you across the face!!"

Rising slowly, Greta said, "Perhaps it is time for you to go home, DJ."

DJ hesitated, lightheaded, already beginning to regret his actions. "What if I don't want to go home?"

"It'll be all right," Greta said, guiding him by the arm to the hallway. Opening the door, she said, "I'll see you soon, DJ. It'll be all right. Goodnight now."

DJ looked at her as he stepped outside. "I, ah—"

"It will be all right," Greta said, patting his shoulder, then closing the door.

He heard her steps as she slowly traipsed back to the living room.

CHAPTER 52

DJ stared at his watch, unsure why he had lost control. Except for the time in Vermont with Monty, he was always in public lock-down.

As he passed the Jailhouse Rock, he saw the parking lot was nearly filled. Rather than have to immediately deal with his father, he entered the bar through the side door.

The place was packed with detectives, local and Nassau County police. DJ edged his way into a corner, eventually catching Thor's eye. "Dale just left," he said. "Want a beer?"

DJ nodded and took a dollar from his wallet and placed it in front of him. Thor returned, sliding the glass to him. "Forget it," he said, "this one's on me."

"Thanks a lot," DJ said, looking around the bar. Besides his own behavior, which he was increasingly regretting, there was something else at Greta's that troubled him.

Something that didn't seem quite right; something out of place.

He couldn't grasp what it was.

If it's important, I'll remember, he thought. Scanning the room, he knew some of the faces, but practically no names until he saw Wendell wedged in the other corner, his shoulder resting against the wall. Catching DJ's eye, Wendell nodded his head, signaling him to come over. DJ took his glass of beer and edged his way past the men until he was next to his uncle.

"How you doing, buster?" Wendell asked. "Glad I saw you. I'm about ready to leave."

DJ nodded.

"Heard about Ike," Wendell said. "Real sorry too. I tell you what, that kind of stuff always shocks you even though you think you're ready for it. Never are, though. Poor kid, that's what Ike was, just a poor kid with a busted-up heart. Course having said that about Ike, nobody was ready for this Litchfield deal at all."

"Have you heard anything new?" DJ asked.

"Nothing," Wendell said. "I tell you what, detectives been at the crime scene all day, but they ain't found a damn thing. So many people behind the school last night for the fireworks, there was a million footprints, plus cigarette butts, candy wrappers, and a ton of dog shit. Way I hear it, nobody knows for nothing. They got zilch."

Thor positioned himself in front of the two. "Another beer, Wendell?"

"Nope," Wendell answered, "like to, but I got to run." He clapped DJ on the shoulder as he stood. "See you, pal. Don't go swimmin' with bow-legged women." As he walked toward the exit, he called, "See you, Thor."

A couple of cops yelled for another beer and Thor turned away from DJ. "I'll be back," he said.

DJ tried to overhear the conversations around him, searching for any scrap of information related to Bobby's death, but all the talk was about the Yankees and how things weren't like they used to be when Mantle first came up to the major leagues.

DJ finished his beer and stood up. He checked to make sure his wallet was in his back pocket, and was about to start for the door when Thor leaned over the bar in front of him. "Just be careful going home tonight. We got patrol cars out, but they can't be everywhere, and nobody knows for sure if some homicidal maniac isn't walking around right now. I've been talking and listening to these guys for hours and they don't know what happened last night, but everybody's nervous. You know what I mean? Real nervous."

"Do you really think Bobby was murdered?" DJ asked.

"Absolutely," Thor answered. "That's one thing there's no doubt about. Question is how and why. Way I hear it, they've got no leads at all. The detectives are keeping me updated and they've got squat."

"They don't have any ideas at all about what happened?" DJ asked.

Thor nodded. "The only thing that I've heard mentioned is this murder is similar to one that happened about a month ago which could mean something." Thor picked between his front teeth using the edge of a matchbook cover. "You probably remember, it was all over the news. A cop was found dead at an exit off the Belt Parkway."

DJ could feel needles surge up his spine and flare across his shoulders. "What do you mean similar?" he asked.

"Don't know for sure, but the way I hear it, and all the autopsy information isn't back yet, is that both the officer and Bobby were killed the same way—hit in the back of the head with some kind of heavy object. Could have been a rock— something like that. Plus there were a couple other similar details, but nothing conclusive yet."

Thor tore up the matchbook cover and threw it in an ashtray. "Tell you the truth, most of the detectives don't think there's much to the one-killer theory because they can't figure a connection between the two. But," Thor said, raising his finger, "if there was something or someone the officer and Bobby both had in common, then the detectives say it's probably one guy who did both jobs." Thor shook his head. "I don't think so though. The two didn't know each other, weren't similar in any way, and lived in different counties.

Nothing at all that links them together." Thor shrugged. "Best guess from most every cop on the job is we're just seeing two random homicides and any similarity is coincidental. Or the other possibility I've heard is that a brand new serial killer is just getting into the hunt. Trouble is, in either case, no one can figure a motive. But then again, I guess serial killers don't need motives, maybe they just need a bad day." He took DJ's glass, and lifting the rag from his shoulder, wiped the bar. "Anyway, sure beats the hell out of me."

"Me too," DJ said, looking around. "Well, I better get out of here."

"Like I said, take it easy going home, DJ," Thor advised. "I don't like the feel in the air. You want me to call one of my boys to drive you?"

"No. Thanks." DJ answered. "I'll be careful."

"Be real careful," Thor said.

∞

Outside the Rock, DJ moved across Main Street and turned left onto Melville Road. As he looked around, there were no cars in sight—none—and all the houses he walked past had their curtains drawn, or the Venetian blinds tugged tightly shut. Occasionally the ghostly shimmer of a TV's blue light peeked out, reassuring him he was not totally alone.

He picked up his pace toward Jackson Road just as two porch lights were simultaneously flicked off. "The news must be over," he said out loud.

DJ thought he heard a car, but when he twisted around, he saw nothing except blackness and a distant traffic light. Further away, he heard the wail of a train. Crickets chirped next to each front porch he passed.

The common sounds, the familiar street sign ahead, eased the tension of walking alone.

He was beginning to relax when high beams suddenly

exploded around him, blinding him, riveting him to the sidewalk! His heart pounded wildly, but at the same time, he was relieved that the police were continuing to patrol the neighborhoods. Turning to the headlights, he waved his hand. "I'm okay, almost home." The high beams were lowered and the car roared up until it was next to him.

A Mustang.

The passenger side window was already rolled down. Carlyn leaned across the console. "Hi, baby, I've missed you. Get in."

DJ was stunned. "I told you this morning, I can't, Carlyn."

"Like hell you can't. Get in, baby. I need you. I want to be with you." Her hair was disheveled, partially covering one eye, and from the faint reflection of the dashboard lights, her eyes appeared sunken, her skin greenish.

DJ hesitated, looking at her.

"Come here, baby," Carlyn coaxed, her voice gentler, yet still tinged with desperation DJ now recognized. "We haven't been together in a while. Come here, baby." She held out a hand to him, smiling, beckoning.

"No, I really can't, Carlyn, I have to go home," DJ answered. He started to walk toward Jackson Road.

The Mustang crept next to him as he continued forward. "What's the big deal, DJ? Is it because I was with Bobby?" Carlyn steered with her left hand as she leaned toward him, speaking through the open window. "That didn't mean anything. It was a mistake. I admit it to you right now, right now as we speak, that it was a mistake. Come on, get in the car. You know we need each other."

"I'm not getting in the car, Carlyn," DJ said over his shoulder, walking more quickly.

"Get in the goddamned car," she screamed. "Do you hear me, get in the goddamned car."

DJ ran.

Carlyn floored the accelerator, her tires screeching after him. When she was alongside, DJ looked over and saw her eyes wide, glaring, then abruptly she swung the Mustang into the center of Melville Road and shot away. The car accelerated and the taillights faded into the night.

DJ slowed, then pulled up and leaned against a tree, shaky, his breathing ragged. I better tell Monty about Carlyn, he thought to himself. Real soon, I better say something real soon.

Away in the darkness, he heard tires screeching again, then saw headlights firing recklessly back up Melville Road directly toward him. Frantically cutting across a driveway, DJ sprinted onto Jackson Road, fear exploding through him. He heard the Mustang tires shrieking as the car made a Hollywood turn behind him, and suddenly he was stabbed with the high beams again.

He scrambled from the sidewalk and tore across a front lawn, dodging a statue of the Virgin Mary as a dog barked wildly inside the house. Seconds later, the Mustang jumped the sidewalk and shot across the lawn after him, ripping serrated trenches in the grass, ramming and crushing the statue of the Blessed Virgin. DJ ran back across the street and through another front yard with the Mustang rocketing after him. As he desperately tried to escape, the Mustang straddled the sidewalk and the street in wild pursuit, the headlights locked on him.

"Come back, DJ, I need you," Carlyn screamed out of the driver's window while she momentarily slowed the car. "Come back now. Do you hear me? Now!"

DJ nearly tripped over a bush, then high-jumped a split-rail fence.

Carlyn instantly accelerated after him, but the Mustang's rear end swerved, and as she struggled to wrestle the car back on to the street, DJ raced over to the front of Leslie's house and dove behind the hedges that lined the front yard. He lay still, gasping for breath, listening.

He heard the Mustang slowly drive up the street, then come to a halt next to the hedges. Carlyn laughed lightly, as she had so often when they had been in her bedroom together—a gentle, sweet laugh, as innocent-sounding as any schoolgirl sharing a private moment with a classmate. How many times he had heard just such a laugh following some acrobatic sexual escapade that she had initiated. How easily he had been seduced. And how so much of him still wanted to forget the past week, the dead bodies, and simply stand up, surrender, and walk from behind the hedges so that it could all start again.

Then she was gone. Carlyn leisurely drove up Jackson Road, proceeded through the stop sign, then quietly disappeared into the night.

Back along the street, four or five lights had been flicked on, and a withered man in a red bathrobe stood on his front porch staring down at a front yard the Mustang had reduced to divots.

DJ waited two minutes, until his breathing was normal, then slowly moved out from behind the hedge and crept home through the shadows.

CHAPTER 53

Inside Van Velsor's Tuesday morning, DJ couldn't miss *Newsday*'s blaring headline *School Star Murdered*, with Bobby's graduation picture centered directly beneath. He picked up a copy of the paper, paid Herman and walked outside to read the article inside the Falcon. The story mentioned Bobby's accomplishments and how he had planned to be the first graduate in Hardscrabble's history to attend Yale. Long on background and short on police detail, the article concluded by stating there were no suspects in the case, but that a team of detectives was pursuing several leads.

DJ stared at the photograph, unable to believe Bobby was gone, unable to believe the insanity in his own life.

When he arrived at Mertz Brothers later, he drove around the employees' parking lot and scrutinized all the cars, but failed to locate the Mustang. Once inside Cliff Collins's office, he still saw no sign of Carlyn.

"The Ivy League Shop," Cliff said, barely looking up. "Stay there until five today. I'll send someone to relieve you for lunch."

"Anything going on?" DJ asked, glancing around.

"Not a thing," Cliff replied.

DJ remained in front of Cliff's desk. "Do you mind if I take Thursday off for the funerals?"

"Nope," Cliff said, "I would expect you to."

∞

DJ waited nervously all day for Carlyn to appear, not knowing what to expect if she did. He arranged neckties on tables and straightened racks of boxer shorts, occasionally looking up to scan the passersby or to catch Carlyn off guard if she was spying from a distance, but during the entire eight hours, he never got so much as a glimpse of her.

At the end of the day, on his way through the employee's exit, DJ caught up with Cliff Collins. "Haven't seen Mrs. Canova around all day," he said cautiously, keeping his voice even.

"No, you haven't, DJ, and it's not likely you will again. She's no longer with us."

"Not at Mertz Brothers anymore?" DJ struggled to keep his voice level. "That's funny, she was here yesterday."

"Yes, she was, but that was yesterday. She's resigned. Called me this morning, gave no notice. She's got a helluva nerve. Very unprofessional. I hope she doesn't intend to use me for a reference." Cliff walked out to the parking lot with DJ following behind. "How's your father holding up with this Litchfield deal?" he asked over his shoulder as he unlocked his car. "I've had two or three customers come up to the office really upset. They liked Bobby a lot. Real good salesman, I guess." He looked over at DJ. "Hard to believe, isn't it? This type of thing hits everybody right in the gut. Takes the wind right out of you. Feels like Kennedy has been assassinated all over again, only worse, because it's closer."

DJ nodded in agreement.

"Take it easy, DJ," Cliff said. "I'll see you in the morning."

∞

A blue sedan DJ didn't recognize was parked in front of the house. Inside, a stranger was sitting with his father at the kitchen table drinking a beer.

"DJ," Dale said, hearing him enter the house, "come here. This is Detective Fagella from the Nassau County Police Department. He wants to ask you a few questions." He stood up. "Want a beer?"

"Yeah, okay," DJ answered.

"No big deal," the detective said, barely moving from his chair as he leaned across the table and shook two of DJ's fingers.

"Another one, Tony?" Dale asked as he crossed toward the refrigerator.

"No go. Thanks, Dale." The detective focused on DJ. "Just have a few questions." He removed a notepad and pen from the inside of his jacket pocket. "This is just standard operating procedure, DJ. I spoke with your sister earlier in the day, along with about ten other people."

Dale placed the beer in front of DJ.

"Tell me what you were doing the night of July 4th, the night before last," Detective Fagella said.

DJ thought for a few seconds, then recounted the events of the evening as best as he could recall, including meeting Maynard, Frannie, Greta, and Patty.

"You had planned to meet them at the Fireama?" Detective Fagella asked.

"Not really. It just worked out that way."

"You'd planned to go alone then?" The detective took a Cigarillo from a pack in his breast pocket and lit it. "You do a lot of stuff alone?"

"Sometimes," DJ admitted, "not always. But the only reason I was alone that night was because Ike didn't want to go."

"Ike?" the detective asked.

"DJ's friend," Dale interrupted. "Kid with a heart condition."

"Where does he live? I should probably speak to him too."

"No can do," Dale answered. "He died yesterday."

The detective stopped writing and looked over at Dale, then at DJ. "Your friend died too? And he was your age?"

DJ had been struggling to keep Ike out of his brain, locked away, beyond reach. He nodded and felt his eyes start to fill. Furious with himself, he coughed.

"That's pretty damn odd," Detective Fagella said. "This Litchfield kid one day and then, what's his name?" He looked at his pad. "Ike, is it, the next? Two high school kids back-to-back. Some coincidence." He looked at his notes. "Anybody find out how Ike died?"

"All indications were heart failure," Dale answered. "He's been living on borrowed time since he was born. Saw him when he was a month old." Dale pointed at the dish rag folded next to the sink. "Blue as that towel. I think the coroner has indicated natural causes. Figures that would be the way he would go. Chances are if they open him up, with everything having been out of whack so long, damn doctors wouldn't know where to begin."

"Jesus," Detective Fagella said, staring, unblinking at Dale. "Jesus, that's something." He made another note, then thought a second before continuing. "I understand there was an altercation the night before the Fourth at the local coffee shop." He looked again at his pad, thumbing the pages backward. "Ah, Van Velsor's. Is that right?"

DJ nodded. "That's right."

"You want to go ahead and tell me about it?" He flipped the pages forward so that he could begin writing again.

"Well, there's not too much to tell," DJ began. "Bobby was out with my sister, Patty." He recounted the events that had occurred in the coffee shop as well as the rest of the evening, leaving out the altercation at home between Patty, his father, and himself.

As the detective thumbed back through his notes again, the Cigarillo slanted out of the corner of his mouth and the smoke curled upward, partially closing his left eye. "Why would someone with a heart condition try to attack a strong, healthy kid? That doesn't make any sense."

"He liked Patty," DJ said.

The detective looked at DJ, then placed the Cigarillo in the ashtray. "So?"

"That's why he went after Bobby, to protect Patty."

"Well, any which way you want to look at it, it doesn't add up no matter how he felt about your sister. Why start a fight you have no chance of winning?" He wasn't looking for an answer. "Damn fool kid. May God rest his soul."

DJ shrugged. "I guess it was just something he thought he had to do."

The detective eyed DJ for a moment. "Bad blood between you and this Litchfield boy?"

"Only because of the way he treated my sister," DJ answered.

"Sure," the detective nodded. "That makes sense. I understand you two worked together at Mertz Brothers."

"Yeah, but we didn't talk much." DJ responded.

Understood," Detective Fagella said. "Okay, I think I got it. Everyone tells the same story. Your sister wasn't hurt by the Litchfield kid, right?"

"No, she wasn't hurt," Dale interjected.

"From what I can tell, it was a basic misunderstanding," the detective said as he picked up the Cigarillo. "No harm; no foul. That about right?"

"That's what I would say," Dale answered again. "That was Herman's read of the situation. Teenagers. You know what they're like."

"Okay, so let me jump ahead again. DJ," the detective said. "The night of the Fireama, you stayed for the fireworks?"

"Some of them. Then I left."

"Why?" The detective inhaled the Cigarillo lodged between

his lips, then exhaled a voluminous cloud creating a Sicilian Wizard of Oz.

"I was tired. I wanted to go home. I've seen fireworks before." He looked over at the detective. "Am I a suspect or something?"

"I have to ask the questions," the detective replied. He flicked the end of the Cigarillo into the ashtray. "Just strikes me as a little unusual to leave in the middle of the fireworks after you had waited half the day to see them." He made a note. "Tell me what you did after you left the fireworks."

DJ explained how he walked home and watched television until Patty arrived. He didn't mention his drive to Carlyn's house, or the subsequent cruising around Hardscrabble in the Falcon. Staring across the table, he was sure his father had no recollection of giving him the car keys.

"What did you watch?" the detective asked.

"A war movie about three guys who came home from fighting and hung around together. One had hooks on his hands."

"*The Best Years of Our Lives*," Detective Fagella said. "I watched it too." He stared away, then glanced at his notepad. "Think that movie was on about ten o'clock, ended about twelve-thirty or so. Coroner suspects that's the time frame this Litchfield boy was murdered, give or take an hour." He glanced again at his notepad. "Then what?"

DJ shrugged. "Then nothing. Patty came home and went to bed, and after the movie was over, I did too."

"And your sister was coming from where?"

"Greta's."

Detective Fagella checked back over his notes. "Right. I interviewed Greta and your sister down at the coffee shop. That all checks out. Pleasant lady, isn't she?" He turned to Dale. "And Dale, you were where?"

Dale nodded toward the bedroom. "Sawing wood. It was a long day, Tony."

"I'm sure," Detective Fagella answered. He turned to DJ.

"Did you see your father at home that night?"

"No, but I heard him," DJ answered. "He snores."

"Me too," the detective said while he wrote an additional note. "The wife wears earplugs. Irritates the daylights out of her." He closed his notepad and pen, then stuck both back into his inside jacket pocket. "Well, that's about all I need for now. Everything seems to fit."

"Beer for the road?" Dale asked.

"I don't think so, Dale," he answered, then turned to DJ as he rose to his feet. "One last thing, son." He thought for a second. "Is there anyone you know who would ever do something like this? Have you heard anybody talk? Any rumors going around?" He stared intently at DJ. "Is there anyone you can think of that would have any kind of motivation to be involved in this homicide?"

DJ stared back at the detective. Slowly he shook his head, "No, I don't have any answers at all."

"Join the club," Detective Fagella muttered as he attempted to button his jacket across his lasagna belly. "No one has a clue. Strangest damn case I've seen in my life, and I've been doing this a long damn time." He tugged at his jacket again. "Too damn long."

CHAPTER 54

Ike's father stood in front of the funeral home puffing on his pipe. "Evening, son," he said, "glad you could make it," then turned away.

When DJ entered the room, he kept his eyes lowered and intentionally out of focus. Mrs. O'Reilly, who had been silently twisting her handkerchief in her fingers, immediately crossed the room. "DJ." She put her arms around him. "I miss Ike."

DJ nodded and offered his condolences. Behind her, it was impossible to avoid the wreaths and flowers surrounding the casket, and the profile, the unmoving, nonliving, plastic profile.

He knelt in front of the casket. As he rose, he looked at Ike for the first time, gradually, indirectly. His best, newly dead friend was tucked into a black suit, his eyes closed, with rosary beads twisted through his fingers. The funeral director had worked fast and done his best cosmetic work, making Ike more life-like in death than when he was alive.

DJ backed away, then stood alone on the side of the room counting the minutes before he could acceptably leave. On his way out, he approached Ike's mother. "Mrs. O'Reilly, what was the name of Ike's doctor?" he asked.

"Dr. Carroll, over at South Shore Medical." She sniffled. "I know he did everything he possibly could."

"I'm sure he did."

"Can I tell you something?" Mrs. O'Reilly asked. "Only because you were his best friend and I know what I say will help you too."

DJ noticed tears beginning to form in the corners of her eyes. He waited although he didn't want to be "helped too." He didn't want to hear a thing she had to say—not one more lousy, supposedly helpful, word about death. Nothing! Nada! Zip! Zero! What he wanted more than anything was to leave—to jump on a Harley Davidson motorcycle and crash through one of the funeral home windows, then roar down Main Street, never looking back! And if Mrs. O'Reilly had somehow managed to be sitting behind him, trying to console him with ancient Ike stories, he'd fire up a shrieking wheelie and power-dump her on the pavement before he sped away!

"Can I tell you something?" Mrs. O'Reilly repeated.

DJ nodded. "Sure."

"This morning, I went to pick up the lawn chair and the blanket Ike used. I also found the front and back covers of the Bible." Her eyes were near the point of overflowing. "All the pages were missing." She fumbled for words. "Ike took the Bible with him to heaven. I know he did. Finding the empty covers was a message to me, telling me I don't have to worry anymore. He's safe. Safer than he could ever be with me here on earth." She fumbled in her pocketbook. "And for that I'm happier and more relieved than I've been in years."

DJ watched Mrs. O'Reilly blot at her eyes with her handkerchief, her nostrils quivering.

"I know you're right," he said, reaching out and touching her elbow.

"You're a good boy, DJ," Mrs. O'Reilly said.

Another couple joined them and a few minutes later, DJ eased away. On his way out, he looked back and saw a profile of Mrs. O'Reilly as she spoke with another mourner. It was obvious that she was pregnant.

"Good night now," Mr. O'Reilly said, working his briar pipe till the tobacco glowed, "thanks for stopping by."

"Good night, Mr. O'Reilly," DJ answered.

∞

When he walked into the Rock, Maynard was sitting at the bar. He had a beer in one hand and a New York Yankees cap resting on the back of his head.

"DJ-J-J-J," Maynard said. "Didn't know you were going to be here tonight. Now that I'm eighteen, I can be here whenever I want."

"Unless I throw your sorry ass out," Thor said, as he passed in front of him on the way to the beer tap.

"Unless he throws my sorry ass out on the way to the beer tap," Maynard said, a smile appearing.

"Be back in a second," DJ said. He walked over to the pay phone. He spoke for a minute, then returned to the bar and sat down next to Maynard.

"Who were you talking to?"

"Monty. He's coming over." DJ thought a second. "Why didn't you go to the wake?"

"Because they scare me." Maynard lit a cigarette. "I miss Ike, probably not as much as you, but I'm not going to help him any by staring at a dead body. If I wanted to stare at a corpse in bed, I could look at Frannie." He slid his glass forward on the bar. "I'll have another if you don't mind, kind sir."

"Don't even think about getting drunk here tonight, Mr. Maynard," Thor said, as he took the glass and refilled it, then walked away.

Maynard pushed his glasses back up onto the bridge of his nose. "You know what bothers me? Who killed Litchfield anyway? That's what really scares me."

314 | Ted M. Alexander

DJ shrugged as Thor brought a beer over to him. "Scares everyone." He looked around the Rock. "I wish I knew the answer."

Ten minutes later, Monty walked in the front door and moved to DJ. "How you doing, cowboy? What's up?"

DJ stood and finished the glass of beer. He fished in his pocket and placed fifty cents on the bar. "I just needed to talk to you. Can you spare a couple of minutes?"

"Course I can, but let's not hang out here. I tend to only stick around bars when I'm playing bass. What do you say we take a walk."

Outside, DJ and Monty moved slowly up a dreary Main Street containing only a couple of parked cars and empty sidewalks.

"The town's really spooked about this Litchfield deal," Monty said. "I'm keeping my fingers crossed the police figure it out in a hurry so everyone can get back to normal. That's assuming the killer isn't someone we know." He glanced around the vacant street. "It's too bad that with everyone so worried, Ike's passing has almost slipped most folks' minds. Were you over at the wake?"

"I went tonight. It wasn't too crowded."

"Yeah, well, Lila and I stopped by this afternoon and practically no one was there." Monty turned to DJ as they walked. "So tell me, what's going on?"

DJ wasn't certain how to begin. He glanced over at Monty, who had turned and was staring at the shotguns in the Army and Navy store window as they moved past. "I think I may know who killed Bobby."

Monty stopped in his tracks, turned and studied DJ. "That right? What do you mean you may know?"

DJ said, almost inaudibly, "I'm not sure, but I think I do."

"Lord, DJ, tell me who it is."

DJ swallowed and hesitated. "I never mentioned this, Monty, but I had a girlfriend who is a little older than me."

"Leslie?"

"No, older; a few years older. Like about ten. Her name was Carlyn Canova. I mean her name is still Carlyn Canova, it's just she's not my girlfriend anymore."

Monty ran his hand across the side of his face. "The one who's your boss at Mertz Brothers?"

DJ was surprised. "How did you know that?"

"Just remembered the name when we were driving to Vermont, and seeing her at the Rock. But I didn't know she was your girlfriend. He shoved his hands in his pockets. "Anyway, I thought she was married."

"She said that, but she wasn't."

Monty resumed walking. "Okay, DJ, so you had a girlfriend a few years older than you who's not married. How does that work with Bobby Litchfield?"

DJ explained about the New York City policeman that stopped them, leaving out what Carlyn and he had been doing, and how Carlyn was angry and had strongly hinted she would get even for being intruded upon. Then two weeks later, the cop had turned up dead.

"Are you positive the murdered policeman was the same one that pulled you over that night?"

"Pretty sure," DJ answered almost apologetically, "but I had been drinking a lot too."

"I have to tell you, my friend, pretty sure doesn't hold up in court. You go around accusing people of crimes, you've got to be more than pretty sure, especially if you've been drinking."

"Then Carlyn was with Bobby, and now he's dead," DJ continued. "See what I mean, Monty, there's a connection. The dead policeman, and now Bobby. Both killed."

Monty frowned. "With Bobby? What do you mean, with?"

DJ turned away. After a minute, he mumbled, "You know what I mean, Monty. She was with me, then she was . . . with Bobby."

Monty hesitated. "Okay, I see what you're saying now." He scratched the back of his head. "Well, that's too bad, I thought you said she was your girlfriend."

"She was, and she wasn't. What happened was Bobby told me about being with Carlyn, and I told her I knew. Next thing you know, Bobby's dead too. She was as mad at Bobby as she was at the policeman. Thor said the police haven't found any solid connection between the two victims, but here it is, right in front of you, here's the connection: Carlyn. She was really mad at both of them, and the two of them died the same way—hit over the back of the head." DJ lowered his voice. "Only nobody knows about it except Carlyn, me, and now, you."

Monty was concentrating. After a few moments, he said, "I don't know, DJ, I can't seem to put this all together to make any kind of sense. A dead New York City policeman that may or may not have been the same one that stopped the two of you shows up dead in Brooklyn, then a month or so later Bobby is killed too. And in both cases, you're claiming it was Carlyn. Where's the motivation? She's aggravated because the cop asked her questions, so she kills him, then Bobby told you about their relationship, so she goes out and kills him too? Those two paid a heckuva large price for not doing very much. She'd have to be a psychopath."

"Then she chased me."

"Who chased you?"

"Carlyn. Last night she wanted me to get in the car with her, and when I wouldn't, she chased me. She tore up Ole Man Bailey's front lawn on Jackson Road in the process."

Monty stopped walking. "Why would she chase you, DJ? Now she's starting to sound like she is nuts."

"That's what I mean. She chased me because she wanted to kill me too, because I was the only one who understood the connection between the policeman and Bobby. I'm the only one who could put the finger on her for being involved in both murders." DJ stared at Monty. "You see what I mean?"

Monty offered a slow smile. "I don't know, DJ. I don't mean to minimize your hypothesis here, but you're talking about a very attractive woman with no record, who has a very responsible job in the community."

"She doesn't have the job anymore. She quit today. Cliff Collins told me she just called in and quit."

Monty frowned. "Just like that, she quit? Heck, that's hard to believe too, especially with an important position like that." He thought for a minute as he stared ahead. "Well, a lot of times in those kinds of work situations there's more going on than meets the eye. Chances are that if she quit, there was a good reason for doing it."

"I'll bet she's taking off and leaving Hardscrabble so nothing happens to her, so she doesn't get caught. I'll bet you a million dollars that's what she's doing."

After a while, Monty replied, "It all sounds a little off the beaten track to me, DJ, but who knows, there may be something to it. Let me do this, let me talk with Thor. Let's see what he thinks. Maybe this is something worth looking into especially because I haven't heard of any other hot leads coming down the pike." He stopped in front of Van Velsor's. "Ice cream cone?"

"No thanks." Inside DJ saw Patty scrubbing the counter. "That's got to be the cleanest place in town," he said. "Herman is a vinegar and water fiend."

"You're right, no one like Herman for keeping things spotless," Monty answered. "Well, I think I'll pass on the ice cream too."

DJ suddenly stopped. "You know what else I just remembered?"

Monty stared at him.

"Back before Christmas, when Carlyn was visiting her sister in Albany, a policeman was killed up there too."

"How would you know that, DJ?" Monty asked. "We don't get any Albany news down here. It's four or five hours away."

"Two hunters came into the Rock. They were late getting back and told Thor it was because of a roadblock on the Thruway. They said a cop had been killed and all cars were being stopped. I was sitting right there at the bar. I remember because I was worried that something might happen to Carlyn."

Monty shook his head, then slowly walked forward. "A lot of coincidences, for sure, but I'll bet you that's all that's going on here." He turned to DJ. "There are tons of weird people in this world, DJ, but very few killers. Know what I mean? Murderers are a breed all their own. There just aren't that many people with that mental instability. And certainly not pretty, blonde store managers, who probably have the world on a string."

"But you'll tell Thor, then let me know what he says?" DJ asked.

"Absolutely," Monty responded, "but I wouldn't get too worked up on it. Sounds kind of iffy to me."

"I know, but I had to tell somebody. I was getting nervous."

"I don't blame you. You did the right thing. And it's got to be tough to do especially when I suspect you probably still have some feeling for her."

"Yeah." DJ nodded slowly. "I guess I'll head home now."

"Fair enough," Monty answered. "But hey, you know what, now that I think about it, I'm going to get that cone anyway. I could get run over by a vegetable truck tomorrow and never have another chance." He turned from DJ, then stopped and looked back. "Watch yourself, partner. Still anyone's guess as to what's going on around this town. And if you see Carlyn in your travels, stay away."

"Okay, Monty, I will." He was relieved he had told someone what he suspected.

As he approached home, he kept a peripheral eye out for a Mustang ready to attack from any shadowy corner.

CHAPTER 55

By noon the next day at Mertz Brothers, it occurred to DJ that he might never see Carlyn again, that lying next to the hedge and hearing her laughter from the Mustang might have been the last goodbye.

According to Cliff Collins, she would never work again if he had anything to say about it. "Totally unprofessional," he had repeated when DJ signed in that morning.

During lunch hour, DJ walked to the pay telephone by the employees' cafeteria and looked up the phone number for Dr. Carroll at South Shore Medical. He deposited a dime and dialed.

"Doctor's office," a female voice stated.

"Is Doctor Carroll in?" he asked.

"Who's calling please?"

"Ah, my name is DJ Elders."

"Are you a patient of Dr. Carroll's?"

"Ah, no, I'm not, but I got the number from Mrs. O'Reilly, Ike O'Reilly's mother, and she said I should call," he lied.

"One moment please." The nurse put DJ on hold. Moments later she returned. "Could you wait for a moment? Dr. Carroll is just finishing up with a patient."

"Okay," DJ answered. He twisted the black phone cord around his index finger as he waited.

"Carroll here."

By the doctor's tone, DJ could tell he was rushed. "Dr. Carroll, my name is DJ Elders, I'm a friend, I mean, I was a friend of Ike O'Reilly's."

"What can I do for you?" Dr. Carroll asked abruptly.

"Well, I was just wondering, I knew Ike for a long time, since we were kids—"

"What is it you're looking for?" Dr. Carroll interrupted.

DJ spoke quickly. "I was just wondering, Doctor, if Ike was ever able to do strenuous exercise. I don't mean all the time, I mean just maybe once. You know how you read about those kinds of people that in an emergency can lift cars off of strangers in a wreck. They can do it even though they're ninety-pound weaklings in real life. Would Ike ever have been able to do something like that, you know if he had a lot of adrenaline running through him? He told me he thought he would be able to."

"Who gave you my name?"

"Mrs. O'Reilly. She said I should talk to you about my questions because you were his doctor."

Dr. Carroll hesitated, then sighed. DJ could almost see him looking at his watch, realizing he had to expend another thirty seconds that he didn't have.

"Some of the medical information is proprietary, and some is just common knowledge that could be determined simply by judging Ike's physical appearance. You're a friend of the family?"

"Ike's best friend. We were like brothers."

"Your name again?"

"DJ Elders."

"Your father the judge?"

"That's right."

Dr. Carroll paused. I'm sorry you lost your friend DJ, but

the truth of the matter is that Ike would be about as successful responding to the type of crisis you describe as a flea would be if it attempted to pick up a dog. You probably know he suffered from a congenital heart defect, irreparable and almost totally debilitating. Our challenge was simply to keep him alive. We all cared about him here at South Shore and did everything possible to help him, but even so, no one expected him to last as long as he did. For all practical purposes his condition was incompatible with life."

"He couldn't say, lift weights or swing a baseball bat, something like that, even if it was just once?"

"Zero chance," Dr. Carroll replied. "Not one in a million."

DJ considered the doctor's comments. It had been a long shot anyway, one he had hoped would take Carlyn off the hook and at the same time supply some answers. "Well, thanks, Doctor," he said.

"Be well," Dr. Carroll replied and hung up.

CHAPTER 56

Even if DJ had wanted to attend the morning funeral, he wouldn't have been able to gain admission. The homicide had been so heavily publicized that besides family, selected well-wishers, and throngs of reporters, the Lieutenant Governor of New York and his entourage also appeared to pay respects, jamming the Methodist Church.

Instead, he watched from across the street, hoping to locate Carlyn in the groups of mourners entering the church's vestibule.

The outer doors closed and he remained ten more minutes, then another five, until he was certain she wouldn't appear.

∞

That afternoon, DJ and Patty climbed the steps to St. Mary's, then sat in the rear of the church. While DJ glanced around, still wondering how he would react to the actual funeral, Patty knelt to pray, her forehead resting against pressed palms.

Moments later, she slid back in the pew. Turning to DJ, she whispered, "Maybe it's my fault that Ike is—"

"Never mind," DJ interrupted in a hushed voice, "never mind."

The townspeople entering the church were stiff, their faces strained, pallid. Dale followed Monty, Lila, and Wendell, then slipped into the pew next to DJ and Patty.

Just before the time DJ dreaded the most, the moment the casket was wheeled down the aisle and met halfway by Father Hill, Greta and Herman sat in front of him.

He thought of his visit with Greta the past Monday night, and was still troubled, not just due to his behavior which now made it uncomfortable to enter Van Velsor's, but also because of the nagging awareness that her apartment had somehow changed.

Something that didn't seem quite right; something out of place.

Yet each time he attempted to grasp what was troubling him, his recall shut down.

The doors of the church abruptly opened and six pallbearers wheeled the casket down the aisle, followed by the mourning wails of the O'Reilly clan.

Patty immediately put her hand in DJ's.

As the casket halted in front of Father Hill, the priest paused, his hands folded across his chest. When he cleared his throat and was about to speak, Mr. O'Reilly suddenly convulsed in tears, then wiped his eyes with a grimy white handkerchief.

Father Hill waited, his front teeth flicking his lower lip, until Ike's father quieted.

DJ stood, sat, knelt, and prayed as he was directed, all the time imagining Ike flat on his back in the wooden box, his eyes, maybe open, maybe closed, his wrists lashed together with rosary beads. As the image grew clearer, sharper, searing through the casket oak, DJ backtracked to a baseball game, or Marty Robbins, or being in Carlyn's bedroom. When nothing

324 | Ted M. Alexander

in his emotional arsenal could blunt the portrait of Ike, to cope with his pain, he watched the remainder of the funeral from the ceiling of St. Mary's.

As if he were a balloon held only by the slightest of strings, DJ was able to view himself below, his sister clutching his hand, a terrified look in her eyes. As the smoke from the incense intensified, rising to the rafters and clouding his vision, he gradually descended outside into a somber cluster of people, then walked with Patty and Dale to the Falcon. They entered the line of cars in the cortège and traveled down a misty Main Street that led to St. Mary's cemetery.

CHAPTER 57

Nine o'clock that night, DJ slipped the car keys off the kitchen table, walked to the garage, then slowly backed the Falcon down to the street.

He couldn't help it. He had to see her.

The rain had ended, but the wind was shifting the clouds, covering and uncovering the full moon.

When he reached Amity, he had second thoughts and intentionally passed Carlyn's street. After a mile, he made a sweeping turn in front of a vacant gas station and headed back, this time turning toward her house.

As he drew closer, he nervously glanced into the rearview mirror. Within three or four houses of Carlyn's, he stepped on the accelerator and drove by at thirty miles per hour. With a quick glance, he saw a dim light extending from the kitchen into the living room, but no Mustang in the driveway. He turned around at the end of the block and drove past again, this time, slower. Still a soft light, but no car. He pulled the Falcon into a neighbor's driveway half a block away, backed out, then inched down the street and stopped opposite her house. Only the faint light was visible, but now he noticed the homes on either side of Carlyn's house were dark and silent. After flicking off the headlights, he sat and stared. No wavering of the light inside the house suggesting movement— no car in the driveway.

The majority of his brain implored him to act logically and go home, to forget the whole thing.

Headlights suddenly splashed into the rearview mirror causing him to jump. As he ducked down in the front seat, he was certain the car slowed as it passed the Falcon, but it continued to the end of the block. Sitting up, DJ could see by the taillights it wasn't a Mustang.

He looked back over at the house.

Taking a deep breath, then counting backward from ten to one, he slipped out of the Falcon, quickly closing the door behind him to extinguish the overhead light. He ran across the street, slowed, then crept across the lawn. After taking cover behind a rhododendron at the front of the house, DJ cautiously peeked in the living room window, again seeing only the same faint light bleeding from the kitchen; no movement, no sound. He slipped from behind the shrub, glanced up and down the street to confirm no cars were approaching, then stepped to the fence gate leading to the backyard. DJ gently opened the latch and moved through, carefully closing the gate behind him.

The wind raced the clouds in front of the moon, darkening the landscape.

A snap!

From somewhere deeper in the yard! As he squatted next to the fence, his heart racing, DJ waited, listening, staring into the backyard darkness, attempting to detect movement.

Nothing.

On his hands and knees, DJ crept slowly forward until he reached the kitchen door. He heard the wind whistling through the trees, but also recognized faint music. Slowly, carefully, he rose until his eyes were level with the door window. As he scanned the inside of the kitchen, he saw a green half-light radiating from the dial of the radio on the shelf over the sink. In a far corner near the floor, a tiny night light carved a circle in the blackness. DJ eased back down into a crouch just as the moon burst from behind the clouds causing him to swivel and stare at the shadows uncoiling from the far corners of the yard. He quickly turned back to the house, reached up and pulled down the handle of the screen door, then holding it with one hand, he reached forward to the knob of the inside door.

It was unlocked.

As the door opened, the radio music rushed forward, surrounding him. He gently closed the screen door behind him and stepped into the kitchen, then waited for any movement, or sound, but saw and heard nothing except the wind bursts and classical music—violins, flutes, harps—filling the background.

His eyes gradually adjusted and he could make out the features of the kitchen. As he surveyed the four corners, the refrigerator clicked on, jarring him.

DJ moved forward toward the living room, his back to the wall, his fingertips gliding next to him. As he peered around the corner, he saw more empty space: windows without curtains and bare wood floors highlighted with moon spots. He crept carefully into the living room and noticed the Falcon parked across the street through the front window. As he inched forward, DJ stepped on a floorboard that creaked under the pressure of his foot. Instantly motionless, he waited.

Nothing.

He cocked his head to one side. Still nothing, only the radio and wind intertwining in an otherworldly melody. He eased his foot from the board causing a lesser groan.

"Carlyn," DJ called softly, "Carlyn, are you here?"

DJ stopped and listened again, hearing the wind—only the wind sweeping across the top of the house and the stream of music from the radio. As he eased forward, the clouds suddenly covered the moon and the living room was plunged

328 | Ted M. Alexander

into darkness. Unable to see more than three feet, DJ left the living room and edged down the hallway toward Carlyn's bedroom. He slowly passed the bathroom and glanced inside, seeing nothing, then continued to inch forward until he was at her bedroom door; a *closed* bedroom door.

"Carlyn, are you in there?" he called, his voice weak and shaky. "Are you in there?"

No sound except faraway violins—distant, fluttery violins barely audible through the wind's velocity.

Carlyn?"

DJ placed his hand on the doorknob, hesitated a long moment, then tentatively twisted it. He slowly pushed the door open into the bedroom.

"Carlyn, are you here?" He took an uneasy small step into the darkness. "Are you here?"

Standing inside the doorway, DJ saw nothing, then the clouds suddenly shifted from the front of the moon, electrifying the bedroom with pale white hot spots, at the same time illuminating a grinning portrait of himself on the opposite wall.

He took a terrified step backward as he stared at his own image across the room, then eased over to the photograph, the one he recognized as the eight-by-ten high school graduation picture, now unframed, he had given to Carlyn. As he studied it more closely in the faint light, he saw the ankle bracelet with the intertwined hearts, the one that had been his Christmas gift to her, threaded through a puncture hole at the top of the portrait and looped over a nail in the wall. Across his mouth was a Marilyn Monroe-style lipstick kiss smudge and along his forehead, in her flowery script, Carlyn had written, *Sorry, baby.*

DJ stared at the photograph, then slowly looked around the empty room.

It seemed small.

He stared back at the photograph.

Sorry, baby.

He lifted his picture from the wall to see if she had written anything on the back, but it was blank. He brought the smudged lipstick to his nose to see if he could recognize the scent, but smelled nothing.

Holding the photograph, standing in the middle of a bare room, in a strange house where he didn't belong, during a no-man's-land summer where he didn't fit, thinking about a woman he didn't understand, DJ identified again the emptiness that had accompanied him through his entire life.

Now she was gone. As were his high school years, as was his best friend, Ike O'Reilly.

Sorry, baby.

And she knew he'd show up and had played him to the end.

DJ eased over to the far wall, opened her closet and saw several wire coat hangers and a bunched-up sweater lying on the floor. He picked it up and looking more closely, remembered Carlyn had worn it once or twice during the winter. He slid the cashmere across his cheek causing a breath of Shalimar perfume to wash over him, resurrecting her as clearly as if they had been together only moments before.

DJ chose the portion of the floor where the bed had been, then sat, his back against the wall, the photograph next to him, the sweater in his hands. The time of day no longer mattered, nor his location, and he figured when he was about to fall asleep, he could just stretch out on the floor, as if it were the bed. He would use Carlyn's sweater for a pillow and it would be almost the way it once was— or as close as he could make it.

Creak!

DJ sat straight up!

The floorboard in the living room!

A brief silence, then, more softly: *Creak*! The floorboard released.

Someone was in the house with him! He hurriedly glanced around, then rose and moved to the far point of the room—the darkest area—and pressed his back against the wall while he strained to hear more. Faintly, faintly, there were footsteps at the far end of the hall: quiet, soft footsteps; menacing, up-to-no-good footsteps. DJ carefully opened the closet door and slipped inside, silently closing it behind him. With his ear to the wall, he could hear the footsteps drawing closer, pausing at the bathroom, just as he had, then continuing toward the bedroom. At the doorway, another pause, then while DJ held his breath, the footsteps moved forward again, quietly stepping into the bedroom, first exploring the far side before moving closer, then next to the closet door.

Squatting in the corner of the closet, ready to pounce, DJ heard the doorknob slowly being twisted, then the door was inched open.

Suddenly, as he lunged forward, the beam of a flashlight flared in his eyes, blinding him.

"Whoa cowboy, take it easy," Monty said, as he caught DJ around the shoulders. "Whoa, whoa, whoa."

"Monty? Oh man, Monty, it's you, thank God, it's you." DJ said. "Thank God, it's you."

"Of course it's me. Strange place to be meeting people though, DJ, in the closet of an empty house."

"How come you didn't turn the lights on? You really scared me half to death."

"No light bulbs anywhere, otherwise I would have. Had to use the old Vermont flashlight I keep in the glove compartment."

"This used to be Carlyn's house. That's why I'm inside."

"I know," Monty said. "Thor knew where she lived."

"But how did you know I would be here?"

"You weren't at home, or at the Rock, so I put two and two together, plus the Falcon's across the street in plain sight. Didn't expect to find you in the closet though."

DJ nodded, then after a moment, thought out loud, "Why are you here?"

"Got some information for you. A few things that will

interest you."

DJ realized he was still holding the sweater and self-consciously tucked it under his arm. "What kind of information?"

Monty picked up the photograph of DJ with the ankle bracelet linked through it. After a moment, he nodded. "Kind of a nasty way to say goodbye, huh?"

DJ looked away.

"DJ, I don't know how to say the kinds of things I have to say so they don't hurt, but I've found the direct way, the truth, is usually the best."

"I'm not sure what you mean," DJ answered.

"Your girlfriend, Carlyn Reynolds, or Carlyn Canova, whichever, is not exactly the true-blue type you would want to take home to mama. And she's not a killer."

"She's not a killer? How do you know?" DJ asked.

Monty walked over to the bedroom window, tapping the flashlight against the palm of his hand. "But that doesn't necessarily make her an upstanding citizen either. After our talk the other night, I spoke with Thor about your suspicions. He's got a line right up to New York City Police Commissioner Biondi, and he was told the NYPD have the cop killer in custody. Same fella they arrested earlier, except they needed more proof. Apparently they got it—I don't know all the details—confronted him, and with what I understand was a mountain of new evidence placed in front of him, the guy confessed. It's all done in black and white, signed, sealed and delivered. Guy was a real nut case with a rap sheet two feet long—should be an announcement in the next day or two." Monty absently ran his fingers along the window ledge. "Thor tells me the police had this guy under surveillance since they put him back on the street, never once letting him out of their sight." He looked over at DJ. "And by the way, the cop that was killed was not the same one that stopped Carlyn and you that night. That's been confirmed by police tour-of-duty records. The two may have looked alike, but Dixon, the murdered policeman was from a Manhattan precinct, his body dumped and discovered in Brooklyn. Your handy-dandy policeman is alive and well and living in Maspeth."

"That's hard to believe, Monty," DJ said. "Really hard to believe. I mean, I was sure it was him." He thought a second. "What about that Albany policeman I told you about that was killed last Christmas?"

Monty shook his head. "Not murder. His buddy accidentally shot him while they were hunting and then was afraid to fess up. Truth came to light the next day."

"Shot him while they were hunting?"

"Happens all the time, DJ. Too many loaded guns with yahoos manning the triggers. Only reason you didn't know about it was because we're outside the Albany news stream."

"Oh," DJ said, unconsciously drawing the sweater to his nose, attempting to revive the fading perfume. "I guess you've got an answer to everything." He paused. "But what about Bobby?"

"Bobby's a different story," Monty said. "Interesting. Police forensic department originally thought the specifics of the New York City and Hardscrabble homicides were identical. Turns out not to be totally true. The city cop was hit in the back of the head with a blunt object—probably a rock or something—and never saw his assailant. Chances are, Bobby never saw it coming either, at least until the last second. What's strange is that it looks like Bobby was hit twice— once on the back of the head—similar to the New York City policeman, but he was also struck with something resembling a crowbar, or baseball bat on the side of his skull. No one is certain if the trauma to the back of the head was inflicted, or the result of a fall, but the crowbar scenario is very real. Looks like he fell, then tried to get up, and collapsed again.

"Detectives have a lot of theories, but they haven't been quite able to figure out exactly what happened, and what's worse, the coroner can't even tell which hit to the head killed him. Thing is though, by some field work and a process of elimination, we know some of the folks who were not responsible for Bobby's murder." He paused. "And as I mentioned, Carlyn falls into that group."

"How could you know that?" DJ asked.

Monty turned toward the window. "Because her activities were checked out. Carlyn quit her job like you said—apparently, it's a pattern she follows when life gets uncomfortable. She was still in town after you talked with me the other night. The police confirmed her whereabouts and she was nowhere near Bobby, or the fireworks on the Fourth of July."

"Where was she?" DJ asked.

Monty looked at DJ. He flexed the fingers of his left hand and shoved them in his back pocket. "She was in a motel with Cliff Collins."

DJ stared at the floor.

"The police have the receipt, the visual confirmation by the motel clerk, and a signed statement by both Cliff and Carlyn. The two had been there since five o'clock in the afternoon." Monty continued to tap the flashlight against the palm of his hand. "I'm sorry as I can be, DJ. But it's only right that I let you know what the truth is."

After a few moments, DJ nodded. "That's okay."

"Carlyn Canova is a psychopath from everything I can tell. Chasing you like a wild woman, tearing up people's property, then spending the night with a married man, destroying more lives in the process. And I would imagine that's just a small part of her history." He shrugged. "Our pal Cliff Collins is going to have to get himself a hotshot lawyer now," Monty continued. "Four kids and a wife with a temper. Shoot-the-wounded-and-keep-on-marching type of gal. I don't envy him."

For a long minute, DJ stared outside at the barren moon, watching, waiting for the clouds to cover it again so he could hide. It was hard to believe it was the same moon that had crept into his bedroom every night of his life. "I guess I should go home now," he said, his voice uneven as he turned to Monty.

"I appreciate you telling me all of this." He loosened his grip on the sweater, letting it fall to the floor.

"Hey," Monty said, stooping and picking it up. "Take it along. Throw it away someday when you can do it honestly, when you don't need it anymore.

"I don't think that's such a good idea," DJ said.

"Not a bad one either," Monty answered. "What's the difference?

"I don't think I should."

Monty put his hand on DJ's shoulder. "Let me tell you something, son. I know it's real hard for you right now. There's nothing finer than your first love, and nothing worse than losing it." He coughed. "I ought to know because I've been there. I'm not trying to preach to you, DJ, but it's a little bit like your mother setting you free for the first time when you were a toddler. She was your whole world, then she let you go on the swing by yourself, or sit on the steps alone while she was doing the laundry in the cellar. You couldn't remember her ever not being next to you, but suddenly there it was, and you know what, you survived. You made it."

"I don't feel like I made it," DJ said. "Anyway, mothers always try to be there."

"Right," Monty conceded, handing DJ the sweater, "but once they leave the first time, it's never quite the same again."

DJ brushed Carlyn's sweater across the side of his face as he stared away.

"I need to ask a favor," Monty continued, dropping his hand from DJ's shoulder. I'm feeling real bad about Ike being gone. I knew him some because he was your best friend, but I'd sure like to know more about him, and I was thinking maybe you could help me with that." Monty crossed the bedroom floor, then turned. "Come on. What do you say we get out of here? Maybe we can stop at the diner and get a bite." He glanced at his watch. "Heck, maybe go totally crazy and even get some ice cream." He looked back at DJ. "You'd sure be helping me out a whole lot with Ike."

DJ studied the bedroom and couldn't quite remember how it used to be. Under his breath, he said, "I don't understand why things don't work out the way they're supposed to."

"Neither do I," Monty said, "neither do I." He glanced at DJ. "How about us leaving now?"

DJ looked around the room a last time. "I guess I could do that."

"Well, let's go ahead then," Monty said, heading out of the bedroom.

DJ followed him through the living room and out the kitchen door. "But I don't understand, then who killed Bobby?"

Monty glanced back over his shoulder. "Lord only knows," he said, "because the police sure don't."

CHAPTER 58

"Hello."

"Hello, I'm trying to reach Mr. Ed Lynch."

"Speaking."

"Mr. Lynch, ah, the reas—"

"Who's calling?"

"Ah, my name is DJ Elders. I don't think you know me. I tried to reach you once before, but there was no answer. I just found your phone number again."

"Is that right? When did you try to get a hold of me?"

"I'm not sure. A couple of months ago. Maybe back in June."

"That makes sense, I was away. Always take the month of June off and head up to South Carolina. Change of scenery. Excuse me a second." He sneezed. "Darn pollen is killing me this season. Where you calling from, DJ?"

"From Hardscrabble. Long Island."

"So what happened, did she break your heart?"

DJ stumbled over the question. "What? I don't know what you mean."

"I'm assuming you're calling about Carlyn. Isn't that right?"

DJ paused. "I guess so, I mean, I guess I am. How did you

know that?"

"Well, I'd like to say beginner's luck, but that wouldn't be truthful. I am surprised she went back home to Hardscrabble though." He sneezed again. "Excuse me for the second time. Sorry to be so rude." He cleared his throat. "I tell you, DJ, I get a phone call about Carlyn every year or so, though it's been a while since the last one. I do try to make an effort to be friendly to the fellas who contact me—seems only right. Once or twice Carlyn's even called me herself. It's strange. I guess I'm a kind of touchstone for her. Something like that." He hesitated. "You sound young though, even for her."

"I don't understand. What do you mean you get phone calls?"

"Easy to say, hard to understand. Sometimes Carlyn gives my phone number to men she's been involved with, though by the time they reach me the damage is usually done. I can't tell you exactly why she does it—just to prove she was married once, that she was credible once, I suppose."

DJ hesitated, considering what Ed Lynch had just said. "That doesn't make a lot of sense."

"It doesn't make any sense as far as I'm concerned. I expect you're calling because you're looking for information, or some kind of explanation for the way she behaves. That's usually the case. Truth is, I don't have any absolute answers about her, and I only have a vague idea how her mind operates. We weren't married very long, you know. It's possible you were pushing her for information, or getting suspicious about her background. For some odd reason, old Ed Lynch's phone number seems to call off the dogs. Somehow it seems to make her believable, even respectable. You know, like she really is what she claims to be."

DJ could barely breathe. Far away he heard the faint hum of the telephone line, a train whistling through the night, and began to feel alone again. "You know her," he said slowly, uncomfortably. "Why did she use me up?"

"That's about as good a way of putting it as I've heard, DJ.

To enlarge upon your question, why does she use everybody up, then discard them as if they were garbage?"

"Why does she?"

"I don't have an answer for you. The reality is she's a sexually aggressive female who frequently moves on to a new conquest, and many times in the process, a new job. She's probably more than just promiscuous—behavior suggests sexual addiction based on the reading I've done. Whether she's hooked on sex, or control, or both, is anybody's guess. And I would imagine her beauty helps reinforce her behavior, just as wealth would reinforce a drug user. He paused. "She is still beautiful, isn't she?"

"Yeah, she is."

"Well, that's right. If Carlyn wasn't so beautiful, she wouldn't get away with half of what she pulls." He paused again. "But being beautiful and smart, which she is, doesn't necessarily mean she's kind. She's not. And her looks will eventually fade, then we'll see what becomes of her."

"Did she drop you too?"

"Like a hot potato, my friend. I was married to Carlyn two months and she was already trolling the male meat market in Hardscrabble. Took me years to figure out that I hadn't done something wrong. Hold it." He sneezed again. "Sorry about that. Damn drugs don't work." He paused. "When I discovered her extracurricular adventures, I was totally devastated, so with the last ounce of pride I could pull together, I went to work one day and didn't come home." He paused. "Of course Carlyn never came after me—she could have found me if she wanted to. I was at my mother's house for a week, waiting for her to call or come by looking for me. But she never did. She was already involved with someone else." He paused. "I have to tell you though, as I look back, getting away from her was the best thing that ever happened to me."

"I don't understand what's the matter with her, Mr. Lynch."

"Call me Ed, DJ." His voice suddenly became solemn. "Look, she just is. Lots of men behave identically and are called Don

Juans and Casanovas. They wear their promiscuity like a badge of honor. You sound like a nice guy, and my advice, as painful as it may be, is for you to move forward. Carlyn's radioactive. You're never aware of the damage as it's being inflicted. Don't forget what's happened, but don't spend time dwelling there. Heck, she broke my heart when I was just a kid out of high school. How old are you?"

"Eighteen."

"Right, eighteen, so you know what I'm talking about."

"Did you think she ever might get really mad and kill you?"

"Carlyn?"

"Yeah."

"I don't know, I never gave anything like that a thought. The only thing I remember for sure is she can't stand it when somebody says no to her, or rejects her in any way. She behaves like a mad woman—overreacts like crazy. Really childish stuff." He blew his nose. "Did you ever have the pleasure of saying no to her?"

"Yes, a couple of times. The last time I wouldn't meet with her or get in the car when she wanted me to."

"What did she do?"

"Chased after me in her Mustang, across people's lawn and stuff."

"And there you have it. Same old girl I grew up with except it sounds like she might even be getting worse. She wouldn't know a boundary if it jumped up and bit her on the seat of her pants." Ed paused another moment. "Is there somebody up there dead?"

Thinking of Bobby, then the New York City cop, DJ answered, "Yes, but she didn't do it."

"That rings true. I've never seen actual physical violence, but anything's possible. With her personality, I'd never say never."

DJ was silent.

"I suspect," Ed continued, "the reality is that she gets away with a lot because we all become entranced by her beauty, then make the mistake of expecting more from her than she's capable of or at least wants to offer. It's most likely that simple."

DJ hesitated, listening to his own breathing into the phone. "I guess that's what happened to me," he said.

"Me too, my friend. And there are probably many more of us out there."

"Were there a lot of others?"

"I'm sure."

DJ stared down at his shoes. "Doesn't seem fair."

"Because it's not fair. But the best thing for you, DJ, is to keep pedaling straight ahead, going your own way. She's probably not thinking about you. Addiction, if that's her problem, is treatable and occasionally people change. Just don't count on it. And be thankful you didn't end up with her. You're better than that. I suspect we all are."

DJ was silent for a few seconds. "This wasn't the kind of talk I thought I would be having," he said at last.

"What were you expecting?"

"I don't know. I think I was hoping to find some way to get her back." After another moment he murmured, "I guess she's not out of my mind yet."

"I understand," Ed said quietly. "Give yourself some time. You'll move on. In the final analysis, you have no other choice. Look at me, I made it."

"Did you?" DJ listened to the train whistle echo through the telephone line again.

"I think so," Ed said finally. "More than likely I did."

DJ nodded to himself, then said, "Thanks for talking with me, Ed."

"You're welcome, DJ. Call me again if you like."

SEPTEMBER, 1965

CHAPTER 59

"DJ-J-J-J," Maynard bellowed as the car screeched to a halt in front of DJ's house Saturday at noon. "Get the hell in here, so we can get the hell out of here."

"Okay, okay. Relax," DJ said, climbing into the passenger side.

Maynard floored the accelerator, burning rubber as he fishtailed down Jackson Road. Reaching across the dashboard, he turned up the radio, then lit a cigarette. "Freedom, huh?"

"I guess." DJ stared out the window, then stretched, raising his arms over his head. "What's the name of this place we're going to?"

"It's a little dump out on the North Fork, right on the water. Quarter beers, pickled eggs—no one to bug you. We can do some serious drinking without anyone giving us any grief. You know, talk about old times."

"We're still in the old times."

Maynard shrugged. "So we talk about some new old times."

∞

An hour later, Maynard left the parkway, traveled through a tiny hamlet, then swung onto a rutted single-lane road for a quarter of a mile until they arrived at a bar with a lone dusty pickup parked in front.

The place was just as Maynard had described: wooden, threadbare, with a pistachio nut machine and a broken-down jukebox full of rockabilly tunes. It was dreary and DJ knew immediately that he didn't want to be there.

After placing two beers in front of the boys, the bartender walked to the far end of the empty bar to read the newspaper he had spread out in front of him.

"So did you find another job?" Maynard asked, lighting a cigarette.

"No, not yet. Just working at Van Velsor's on Sundays. I have to find something pretty soon though. In college, you need money."

After he'd learned about Cliff Collins and Carlyn being together, he never went back to Mertz Brothers despite his father's threats. He didn't even attempt to call. Cliff could insinuate he was unprofessional for the rest of his life—he didn't care. The store was alive with too many ghosts of Carlyn, too many shadows in the back room of Basement Shoes.

DJ picked up his beer and walked over to the jukebox. He played a quarters worth of songs and crossed back to the bar. "You know what I can't figure out? How come they never caught the guy who killed Bobby? I thought detectives were supposed to be good like on TV. One clue, case solved."

"I know what you mean," Maynard answered after firing out a succession of smoke rings. "What did the cops finally say, random homicide? I bet that makes Bobby's parents feel real good. Doesn't make me feel so secure either."

"Nope," DJ said, "it sure doesn't."

∞

An hour later, DJ nudged Maynard. "Let's hit it."

"Amen, brother," Maynard answered. "Need some fresh air myself."

Back in the car, Maynard screeched around the parking lot initiating a massive dust tornado. Before he headed for the road, he flashed the bar a traditional obscene gesture from the arsenal of insults so readily available following a beer holiday.

As they approached the tiny town perched near the parkway, Maynard groaned, "Ah-h-h, man, look at that, the oil light's on." He slapped the dashboard.

"What's the big deal?" DJ asked.

"I'll tell you what the big deal is. It means we have to pull over and get some oil unless you want the engine to seize."

Moments later, the car pulled into a Gulf station. DJ and Maynard stepped outside and walked to the front of the car.

"Help you, sir?" A teenage boy approached Maynard.

Maynard turned to DJ. "Believe that, he called me sir? I must be getting a beer belly." He turned back to the attendant. "Quart of oil—cheapest you got."

The boy jammed a funnel into an oil can while Maynard lifted the car's hood. He held it open with one hand, unhooked the prop-rod, then inserted it into the hole on the hood's inner edge. His hands free, Maynard took the oil from the attendant, unscrewed the crankcase lid and poured in the oil. He replaced the cap, then slid into the front seat, started the engine and studied the dashboard. "No problem, oil light's off."

Maynard stepped outside, paid, and lowered the hood. "Let's blow this dump," he said as the two jumped back into the car. As he screeched out of the Gulf station, he lit a cigarette. "Hey, we could have been screwed if we hadn't found the gas station. Yup, that shows I'm just born lucky sometimes. Lucky, that is, if you don't count Frannie getting pregnant. I wonder if she'll ever want to do the dirty deed again?" He reached over and punched DJ in the arm. "Kidding, just kidding." A frown crossed his face. "Not really."

DJ barely heard Maynard's running monologue. He could feel a slow iciness crawl across his shoulders. The prop-rod that kept the hood open; the diameter; the crook at the end; the way it fit into the hole; the purplish blue color.

He'd seen a similar piece of steel before

Something that didn't seem quite right; something out of place.

The last time he had been at Greta's, more than two months ago, when he had cried about Ike's death, then called her a liar . . . after she had escorted him out the door, he had stood on the landing . . . and he hadn't heard the bar from the lock being slipped into position as was her custom.

Something that didn't seem quite right; something out of place.

He thought back. When Greta had opened the door to let him in, she had not removed the steel bar from the lock and placed it in the corner as she always did. Ike had died the day after Bobby's July 4th murder. That was the day he visited her, July 5th, and the steel bar that angled from the double bolt lock to the floor had been missing. He was sure! What had Monty said? "What's strange is that it looks like Bobby was hit twice—once on the back of the head, similar to the New York City policeman—but he was also struck with something resembling a crowbar or baseball bat on the side of his skull!"

DJ had observed Greta's anger before. He had watched her destroy a Christmas tree with a broom handle simply because it would not stand up straight. He'd heard all the unbalanced lies about a deceased poet being her friend. He had seen her sit alone in a booth at Van Velsor's, either staring at an empty checker board, or vacantly off into space.

And?

And what? Did that make her a killer, or even a suspect for

that matter? Would she, no, could she, ever have such violent inclinations?

DJ struggled with his thoughts. Greta had witnessed Bobby mistreating Patty that Saturday night in Van Velsor's. Was she so protective of his sister—were the two so close—that she would stray from a system of laws to commit a murder? Was she even capable, mentally or physically, of such a deed?

DJ stared out the side window, then slowly relaxed. He was barely eighteen and already felt like he needed a vacation from life. Greta had probably thought she was too security conscious and had decided to stop using the bar. That had to be it.

"Want to stop and say hi to Thor?" Maynard asked as they drove down Melville Road toward Hardscrabble. "I've developed a healthy thirst on the way back."

"Tell you what," DJ answered. "You go ahead. I've got to stop at Van Velsor's."

CHAPTER 60

DJ was uncomfortable walking in the door. He hadn't spoken with Greta since the night he had come unglued in her apartment. Nothing between them had been resolved and she no longer appeared in Van Velsor's on Sunday mornings when he assembled newspapers.

Herman was on his way out the door. "Ah, DJ," he said, stopping, "I'm going over to the auto parts store to see if I can get some change for tomorrow. Didn't get to the bank this morning." He paused. "Don't forget to come in early so we get a good start on the papers." He glanced at his watch. "That's not too long from now. Never hurts to be one step ahead, eh?"

"Okay, Herman," DJ said.

Herman looked over his shoulder. "Greta, please watch the front in case any customers come in. I'll be back in a few minutes." He walked out the door onto Main Street.

The coffee shop was empty except for Greta, who was in her booth studying the checkerboard, her empty ivory cigarette holder between her fingers, a cup of coffee sitting to the side.

DJ stopped once he was in front of her.

Slowly, carefully, Greta looked up from the checkerboard, her eyes meeting his. "Hello, DJ," she said.

"Do you mind if I sit down?"

"You won't win," she answered, nodding at the checkers.

"I don't expect to." He slid into the booth opposite her.

"I just finished looking at Patty's yearbook. She brought it with her today," Greta said. Opening the front cover, she thumbed through the pages, then stopped at one. "So very sad." She slid the book sideways so DJ could see a picture of Bobby and Lisa being crowned king and queen of the Inaugural Ball.

DJ studied the photo closely as if he were an outsider viewing it for the first time. He could see that all the media hype had been correct. Bobby had been handsome and athletic with worlds at his disposal.

"Just like that, life changes," Greta said, "and we don't know when we are facing a last goodbye."

DJ met her eyes, then looked back down at the yearbook.

"And you," Greta continued, "on this donkey." She turned the page, then pointed at the picture that had appeared in the school newspaper showing him making the final shot at the wrong basket, losing the game for the senior class. "You thought you would never survive after that incident." She smiled. "And look, here you are."

DJ reached across and leafed through several more pages, unsure how to initiate his conversation. He saw a candid shot of Rocco sporting a sour disposition, glowering at one of the teachers in the cafeteria, and a picture of several cheerleaders talking with muddied football players in front of the team bus. Toward the end of the book, just past the homeroom pictures of the freshmen, he saw a photograph he had nearly forgotten, one that Ike had pointed out, showing students traveling between classes in a crowded hallway. When he looked closely, far into the background, he could see Ike leaning against a bank of lockers, waiting for the crush of people to lessen before he walked quietly to his next class.

DJ wondered what Ike had been thinking at that exact moment he had become immortalized in time. He looked away. It was too sad.

"And you, dear boy, how are you?"

Not acknowledging Greta's question, DJ turned to the first page of the yearbook which contained Robert Frost's "Stopping By The Woods On A Snowy Evening" superimposed over a frosty, snow-laden image of the public golf course. He figured it was as close as the photo editors could get to a genuine country winter scene near Hardscrabble's area of Long Island—though the ball-washers sticking out of the snow like lollipops tarnished the mystique.

Sliding the picture to Greta, he pointed to Frost's name, "Did you know him too?"

Greta inserted a Players cigarette into the ivory holder and lit it, ignoring his question. "And you, dear boy, entered my world because I allowed you to, because I care for you, then you choose to flaunt its inadequacies to me."

"Only because it wasn't a real world," DJ said.

"And yet, in many ways I am grateful to you, dear boy," Greta continued, staring away, dismissing his response as she twisted a lock of hair around her forefinger. Resting the cigarette holder on the lip of the ashtray, she folded her hands. "You have, perhaps, awakened me." Her eyes met his. "But contrary to what you may believe, the photograph in my apartment was indeed signed by Rupert Brooke. I was a mere child, intrigued by his poetry, and sent him what I suppose you might refer to today as a fan letter. He was kind enough to respond with the picture. For reasons that are mine alone, but primarily due to a self-inflicted fear of living in the real world, I subsequently created a lifestyle of my choosing revolving around the photograph. It was easy, safe, and beautiful." She hesitated, "Though now I realize it was also quite empty."

Greta nodded in DJ's direction. "You were perceptive enough to point out my fabrications, for which I am grateful." She paused. "Perhaps Nureyev and Fontane will never again leap with such abandon, nor will Mendelssohn's 'O for the Wings of a Dove' be as pure, but I will survive, dear boy, and I shall now continue to move forward, absorbing whatever life has in store for me." She hesitated. "Yet sometimes I—"

"What happened to the bar from the lock in your apartment?" DJ interrupted.

"Why do you ask, dear boy?" The crow's feet at the corners of her eyes suddenly resembled war paint, the loose flesh below her jaw, a reflection of tribal wisdom.

"Because it's not there anymore."

"And you would know that how? Certainly not by visiting me."

"On July 5th, I did visit you, and the bar wasn't there when I came in and went out. That was the day after Bobby Litchfield was killed."

"And therefore, what?" She picked up the cigarette holder and inhaled. "What is it that you are suggesting?"

"Thor told Monty that it was a crowbar, or a baseball bat, or something like that may have killed Bobby."

"And therefore, what?"

DJ wasn't sure how to proceed. He hesitated, then said, "Just tell me, what happened to it?"

Greta dropped her gaze and moved a checker forward, then slid it back. Lifting her eyes, she said, "I don't know."

DJ leaned forward. "What do you mean you don't know? It was part of the lock in your apartment. It was always there. What do you mean, you don't know? Where is it?"

"You would have to ask your sister. She's the one who borrowed it from me."

DJ was shaken. He stared at Greta. "Patty? Borrowed it from you? When?"

"After the fireworks. After she left my apartment the night of July 4th."

"That's not true. That's totally untrue."

"Is that so?" Greta rolled the cigarette holder between her forefinger and thumb. "Ask her."

"I don't have to ask her. She would never even consider what you're suggesting."

"And what is it that I'm suggesting?" Greta inquired.

DJ's eyes locked on Greta's.

"Ask her," Greta continued. "Don't take my word for it. Ask her."

"I don't have to ask her anything."

"Did she ever tell you what happened that night out with Bobby? I believe it was July 3rd," Greta continued. Her voice grew cold, removed. "Did she ever explain to you what happened?"

"Of course she did. You know she did."

"Tell me," Greta said. "Tell me what occurred."

DJ hurriedly recounted the lurid details Patty had revealed about the evening. When finished, he said, "That's the story."

Greta shook her head. "You know nothing, dear boy. Nothing at all."

"Then what don't I know?" he asked, his voice less confident, a vague sense of dread now approaching.

"You don't know that your sister lied to you through omission. That what occurred was far more serious than Patty would ever admit to you." The muscles around her jaw tightened. "That against her wishes, Bobby had his way with your sister, then brought her here as a conquest, a personal trophy, if you will, but grew irritated with her attitude. Imagine that, irritated with *her* attitude."

DJ could not speak, would not believe her.

"Patty was unable to tell you for fear of what you might do to Bobby or what you might think of her. And when she approached your father, I'm told his grasp of the situation was a little less than sympathetic. Is that not correct?"

"She would have told me if something more had happened," DJ said, his voice tight.

"So she ended up telling me," Greta continued. "I suppose as a type of Mother Confessor because she knew I would never condemn her or think less of her."

"You're making this up. Just like Rupert."

"Am I?" Greta shrugged. "Ask her. I wasn't there. I'm just repeating what was told to me and only because you are her brother and self-appointed protector." She paused briefly. "But I assure you I will never mention these words to anyone ever again and deny to all who inquire that they were ever spoken."

"Let me make sure I understand. Are you saying th—"

"I am saying nothing, dear boy, only repeating what has been told to me."

DJ hesitated. "If Patty did do something," he said looking quickly around the coffee shop, assuring himself that no one was present to overhear the conversation, "then she'll end up going to jail." He felt lightheaded. "If she's lucky, she'll *just* have to go to jail."

"And I wonder for what," Greta responded matter-of-factly. "For avenging the savagery that violated and humiliated her? For responding in the same manner in which she was attacked? Your sister is barely seventeen, a child herself, and you are suggesting she spend the rest of her life stamping out license plates in a corrupt corrections institution, fighting off more aggressors in the process? Please, spare me."

"I'm not saying anything other than she may have broken the law, Greta." DJ paused, the ends of his fingers nervously tapping the edge of the table as he thought. "Why did you ever let her take that bar from your apartment in the first place?"

"Your sister took it and left when I was in the bathroom. Although she had never before departed so abruptly, I knew she was seriously upset so I could understand the unusual behavior. I didn't notice the bar was missing until I was ready to go to bed." Greta absently ran the palm of her hand across her cheek. "Certainly, I had no idea of her intent. And I never would have guessed." Greta locked her eyes on DJ. "But the law is the law, and your sister is your sister. The law, for all its claims to the contrary, is subjective, but your sister is everything."

"But you can't take the law into your own hands."

"Ah, yes, a familiar and tattered cliché of the worst kind. You can't take the law into your own hands. What might I ask did Bobby do? Why is his crime any less than Patty's? Is it because she had the good fortune to live and now must suffer with the memory of his brutality the rest of her life?" Greta shook her head. "Had Patty brought criminal charges against Bobby, his father, a lawyer himself, would simply have purchased the necessary justice, a 'he said-she said' defense. For the rest of us there is only the law. And whose hands should that law be in? Lawyers? Perhaps judges?" Her eyes pierced DJ's. "I understand your father has been awarded the patronage-based Liberty Party nomination for a state judgeship, which is tantamount to winning. From what I've read, he will be ruling in matrimonial and child custody cases. Yes, how about judges?"

DJ's voice was barely above a whisper. "If Patty did it, she broke the law in the worst way. You can't kill somebody and get away with it, or pretend it didn't happen."

"Obviously, the police have no evidence and I assure you the only story they will ever hear from me, the only story you will ever hear from me from this point forward, is that Patty was in my company the entire evening until the moment she departed for home. We have coordinated the time so there is no disparity." Greta tamped out her cigarette. "And, dear boy, that is all there will be. As I enter your world, your so-called real world, I will, nonetheless, make certain poetic justice does and will prevail. While the detectives and commissioners and politicians are posturing, battling hangovers and calculating power grabs ad nauseum, Patty shall continue on with her life as if nothing happened."

DJ stared at Greta. Slowly, he thought out loud, "I wonder if she can."

Herman appeared in the front of the coffee shop carrying rolls of coins. "I'm back," he called, parking himself behind the cash register.

Quietly, almost to herself, Greta said, "We attempt to live

our dreams and end up being destroyed in the process." Lifting the checkerboard, she slowly folded it in half, allowing the checkers to slide down the crease and clatter onto the table. "So you will do what you will do, DJ— without any help from me." She placed the checkerboard and checkers in a box. "I'm an old woman, and I'm weary, and you will do what you will do."

"Where is Patty?" DJ asked, looking around.

"Where she always is on Saturday, at five o'clock Mass over at St. Mary's."

DJ looked at his watch. "It's four-thirty."

"Your sister is always early. Herman allows her this freedom because it's a slow time here and he knows it's important to her. But you knew that." Greta slid from the booth, picked up the box, and not looking back, walked to the side of the counter and removed her coat from a hook. As she approached the cash register she handed the checkers box to Herman and slowly hobbled toward the door. "Goodbye. I think I'll go now. I'm not feeling well."

Herman looked up briefly. "Okay, Greta," he said. "You'll call me if your condition worsens?"

"Yes," Greta responded. "I'll know soon enough." She crossed to the door and left the coffee shop.

DJ continued to sit, deep in thought for several minutes, then as he rose to leave, Herman beckoned him over to the cash register. "So, DJ, why do you torment Greta?" he asked.

"I don't know what you mean."

"She's my sister. You have most certainly noticed she has always been, well, different, which is why she lives as she does."

"Yes, I know that." DJ hesitated, "And she doesn't always tell the truth."

Herman shrugged. "And who does? You, maybe? Me? I don't think so." He brushed crumbs from behind the cash register onto the floor. "Have you never had imaginary friends for comfort?"

"I was younger."

"And she is older. So what?" Herman reached into his front pocket and extracted a roll of bills, then began sorting them by denomination. Not looking up, he continued, "Greta has fantasies that occupy her life, but she also possesses a wisdom that surprises me. That insight is, I believe, genuine, and a gift." Herman stopped sorting and looked at DJ. "In her heart, she knows her poet relationship does not exist, that it is merely a source of comfort to a woman who has had very little in the way of companionship over the years. Accept her for who she is, DJ. She's harmless and has much she can teach you. Take what you want and leave the rest behind. Just be kind to her."

"I've been kind to her. Except for once or twice."

"Once or twice is too much." He stretched a rubber band around the roll of bills and shoved it back in his front pocket. "You know what I'm talking about."

DJ rubbed the back of his hand. "I didn't know. I didn't know that she wasn't telling the truth. For a long time I believed her about Rupert Brooke."

"You're young. You'll learn everything in life isn't as it seems. Your friendship, Patty's, both have meant a good deal to her. Greta and I think of both of you as part of our family."

DJ nodded.

"So what do you say? Can you be kind to an old woman?"

DJ stared out the front window. After several moments, he mumbled, "Okay, Herman, I guess I just didn't understand the rules."

"So now you do." He reached out with his open hand and tapped DJ lightly on the cheek, then ran his eyes around the coffee shop. "Come in early tomorrow. I want to make sure we've got all the newspapers together at least a half hour before opening time."

"Okay, Herman," DJ answered. "I'll be here early."

"I know that," Herman answered. "You're getting better. Maybe someday I won't have to remind you."

CHAPTER 61

DJ stood in the vestibule and allowed his eyes to adjust to the dimness. A faint branch of sunlight speared through the stained glass, skated across the altar, then disappeared into the wood flooring of the empty, hushed church. Moving forward through the vestibule, quietly entering the nave, DJ saw Patty in the far corner of the rear right-hand pew, kneeling, her hands tensely folded, her eyes clenched shut. He moved across the pew, knelt next to her, then reaching, placed his hands over hers.

After a moment, her eyes still closed, she whispered, "I knew you would come."

"I'm here," DJ answered.

Still kneeling, her eyes slowly opened and she whispered, "Do you remember the colors of the Maypole?" She stared at the stained glass and smiled—a small, tentative smile. "I could smell the flowers, and I was so happy. Then as I was skipping, winding the ribbons together with the other girls from my class, their mothers began to take each one away until I was alone with the empty Maypole and my teacher. She said to come inside with her, but I said no, that you would be there soon. I stood under the schoolhouse ledge in the shade, hoping it wouldn't be you, but instead our mother." Patty hesitated. "I wouldn't recognize or remember her, but somehow I would know it was her."

"I remember the Maypole. I remember you waiting under the ledge."

"But she didn't come, and you did. You walked over and put your arm around me, and we went home."

DJ gently lifted his hands from Patty's. "I remember."

"That was the first day I realized how I needed her. I had always missed her—I had gotten used to that—but I never knew I needed her. All these years I've waited for her to come back to me, but she never has." Lowering her head slightly, she quietly slid back and sat on the bench of the pew, her hands folded on her lap.

DJ moved back next to her. "She's not alive, Patty. You know that."

"I know. I know, but I still pray for her to be here. I can't stop that. Every Saturday, sometimes in the morning too, I'm in church by myself so that my voice will be the only one God hears. And I don't want to be angry when my prayers are unanswered, and I always am." She brought the knuckle of one thumb to her mouth and a slight smile appeared, then just as quickly departed. "I've even imagined that beyond the school was a seawall where she and I sat and watched the ocean waves, with the wild daisies and beach plums in the field behind us. And I could rest my head against her shoulder, unafraid, and tell her about the Maypole."

DJ saw her hands knotted on her lap, chapped from all of Herman's vinegar-and-water scrub sessions, and strands of hair, loosened from beneath a barrette, scattered across the back of her neck. And no earrings. Patty never wore earrings because no mother had been present to teach her. "Maybe Greta is like a second mother for you," he offered gently.

"I don't know," Patty said. "Maybe she is."

"It could be what she believes."

Patty turned to DJ, tears filling her eyes. "I couldn't tell you or Dad what Bobby did to me." She reached in her pocketbook for a tissue. "I wanted to tell you. I tried." She looked away. "I couldn't."

"I know."

Patty stared at her fingers, now twisting in her lap. Her voice barely a whisper, she murmured, "Bobby said he wanted to park and just talk. He said he wanted to get to know me better. And then, once we were there, he wouldn't leave me alone. No matter what I said, he wouldn't leave me alone." Patty's eyes overflowed. "I tried to push him away, DJ, I did. I screamed for him to stop, but he wouldn't. And he was so strong, he forced my arms back and held them behind my head, and he wouldn't stop." The tears ran down Patty's cheeks. "Then he hurt me and I didn't know what to do." She rested her forehead against DJ's shoulder. "I thought I was going to die."

DJ placed his arm around her.

"And when he was finished, he said he was going to tell everyone on the football team that it was my idea—so that after he had gone to Yale, they could get a turn too." Patty lifted her head so that her face was inches from DJ's. "He was going to do that to me."

DJ stared forward, unable to respond, his internal rage howling.

I begged him not to. I begged him not to tell anyone," Patty repeated, "and finally he laughed and said he wouldn't as long as I kept my mouth shut and let him do it again."

DJ involuntarily jerked.

"I didn't let him," Patty whispered. "And he didn't try to force me the second time. I don't know why. He just laughed again, then told me we were going to Van Velsor's as if it was all normal. He said that if I went with him and didn't say anything, he wouldn't either." She looked away. "I don't even know why I did go. It was as if I was in a dream. But once we were there, he started making fun of me, then getting mad with me, and I knew he would eventually tell everyone." Patty slowly rocked back and forth. "And I couldn't live with that, DJ. I could never live with people thinking that about me."

DJ silently nodded. "I know you couldn't."

"And Dad wouldn't even believe me." She turned. "Even Dad, DJ."

"I know."

Patty slowly straightened in the pew. "Then the next night, the Fourth of July, I didn't think I was going to do—what I did."

DJ stared straight ahead.

"When Greta went into the bathroom, I took her security bar that fits in that lock on her door and walked outside. I took the flag that was in front of her apartment and rolled it around the bar to hide it." Patty shivered slightly. "I wasn't sure what I was going to do, but in the back of my mind, I think I was planning. I was so angry, DJ. It felt like a delayed reaction to what Bobby had done to me. And I kept getting madder and madder with each step."

She hesitated. "Then I saw Bobby in town and I walked over and asked him to meet me by the lake."

Patty halted, then sighed, her eyes cast downward. After a moment, she continued, her voice shaky. "He said he didn't want to meet me anywhere, so I told him . . . I told him . . . we would have a better time than the night before." She hesitated briefly, her breathing uneven, her eyes still lowered, before continuing. "I remember he stared at me, then said, okay, he would be there in a couple of minutes. I went and hid by the lake until no one was around except Bobby looking for me. When he was facing away, standing next to the water, I sneaked up behind him." Patty stared at her brother, her eyes faraway. "And then, and then it felt like everything was in slow motion when I was swinging that bar. And at the same time, while it was happening, I knew what I was doing was wrong."

Patty leaned back, looking away again, and with her voice barely audible said, "Bobby must have heard me at the last second because he started to turn in my direction. I couldn't stop the swing—I tried to—and I hit him on the side of the head. Not hard, but hard enough. He lost balance and stumbled, then fell. And I heard this loud thud when the back of his head smashed against one of those big rocks next to the water.

"I stood there and watched—I must have been frozen—not believing what had just happened, when very slowly, Bobby began to move. And when he had gotten to his knees, I was so afraid of what he would do if he got his hands on me, I grabbed the flag and wrapped it around the bar while I ran behind the lake and out the back way."

She paused, placing her fingers against her mouth, then slowly shook her head. "I only wanted to hurt him, DJ, like he did to me. I never even considered—until you told me that morning—that he might be dead." She closed her eyes.

"Where are the flag and steel bar?" DJ asked.

Patty slowly reopened her eyes and studied the wooden floor below her feet. "They're behind the sleds in the garage." She peered at DJ, the skin beneath her eyes as raw as her hands. "I should have gone back. As much as I hated him, right away, I should have gone back." She unconsciously pressed the palms of her hands together. "But, DJ, I was so afraid—afraid of what I had just done—and Dad would never help me." Patty placed her hands at her sides. "So the next day, Greta and I figured a time line showing I was with her the entire night except for the ten minutes it took me to walk home from her apartment."

DJ sat, unmoving, watching his sister. To escape the pain of the conversation, he floated overhead from what he figured had to be at least three stories. Below, he studied a tiny girl in a nightgown, fresh from her bath, her damp hair parted in the center. She rested her elbows on the window ledge behind the screen and laughed with delight as she pointed at the neighbor's orange tomcat that bounded back and forth across the backyard, leaping, diving, and tumbling after fireflies. And he remembered her closed bedroom door and the darkness that seemed to invade her soul, her unending quest to locate the Christmas spirit, and the sweetness of Johnny Mathis's voice which seemed to comfort her.

"Do you believe I didn't want him to die?"

DJ gently nodded to his sister. "Of course, I believe you," he whispered. "Sure I do."

"You won't tell?"

DJ stared at the stained glass, then back at Patty. He shook his head. "No, I'll never tell."

A door opened and Father Hill appeared in the sanctuary. He walked to the front of the altar, genuflected, then crossed to the choir screen.

Patty began to sob quietly again. "But how do I live with myself? I have to confess to be free of my sins."

"You have confessed," DJ answered. "To both Greta and me."

"Anyone back there?" Father Hill called, his hand over his eyes as if he were staring into a blazing Amazon sun.

"DJ and Patty Elders, Father," DJ called back.

"Very well," the priest responded. "You're early."

"Forgive us, Father," DJ answered.

"You are forgiven," Father Hill answered good-naturedly as he reached into his pants pocket for a pen, "as we all shall be."

"Do you hear what he said?" DJ whispered. "You will be forgiven. You are forgiven, Patty."

"Is it that simple?" Patty asked.

"For today," DJ answered.

"Am I really free of what happened, DJ?"

"Yes, you are." He looked into her eyes. "You are."

As he sidestepped across the pew toward the aisle, he saw his sister shift forward to her knees, her palms pressed together in prayer.

CHAPTER 62

DJ walked down to the high school, then around the building and toward the football field where Bobby had once run for touchdowns and glory. What had Greta said? "The law for all its claims to the contrary is subjective, but your sister is everything." He considered her words, and now, after seeing Patty, understood the truth behind them.

Nothing could change what had happened and nothing would return Bobby to life. And though DJ's own conscience might have to endure the unsolved death persisting for decades, he knew he would be able to roll with the tides—today, tomorrow, next year—forever locked in a secret pact with Greta and Patty. And, yes, sometime in the future, when the moment was right, he would burn the flag, then slip the lock bar from his garage, clean it, and return it to Greta.

Because his sister was everything and she would prevail.

As he approached the field, DJ knew the football game was over. The stands were empty and he'd heard the honking bus take a victory lap through town. In a far corner, four grade-school boys wearing football helmets practiced slashing and running down the sidelines in front of an imaginary crowd bursting with applause. As he climbed the bleachers, then sat, his elbows resting on his knees, DJ could feel the echoes the boys heard, could sense the dreams they envisioned. It had been less than a year since he had been in the stands as a student, and now he was returning to a place he no longer belonged and, like Carlyn's bedroom, to a place he could not quite remember.

As an outsider, he remained and watched the boys until they collapsed in a pile, grinning and breathless.

After he descended the bleachers, DJ paused to watch bits of green and white confetti dance in the breeze across the length of the tiered boards, and then as he walked away from the field, he spotted a metal gold lipstick that had fallen from someone's purse into the grass, and stepped over it.

He crossed the field and walked to the front of the high school building on Main Street, then climbed to the top of the entrance stairs and sat down.

The leaves were beginning to change color. DJ looked up at the maple towering over him. It was too soon, or like everything else around him, too fast.

If I carve my initials in the tree today, up near the top, the part that's hidden from the street, will the letters still be there in twenty years? In forty years? If I came back and looked for them, would I ever remember being seventeen? Or if I died in a car accident, or in a remote corner of the world during some bloody war, would the initials ever be seen again by anyone?

Reaching for a twig that had fallen at his feet, he snapped it in half.

And Carlyn.

Always Carlyn. She crowded every room he entered and occupied each street he walked. Maybe when he grew older, wiser, he might see her again, he thought. She could have changed a little too. And maybe she'd even find a way to love him.

And Patty.

Always Patty. Maybe one day his sister's prayers would be

answered and their mother would reappear. She'd be wearing her blue dress and when she saw her daughter, she'd wrap her in her arms, smooth her hair and seek to calm her trembling heart.

And when that day arrived, he too would be free . . . yes, he would be free.

DJ tossed the pieces of the twig away and stood.

Across the street, he saw Wendell shuffling up the block, whistling softly to himself, his hands stuffed in his front pockets. As his uncle passed in front of Captain Leo's Seafood Restaurant, for a second, the reflected image reminded DJ of the boys swimming like fish across the front of the window with Ike following as King Neptune.

DJ moved down the steps and crossed the street. After stopping in front of Captain Leo's, he quickly swam a three-step breast stroke across the front of the glass. Completing the lap, he circled back to the start of the window, then vigorously swam across once more, this time, the final time, as a vital, healthy fish.

For Ike. A wish. A last goodbye.

CAPTAIN LEO'S SWIM TEAM 1957

Ted Alexander grew up in Vermont and Long Island, New York. He won a Shubert creative writing fellowship, completed his Masters Degree, then joined a rock band and toured America for five years. He later worked as an account supervisor and media director for two Manhattan advertising agencies, followed by a career in publishing. He is currently a columnist for the Asheville Citizen-Times in Western North Carolina.

His second novel, *After & Before* is scheduled for publication in 2015.

Visit the author's website at TedMAlexander.com.

CPSIA information can be obtained at www.ICGtesting.com
Printed in the USA
BVOW03s0904090215

386923BV00001B/2/P